NICK AUCLAIR

STEEL'S TREASURE

Steel's Treasure
Copyright © 2013 by Nick Auclair. All rights reserved.
First Print Edition: April 2013

Cover and Formatting: Streetlight Graphics

ISBN: 978-0-9891736-0-5 (print)
ISBN: 978-0-9891736-1-2 (eBook)

steelstreasure@gmail.com
http://www.steelstreasure.blogspot.com

No part of this book may be reproduced, scanned, or distributed in any printed or electronic form without permission. Please do not participate in or encourage piracy of copyrighted materials in violation of the author's rights. Thank you for respecting the hard work of this author.

This is a work of fiction. Names, characters, places, and incidents either are the product of the author's imagination or are used fictitiously, and any resemblance to locales, events, business establishments, or actual persons—living or dead—is entirely coincidental.

DEDICATION

To Tony and all the displaced Aeta people whose way of life was greatly disrupted by the eruption of Mt. Pinatubo and to my friend, Kuntaw Master Maximo "Jo Jo" Abarquez—Jo Jo, give me a call; I have a map I want to show you.

PROLOGUE

25 May 1985, Republic of the Philippines, somewhere west of Clark Air Base in the remote Zambales mountain range, twenty-seven-year-old U.S. Air Force Capt. William "Will" Steel paused, and with a rag wiped the waterfall of sweat running down his face, trying to stop the burning in his eyes. He pulled out a fresh bandanna, tied it around his head, and grabbed a green canteen, taking a long drink of lukewarm grape Kool-Aid—the Kool-Aid was a necessity; water boiled over a campfire tasted like shit.

He holstered the canteen and tried to shift the nylon shoulder straps of the forty-pound pack on his back. One of the straps dug into his shoulder. He noticed blood on his shirt under the strap—two days into the jungle, he couldn't afford a raw skin-ulcer, festering. He looked at the burning sun set up high in the sky and guessed it was noon. He checked his watch—eleven a.m.

They had marched seven hours into the mountains the day before and overnighted along a small stream. They had gotten up early this a.m., had a quick breakfast, and hit the trail—marching their way through thick groves of elephant grass and thorny, scrubby brush. They had just hacked through a lush grove of twenty-foot tall bamboo. Despite its near impenetrability, the shady green thicket was actually a welcome relief from the dry, hot, eight-foot-tall sea of elephant grass—

brown, brittle, with razor sharp leaves—that they had spent the last three hours walking through. It was the height of the dry season.

Even with the heat and grueling conditions, Steel was happy to be out of the office and in the mountains, flush with seven days of vacation. Steel glanced over at Jo Jo—his Filipino aide-de-camp—who had taken Steel's cue and rested for a moment. Jo Jo was essential, a strong and intelligent companion, the voice of reason. He kept Steel grounded.

Ahead of them, almost out of sight, Steel could see three Negrito pigmy tribesmen—shirtless, shoeless, and dressed in loincloths. They were primitive mountain people, expert guides, and his porters. He had hired a total of six for this expedition. Not wanting them too far ahead, Steel yelled angrily in Aeta at Tony, the head Negrito, to slow down. Unlike Steel and Jo Jo, the Negritos were tireless hiking fools, even with their towering backpacks, heavy with food and equipment.

They had two objectives this trip; the first was to explore a large World War II Japanese bunker in a cave that Tony had found earlier that month. Maybe they'd find some gold this time. Steel had brought his metal detector and digging equipment. Legend had it that Japanese General Yamashita, the infamous Tiger of Malay, had buried a king's ransom of gold and precious gems someplace in the mountains and taken to his grave its secret locations. Over the last two years, Steel had spent a good chunk of his free time roaming the mountains trying to find the gold.

The second objective—which Tony assured him was on the way to the cave—was a crash site for a World War II Japanese Zero fighter aircraft, the dead pilot still strapped into the cockpit. Steel was apprehensive about this part of the trip. Tony had introduced Steel to the slimy, cashiered Phil army scout ranger who had reportedly found the crash site. Like Steel, Jo Jo had taken an instant dislike to the guy.

Steel had never used a non-Negrito as a guide. The ranger wanted a lot of money to lead them to the Zero—the bulk of it paid in advance. In the end, Steel's desire to see the Zero and salvage souvenirs won out over Jo Jo's objections, and Steel reluctantly paid the ranger what he asked and went for it.

With his pack readjusted, Steel walked over to Jo Jo, and together they marched off to join Tony and the antsy Negritos waiting for them. Steel did a quick headcount—all the Negritos were accounted for—but where was the scout ranger? Steel was pissed when Tony told him the ranger had gone on ahead without them. The ranger said he wanted to check out the area before they arrived.

After another ninety minutes of uphill hiking, Steel yelled for Tony to stop, and they rested in the shade at the bottom of a big ravine. A gentle breeze rolled through. Tony approached Steel, who was getting some food from his pack, and expressed concern that they had not seen the ranger yet—that something was wrong—that he sensed some bad wind.

Steel rolled his eyes—the Negrito jungle spirits were at work again. Before he could roll his eyes once more, a huge troop of spider monkeys raced overhead in the jungle canopy, screaming and chattering, trying to outrun something or someone. The simian riot left a path of broken tree limbs and rained down leaves on Steel. He glared at Tony, who shrugged his shoulders and spoke rapidly to his comrades in a dialect that Steel didn't understand.

A wide-eyed Tony wanted to go and see what the problem was. Steel, surprised by the crazed monkeys, agreed and sent Tony forward. Steel didn't have to wait long. Five minutes later, a flustered Tony arrived yelling in high-pitched Aeta, then Tagalog, and finally in broken angry English. The son of a bitch ranger had set fire to the jungle—he was trying to clear brush so he could find the plane, or maybe he was trying to kill them because he was lying about the plane.

3

Steel swore at Tony for introducing them to that fucking ranger and watched as the Negritos grabbed their gear and yelled for everyone to run. Steel smelled smoke and heard a roar, like a freight train bearing down on them. As he gathered his gear, four huge wild pigs erupted from the brush in a primordial panic and bolted through the men.

Steel threw on his pack, glanced over his shoulder, and saw Tony's bad wind—a twenty-foot wall of flames blasting through the dry brush and trees. The fire crashed into the ravine like a tsunami wave. Jo Jo grabbed the stunned Steel by his pack frame, and together they ran after the Negritos.

With men and monkeys screaming and wild hogs squealing, the fire flew at them. Since ancient times, man and beast feared fire. Steel ran through the jungle hoping like hell he'd live long enough to find the treasure he knew was out there—or at least long enough to kick Tony's Negrito ass.

1

February 1946
Los Banos Laguna, Philippines

LIEUTENANT GENERAL TOMOYUK YAMASHITA, THE Tiger of Malay, sat at a small rattan and narra wood table scribbling notes onto a thick white legal pad. Early in the morning, he was alone in his cell at the civilian prison in Los Banos, south of the Philippine capital Manila. The sixty-one-year-old general was dressed in simple white cotton western-style pajamas; a sheen of sweat glistened on his bald head, evidence of his earlier sword-less Kendo workout. Kendo helped focus his thoughts and reinvigorate his flagging Samurai spirit.

He had fashioned a seat for the hard metal folding chair from a spare bed pillow. It eased the arthritis in his back and legs, pain hatched over too many years in the cold, squalid military encampments of Manchuria and fledged during hours on hard wooden chairs before his American captors.

He had placed his table parallel to a small barred window, which let him look out over the lush jungle surrounding the prison. He smelled tropical flowers on the slight morning breeze and sighed, glad to be out of the circus that was his military tribunal trial in Manila. His execution date was less than a week away, but he pushed thoughts of it aside, sat quietly, and began to write.

The war was over. He had eaten well the last month, slept on comfortable beds, bathed with hot water, luxuries he could not have imagined during his march into the Philippine countryside more than a year ago.

He was handed command of Japanese forces in the Philippines in October of 1944, two weeks before the massive U.S. invasion at Leyte. Revisiting the hastily organized defense plans upset his stomach. He wished for a peppermint to settle it or his kendo sword to relieve the stress.

He roughly rubbed his hands over his face: if only he had been given more time, he could have mounted an organized defense, possibly even turning back the American invasion. But Tojo, the prime minister, had decided too late.

He had been friends with Hedeko Tojo when he was a young army captain, but they fell out long ago. Tojo was a misguided adventurist who led Japan to defeat. He shamed the Japanese people and the emperor.

Tojo had even botched his own suicide. The fool. He had shot himself instead of committing ritual seppuku. Unthinkable. And now he waited his turn for trial.

Yamashita had also briefly contemplated suicide to avoid the humiliation of trial. But in no circumstances would he let an inconsequential junior subordinate hang for his orders. It was only honorable for Tojo and the others responsible for the war to be held accountable.

Yamashita and Tojo had bonded during the cruel rigors of the military academy. But once graduated and serving as a junior officer, Yamashita grew increasingly tired of Tojo's political schemes. Instead of pursuing plum staff jobs like Tojo, Yamashita focused on acquiring wartime operational commands.

Tojo had always been intensely jealous of Yamashita's wartime fame and the loyalty of his subordinates. Yamashita commanded the Japanese forces that defeated the British in

Singapore—Winston Churchill had called it the worst British military disaster in history. Yamashita's victorious troops smashed the white colonists, and Japan had scooped up all the treasures of Asia—enough to finance an empire.

He was proud of his title: the Tiger of Malaya. But Tojo had seen to it that Yamashita was banished to insignificant units in Manchuria and denied the spotlight. He ground his fist into the table thinking of Tojo's treachery.

Breathing deeply, Yamashita gazed at the verdant jungle. How little that matters now. History has recorded his victory in Singapore and will ultimately hold Tojo responsible for Japan's downfall. No one will recall the petty rivalries.

Yamashita stretched his back and fought a yawn. His sleep was fitful, full of strange dreams. He saw the faces of comrade's long dead, and the specter of the atrocities he heard his men had committed against the Filipino people.

He had not witnessed those horrors, but during his trial, hundreds of eyewitnesses testified to them. One beautiful young Filipina described how drunken Japanese soldiers skewered her two babies on their bayonets. Lately, she visited his dreams, her naked body sliding across his scarred torso, soft hands stroking inside his aching legs. But her teasing tongue would too quickly turn sharp, and the face she lifted from his lap was a monster's visage with murderous eyes.

Last night he had dreamed of his boyhood school in Hiroshima, the smell of cherry blossoms and a stolen kiss with Miaoko—his first girlfriend—then the flash of the atomic bomb. People burned quickly, disintegrating as if they were paper dolls. Did Miaoko make it out alive, or was she, too, just part of the clouds of ash that haunted his nightmare?

Never had 70,000 souls gone so quickly—in an instant. Yet the Americans dared to call him a monster, a war criminal. Would they pay for their war crimes? He laughed a tight, bitter choke. The victor tries the vanquished.

The Americans did provide him with a surprisingly competent legal team. But they had told him the trial was not bound by any laws or rules of evidence; it was merely meant to set the precedent by which more enemy officers could be hanged. MacArthur wanted vengeance for his humiliating defeat in the Philippines, and humiliation it was. No wonder MacArthur made sure that the British General Arthur Percival, whom Yamashita had beaten in Singapore, had a seat of honor at his trial, a perch from which to gloat when the guilty verdict was read.

There was no changing history. Yamashita had defeated Percival's 85,000 troops with only 36,000 men, most of whom he transported on bicycles. The one-hundred-day campaign cost him 10,000 of his men compared to 138,000 lost by the British. What could that fool Percival possibly have had to gloat about?

The cell's heavy metal door banged, and Yamashita checked his watch: 0800 breakfast. He hoped the tea would still be hot.

He was surprised to see Tomas Abucayan next to the silent and wizened orderly who stood awkwardly holding an unusually large tray of food. It must be food for two.

In a short time, Yamashita had grown fond of the young, bespectacled priest who after three years of missionary work in Japan spoke passable Japanese. Yamashita enjoyed Abucayan's company, not for his religious views but for news from Japan, sharp political discussions, and the game of chess.

On some level, the young priest made Yamashita wish he had had a son; he would have been around Abucayan's age. Of course, he would have joined the military and no doubt been killed in battle. Morbid thought, the musings of a man slated to die.

Yamashita stood and cleared off his table to make a place for the bamboo tray. He acknowledged the attendant with a silent nod, and the aged jailer exited quietly leaving Abucayan alone with the general.

Yamashita and Abucayan faced each other and exchanged bows. Abucayan's bow was polite and respectful, showing deference to the general's rank and age.

"Tomoyuki, it is so good to see you." Abucayan reached forward and held his hand. "There isn't a day I do not think of you and say a prayer for your everlasting soul." Abucayan spoke the words in Japanese slowly and precisely, as if he had practiced in the hall.

Yamashita enjoyed hearing his first name spoken. It added a comfortable familiarity to their interaction and proved that at least one other knew him as more than just a brutal occupier. "Tomas, the pleasure is mine to see you, my friend. What brings you from Manila to Los Banos?" He asked this knowing the answer.

Abucayan smiled. "Why of course to see you and try to win a game of chess, before……" He paused delicately.

"Before I am hanged."

"Before your journey for salvation begins my friend."

"Sit please. You come a long way to win at chess." Yamashita picked up the pot and poured the tea.

They ate bread, pork sausage, and fruit and chatted about the news from Japan. When they had finished the food, Abucayan stood, cleared the table of the plates, and reached for his satchel. A smile erupted on Yamashita's face. He loved board games.

Go was his passion. He had played thousands of games on a worn board with black and white tile pieces fashioned from black stone and shells, a handmade gift from his men on his birthday many years ago.

He wondered what had become of his board. He doubted the Americans who raided his office would appreciate its beauty. Such a pity.

They set up the game. Yamashita drew a white piece from one of Abucayan's closed fists. After several quick moves, they settled into a comfortable rhythm of play. Conversation was at a minimum.

Abucayan broke the silence. "Tomoyuki, I will not insult you with any more religious discussions, but I would be remiss if I didn't ask you one more time to...." He paused to compose his thoughts, making sure his Japanese grammar was correct. "....to see if I can ask God to forgive you for your sins." He bowed his head and lowered his eyes.

Yamashita smiled. He was full of good feelings for his friend. "Tomas, please ask for my forgiveness, if it would make you happy. I would be honored."

"Yes, Tomoyuki. It would," Abucayan spoke in a hushed voice. They resumed their game.

Yamashita was surprised at how deeply Tomas' simple kindness moved him. "Tomas I want you to know," he struggled for the words. "What Wabuchi and his men did to the city of Manila and its people disgusted me. It dishonored the Japanese army. It is one of my biggest regrets that I lost control of my command. My command and control structure was so weak." Yamashita closed his eyes tightly and pushed his forehead with clenched fists. "I just did not have time to consolidate my command before the American invasion. Wabuchi and his men behaved like animals and for that I am truly sorry."

Abucayan looked at the old man. At first, he had not wanted to minister to the general. The Japanese occupation had been so brutal. Abucayan had lost many from his rural parish to the depraved acts of crazed Japanese soldiers. They had seemed like the devils and invincible.

But when he met Yamashita, Abucayan had not found Satan, just a tired old man in his prison pajamas. How could the Americans have lost the Philippines to such ordinary men?

His friends, family, and parishioners were outraged by his visits to the prison. He had not told them of his and the general's growing relationship or their chess games. The rest of the world was not prepared to offer forgiveness, even in God's name.

The game lasted for nearly an hour before it became clear that Abucayan would win. Only once had he played down his game against the general, an insult the priest blushed to remember.

After he had put his board and pieces into his bag and prepared to depart, Yamashita faced Abucayan and whispered hoarsely, "Tomas, I want to tell you something I have vowed to the emperor I would protect with my life. I have been entrusted with a great secret I will take to my grave. But, my friend, if it is ever discovered, I hope the people of the Philippines are given a great share, so that they may experience some prosperity in their lives—a minor amends for the injustices we have dealt them." Yamashita bowed to Tomas with great reverence, walked to the window, and stared out into the hills.

Tomas bowed and exited the room, promising to return for another game, not knowing what to make of the general's last statement. He would query him more next time.

2

**1985
Clark Air Base
Republic of the Philippines**

MAJ. GEN. MALCOM SMITH LOOKED up from the papers he was shuffling. He was desperate for a cigarette. He scanned around his big mahogany desk, piled high with folders, hoping that a pack was hidden amongst the mess. Of course there wouldn't be. His executive officer Maj. "Bucky" Bart was hiding them; he thought smoking wasn't the image a general officer in the new Air Force wanted to project. Smith gritted his teeth, muttering at Bucky's efficiency. He knew Bucky was right, but this new, politically-correct Air Force was constantly at odds with Smith's old school fighter jock mentality.

Bucky, a politically shrewd academy graduate, had shaped Smith's career over the last five years. It was Bucky who had scored Smith his second star and this new command position. But damn him. Smith needed a smoke.

The stress of learning the ropes as the 13th Air Force commander was fueling his cravings. He thought he could easily transition from the Pentagon J-8 job; yet here he was, a month later at Clark, faced with completely unfamiliar political and military problems. He smiled to himself. The big difference, however, was that being a two-star general at 13th meant something—unlike at the Pentagon where one- and two-stars had shitty management positions.

Unfortunately, his previous visits to the Philippines had clouded his expectations about this current assignment. His early Philippine memories were from 1968, when he deployed through Clark in route to Thailand and Vietnam, where he flew more than two hundred combat missions in F105s. Life was simpler when he was a swaggering young buck, enjoying the rest and recreation the Philippines afforded.

It wasn't the same carefree place anymore. Smith felt old and tired. He craned his neck, peering around the corner. Bucky was away from his desk. Smith walked over to a big wooden display shelf and peered into several ceramic mugs, souvenirs from previous assignments and his secret cigarette stash. Bucky had missed two crumpled Marlboros.

With his smokes in hand, he moved quickly through a small hidden side doorway in his office onto a fire escape. He felt like he was back in high school.

It was early in the morning, and the humid tropical heat had not set in; in fact, there was a refreshing breeze blowing, courtesy of a big rainstorm during the night. Smith pulled out his favorite Zippo lighter. It had his old "Wolf Pack" fighter squadron's emblem on it, a token of his tours in South Korea. He carefully straightened his cigarette and flicked open the lighter. He loved the smell of the lighter fluid and the sound the flint made when his thumb flipped the metal wheel. He inhaled deeply, relishing the smoke as it filled his lungs.

Smith felt safe surrounded by a barrier of seven-foot-tall tropical hibiscus bushes. The only sounds were the shrill chirping of tropical birds and the whine of the air conditioner units. He wished he had a lawn chair and his cup of coffee.

He was halfway through his first smoke when he heard

voices. He strained one ear. Shit. Must be Bucky. Reluctantly, he extinguished his rumpled smoke.

The air conditioner unit kicked off, providing a few minutes of silence. He was relieved to hear the local language. He intently listened and picked up a word or two, enough to be certain they were speaking Tagalog.

He had ordered some language tapes from the library at the Pentagon and half-listened to them as he commuted to work. Still, he had only mastered a few simple phrases; no time to study with his sixteen-hour workdays. The Air Force never had enough qualified linguists. It was one of his pet peeves—probably started during his liaison duty with the Thai air force more than a decade ago. The language barrier made it nearly impossible to deal with foreign militaries.

Smith thought he recognized the voice of one of the several Filipino houseboys and gardeners who were assigned to his building. Joe, who emptied his trash and cleaned his office, was senior; he had been Douglas McArthur's shoeshine boy.

Smith listened more closely. Along with the Tagalog, he could hear laughter and sporadic hand clapping. He quietly pushed his way through the bushes. Twenty feet in front of him, hidden from public view by a ring of lush vegetation, were four figures.

They were sitting on their haunches, engrossed in a lively game of cards. Including Joe the houseboy, three were Filipinos, and, to Smith's surprise, one appeared to be a Caucasian, judging from the short brown hair. As he peered closer, Smith noted with interest that the brown-haired man was squatting like the natives but dressed in the Air Force's blue class-B uniform.

Smith couldn't see the man's rank or his face but could hear the American speaking fluent Tagalog. He was clearly enjoying himself, slapping cards down as he smoked and laughed, a small pile of colorful crumpled paper bills and coins piled in front of him.

As commander, Smith knew it was his duty to march over and chew the airman out. Christ, he was absent from work and gambling to boot—not exactly action becoming an airman. But Smith hesitated.

Damn it, he thought, it was a nice morning, he was in a good mood, and on some level, he envied their fun. Just as Smith turned to go back inside, Joe spotted him.

Joe stared at the general in disbelief, then horror. He turned to the American. The general's discovery of their sanctuary was sure to have a dire impact on his friend's reputation and career.

General Smith, amused, put a finger to his lips. Joe, unable to stop himself, jerked to attention and watched the general approach their group. Joe's two Filipino companions, taking a cue from him, jumped up leaving the hapless American still squatting on his haunches, his back to the general.

Capt. William 'Will' Steel was surprised by Joe's rapid movements and twisted around to see what rousted his pudgy friend. Steel saw the highly polished shoes and pressed blue Air Force pants first. He followed the knife-sharp creases up to a shiny belt buckle embossed with two silver stars and up further to the general's glaring face.

Steel jumped up and locked at attention, as if a demonstration of crack military posture would atone for the situation, the cigarette, smelling of pungent local tobacco leaves still pursed between his lips.

The general was surprised that Steel was not an airman, or even an NCO, but a captain. He recognized him as one of his intelligence officers.

Steel grabbed the cigarette, burning his hand, and dropped it to the ground. "Good morning, sir," he barked as he snapped a salute.

"Good morning, Captain," the general gave a quick salute back and spoke slowly and deliberately, jealously savoring the lingering cigarette smoke. "What do we have here?" He paused for effect. "Let me guess. You were gathering intelligence from Joe."

Steel thought for a moment—no jokes. "No sir, just a smoke break. I came in early to work on your briefing."

"Do you speak Filipino, Captain?" The general eyed him.

"Yes sir—a little."

"Are you fluent?"

Joe piped in trying to help. "Oh sir, Captain Steel speaks several of our languages."

"Captain, how long have you been stationed at Clark?"

"Almost three years, sir."

"You must like it here."

"Yes sir, it's a great job and place to live," Steel said, not sure where this line of questioning was going.

"Well, from what I've heard you have a minority opinion."

"I'm afraid so. Most American's feel too far from home here."

The general eyed Joe, who was squirming uncomfortably next to Steel. "So, Joe, his language ability must come in handy, huh?"

"Yes sir, he has a gift from God."

The general smiled and nodded approvingly, "From God, you say Joe. Nothing wrong with that." Smith checked his watch. "Let's see, a 0900 brief. I guess we'd better both get back at it...right, Captain?"

"Yes sir," Steel saluted smartly and watched the general leave. Steel inhaled deeply, stunned by the general's relatively easygoing manner. Although, he knew it probably wasn't over. Should his boss, Lieutenant Colonel Kuncker, find out, Steel was a dead man.

Smith headed back to his office, amused by the young

captain. He paused for a moment before he went back inside—checked his six—no one around. He pulled out a second smoke and quickly lit it. He was not looking forward to the morning intel briefing. It was outlining new threats against American personnel from by the New People's Army, also known as the NPA. Heavily armed guerrillas were threatening violent acts against his people, and he had lots of men, women, and children he was responsible for. In the distance, he could hear the roar of jet fighters taking off and looked into the sky. Must be the morning training missions scheduled to fly the Crow Valley Bombing Range. He wished he were with them.

Forty-year-old Lt. Col. Russ Kuncker, the chief of the 13th Air Force Intelligence Division, wiped his brow. Damn Philippine heat. It was noon, and he was sweating. He brushed his short thinning red hair with a free hand and straightened his shirt as best he could before leaving for Bucky's office. Tucked under his arm was a brown file folder jammed with intelligence reports.

Bucky had called earlier to tell Kuncker that the general wanted to talk about the a.m.'s stand-up briefing. Kuncker was pleased the general had been making a great effort to grasp the complex local, political, and military situation since his arrival last month.

"Hey, Bucky, the general still wants to talk?"

"Yeah. He's anxious over the increased NPA sightings."

"I see," Kuncker nodded.

"He says the number is giving him second thoughts about reducing the threat level on base. He hoped to drop some of the restrictions on personnel and their dependents. He's taking pressure from everyone, from the Philippine president right down here to the mayor of Angeles City. The mayor's upset because a lot of businesses are hurting."

"I'll be glad to go over what we've got. Unfortunately, the reports are pretty credible and so far, knock wood," he rapped his knuckle on the desk, "we've been calling them pretty closely."

"Personally, I have everything I need right here on base. No need for me to leave. If there's any threat, I want to know about it. I don't want to end up like those poor bastard airmen, with .45 rounds in their heads," Bucky emphasized his point holding up a finger gun. "The NPA mean business. Let me check on the general." He walked into the Smith's office.

Of course, the NPA means business, Kuncker thought. The New People's Army, the armed wing of the CPP or Communist Party of the Philippines, had been waging a more-than-two-decade bloody and violent struggle against the government. And now their strategy was assassinating American servicemen. Six months ago, three 8th Tactical Fighter Wing airmen who had been deployed to Clark from their air base in South Korea were gunned down by an NPA Sparrow hit squad. The CPP wanted publicity and targeting Americans was the way they got it. Pictures of the dead airmen sprawled out on the pavement were published in papers around the world.

The Communists had pushed ending what they called "the U.S. imperialist presence in the Philippines" for years. The Philippine government received hundreds of millions of dollars in outright payments and military equipment for letting the U.S. operate several large military bases there. The CPP believed that the government, if deprived of the U.S. financial support, would weaken to the point that it would fall.

For the Americans, the NPA hits were a security nightmare; any one of the 30,000 U.S. military personnel and dependents around Clark Air Base could be targeted. All personnel had been restricted to either the base or their quarters off-base after duty hours. The Philippine government increased its military and security force presence. Fortunately, there had been no additional killings—plenty of threats, but no more killings.

Now, after three months of quiet, various Filipino groups were pressuring the U.S. Command to drop the restrictions. At the national level, President Marcos wanted the Americans to acknowledge that Philippine security forces had reestablished law and order. The restrictions had become an embarrassment for his government. At the local level, Filipino politicians complained that businesses around the bases were suffering because they had lost their American patronage.

For the Americans, however, the biggest reason to eliminate the restrictions was to improve morale. American personnel were tired of being restricted to quarters. Shopping, vacations, or sightseeing were forbidden, and the young single G.I.s longed for Angeles City's raucous nightlife, with hundreds of bars and brothels employing thousands of available girls.

Bucky approached, "Yes, come on in. He has fifteen minutes before lunch at the club."

Kuncker loved visiting Smith's office. Aside from the face time a visit offered, the office was impressive, even by general officer standards. Its walls were paneled with dark colored old Philippine narra hardwood. The floors were wood as well, and covered with rich oriental carpets, a pre-World-War-II colonial-America- in-the-Philippines look. Of most interest to Kuncker, however, was General Smith's personal touch.

During his last assignment in Washington, Kuncker always took time to scan a general officer's décor as he made calls around the Pentagon; of course, the higher the rank, the bigger the office and the more room to hang memorabilia. He always wondered what the generals did with their professional junk when they retired. They must have had huge dens reserved, or big fights with wives who relegated the plaques to garage walls.

General Smith, as a two-star in the Philippines, had a much

better floor space situation than his peers in the Pentagon. He had four walls full of plaques, framed photos and paintings, several tables of aircraft models, and bookcases full of military history books, mugs, and memorabilia.

"Hi, Russ, thanks for coming over," the general said motioning for him to take a seat. Bucky sat next to Kuncker, with a yellow notepad and pen in his lap. "So you play some over the weekend? Sure was beautiful."

Kuncker liked the general. He got along well with fighter jocks. He let them think he knew his place. "Yes sir, had a wonderful round on Saturday. How about yourself?"

"Just hit a few on the driving range; next weekend for sure," Smith nodded. He leaned back in his chair, and it creaked softly. He picked up a pen and began twirling it between the fingers of one hand. "So, this information on NPA numbers in the briefing this morning. Are you sure about these reports of NPA guerrillas massing north of us? Sounds like Communist propaganda to me. Mayor Diaz assures me that his constabulary and regular army units have a handle on the situation."

"Well sir, to be frank, I really do not have much confidence in the intel reports the mayor gets. They're under pressure to reduce the threat. We've had to rely in part on our own intelligence nets—mostly to check out what we're getting from our Phil counterparts. Our sources are reporting increased numbers of NPA patrols in some of the remote *barangays* to the north of us. They are procuring food and intelligence on the Phil army units in the area. They still have a large support base in the Zambales area."

"Who are these sources the U.S. is relying on?" Smith asked skeptically, recalling how the intelligence provided to him for mission prep flying over Vietnam nearly killed him several times.

Kuncker thought for a moment before he spoke. He recalled

the words of Col. Bill Morgan, the chief of the local Air Force Office of Special Investigation or OSI, who ran the nets of paid informers and intelligence collectors. Morgan had said, "Generally, you get what you pay for. A can of ham, golf clubs, or cash can buy you a wheelbarrow full of shit or some nuggets of info. You got to remember that sometimes our sources are not necessarily upstanding citizens. These individuals are willing to divulge information for a variety of reasons—some political reasons—but most are willing to betray their country simply for financial gain."

Kuncker gave a slightly edited version. "Quite frankly, the sources range in reliability, but the OSI feels that they have gotten some good info from their established sources. Overall, the big picture seems to indicate something is up, particularly to the north of us. The OSI has also queried their sources close to the CPP in Manila. We've got some good CIA reporting from the Manila station as well. The CPP has not stopped targeting Americans. It just seems on hold."

"Bucky, where's Morgan? I thought he was supposed to be here. I've got to make some kind of decision today," the general sighed deeply.

"He's in Manila," Bucky reported.

Kuncker jumped in. "Yes sir, he's personally following up on the CPP collection operations—trying to get a read on what their targeting policy is. Some folks think that the CPP isn't going to target more Americans because of the bad feelings the killings generated amongst the Phil population around the bases. The restrictions have really hit them hard in the wallets. No G.I.'s, no cash. It's a pretty simple equation. NPA tax collectors have been getting the same story when they've tried to extort money from the local businesses. Ironically, for all their bad mouthing of Uncle Sam, they collect a hell of a lot of cash because we're here."

The general paused for a moment, carefully considering what he had just been told. "I'll be anxious to hear what Bart has to say when he gets back from Manila. I'm intrigued by the idea that the NPA is getting hit in the purse strings. Not much for winning their hearts and minds, right Kunky?"

"That's right, sir," Kuncker grimaced inwardly at the moniker. The general, like all pilots, loved nicknames. Pilots were a fraternity of grown men with names like Spiker, Spunky, or Buff. He wished he had a better nickname than Kunky. Maybe something intel-related, more James Bondish, like Spooker or something.

He refocused on the general's question. "Sir, the Phils think the restrictions have made the local populace realize just how monetarily important the Americans are to them."

"Sounds reasonable, but I just don't know." The general sat back heavily in his chair. He was torn. "Kunky, I'm under some heavy pressure here to open up. It's been three months since the last attack. What makes you so confident?"

Kuncker thought for a moment. "Sir, our track record's pretty good. I've got my best analyst on the issue. He's been following it for a couple of years now. He's really wired into the local scene and—"

"You mean Steel?"

Kuncker tried to not look too surprised. "Why, yes sir, er…. Captain Steel is an excellent analyst, he—"

"I know. I've seen him in action with the locals, he has a gift from God," he smiled and nodded.

"Excuse me sir, gift from God?"

"Nothing. What's his story?"

"Well sir, he's very knowledgeable about the NPA. He speaks several Philippine dialects fluently. He's traveled widely in the area and has numerous contacts in Phil military intelligence. Prior to the assassination of the Korea guys, he had warned of the potential for increased attacks, just that sort of thing."

While Kuncker watched for a reaction, he thought about Steel's warnings. He had said that there was a power struggle in the local NPA organization. One particularly ruthless commander was out to make a name.

The general pursed his lips and closed his eyes. Kuncker was nervous that he could be putting too much faith in his young captain's analysis.

Overall, he admired Steel, trusted his judgment and expertise. What rankled Kuncker, though, was that Steel was a lousy officer, sloppy in appearance and bearing and rebellious. He just didn't fit the Air Force mold. Consequently, Steel's promotion potential was limited, not that it seemed to bother him, thought Kuncker.

Bucky, who had sat quietly through the conversation, stood up. He checked his watch. "Sir, you have to leave soon."

"Yeah I know," the general sighed. "I'll see what Morgan says. I'll make a decision by tomorrow a.m. Thanks for coming, Kunky."

"No problem, sir," Kuncker exited the office.

Bucky closed the door. He had listened to Kuncker and considered the ramifications of opening up and what more killings would do to his boss's career. "Sir, to be honest, any potential for loss of American life is a really bad risk and—"

"Damn it! I know that. I don't want to put U.S. personnel at unnecessary risk."

"Sir, if I may," Bucky visualized the message that they could send up the chain to Pacific Command Headquarters in Hawaii. "I think you should continue to warn PACOM that the situation seems quiet, but there is an undertow. Some

NPA threats, etc. But extreme political pressure from the Phil government warrants an opening—suggest a gradual approach. Suggest that PACOM take the lead and have us open up somewhat to keep the Phils happy. Make PACOM keep up the military and political pressure on the government to cover our asses."

The general slammed down the pen he had been chewing on, "You know, I like that. Let the Navy brass at PACOM make the call. Dealing with political pressure from Marcos's office is above my pay grade. Let's get some lunch."

3

Pangasinan Falls

STEEL SAT UNCOMFORTABLY IN THE rear compartment of the jeepney passenger taxi. He was hot, sweaty, and covered with a fine layer of volcanic pumice. He ran his tongue across his teeth—even they felt gritty. The jeepney was brightly painted in a rainbow of colors with the words "Playboy Bong" emblazoned on side panels. It could hold ten passengers seated on two long benches in an open-air rear section. Steel had bounced back there for two hours, while the driver stopped to drop off and pick up other riders.

Despite the heat, dust, and bad shocks, he enjoyed riding in jeepneys; they were ubiquitous, cheap, and most important, offered the anonymity he wanted. His own vehicle sat under the carport of his home, outside the base. He was being careful. The restrictions had only been partially lifted. It was an automatic Article 15 offense if he was caught this far off base.

It was, however, a three-day weekend and more than a month since he had last violated the restrictions. He was ready to get out of town. His maid Rosa was covering for him. He'd call her later and check to ensure that no one was looking for him.

He stretched out his arms and rubbed the back of his neck. He was stiff and tired. It had been a long day: first a bus ride and now, the jeepney. He hoped they were getting close to Pangasinan Falls.

The falls and the river area surrounding them were spectacular: white water and rugged lush jungle. *Apocalypse Now* had filmed scenes there. The area's other claim to fame, or infamy, was as a haven for pedophiles: European and Japanese men preying on hapless Filipino children. The thought repulsed Steel.

To his right, his companion Jo Jo sat with his head slumped forward, dozing. He could sleep anywhere. Maximo "Jo Jo" Bato was short with a heavy muscular build and dark complexion by Philippine standards. His hair was crew cut and peppered with gray. He had a scraggly mustache and goatee, which he claimed made him look distinguished. Looking at it now, Steel thought it just added to Jo Jo's already menacing demeanor, even while dozing. Even dressed casually in jeans and a white polo shirt, Jo Jo looked older than his thirty-five years.

Jo Jo had a degree in political science and history from the University of Philippines. Like thousands of overeducated Filipinos, he had never worked at his vocation, instead taking manual labor jobs when he could find them. There were literally thousands of Filipinos with college degrees reduced to working manual labor jobs. The alternative was to flee the country: victims of the so-called brain drain.

Jo Jo was too proud to leave and become a slave to a Saudi Arabian master. He said he would rather be a poor Filipino in the Philippines than be sodomized by a rich Arab. Pride, however, did little to put food on the table. Fortunately for him, his wife did not share his beliefs.

Carmelita, or "Baby," was the primary breadwinner for the family. A nurse, she had followed countless other Filipino professionals to the job opportunities in the Middle East leaving Jo Jo to play mother and father to their two teenage girls and husband and lover to a string of difficult girlfriends. Baby's future plans involved trying to get a visa to Canada and applying for permanent residency, eventually bringing her husband and daughters over. Some of her nurse friends had already taken this path. Jo Jo didn't want to leave his country, even if it was for the better.

He had a third degree black belt in kuntaw, a Philippine mix of kung fu and Korean karate. To earn money, Jo Jo taught kuntaw to G.I.s around the base, including Steel. They had met first as kuntaw student and teacher, but Jo Jo soon added language lessons in the commonly spoken Tagalog and the dialect Pampangan as well as guide services for Steel during his forays into the countryside. As their friendship and partnership deepened over the last three years, Steel began to pay Jo Jo a monthly stipend to act as Steel's aide-de-camp and companion.

Today they were traveling to meet Dr. Arturo Abucayan, a renowned expert on the Japanese occupation of the Philippines during WW II and a retired university academic. Steel had asked his history professor at the University of the Philippines in Manila to set up an interview. Abucayan, who lived in Manila, resided for several months out of the year at a family home near the falls. Steel wanted to find out if it was true that Abucayan had spoken with General Yamashita, the infamous Tiger of Malay, the night before he was tried and hung for war crimes in 1945.

General Tomoyuki Yamashita and his men had arrived in the Philippines in 1943 after raping, pillaging, and plundering their way through French Indochina, Burma, Thailand, Malaysia, and Singapore. They were said to have brought with them to the Philippines billions of dollars in looted gold and gems from the temples, palaces, and capital cities of Southeast Asia.

Their plan was to store the treasure in the Philippines and draw on it to finance Japan's dream of an Asian empire known as the "Greater East Asian Co-Prosperity Sphere." But after the end of the war and Japan's designs, the hidden fortune was never found—but not for lack of trying on the part of opportunistic adventurers and treasure hunters, including Steel.

Steel smiled at the pretty young Filipina sitting across from him. She pretended to ignore him, but he caught her sneaking glances his way. He figured she was around twenty-years-old, an office worker or a shopkeeper from her dress, which was neat and pressed.

Probably heading home to her *barangay*, he thought, wondering how she managed to keep so clean, when he felt blown, dirty, and stinking of the skinny chickens that were crammed in a bamboo basket on the bench next to him. "I am truly fowl," he joked to himself.

He checked his watch: six p.m. He would be at Jo Jo's cousin's house before dark. It wasn't a good idea to be out on the roads after that. The NPA, the "Nice People Around," as Jo Jo referred to them, ruled the night. They set up impromptu roadblocks, soliciting "donations" and assassinating off-duty cops and military men.

The jeepney driver called out to the passengers that he needed to stop for gas and pulled into a station. By Third World, and especially Philippine, standards, the jeepney seemed mechanically sound, unlike most on the road. Steel and his buddy Rand had a running bet, ten dollars to the guy who found the biggest jeepney death trap. Steel had won six months ago. The jeepney, "Lover Boy" painted on the side, hadn't had a functioning brake pedal. Instead, the owner improvised a cable attached directly to the braking system, that he pulled by hand—one step above Fred Flintstone's foot break.

"What's up boss?" Jo Jo whispered, shaking off his grogginess.

"Getting gas."

Jo Jo brushed a chicken feather off his shirt and said to Steel in Tagalog: "You're too good to me, with these first class accommodations. We are not far now, maybe twenty minutes, then a ten-minute trike ride. My butt's already sore just thinking about the trike."

Surprise showed on the three other passengers' faces as Steel answered in Tagalog: "At least you have big padding on your ass...mine is skinnier than yours."

The pretty office girl politely covered her giggling with her hand.

Steel smiled at her, "I hope the trike has good shocks." At least it was only a ten-minute ride, he thought.

Steel casually eyed the driver as he switched off the engine, which died with several heaving chugs. The driver had lit a cigarette then reached down next to his legs and pulled out a bright yellow plastic anti-freeze jug, unscrewing the cap and examining its contents. A skinny black rubber hose connected to the cap led under the dashboard. Now I've seen it all, Steel thought, a jeepney with windshield washer fluid. But then, the driver got out and filled the jug with gas, the lit cigarette still precariously dangling from his lips. Damn if it wasn't the vehicle's gas tank. Rand would owe Steel another ten dollars. He nudged Jo Jo.

"Jesus Maria Joseph! You have to at least admire the clever nature of my fellow countrymen." Jo Jo made the sign of the cross.

"It is easy to tell when you're getting low on petrol." Steel laughed as the jeepney—tank full, driver smoking, and vehicle miraculously not engulfed in flames—pulled out.

Jo Jo's cousin Felix Bato was a rice farmer and the *barangay* captain, or headman, for the small village where he lived. Most of the villagers farmed; others ran the tourist business that the falls brought in. Some piloted the boats that took tourists down the white-water rapids.

It was an honor for Felix to host the American Air Force captain, and he played his role to the hilt. A parade of villagers passed through his house to meet and greet the American visitor, the village's first ever. Steel, accustomed to being the only white man, acted as an American ambassador of good will, kissing babies and joking in Tagalog.

Gawkers gone, Steel and Jo Jo relaxed on the porch of Felix's bamboo, wood, and thatched-roof house. As candles flickered around them, they could look down the hillside to flooded rice paddies. The smell of the jasmine, burning trash, damp jungle, and smoldering mosquito coils scented the warm breeze.

Steel laid back on a bamboo bench, while Jo Jo lounged in a hammock, both dazed by the dinner they just completed: wild pig, rice, fish, and fruit—all prepared on a smoky kitchen hearth and eaten with fingers off huge wooden platters.

"Ah, Captain Steel, please have another beer." Felix approached and handed him and Jo Jo a cool San Miguel.

"Ah *Salamat*, thanks," Steel acknowledged. The San Miguel was doing internally what the cool bath under the hand-cranked well pump had done externally. He finally felt clean.

He watched the candle flame nearest him jump—so peaceful in the provinces after dark. Jo Jo always joked that the lack of electricity here was the reason behind the Philippines' high birth rate. After dark there's nothing else fun to do except screw. Steel thought about the pretty young woman from the jeepney, and how he would like to share his bamboo bed with her. Her soft brown skin and—

"Hey boss, what time are we meeting Professor Abucayan?"

Steel snapped back, "We need to be there at nine a.m."

Jo Jo raised his head slightly, checked his watch, and said, "I will awaken us around seven a.m., since I doubt if either of us will be lucky enough to find a horny provincial girl. Most, unfortunately, are too virtuous; I have no choice but to go to bed now." Jo Jo tried to exit gracefully from his hammock but failed and fell to the floor. "Maybe I should just sleep here, but unfortunately I have to go to the comfort room now."

Steel walked over to him with extended hand and pulled him up. "Come on, *Lalo,* grandpa, time for bed."

"Grandpa! I'm very insulted. I'm just resting to be ready to meet the professor so I can engage him in thoughtful conversation."

"Good."

"I can't wait to see Abucayan again," Jo Jo said.

"You know him," Steel was surprised.

"No, not directly, but I listened to him speak at lectures and at political rallies. We were all highly motivated back then to break the Marcos's dictatorship. Now *Bahal Na,* so be it. The fire is gone. Gone. Gone!" The alcohol slurring Jo Jo's words.

Steel laughed, aimed Jo Jo toward the outhouse, and headed for his bedroom.

Steel and Jo Jo stood as Professor Arturo Abucayan approached their table. They had arrived at nine a.m. and ordered cups of strong local coffee. True to his heritage, Abucayan operated on Filipino time and ran thirty minutes late.

He looked like a textbook academic—wispy, stooped, and except for a few strands of white hair, almost bald. He had been a Fulbright scholar and had done some undergraduate work at Harvard. He was known for his radical left-wing views of Philippine politics and history.

During the 1970s, he had organized anti-U.S. protests in Manila and written at least a dozen books on various aspects of Philippine history, but his expertise was twentieth century foreign occupation of the Philippines. None of that explained why the professor had been so anxious to meet Steel, Steel thought as they took their seats around the small wooden table.

They ordered breakfast: papaya fruit, fried eggs, and *tocino*, sweetened pork meat, along with more coffee. Abucayan entertained them with stories about the Japanese occupation. Steel listened anxiously, waiting for the right moment to press the professor about General Yamashita.

"So professor, I was told that you were one of the last people to interview General Yamashita, the Tiger of Malay."

"Ah yes, you must have been talking to Professor Salamanca," Abucayan eyed Steel and sipped his coffee. "Good, yes?"

"Yes, really strong, the way I like it," Steel held up his cup.

"So you are interested in the Tiger." Abucayan stared at his coffee cup with unfocused eyes. "Salamanca did not exactly have the story correct concerning my connection with Yamashita. It is interesting that you should inquire about him. I have been writing about him in my latest book."

Jo Jo leaned forward. "I'm curious. I've read your books, and you only mention him in passing. He was such a pivotal character in the period. Why is that?" Jo Jo asked.

"Ah, I guess I was saving the best, or maybe worst, for last," Abucayan set the cup down gently, eyes still on it.

"You were a journalist during the war, is that true?" Steel asked.

"Yes, a seventeen-year-old one, though. I think now that it was God's will that I have a connection with the Tiger. It was February 20, 1946 that my brother asked me to come to Los Banos. I arrived a day after the Tiger was executed."

Steel had to ask. "Are the stories about the Tiger true? That—"

"That he buried a king's ransom in treasure," Abucayan smiled sadly.

"Yes."

"Ah, Captain Steel, you are seduced by the Tiger. I'm afraid the treasure is no more. Marcos took it. Maybe it has paid for Mrs. Marcos's shoes." He balled up a napkin and angrily ground it into the table. "You know, the treasure would have meant so much to the Filipino people, but instead it was squandered. I wish I had done something to find it. I did some research, but lacked the guts to go out and really look. I'm the academic type, not the Errol Flynn swashbuckler." After a moment, he swatted the napkin to the floor. "Marcos could have helped our people."

Steel wondered whether this was the root of the anger that had fueled Abucayan's involvement with the radical left during the tumultuous 1970s. He had no love for Marcos.

"Sir, why do you think the treasure is real?" Jo Jo asked.

"He told my brother, who was by his side at the end."

"If you don't mind my asking, why was your brother there?"

"He was a priest."

"The Tiger was a Catholic?" Jo Jo's eyes widened.

"No, he was a Buddhist. A Catholic father was provided for him prior to his execution. My brother, who had been in Japan before the war and spoke Japanese, tried in vain to convert him and save his soul. Yamashita refused to acknowledge his crimes or repent. He did, however, make reference to the treasure, at least in vague terms. He said something like: 'Japan's future will lay in the Philippines undisturbed until Imperial Japan rises once again.'"

"You never spoke directly with Yamashita then?" Steel stared intently at the professor.

"Correct, Captain."

"I'm really surprised that MacArthur didn't put him to the thumb screws in order to find out where he buried the loot."

"Oh, come now Captain, the U.S. military was not about to beat a confession out of him. Besides, at that point, there really wasn't any evidence or even rumors that a treasure existed. It wasn't until much later that the stories began to surface."

"I wish I had some more to read on the general and his activities in the Philippines. There's only a limited amount available."

"Yes, there really hasn't been a lot written about what he did, though there are several good books on what he did in Singapore." Abucayan took a long sip from a glass of mango juice.

Steel pressed: "Sir, for your book, and the part on the general, if you don't mind my asking, what will your sourcing be?"

"I have some old papers from the Philippine army archives. A colleague of mine, who works for our government's army, found imperial Japanese army documents buried in their files. Some were purportedly at Yamashita's headquarters when it was captured."

"When will your book come out?"

Abucayan smiled. "Oh, not for a while. I'm afraid I haven't even finished writing it yet."

Steel's shoulders sagged. "What a shame."

"Now, Captain, surely you are not such a great fan of mine that you can't wait until it is published?"

Steel paused. "To be honest, I'd love to see an advance copy. I am really interested in the sections on the Tiger or any documentation that you've found related to him. I'd be willing to, er, compensate you for your academic research time."

Abucayan smiled, then looked at Jo Jo and said in Tagalog, "Your American friend, I believe, thinks he can find the Tiger's treasure. At least he is willing to buy my time. Has he been looking?"

Jo Jo glanced over at Steel, searching his eyes. Steel jumped in, answering Abucayan in Tagalog. "Sir, I have been looking, and I think the stories of Marcos finding it aren't true. Or at least, they may be true in part only. I really don't think he found all of it."

Abucayan removed his glasses and rubbed his eyes. "I'm impressed. Your Tagalog is as good as Salamanca said. He exaggerates at times, you know. So what will you do with all this treasure if you find it?"

Steel answered readily. "I think it's a legacy for the Filipino people. They should have their share."

"So, of course you want a share for yourself."

Steel laughed. "Of course."

Abucayan nodded. "You're honest; that is good. Yes, that would be only fair for the finder to share in the wealth. Have you been to the mountains looking for it?"

"Yes, we've been making trips for about a year now. We've been in a lot of caves and done a lot of digging. Unfortunately, without some sort of clues, all we've come up with is dirt."

"But Captain, isn't this just daydreams? The treasure is long gone, and the men who buried it are dead."

"We don't know that for sure. Many of Yamashita's men survived the war. And maybe there is some documentation that points us to where it once was, even if it is gone or mostly gone."

"I am inspired by your faith that the treasure exists. Maybe I can give you some direction. When I return to Manila next week, I will have the translations of the final set of documents. Maybe we can come to terms and work together to find the treasure."

"That's good news."

"Don't get too excited. The documents I have seen thus far have been nothing more than supply orders and routine administrative paperwork."

"Frankly, sir, it is much more information than I, we…"

Steel pointed to Jo Jo, "have had thus far. It is possible that even the most seemingly trivial tidbits could shed some light on where to dig."

"Come now. We are probably not talking about simple holes dug in the ground, more likely an elaborate system."

"Or maybe not Professor, we really do not know what to expect."

"True, but it would seem likely that Yamashita would not have just buried his treasure in the ground like a pirate. I imagine that he had special engineering units building elaborate underground shafts, with booby traps."

Steel was surprised. He wondered what other details Abucayan knew.

The professor tipped the last drop of coffee into his mouth. "Captain Steel, I will agree to help you, but only on one condition: that should this crazy idea bear any fruit, the fruit be given to the Philippine people."

"Some of the fruit—at least a banana or two," Jo Jo said, shrugging his shoulders.

"I think we can agree to that." Steel nodded.

Abucayan extended his hand. "Then we must shake on it, and I will take you at your word as an U.S. military officer."

As they clasped hands, Steel's initial excitement was dulled some by a stab of guilt. Would he really be able to give up the treasure if he found it? What the hell was his motivation? Maybe it was just the adventure—or maybe it was growing up not ever having enough money, scrounging his way through college. It would nice to be filthy rich.

As the three men gathered their belongings, Steel watched Abucayan fuss with his briefcase. Did Abucayan really believe there had been a treasure? Did he find something in those files that convinced him?

Abucayan stood. "Well, Captain, Jo Jo, it was a pleasure to meet you. If I could have a telephone number where I could reach you, I will give you a call next week so we can arrange a day for you to come to Manila. I will show you my files."

"That would be wonderful. It was an honor to meet you." Steel gave the professor his business card and walked with him out of the cafe.

"He was a driving force in the leftist movement, the senior radical academic of the time. I heard him speak several times. He was very inspirational," Jo Jo said as they watched the crowd in the market place swallow up Abucayan's small frame.

"Yes, very interesting, but what about those papers from Yamashita's headquarters?" Steel imagined vaults of gold bars and precious jewels, a comic vision of endless treasure out of a long-forgotten Saturday morning TV show.

"So, boss, let's grab some fruit and food from the market to take home with us, cheap to buy here," Jo Jo motioned to the bustling market ahead of them.

"Sure. But don't go overboard unless you're willing to carry it back on the bus." Steel reached into his shirt pocket, put on his sunglasses and followed Jo Jo into the market.

U.S. Air Force Lt. Col. Arthur Snowden, vice-commander and special agent of the office of special investigations division at Clark Air Base was in an upbeat mood as he walked slowly around Pagasinan's Sunday market. He was tall and broad chested, proud of the physique he had built playing several varsity sports at the Air Force Academy, maintained still twenty-one years later. He kept in shape with regular runs and basketball.

He was dressed casually in civilian clothes, dark sunglasses, brown sandals, and a native-style *barong tagalog* shirt untucked from his khaki pants. The only vestiges of a military career were his brown hair cut short in a crew cut and a .38 caliber snub-nosed pistol concealed in a leg holster around his sock. Despite the awkwardness of the pistol, he had a relaxed and satisfied stride.

The market was packed, throngs of people fresh from church milling in a circus of mobile *carabao*, water buffalo, carts, and temporary tables piled high with food and wares. He hadn't seen a white face since he left his home outside Clark two days ago. As he pushed through the crowds, he was relaxed and felt more like a tourist than an agent. He nodded nonchalantly to an old tired Filipina woman, who sat behind a table full of brightly colored tropical fruits.

Mangos were in season, and he loved the sweet taste the orange, fleshy body. He picked out a small yellow-skinned one, squeezed it gently, and smelled it. It was almost perfectly ripe. A thrill shot through him; the touch and smell reminded him of the sensual pleasures of the weekend past, but so did everything—it had been that good. How he relished forbidden fruit, he chuckled to himself, handing several mangos to the old woman to bag.

He had been stationed at Clark for almost three years. He should have gone to a new assignment by now, but he had applied for, and had been granted, a one-year extension, a request that surprised his superior who had expected Snowden to move to a key position in D.C.

Snowden was pleased with his near perfect military career; without doubt, he would be promoted to full colonel. He knew that the OSI personnel folks were perplexed by his request for assignment to Clark; in fact, one colonel had called him to try to talk him out of it. Snowden had been bored with his last assignment—a year in South Korea at the U.S. airbase at Osan. Korea and especially the Philippines seemed to everyone a step down from his assignments in West Germany where he had used his German language proficiency and counterespionage skills with Soviet and East German agents.

But now, at forty-three, Snowden was tired of Europe and had few family members in the States. He had not lived in the U.S. for more than a decade. In any case, it was not a society that treated those with his special interests and appetites with any understanding.

When he first arrived in the Philippines, he had hoped he had not made a huge mistake; he was afraid he would be bored with his job. As vice-commander he was mostly removed from field work, more directly concerned with the administrative side of the seventy-five-man division.

There were minor espionage forays here and there with Chinese, North Korean, and Soviet Embassy personnel. And, of course, the threat from the New People's Army, as well as a hodgepodge of political intrigues with the Philippine military. However, the bulk of the division's time was spent on the common day-to-day crimes and petty larceny cases of U.S. servicemen and their spouses.

He was surprised at how intriguing he had come to find those cases: squalid little windows into the corrupt human heart. He relished secretly watching video tapes of the OSI's criminal interrogations, intently seeing if he could tell truth from lies. It was fascinating to see the faces of individuals when interrogation brought to light their ugly inner demons. He sometimes even wished he had pursued criminal investigation instead of counterespionage as a career.

The old woman bagged his purchase, and he smiled at the thought of those who were surprised when he chose to extend his stay at Clark. Imagine their shock when they found out he soon planned to hang up his military uniform for good. With twenty-one years of service, he was eligible to retire. He would wait until he was in his fourth year at Clark before making that announcement. No one liked a ROAD officer—retired on active duty.

Several years ago, he had decided that the Philippines would provide the perfect venue for his golden years. On a lieutenant colonel's pay, plus his enormous savings accounts courtesy of a rich spinster aunt, he could live like a king. Oddly enough, he found himself wanting the stability of a family.

Maybe he could find that here in the free-wheeling Philippines. Of late, he had been uncharacteristically soul searching. His dutiful, once-a-week trips to church were an exercise in reconciling his relationship with God. Long ago, he had seized upon the biblical teachings that God had made man, including Snowden, in his image. And God had put all of these feelings in him. God had to understand why he longed for the affection of children. How they pleased him. Why their trusting innocence was so appealing. Yes, they pleased him sexually, but he gave them so much love back. Still, he felt terribly alone. Few adults shared his desires—or at least few adults would dare to admit it.

Yes, he thought, if there was any place where he would be welcome, it was here. Plus, he had his friend Ramos who lived in Manila. He was the closest thing to family Snowden had. He made a mental note to call Ramos later and tell about this latest adventure. Snowden grabbed a small bunch of bananas and smelled them—they too were perfectly ripe, and he handed them to the woman.

He paused for a moment, a sense of foreboding flashed through his brain; similar instincts had saved his life on many occasions in Europe. He methodically scanned the area around him from behind dark sunglasses.

He was being an absolute idiot. Here in broad daylight, his exposed, tall, white frame an available target for any would-be NPA assassin. He slapped his forehead, angry at his carelessness.

He had concocted an excuse for violating the restrictions—meeting a high-level source—but he hoped he would not have to use it. He preferred to rely upon his training to mask his movements. He winced and again checked his surroundings, feeling conspicuous and large.

His head again screamed a warning. Snowden reached into his shirt pocket and threw a wad of pesos onto the table, grabbing the bag of mangos from the old woman, not bothering to ask how much he owed or collect change. From the corner of his eye a white shape caught his attention. The shrill voice in his brain was right—it was always right.

A Caucasian head bobbed above the crowd no more than thirty feet from him. Snowden ducked, trying to drop his height below the sea of black-haired Filipinos. Sunglasses covered the man's eyes; he turned toward Snowden and stared. Did the man seem shocked as well?

Horror gripped Snowden as he grabbed a large straw hat off the table and put it on. Shit. He had been seen. Or worse, followed? It had to be a tourist; everyone else on base was on lock-down.

For a large man, Snowden effortlessly disappeared into the crowd then hid in a wall of tall carts loaded with baskets, pausing only momentarily to catch his bearings. He wanted to return quickly to his hotel and retrieve his car. He racked his brain trying to figure out if he really knew the man, or if he had just imagined it.

The voice in his head sounded out. Hey, asshole, just focus for a second and recall the face, without the glasses. Snowden concentrated, smacking his forehead with his fist. "Fucking Steel, the intel guy," Snowden grunted aloud. Steel had seen him. Bad enough, but how long had he been following? What had he seen?

The woman at the fruit table tilted her head at the sudden, strange behavior of the Americano. She grabbed the wad of money off her table and counted it, way more than enough for the ratty hat and small mangos. She shrugged at his stupidity for not haggling and grossly overpaying. The rich Americano disappeared into the crowd so quickly, as if he had seen the devil. "*Loco loco Americano,*" she muttered to herself.

The mango lady wasn't the only one watching Snowden. Lee Chang-dong had been silently standing in the dark shadows of a scrubby acacia tree. He was pleased to have some shade. His skin was unaccustomed to such a harsh tropical heat. After two days of tailing Snowden, he and two other operatives were hot, tired, and bored.

Like the mango lady, Lee was stunned by Snowden's sudden, erratic behavior—ducking and hiding—as if he feared being seen. Lee scanned the crowd of brown Filipino faces, looking for the source of Snowden's angst. Suddenly, one white face emerged. Had seeing this Caucasian caused Snowden to flee? Lee nodded to his associate who quickly pulled a camera from a waist pack and snapped a picture of the unsuspecting young man in dark sunglasses. Very curious indeed, Lee thought.

Lee, a twenty-five year veteran of North Korea's intelligence service, had only recently been assigned as a cultural affairs officer in North Korea's embassy in Manila. At fifty, he was old for this profession compared to his foreign contemporaries, but Pyongyang insured that its overseas cadre were party loyalists and had a vested interest in returning home, not political asylum seekers and not those easily turned as a double agents. Lee had a wife and four children in top schools in Pyongyang and Beijing. All of them economically benefited from being part of the elite of North Korean society.

For the last five years he had been a specialist in North Korea's powerful overseas intelligence collection service, working various nuclear weapons' acquisition programs in the Middle East. He had made his name running several renegade Pakistani nuclear scientists and negotiating deals for missile warhead weapons systems. He had thought these successes would have assured he could take a comfortable position as head of one of the civilian intelligence agencies close to his home. He was tired of foreign travel and strange food, and he missed his wife and children.

He tried not to entertain the idea that his assignment to Manila was because of political problems within the party. He had heard that "Great Leader" Kim Il-song's deteriorating health had created a power vacuum within senior ranks of the regime. For the past several years, "Great Leader's" son, Kim Jong-il, known to the masses as *"Ch'inaehanunjidoja* 'Dear Leader,'" had been ruthlessly consolidating his power. Lee also fought thoughts of scurrilous stories that "Dear Leader" was prone to bouts of mental illness and shuddered—daring to even think the "Dear Leader" was afflicted by such problems.

Thoughts of "Dear Leader's" mental health had only popped into his mind because it was rumored Kim Jong-il was obsessed by a recurring dream of U.S. plans to turn the North into a sea of fire, launching hundreds of nuclear weapons hidden in South Korea. "Dear Leader" had demanded that his spy agencies confirm whether or not the Americans had a nuclear arsenal bunkered in South Korea. Reportedly, individuals who had previously failed "Dear Leader" were now dead or locked away in labor camps. Thoughts of failure obsessively crept into his Lee's mind, clouding his analytical judgments. He feared for his family if he failed.

His boss had toyed with the idea of finding senior U.S. Air Force officers who had recently been stationed in South

Korea—ones who were believed to have had access to nuclear war plans. Such officers were available in the Philippines, many assigned to the fighter squadrons at Clark Air Base, and that explained Lee's transfer to Manila. Lee's boss hoped that away from the intense wartime atmosphere in South Korea—here in the relaxed Philippines—these officers would let their guard down.

Lee knew that Snowden was a counterintelligence officer with recent South Korea experience, but Lee doubted Snowden had any specific knowledge of nuclear-related value since his career was mostly espionage. But Lee's Philippine sources had reported something very interesting—Snowden might have an unnatural fondness for children—and that could provide valuable blackmail material. Lee pushed forward through the market crowd to try to continue to watch Snowden. He wasn't worried if he lost contact. Snowden was a sideshow. Lee's real target, and best chance for getting actionable intelligence, was a much bigger American fish—one that would require a different sort of operation, one that Pyongyang was pushing him to organize. He had no idea how to go about doing it.

4

Angeles City

It was six a.m. and Steel had two miles left to go in his ten-mile course. He was dressed in shorts and a T-shirt and carried a military-issue backpack. He liked walking in the early morning as the town woke up. His route was circular, running along the perimeter of Clark Air Base past a line of souvenir stores, rattan and bamboo furniture shops, and Chinese and Phil restaurants and bars.

He walked on the side of the creatively-named "Perimeter Road"—a road in name only, not paved and comprised mostly of gravel, chunks of concrete, and volcanic dust. Clouds of thousand-year-old ash blew around it in the dry season and with the monsoon rains came enormous puddles of foul-smelling water and ruts large enough to swallow a small car.

The shoulder straps on his green pack dug into his shoulders. The pain wasn't too bad. The pack held forty-five pounds of exercise weights wrapped in foam rubber. Between Jo Jo's martial arts training and this forced march routine twice a week, his twenty-eight-year-old body was in top shape.

Steel had been waiting two weeks for Professor Abucayan's call, anxious to see the Yamashita papers. Steel cursed himself for not getting the professor's number. Salamanca would have it, of course. Steel would give it another week.

He wiped the sweat from his brow with his T-shirt; only one more mile to go. In the distance the mountain range rose south of the base. He traced its line until he reached Mount Pinatubo, the largest peak and a dormant volcano. He had climbed it last year, quite a view from the top.

He glanced over to the Zambales Mountains, clearly visible this morning. Steel was hungry to mount another expedition through those lush jungles. It had been months since his last one. Maybe Friday evening, two days from now, he could squeeze in a quick overnight hike. That was why he trained after all: to be able to carry a fifty pound backpack full of equipment on quick trips into the rugged mountains. But, with the restrictions, he'd better lay low, at least for a short time.

Up ahead, Steel could see one of the three gates—this one known as Friendship—that allowed access to and from the base. He was so glad to live in town. It would have been god-awful on base, especially now.

Unlike Steel, most Americans assigned to the Philippines fought desperately for a base house; the waiting list ran for pages. On base, you could have central air conditioning, movie theaters, pizza places, sports fields, and lots of Americans to socialize with. Might as well stay in the states, thought Steel.

As he got closer to the gate, a lone G.I. exited on foot.

"Hey Captain," he called out.

Steel looked over. He instantly recognized the short, stocky African American dressed in camouflaged fatigues: Staff Sgt. Curtis Washington, Steel's favorite of four NCOs who worked with him in the 13th Air Force's Intelligence Division. Curtis was sharp, street smart. He had been persuaded by Steel to take night classes and work on an associate's degree. At work, Steel included Curtis in his projects and briefings, pushing him to assume duties more challenging than the usual NCO administrative jobs.

"Nice camouflage job, Curtis." Steel returned a salute. "I could hardly see you coming. You really blend into the street. Why don't you find some real jungle?"

Steel found the Air Force's policy requiring office workers to wear camouflaged fatigues utterly ridiculous. The only thing stupider were the Air Force guys who walked around the Pentagon in them. If they were really trying to hide, they ought to dress in suits, ties, and white shirts to blend in with the civilians.

"Sheeet Cap, my mama didn't raise no fool. No way I'm hauling my black ass up in them boonies with you."

"Well Curtis, you said 'boonies.' Did you know the American slang 'boondocks' is an appropriation of the Tagalog word '*bundok*,' which means mountain? During the Spanish-American war—"

"Cap- this going to take long?" Curtis rolled his eyes.

"You see, U.S. soldiers picked up the expression 'going to the boondocks' when they went off to fight the Filipino rebels in the mountains."

Curtis laughed. He liked Steel. Most of the NCOs at the headquarters unit liked him. Steel was good at his job and wasn't arrogant like some of the other officers.

"Did you hear Captain? They lifted the restrictions," Curtis threw his clenched fists into the air.

"Curtis, tell me you're not shitting me."

"No sir. I wouldn't lie to you about that. As of 0700 we are free to roll into the vil. Party time tonight."

Steel grabbed his arm and shook his hand.

"You can say that again. Maybe I'll see you out there later."

Curtis gave him a hard look. "I doubt that Cap; we don't run in the same circles. I'm taking a couple of days leave. I've got to get out on the town. Watch yourself Captain, all the amateurs be out tonight."

Thank God, Steel thought. He could plan a trip this weekend. But deep inside, his analyst voice called for restraint. The NPA weren't going to give in this easy. They'd lose face. They had to kill again. He just hoped it wasn't him or Curtis this time.

Steel picked up his pace until he passed the entrance to the Flying Machine bar. He noticed the doors propped open and moved to look inside but quickly changed his mind. The place had to be scary during the daylight. At night, pulsing interior lighting, loud music, and ample amounts of alcohol masked its seedy décor. Tonight it would be bustling with eager, rich, and horny G.I.s.

He eyed a tiny old lady, bent over at the waist, sweeping the cracked sidewalk leading up to the entrance. Bone thin, she wore a long skirt and white blouse, her gray hair tied back in a bun; her short, stiff bristled broom rhythmically moved across the pavement. The swish-swish was just another voice in the chorus as every maid and houseboy hit the sidewalk for this morning ritual.

The Flying Machine was one of probably fifty bars in Angeles City that catered to a mix of American G.I.s, retired G.I.s, and a few foreign tourists. Angeles City was the wildest party town in Asia. Sodom and Gomorrah, or at least Saigon at the height of the Vietnam War. The only other competitor for the title was Olongapo City, the town outside the U.S. Navy's base at Subic Bay—about fifty miles northwest from Manila.

The bottom rung of the Angeles bar scene were the seedy dives, grouped in an area known as "blow row." Barely legal girls and aged hostesses provided the namesake blow jobs. It was not unusual to see eight G.I.s sitting around laughing, talking, and drinking beer while two or three girls under the table provided free samples. Rooms were available in the back of the bars to complete the transactions.

The relatively classier places were the discos, featuring huge dance floors and the latest music. There were country and western saloons, heavy rock hangouts with names like Superhead, Red Lips, and Pussy Galors, and even one bar where hostesses paraded around in sexy underwear. But among all these niches, Steel liked the Flying Machine best.

He smiled at the old woman. "*Magadang Umaga*, good morning."

She looked up surprised.

"Good news, no more restrictions. Tell Mamasan to get ready for some business tonight."

The old woman dropped her broom, clapped her thin leathery hands together, and gave Steel a toothless grin.

He called over his shoulder, "Yes. We got the news this morning."

The proprietress of the Flying Machine was from Cebu in the Visayan Islands, and she recruited the most beautiful women from her province to work for her. Steel liked Visayan women, taller than the average Filipina and light-skinned, attributes inherited from Chinese and Spanish ancestors.

On any given night at the Flying Machine, as many as thirty women, dressed only in string bikinis, gyrated to pulsing rock music on raised stages around the bar. Early on in his tour, he was here every other night; so many beautiful women, any of them yours for a twenty dollar bar fine. He had been a kid in a candy store.

For the last five months, though, Steel had taken a break from the bar scene, in part because of the restrictions, but also to do a little soul searching. It had given him a chance to focus on his work, school, and the treasure. He had also thought about trying to date women in the traditional manner, but he worried he was sorely out of practice. Not that he actually had been successful at dating women before he started just paying for them.

Looking at the empty Flying Machine, imagining the girls who in a few short hours would be tempting customers with bouncing breasts and tight asses, Steel felt a welcome stirring in his gym shorts. Whatever the psychic benefits of his monastic living these last months, it had been too long. He knew he was headed to the bar tonight.

Steel walked the last fifty yards of his circuit at a slow pace, cooling down in more ways than one. The subdivision where he lived was called Vila Sol. It housed the families of enlisted G.I.s, upper-middle-class Filipinos, and some retired Americans—unlike the majority of off-base housing, which held Americans only.

He stopped at the high metal gates protecting his driveway—the only access through the seven-foot-tall cinder block wall that surrounded his house. Though ugly, the wall was necessary in this high-crime area. He opened one of the gates and walked into his tranquil safe haven.

The house was large and airy with high ceilings and an abundance of screened windows. He had three bedrooms and a large living room. His rent was nothing, one hundred dollars a month, a price low by even Philippine standards.

He paid his rent in U.S. dollars, technically illegal under Philippine law. His landlord got a higher pesos exchange rate when he traded the U.S. dollars on the black market. Steel also provided his landlord a monthly allotment of two bottles of good American scotch and two cartons of cigarettes; while it was a violation of Air Force rules, Steel saw no harm in the transaction. He didn't drink scotch or smoke American brands.

With his captain's salary, housing allowance, and overseas cost-of-living allowance, Steel lived like a king, supporting a motley crew of household help and, of course Jo Jo and his daughters. Steel paused for a moment and watched his yard boy Joseph push a cart of stones toward the beginnings of a Japanese garden and pond.

"Good morning sir," the boy called out, "I hope you enjoyed your exercise?" Joseph was in his late teens, short, skinny, and dark-skinned from working outside. Today, he was barefoot and shirtless wearing only an oversized pair of ragged gym shorts—formerly Steel's.

Steel waved and thought about going to inspect how his latest beautification project was coming along. When he first acquired the house, he bothered little with the extensive garden. But after a few months, he started to take interest and buy plants, trees, and flowers. He knew it wasn't financially practical to make improvements to a house he didn't own, but the order inside his walled yard appealed to him. When he was out amongst the plants, he had a feeling of home, something he had not experienced since he was a small child.

He walked over to the section of the wall in front of his bedroom window. He examined an orchid growing on a tree branch he had nailed there. It had recently flowered for the first time, a delicate yellow and red—amazing how an ugly clump of vines and green leaves could produce such a beautiful bloom.

He examined the bush he had planted below his bedroom window to perfume the evening air. He got it from his neighbor Teddy who said it was quite rare.

Teddy Lacson, a retired attorney, grew hundreds of orchids, each anchored to a vertical log pole on the other side of their shared garden wall. A tent of black mesh net hung over Teddy's yard, cutting down on the direct sunlight and providing some shelter to the orchids during the scorching noon sun.

Steel only cultivated about two dozen varieties of orchid, some common, others highly prized by collectors. He had found some on his forays into the mountains where they grew high up in the canopies. Others, he had bought from mountain tribesmen who came by his house.

His maid, Rosa, was waiting for him at the door, annoyed.

"William, did you call Father Rudy back yet? Remember, he called yesterday afternoon."

"No, I forgot. Maybe I could go over there after work today." He checked his watch.

"William, that would make me very happy. You have plenty of time, and you should be feeling so full of goodness after your nice exercise." He ignored her sarcastic tone. She was the only one who called him William.

"Do you want some breakfast?"

He eyed her, shaking his head no. She stood with her arms folded across her chest, blocking his access to the house. She was dressed in her white maid's blouse and skirt, looking as always, neat and clinical. In her early fifties and tough as nails, Rosa was a widow who had raised three children on her own.

Steel was thankful to the instinct that led him to hire Rosa three years ago rather than one of the admittedly pretty but usually incompetent house girls favored by most G.I.s arriving in the Philippines. Their maids were not only lousy at their jobs, they were often trouble as well. Last year a senior airman found himself in nasty divorce after he impregnated both his wife and house girl in the same month. No chance of that with Rosa.

In fact, Rosa was also one of main reasons he didn't get into as much trouble as he could have. She was never one to keep her disapproval of his choices in female companionship to herself. There was nothing worse than trying to deal with a morning hangover while listening to her commentary, "It is such a shame that they think they have to sell themselves in order to survive in this life." He only had overnight guests on Saturday nights; Sundays were her day off.

He walked around her, hurrying to get cleaned up and into the office a little early. He planned on leaving work on time this afternoon because tonight he was headed to the vil.

Steel pulled his dark blue Datsun 4 x 4 truck into an empty parking spot in front of the Flying Machine. The blaring heavy metal rock, with bass booming, spilled out into the street. Jo Jo eagerly jumped out of the passenger seat. It hadn't taken much convincing to get him to come along. It had been a dry spell for his love life too, although not as long as Steel's.

The blue-suited security guard greeted them with a wave. Shouldering an old Remington pump action shotgun, the one-eyed, greasy-haired old man reached to open Steel's door, smiling disingenuously.

Steel beat him to it, quickly jumping out. He tried, unsuccessfully, not to stare at the guard's badly scarred eye socket. What had caused such a jagged wound? Steel stared instead at the guard's nametag which read "Santos."

"Whenever I see that guy, I wonder what the hell happened to his eye," Steel muttered quietly as they walked.

"Last time when we were here, I asked him. He said he lost it in the army down in Mindanao. A Muslim guerrilla with a kris blade tried to kill him," Jo Jo made a stabbing motion with his hand.

"Jesus."

Jo Jo continued. "He's moonlighting at this job. Believe it or not, he is a corporal in the local Philippine constabulary. He is too old and lazy and low rank to make good extortion money as a cop and more importantly, he's related to the club owner; that's how he got the job."

Steel knew the job was plum. Americans paid Santos to provide a little extra security for their cars, probably doubling his day job's salary of eighty pesos or about U.S. four dollars. Steel didn't like him, not because he was lazy or had an ugly eye, but because he was rough on the street kids who hung out in front of the bar.

Once inside, Steel took a few seconds to adjust to the darkness. The place was packed, but they found two seats at the bar. Behind the bartenders, a raised wooden platform held a dozen girls in bikinis dancing to a blasting Van Halen song.

The two scantily clad dancers directly in front of Steel shared one wooden pole; he watched with appreciation as they gyrated their tiny hips to the thumping guitar riff.

He and Jo Jo ordered beers from the short, butch woman behind the bar. Steel held his bottle up to the dim light—nothing floating inside the bottle. Jo Jo followed suit. Once, Steel had found a huge dead cockroach in his beer after he had already drunk half of it.

"I think I'm already in love," Jo Jo leaned on the bar and called out to the girls sharing the pole. "Hi *maganda,* beautiful, don't fall too hard for my Filipino good looks. Let us buy you drinks when you finish your dance," Jo Jo turned and whispered to Steel: "So boss, it would be good for you to buy drinks for them."

"Thanks for the honor," Steel eyed the women closely. The one to his right, the shorter of the two, had an incredible body. As they say, stacked like a brick shit house. She belied the stereotype of the Asian woman with small breasts. Take her to the states, put her in a pair of jeans and a tight top, and she wouldn't give you the time of day. Here for a few dollars, she would be yours for the night, or the month. The one on his left, taller and thinner, was more his type.

Steel drank several more beers, chatted with the girls behind the bar and with a half-dozen dancers who sat with them between sets. Steel's language ability was a source of great amusement and fascination to the girls.

He could speak two dialects with near fluency and play around in several others. Earlier in the evening, one girl began chatting to her friend in the *Pampangan* dialect within earshot of Steel. She thought he could be handsome; maybe his nose was too big and his arms were too hairy.

Steel responded in *Pampangan* that his mother was part spider monkey and he had a great fondness for bananas. The girl buried her face into her hands as the bartenders laughed.

The place was wild tonight—six months' worth of testosterone and cash flying. Half past midnight, Steel got up to leave; he had already drunk way too much.

He had enjoyed himself immensely playing grab ass for an hour with a beautiful dancer named Lychee, who perched for a while in his lap. He even thought about taking her home, but he had to get up for work in the morning. He told her he'd see her on the weekend.

Jo Jo grabbed the keys, thinking it would be better if he drove his happy boss home. Santos waited for them at the truck, a big smile on his scarred face. Steel reluctantly began to fish around in his pocket for pesos for the expected tip.

Before they could reach the truck, two street kids scurried out of the shadows. They were maybe eight-years-old, dirty, shoeless, and ragged.

The larger of the two approached Steel with one hand out, the other on his friend's shoulder, "Please sir we're hungry and would like to buy some food."

In his time in the Philippines, Steel had seen hundreds of begging street kids and adults too, for that matter. Some were horribly disfigured, crippled, crawling. He had become hardened to the routineness of it. But for a brief moment, this particular child, lacking the pathos put on by so many beggars, grinning and looking Steel in the eye, connected.

"You get out of here!" Santos yelled, upset at being upstaged.

Steel smiled and handed the boy a wad of pesos. "What's your name?"

"Renaldo, sir," his grin widened to a full smile and he flashed a mouthful of badly rotted teeth.

Santos grabbed the child behind the neck.

"Let him go," Steel ordered.

Santos looked confused. These kids were barely even human. He tightened his grip on the boy, who stood grimacing. "But sir, these street boys are causing trouble and damaging customers cars."

"Let him go." Steel's tone of voice was low and menacing. Santos was lying about the boy, probably to trump up his claim that he deserved payment for extra protection for the cars.

Jo Jo quickly moved forward. "Why don't you just let the boy go, okay."

Santos hesitated for a moment, then released his grip. The boy quickly moved out of reach.

Steel glared at Santos. "You motherfucker," he hissed.

Jo Jo quickly put his arm around Steel. "Okay Captain Steel, we'd better go home now." Jo Jo repeated the title loudly so Santos would know he was messing with an officer.

Steel was still pissed and still drunk. He thought for a second. If he couldn't beat the hell of Santos, the next best thing was public humiliation. He reached into his shirt pocket and pulled out some more cash. Santos eyed the wad of bills. Steel held it into the air, examining it under the light from the bar, putting on a show for a gathering crowd. Steel fished out a bill and dramatically handed Renaldo one hundred pesos.

The boy looked at Steel, and then Santos, slowly taking the bills. He looked at them in disbelief. "Thank you, sir," he smiled and disappeared down the street. Steel then peeled off more bills, again waving at the crowd, who had started to laugh, wondering how much more the drunken G.I. would hand out. Santos grinned and waited, hand outstretched. Steel handed him a single bill and turned to the truck, leaving Santos staring in disgust at the two peso note with the taunts of the onlookers ringing in his ears.

The ringing phone pulled Snowden out of a deep sleep. He stood up and stumbled across his bedroom. A familiar voice called out a greeting, "*Kuya, kumosta kayo*, Brother how are you. Sorry to call so late I just got your message. I hope all is well. Your message sounded urgent."

"Sorry, I had a few drinks and something has been weighing heavily on me," Snowden sat down in a comfortable lounge chair next to the phone stand.

"Ah, you know *kuya* you shouldn't drink too much. So the restrictions have been lifted. That is good news. Did you go out? I can tell Romeo that you might want to visit the club in Manila."

"No, I'm not in the mood," he grimaced, remembering the incident with Steel.

"You sound troubled. We should talk about this when you come to Manila this week. I'm sure it is nothing," the calm voice reassured.

"No, I think it might be a problem. I've got a bad feeling. I'm laying low until I've worked this out."

"Yes, we'll work it out. It is a shame it has put a damper on your memories of Pangasinan."

"Yes, it was incredible. Thank Miguel for me for the arrangements. They were perfect. Look, it's late. Thanks for calling. I'll talk to you more in Manila in person."

"No problem *kuya*. We can talk."

"Good night." Snowden hung up the phone, fighting waves of anxiety about Steel. What was Steel up to?

5

Barangay Sampang Bato

STEEL LEFT WORK AT NOON the following Friday and set off to Barangay Sampang Bato to meet their guides and porters. Taking advantage of an uncharacteristically smooth section of the dirt road, Steel took a corner quickly, skidding, and watched in his rearview mirror as twin dust clouds trailed behind.

"Ow! Shit," Steel's head hit the roof as the truck jolted onto a straightaway full of holes and erosion cuts. A long rainy season had taken its toll. "Fucking road."

He checked his watch. 1:30. They were making great time. Jo Jo had been prepared when Steel got home from work, standing ready with packed gear, food, and water. They quickly loaded the gear into the truck and headed off.

"I swear this road gets worse every time we come down it," Steel said, swerving to miss a boulder in the middle of the road.

"I'm tired of paying the mayor taxes for repairs to the roads that never get fixed." Jo Jo rocked with the swaying truck.

"I'm sure his mistresses would be enjoying your tax money, had you actually paid any."

"We wouldn't want to keep them from their nail appointments," Jo Jo said, examining his own finger nails.

"Maybe you should try your hand at politics. You'd make a good man-of-the-people mayor. Honest and intelligent. That would be a change."

"You're right. I could be happy with half as many mistresses as the mayor and still manage to repair the roads."

Steel looked over his shoulder into the bed of the truck. "Mr. Mayor, hope we got everything, especially the extra batteries for the metal detector."

"Yes boss, and the big one for the flashlight."

"Good. Hate to be out there and have a dead battery. I'm really looking forward to this. Probably change my tune on Sunday afternoon, though, when I'm about dead from heat stroke."

"Or maybe on Saturday night when you will wish you had kept your appointment with sexy Ms. Lychee at the bar."

Steel ignored Jo Jo and savored the simple pleasure of getting off work early. It had been a slow day, mostly spent filing copies of intelligence reports and plotting NPA incidents on the huge map of the Philippines on the wall next to his desk. He had paid particular attention to the mountain area east of the base, where they were heading now.

Lt. Lenny Mitra, his Phil army intel friend at the sprawling Camp Aquinaldo, had assured him that Communist activity in that area was low. He and Mitra, or "Boy" as his close friends called him, had an understanding. Boy found subtle ways to distinguish for Steel between the officially party line and the actual story.

Even without NPA in the area, Steel had to be careful. He was violating the modified restrictions. Nobody was allowed beyond a five-kilometer radius of the base. But he wasn't worried about being caught: There wouldn't be anyone to observe him where they were going.

Twenty minutes later, they pulled into Sapung Bato. The

village was the last vestige of civilization before the foothills and attracted hill people who sold items ranging from rattan to monkeys or bartered for modern products from the lowlands. Must be what an eighteenth century American frontier fort would have been like, with white trappers and American Indians trading animal pelts and gold.

They drove to the small cinder block structure topped with a tin roof and TV antenna where Tony, his main guide and porter, lived. Steel eyed the dwelling suspiciously. "I hope that little son-of-a bitch got organized. He's supposed to have five porters and diggers lined up and have their damn food too."

Jo Jo defended the guide. "Spoke with him yesterday. He said he'd be ready."

"I've heard that before. I hope he wasn't bullshitting me about the cave either."

"No, he's serious." Jo Jo tried to sound confident. He, too, hoped Tony had his act together. It wouldn't be the first time Tony had lied to them about finding a new cave or bunker to explore or failed to pull together the crack team he always promised. He hoped Steel wouldn't bring up the stupid Japanese Zero aircraft again. Unfortunately, Tony was the best guide money could buy, at least according to Tony.

Tony emerged from his house—a Negrito, not five feet tall, with black skin and short kinky black hair. He was dressed in western clothes: blue jeans, tennis shoes, and a polo shirt. Steel had never asked, but guessed Tony was probably in his late thirties.

Tony waited for Steel and Jo to exit the truck before he approached them.

"Glad to see you remembered to be here," Steel grunted, recalling Tony's last no-show. "Is everyone ready to go?"

Tony nodded his head.

"How many porters?" Steel asked in Aeta, Tony's native dialect, to emphasize he wanted a clear answer.

Tony pointed with chin towards the mountains and mumbled. "*Doon,* Over there."

Steel squinted in the direction indicated by Tony's chin. "Are they waiting at Barangay Magalang? How many are there?"

Tony paused, "Maybe four, sir."

Steel took a deep breath, gritted his teeth, and grunted at Jo Jo. "Talk to him."

Steel walked to the back of the truck as Jo Jo took Tony aside.

After a few minutes, Jo Jo returned. "He says he's pretty sure he has four men. Three for sure."

Steel took another deep breath. Three plus Tony was barely acceptable. He needed manpower for carrying and digging if the site proved promising; they only had one day to dig. More importantly, he didn't want to end up carrying all the extra gear. Five plus Tony was ideal. He had asked for five hoping for at least four.

"Why the shortage of bodies?" Steel asked through clenched jaw.

"Tony said there is a big problem between two Negrito families. Someone insulted someone and now they are fighting each other. No one wants to get involved or go up in the mountains right now."

"Great. Feuding Negritos. Let's just load up and get moving."

They pushed through a crowd of neighbors who had gathered around the truck to watch the American. Most were Negritos, a few Christians, Mestizo-Negritos, and other lowlander mixes. Before the restrictions, Steel had been a familiar sight around here, hardly worth a second look; but today everyone wanted to see the Americano.

Tony threw a large woven sack into the bed of the truck and waved to a small group, two adults and three children, who were quietly standing in the shade of several large banana trees. Steel watched as they stood among their possessions, nervously eyeing the truck. Their simple dress and skittishness pegged them as hill folk. They had an air of wildness about them. Tony waved again, motioning forward.

Steel guessed the female of the group was in her early twenties. No more than four-foot- three inches tall, she had a pretty face, ample breasts, and wild kinky black hair tied back in a ponytail. She picked up a large cloth bundle, and, with one graceful movement, balanced it on her head.

The man next to her hoisted a big pack on his back. Must be the girl's husband, thought Steel, and related to Tony, whom he looked like. Following their parents, two children hosted their bundles. The troop moved quickly to the truck, silent except for the jangling of the metal pots and plastic water jugs that hung from their bundles.

" Relatives of yours?" Steel asked.

"My cousin and his family."

"Where are they going? And don't tell me *doon*, over there."

Tony smiled. "They are going to walk maybe three days to their village at the other side of Mount Pinatubo."

"That's a hike." Steel marveled at the tough little kids and bent down and spoke to the smallest child, a girl of five or six. "What's your name, sweetheart?" he asked her in Aeta. She ran and hid behind her mother. No way she was going to speak to a scary white giant.

"Ponita." Tony answered for her.

Steel waved. "Hi everyone, my name is Steel and that is *Lolo*, grandpa Jo Jo," Steel pointed at Jo Jo, who waved. "Please take your seats, we are ready for take-off. Jo Jo will be your stewardess and I'm your pilot. Flying time to our destination is lord knows how long." Steel's humor was lost on everyone except himself.

Tony helped them stow their gear and got them settled in the back of the truck.

"Are we ready?" Steel looked at Jo Jo.

"Let's go."

Steel shoved a tape into the cassette player and they drove off, Dire Straights blasting.

Half an hour later, the road narrowed to the width of a footpath—with deep ruts worn by years of *carabao*, water buffalo, drawn carts. Steel tried to avoid the biggest pot holes and trenches in deference to his passengers in the back. He picked up anyone they found walking along the trail. He stopped counting at a dozen.

Around the next bend the trail ended at Barangay Magalang, a grouping of small huts. They would leave the truck here.

A group of Negrito men, naked to the waist and loaded down with bundles of eight-foot-long cut rattan poles, darted to the side of the trail as Steel slowed the truck to a crawl. "I wonder how far they've come?" He waved to the stunned men.

Jo Jo eyed them. "Judging from the quality of that rattan, probably a long way."

The men were headed out of the village, making the last leg of their long walk to Sapung Bato. Steel marveled that the rattan bundles on the shoulders of these Negritos could one day end up as furniture in an expensive showroom in New York City.

Jo Jo peered at the rattan. "Not much rattan left around here, probably more than a week's walk to find some. That could be a business for us. We could buy the rattan from the Negritos before they take it to Sapung Bato. We could make a nice profit."

Steel shook his head. "Take a hell of a lot of rattan to make any money."

He pulled in front of Old June's hut where the shriveled

Negrito barrio captain waited for them. Around him stood several of the village elders. Word traveled fast.

June stood at attention, an old World War II Garand M-1 rifle strapped on his back. He was dressed in shorts and a faded, stained white T-shirt, with CHDF printed in large letters on the front. He was happy to see Steel for a variety of reasons, the primary one being that June was well paid to watch the truck.

June was the village's leader and, for three decades, had constituted the entirety of the government's law and order in the area.

President Marcos created the Civilian Home Defense Force, the "CHDF," as advertised on June's shirt, similar to the U.S. strategic hamleting doctrine during the Vietnam War. The Marcos government fortified villages and armed citizens to defend against Communist aggression. Like in Vietnam, the program was a failure.

The CHDF suffered tremendous losses; their weapons' stockpiles turned into a personal armory for the NPA during their *Agra armas,* or arms-grabbing campaigns. Those CHDF units that weren't overrun ended up, in most cases, as private militias, serving the interests of wealthy landowners. It was debatable which group violated human rights more often, the NPA or the CHDF.

By the early 1980s, the official organization faded and regular army and constabulary units filled the void. June, however, dutifully kept the CHDF torch burning, proudly wearing his T-shirt. Steel wondered if he still collected a monthly stipend. It was possible the local army police units relied on June for intelligence and support. Steel chuckled. In all likelihood, the NPA relied on June too.

The NPA had tried in vain to win the Negritos over to Maoist doctrine, but for the most part, they were immune to the propaganda, and the NPA avoided confronting them. The NPA knew that a warring or vengeful Negrito tribe could play havoc with units trying to operate in the area. The NPA's begrudging respect for the Negritos fighting prowess was the main reason why Steel felt safe traveling in the mountains under their protection.

Tony appeared in his mountain clothes, a huge leather-sheathed bolo dangling from a rope around his tiny waist. The cloth sack slung over his shoulder held his team's store of rice and dried fish. They would barter with mountain Negritos for additional supplies like sweet potatoes or would forage for wild vegetables and animals.

"Ready now?" Steel called out to Tony.

He nodded and reluctantly picked up the huge army pack. The big pack was the only way to slow Tony down to a pace that wouldn't kill his white benefactor. Tony called out to the crew, and they shouldered their own packs and started for the edge of the village where the scrub jungle began.

Steel and Jo Jo hoisted their own equipment and followed. "I really feel overdressed for the occasion," Jo Jo said as they passed a clump of mostly naked Negritos. On the way out of the village, the men had stripped off their town clothes and were now bare-chested, sporting white loincloths that covered very little. The one woman in the group remained clothed in a modest, old, faded skirt and blouse.

"Maybe this will be our lucky weekend. Maybe we shall return as rich men," Jo Jo laughed.

"To the treasure." Steel held out his hand and Jo Jo slapped it.

Steel adjusted the strap of his pack. It didn't feel too bad. He had offloaded most of the bulky items to the Negritos. The heaviest weight was his water; it would be lighter on the return trip.

The Negritos drank water they found along the way. No way was Steel going to do that. He had spent too many days after these expeditions nursing violent stomach cramps.

Steel lifted his straw hat and mopped his brow with the end of the small towel tied around his neck. "Do you think Tony's lying about the cave?" Steel asked.

Jo Jo answered, "I don't think so. He's had months of hiking around. I think this might be a good one. Although one thing is odd; he keeps talking about *hangin*, wind coming out of a small hole near the cave. Very strange."

Steel thought for a moment. "Wind. Maybe geothermal."

He could just see the last Negrito porter walking ahead at a fast clip. He checked that his compass was still hanging around his neck and patted the cargo pocket on the side of his green jungle fatigue pants; the plastic bag holding his map was still there. "I want to plot our course in case we want to return to the spot someday."

"Yes, if you end up killing Tony I want to be able to get back alive."

"Your confidence level in Tony's story dropping?"

"I hope not," Jo Jo shrugged.

"Yeah, me too."

Jo Jo struggled to adjust his shoulder strap. "Think I could pay that Negrito woman to carry my pack. She looks stronger than both of us."

"Not a bad idea, except if she carries anyone's pack, it's mine. I'm the ugly American here."

He checked his watch. "It's two p.m., six hours before we camp. If we get up at 0500 tomorrow and are on the trail by 0600, we can be at the cave by ten, assuming Tony's right about the distance. Then we work all day on Saturday and a little on Sunday morning and leave around eleven to hike back."

"Good plan." Jo Jo exhaled deeply. He was already tired.

The trail into the mountains was well worn, winding along a rocky ridgeline and through a sea of waist-high elephant grass, then narrowing. The late afternoon sun was angled low enough that the hills provided some shelter from the burning rays.

There were few trees or shrubs, only scrub grasses and patches of banana trees. Most of the hardwoods had been cut, long ago, used for firewood and building materials.

The motley parade fell into a steady pace, Tony and the Negritos one-hundred paces ahead of Jo Jo and Steel. Steel was thirsty even though he had already emptied and filled his canteen twice, refilling it each time from a big plastic jug a Negrito carried. Sweat washed down his face; salt burned his eyes. The farther they left the village behind, the thicker the jungle became.

There was another hour before the sun set behind the mountains. Steel told Tony he wanted to camp near some water. He had to get out of his sweaty, filthy clothes and bathe. Tony knew of such a place.

As dusk darkened the sky, they marched into a lush grove of trees and bamboo plants with a stream running through it. Steel checked his compass, then pulled out his map. He had a rough idea where he was, but the stream was too small to make it onto the map.

Up ahead, Tony was talking to his relatives, stopping as Jo Jo and Steel approached.

"Dom Dom and his wife are leaving us now."

"Aren't they going to camp here for the night?"

"No. They want to walk some more. They will stop later. They still have far to go."

"They don't mind walking at night, I take it. They're welcome to stay and to share some food with us."

"I offered, but Dom Dom is concerned about his mother who is sick. He brings medicine and food for her."

Dom Dom thanked Steel for the car ride and waved goodbye. His wife smiled shyly. Steel wondered what medicine they carried. No doctor would have examined his mother. The village medicine man used native herbs.

Tony gazed after them as they silently disappeared in the forest. Steel asked him, "How much farther to the cave? How many hours walking?"

Tony paused for moment, calculating how long it would take the white man to walk it. "I would say less than five hours. We could do it in four if we go fast."

"Five hours is fine," Steel put his hand on Tony's shoulder. "I'm hungry. How about you?"

Steel and Jo Jo had quickly set up the small tent they shared so Steel could get his bath in the cool stream water. Clean and refreshed, he devoured a fat chicken Jo Jo had roasted in the coals with some sweet potatoes. Raising two picky teenage girls had done wonders for Jo Jo's cooking.

As night fell, Steel could see Jo Jo's profile against the glowing orange of the tent. He was reading by flashlight. A chorus of frogs and the laughter of the Negritos were the only sounds.

The Negritos had started their dinner late, heading out first to do some hunting and gathering. They lay around their fire laughing and talking in whispered voices. Steel could hear them plan what they were going to do with the money they made. He wondered what Tony was paying them.

The tableau could have been from a museum exhibit on primitive man. Tony stirred a big, black pot of water and rice. Impaled on sticks angled over the fire were a dozen tiny birds and one large snake: a four-foot boa, Steel guessed. The sweet potatoes were probably already buried in the coals. Tony's ancestors had no doubt prepared countless identical meals over the last thousand years.

Steel stretched, ready to turn in after one more trip to the stream. He draped his bath towel around his neck and reached for the U-shaped handle of an aluminum cooking pot; inside was his toilet kit, a clean pair of shorts, and shower thongs.

In his other hand he held a large flashlight. He flicked it on and scanned the ground ahead of him. He didn't want to surprise a cobra or any of the scores of other poisonous snakes indigenous to the area. He was not the only creature who enjoyed a cool stream.

"Sir." A whispered voice cut the still night air.

Steel's heart skipped. A Negrito approached, carrying a small water jug filled with water from the stream. "Christ, you scared the shit out of me."

The Negrito smiled and hurried back to the fire to get his share of food. "Scared the shit out of me," Steel muttered again. Tony did the same thing, always appearing from nowhere, then disappearing just as silently. More than once Steel had been giving instructions to Tony only to find out the small man had slipped away, leaving Steel pontificating to an empty jungle.

The Negritos were famous for their stealth. During World War II, the U.S. had used them to infiltrate Japanese barracks or encampments at night and slit the throat of sleeping Japanese soldiers. Or they would sneak up and mark an X on the boot of a sentry as he stood on duty—a lesson in how vulnerable and helpless the invaders were.

Steel shined his light around him to ensure no more Negritos were about and headed for the stream.

Back at the fire, they all laughed when Remi told about scaring Steel. Remi passed Tony a plastic jug of *tuba*. The coconut-based alcohol drink was getting them drunk.

"Why does Steel come to the mountains?" Remi paused and took a bite of boa from the stick. "I hear he is looking for trash we dig out of the ground and Japanese money."

Tony passed the jug to Pitpit who was half asleep. "Yes, he looks for lost Japanese money, but Jo Jo told me he looks for the bones of his dead father too. He was killed in the great war," Tony said in a whisper.

Remi looked surprised, then nodded somberly. "Oh, that is a sad thing to not have a proper burial for your father. It is no wonder that Steel is always sad-faced."

"I thought that was an angry face from too much money," Pitpit slurred sleepily.

"He is not mad-faced all the time, just when he looks for the money, and the bones," Tony noted.

"With so much money, I could have a happy face all the time," Lindom piped in, poking the coals with a stick looking for his sweet potato. "I would buy a big house and have a wife in Sampang Bato and have two more wives in the mountains."

"Yes, and pray they never meet," Tony mused.

They all laughed.

6

The Bunker
Zambales Mountains

STEEL ZIGZAGGED ALONG THE RIDGELINE, following a narrow path traveling above a thick grove of bamboo and bananas and a few large trees. The path provided spotty shade from the morning sun, already scorching below.

Steel scanned the trees. One thin one with a tuft of small scraggy greenery at its top caught his eye. It had grown skyward at extreme angles, first left, then right, as it competed for sunlight among its larger and fuller neighbors. Perseverance paid off as it secured a place high in the sky where it could display its handful of foliage. Its branches, Steel could see patches of different shades of green. He pulled out his binoculars; maybe an orchid? He thought he could see yellow flowers.

Steel called to Tony. "What do you think? Are they too high?"

Tony shielded his eyes. He shrugged his shoulders, not as excited by the small plants as Steel.

"You want some rope? It's a pretty tall tree."

Tony shrugged again. Steel dug in his pack, found his rope, and hacked off a six-foot section. Tony dropped his pack, strapped his bolo across his back, and climbed up the tree. He tied the rope in a large loop around his waist and the tree, leaving a space between his belly and the smooth bark.

Tony hopped frog-like to the tree's first bend, an almost orthogonal angle. He sized up his path and climbed the rest of the way to the top, probably seventy feet. Pulling out his bolo, he chopped at a branch where a cluster of orchids had taken root. The branch crashed to earth. Tony chopped again and a second branch fell. Steel wanted to leave some of the flowers to continue to procreate, so he yelled at Tony to stop.

Steel retrieved the branches while Tony descended. He examined each plant—they were healthy. Steel trimmed them and placed them into a large plastic woven rice sack he had brought along to carry orchids. He sprinkled water over them and secured the sack to the outside of his pack. The plants could easily weather the trip back to town.

Steel knew Tony and the others did not understand all the effort to gather and transport what to them were common forest flowers. But Steel relished finding something European collectors would pay top dollar for, even though he had no intention of selling them. For him, it was just another way to satisfy his urge to hunt treasure.

Four hours of walking through spiny scrub trees, brush, and dense groves of bamboo later, Steel was lacerated and bleeding where sharp thorns had ripped through his clothing. But he and Jo Jo had kept up with the mini-iron-man Tony, their rigorous workouts paying off.

Tony had led them to a lush canyon filled with large boulders strewn along a small dry stream bed. He silently pointed to a large boulder and stopped.

Jo Jo looked at it. "Sort of looks like a big parrot head."

Steel agreed.

Tony slipped his backpack off, dropped it to the ground, and disappeared behind a boulder. The other Negritos dropped their gear too.

"Looks like we stop," Steel thought as he laid down his

pack. He scaled a steep incline to find Tony squatting next to a hole in the side of the rock cliff. The hole was smooth-walled, as if chiseled by man rather than nature. Tony put his hand in front of the hole and motioned for Steel to do the same.

Steel put his face in front of the hole. Cool air streamed out as if fanned by machinery. Steel peered into the blackness. "Jo Jo, come up and bring the big flashlight."

"Sir, what can this be? Where is the wind coming from?"

Steel spoke, more to himself than to Tony, "I'm guessing that this is a vent system for an underground bunker." Steel took a step back and peered upwards. "I bet that on the other side of this hill there is an intake vent. Air travels right through the hill providing oxygen to the interior. There are probably more of these vented shafts. What an amazing engineering job. Jo Jo, where's the light?"

"Here." Jo Jo appeared at the top of the incline. "What is it?"

"Check this out," Steel indicated the hole. "Air conditioning."

Jo Jo pushed his face toward the vent. "Incredible—an air well?"

"A command post ventilation system. This is no ordinary bunker." Steel pushed the light into the hole and tried to peer in as far as he could. He could see about five feet. He pulled back and looked at the diameter of the hole, then sized up Tony. "Have you been in there?"

Tony nodded. "The roof has fallen maybe ten meters inside. No room, only for tiny hole." He measured the diameter with his hands.

"There's probably a bigger entrance down around the bottom," Jo Jo piped in.

Tony pointed to the bottom of the hill. "Yes, I think we know where it is, but it is buried in by dirt and rock."

"Let's have a look." Steel climbed back down the hill.

Tony led them into a flat, shady area beneath some acacia trees. He stopped and Steel walked up beside him. Tony pointed to the ground. Among delicate green ferns, Steel could see shallow depressions in the rich, brown dirt. He had seen this before—graves, likely the graves of Japanese soldiers.

A white elongated object, partially buried below the surface, caught his attention. He pulled a knife from a sheath on his boot and dug—a human bone. He gently put it back.

"Judging from how shallow these are, I guess there are at least thirty or forty graves," Jo Jo noted, making the sign of the cross on his chest.

"Yeah, biggest graveyard we've found yet." Steel stood up and brushed the dirt from his hands. "These are likely Japanese soldiers. With a site this big, our guys would have returned later and dug up their U.S. dead."

"Tony, where's the entrance you found?" Jo Jo asked.

"Over there," Tony pointed to the hillside.

"Are we going to dig up any of the graves?" Jo Jo asked.

"No, but I'll mark the map and provide the location to the Japanese Embassy in Manila."

Normally the Japanese Embassy wouldn't send anyone into the mountains for a couple of bodies, but with the size of this graveyard, they might make an exception. Early in his treasure hunting days, Steel had made an effort to haul back to town the bones of Japanese soldiers he found, at least those who had their metal dog tags. Initially the Japanese Embassy would send someone down to collect them, but after a while, they lost interest.

At one point, Steel had the bones of about fifteen Japanese soldiers in shopping bags in his house awaiting pickup from the Embassy. Rosa had found them, and it took two days to calm her down. She refused to go anywhere near the closet where the bones were until they were removed. She still gave the sign of the cross every time she entered the room.

Rosa told her story to the neighbor's house girl who in turn passed it on to her employers. An agent from the Air Force Office of Special Investigations was sent to Steel's house. When Steel explained, the agent shook his head and laughed. It was the first time he had literally found skeletons in someone's closet.

A Japanese councilor officer eventually candidly explained to Steel that most of the military records of the soldiers were lost or destroyed after the war; consequently, the chance of reunification of the body with the family was almost nil.

Tens of thousands of Japanese soldiers, sailors, and airmen had died in the Philippines. Their bodies were scattered around the old battlefields in unmarked graves. No attempt was made to identify what bones they could find. Instead, they were cremated in Manila in a mass Buddhist ceremony and returned to Japan.

This stunned and angered Steel; it was so unlike America's desire to find World War II MIAs and return their bodies. He assumed that families of the Japanese soldiers would have felt the same way. He wished he could have sent the bodies he found back.

Tony led them to what looked like a large doorway. Steel placed a hand on Tony's shoulder said, "Shit. I guess I'll have to take back some of the names I've called you. Looks like an entrance to me."

"Definitely been sealed up though," Jo Jo noted.

"I agree. Looks like we dig."

The Japanese had built an extensive network of bunkers and command posts in these and other mountains. When the American and allied forces invaded the Philippines in 1944, Japanese soldiers died by the thousands in the caves, most killed in battle, others taking their own lives rather than face the dishonor of capture.

In many cases, American military forces simply blasted shut command bunkers, sealing the Japanese inside, preferring not to face suicidal soldiers aching for one last battle. Steel thought, that's what happened here. The cave probably hadn't been opened for forty years.

They dug in shifts. There wasn't enough room for more than two men to work at one time. Steel had just finished his turn and was squatting on his haunches. "So how far do we have to dig before we get through?" he said to Jo Jo.

Jo Jo looked up the hill and down, trying to gauge the distance. "I have no idea. I guess it would depend on how much explosives they used. Most of it seems to be loose dirt and rock; fortunately, no big boulders."

"I say no more than ten feet. Just a hunch. My guess is that beneath this initial rubble, we'll find a solid rock shaft." Steel turned back to his digging.

Four hours later, they did come on a solid granite interior tunnel. The entrance was bigger than Steel had expected. After another hour of digging, one of the Negritos yelled out that he had punched through into a tunnel. Steel shined his light inside and watched two Negritos crawl until they disappeared into the darkness. Steel glanced at the clear blue sky and took a deep lung full of fresh air before he entered the tunnel. He pushed forward, slithering on his belly like a limbed snake.

The tunnel was narrow and smelled of fresh dirt. The air was musty and needed more oxygen—definitely not a place for the claustrophobic. He thrust one arm forward and crawled along, flashlight in hand, trying to see the path ahead. The tunnel appeared to dead end. He wrenched his body, feeling blindly with his hands, and came on a sharp left bend. The Negritos who had cleared the way had apparently hit solid rock. After the detour, the passageway narrowed significantly. It became Negrito-sized, not measured for Steel's large frame.

Steel paused and took another gulp of stale air. It had taken him an eternity to get this far. But the way forward was too tight. How the hell was he going to get through? He twisted over onto his back and crept forward until the top of his head hit rock.

He worked his arms up over his head, feeling in the darkness for something to grab hold of. "Damn shoulders," he thought. "I'm too wide. I'm stuck." Steel fought off a wave of panic and tried not to think of being buried alive. He sucked in a deep breath—"I'm not stuck"—and exhaled loudly, collapsing his ribs and shoulder blades, again moving ahead.

Dirt and dust clogged his nose and mouth choking him. He dug in his heels and scooted a centimeter, repeating the process dozens of times. Exhausted, he lay for a moment in the dark and rested. He stared at the dirt ceiling directly above him. It was the second time in his life that he had endured the birth process. In the silence, he could hear Jo Jo grunting and cursing directly behind him.

"Jo Jo, hang in there. I've made it through the worst. It shouldn't be a problem for you. You're smaller."

"Okay," came a muffled voice. "Jesus Maria Joseph, what the hell am I doing in this dirt vagina?"

Steel had already moved ahead. The tunnel widened slightly, maybe to three feet in diameter, but that felt huge. Steel slipped over to his stomach, coughing up a pound of dirt, and crawled, his ass bumping the ceiling.

Ahead he could see a flickering light. He was anxious that Tony not get too far ahead. Steel caught up with Tony and Remi standing in a chamber with a five foot tall ceiling. Steel was stunned that Tony had not rushed off to explore.

"Goddamn, that was a squeeze." Steel choked and banged the dust and dirt off his shirt and pants.

Behind him, Jo Jo popped out of the tube, relieved to be free of it. "That was too tight. I am too fat. No more extra helpings of rice for me." Tony and Remi laughed loudly.

They waited for two more Negritos carrying more equipment to emerge. One Negrito remained outside to show rescue teams where to look.

Steel shined the beam of his lantern on the ground ahead of them. The solid rock walls and ceiling were smooth as if carved by a big drill bit. This must have taken thousands of hours to build.

Steel and Jo Jo had been in many different caves and bunkers, but none as large or well-constructed as this. They moved quickly, Steel stooping over while the Negritos walked comfortably upright.

Steel stopped to examine a piece of rotted leather lying on the soft, dusty floor—the sole of a Japanese imperial army boot. He pointed to it with the tip of his own boot and identified it for the rest. Tony picked it up and put it in his backpack.

Up ahead the tunnel split into two passages. Steel shined his light to the right and then to the left. The light beams briefly danced around the walls, then disappeared into the black abyss. Which to take?

"Who votes left?" Steel asked.

"Sounds good," Jo Jo piped up.

Tony nodded yes.

Steel checked his compass, then pulled out a small can of white spray paint and scrawled a large X and an arrow on the wall. He wanted to know just where the hell they had been, or more importantly, where they hadn't.

"Maybe we should split up," Steel thought aloud. "Naah, we'd better stay together."

The group moved left and walked about a hundred feet. There were a few signs of human habitation: broken glass from a Japanese beer bottle, some empty 7-mm rifle shell casings, and a metal part from the rubber hose of a Japanese gas mask.

Farther down, the path seemed to rise slightly; Steel thought he saw a light. He blinked his eyes hard, turned off his flashlight, and stopped. The flicker remained.

"Jo Jo, what do you see?"

Jo Jo drew up next to him and stared. "Looks like a lantern. Looks like light."

"A lantern, now that's creepy. Can't be. Must be an opening."

"Let's go and see." Jo Jo led the way.

A small hole near the roof of the cavern let bright morning sunshine stream in. They stood squinting, trying to accustom their eyes to the light.

Steel scrutinized the wall nearest the opening. Rough stairs were cut into the rock. He called out, "Tony, you and the boys stay here while Jo Jo and I have a look out the hole. Don't wander off." Switching to English, he said, "C'mon, Jo Jo."

They climbed up the side of the wall and into the daylight.

Steel pulled himself into waist-deep grass on the top of the hill housing the command bunker. Fresh air rushed into his lungs, making him dizzy with oxygen. He shielded his eyes from the sun with his hand, looked into the distance, and blinked at the sight of Clark Air Base.

Jo Jo whistled loudly as he popped from the ground next to Steel.

The exit hidden in the grass was barely large enough for a man to squeeze out—almost like an animal burrow.

"Must be a sentry outpost. Look, there's Clark Air Base," Jo Jo pointed. "Jesus, we're on top of the command post hill. I didn't realize we were climbing inside."

"It wasn't much of an incline. I didn't think we were

close to the top of the hill. But more importantly, this hole is fucking good news. We don't have to crawl back out through that narrow slit."

"Amen to that," Jo Jo nodded.

"This is definitely the biggest, most developed bunker we've been in," Steel said. "Had to be a major headquarters. I'm anxious to get back in there and look around. There must be some big rooms."

"Yes. Although, this hole makes it obvious that none of the Jap troops were trapped inside. They must have left after the Americans moved on."

"True."

"Let's get back in there." Jo Jo moved forward.

Again inside the tunnel, the air was dank but cool. Steel's mood was light as he contemplated an exit much easier than their entrance.

They marched forward into another tunnel. Once Steel's eyes adjusted back to the dark, he resumed scanning the floor which was littered with broken beer bottles, sake bottles, and medicine vials. As they moved on, rifle magazines—some loaded with rounds, others empty—and several Jap helmets appeared in the scattered trash. Steel bent down and examined a small green bottle. It was sealed with a cork and held tiny white tablets, still fresh—looking as if they had been packaged yesterday instead of 1942.

Steel checked his watch. He was tired and filthy with dirt caked in multiple layers. Thankfully, he had gotten an adrenalin rush from the possibilities the command post provided and was eager to push forward.

They entered a room off the tunnel. It took a few seconds before Steel's narrow flashlight beam could expose the entirety of the room. It was large with thirty-foot high ceilings, a natural cavern.

"My God," Jo Jo gasped as he stood looking around. He quickly made the sign of the cross on his chest.

"It's like a bad horror movie," Steel exclaimed in disbelief.

7

Manila

It was late Saturday afternoon, and Snowden was enjoying his stay at the Peninsula Manila Hotel in Makati, Manila's business district. He frequently booked himself the same enormous suite; as a returning gold-member guest, he was treated like royalty.

Earlier in the afternoon, he had worked out in the hotel gym and then soaked in a hot bath in the large tub in the suite's bathroom, enjoying its vast expanse of Italian marble, huge fluffy towels, and bouquets of fresh tropical flowers.

He felt clean and refreshed, lying naked on the silk sheets of his king-sized bed. The air conditioning was cranked down low and the coolness of the room invited him to nap, burrowing deeply under a thick layer of sheets and a comforter. If there was one thing he missed about Europe, it was the winters. The Philippine heat normally precluded snuggling under the covers and he did like to do that, especially with the little girls—and sometimes little boys—so available on the streets of Manila for just a few pesos.

He hugged tightly to his chest the two large pillows that the hotel made especially for him, embroidered with his initials and always plumped on his bed when he checked in. He gave a small thank you to Aunt Ruth for making this life possible.

She had been his rock when she was alive. For years, she cared for him and protected him, like no one else.

She saved him from his abusive father—threatened to report him to the police. Snowden moved in with Aunt Ruth when he was nine-years-old and stayed with her until he left for the academy. In fact, she still cared for him from the grave.

The inheritance was a surprise. How a simple librarian amassed $1 million in investments, Snowden never figured out. But she left it all to him. She was a financial genius and a saint.

He rolled over and checked the clock. His good friend Ramos would be by later. They would go out to dinner at an excellent seafood restaurant and then likely catch a show. Even in the cool room, the thought of those tiny children dressed as strippers and whores—the little boys in thong panties and high heels—made him sweat. The club must have kept a bevy of tailors making child-sized lingerie. They could afford it with the prices they were charging the elite, mostly foreign, clientele: wealthy Middle Eastern men and smattering of Europeans.

Snowden pulled the heavy pillows tighter against his body, squeezing one between his thighs. Maybe after dinner, instead of the noisy club, just a massage with two or three naked children all oiled up and sliding over him. Sometimes Ramos could find them as young as five or six; Snowden liked it if they were still fresh enough to look a little scared. He bit down hard on the pillow, savoring the image.

But too soon, choking anger replaced his excitement. Damn, he hadn't felt this way for twenty years, almost constantly in a state of panic, near hysteria. That bastard Steel was to blame. What was his game? He was following Snowden. Why? He had been so careful to conceal his sexual predilections from the Air Force and from the world.

Ramos would help him deal with Steel; then he could go back to enjoying himself. Yes, Ramos would help. Ramos would help. Snowden repeated over and over the soothing mantra. He felt the anxiety easing from his body as his thighs relaxed their death grip on the pillow, and he let himself drift off into sleep.

8

**The Bunker
Zambales Mountains**

STEEL WAS STUNNED. Dozens of wooden beds lined the floor, some with human remains, some with full skeletons stretched out on them. A few of the bodies were rested peacefully; others lay contorted or in the fetal position. Most were dressed in rags, remains of uniforms. Glass IV bottles hung on wooden poles, filled with clear liquid, waiting to revive the long dead patients. This was the central hospital, thought Steel.

"This place is filled with spirits of the dead," Jo Jo whispered.

"This is very good place," said Tony cramming a Japanese helmet into his backpack.

Steel bent to peer at one of the corpses laid out on a wooden bed as if at attention. He reached down and gently lifted a white string from around its neck.

He fingered a small, round brass medallion, an imperial Japanese air force dog tag. Poor bastard was a long way from the airfield. The army had forced many airmen into the hills for their last stand.

They stayed in the room searching more than an hour but found nothing valuable. Tony and the boys began to organize and pile things in preparation for their departure. They'd never be able to carry it in one load, but for now they would fill every available space in their packs.

Steel wasn't interested in souvenirs—he wanted treasure. But the closest they had come to gold were the gold fillings in some of the teeth in the corpses. He had told Tony to stop prying teeth out of the skulls. Tony was miffed, but there would be no desecration of bodies on Steel's watch. He didn't hold it against Tony. He'd do the same if he were as poor.

"All right, guys. I know you hate to move on, but I want to explore the rest of this place." Steel headed back into the main tunnel with the lantern, leaving the Negritos yelling in the dark, unhappy with only one old flashlight between them. He turned to Jo Jo. "I bet Tony wished he had opened this baby up instead of waiting for me."

"He won't wait for us again. Where now?" Jo Jo asked.

"There's got to be a lot more."

They backtracked to the fork in the tunnel and headed this time down the right passage, where they found a catacomb with at least a dozen rooms. Most were empty. Some, however, had makeshift tables, chairs, and beds. It appeared that the last Japanese soldiers to leave had managed to take most of their belongings with them.

"This place is pretty much cleared out except for junk. What about that last room? The tunnel seems to dead-end there." Steel checked his watch. It was already five. He was tired, hungry, and thirsty. He'd drunk most of the water he'd brought with him.

Jo Jo led the way. Steel saw him disappear into the room then almost instantaneously pop back out.

"Not a good room to be disturbing," Jo Jo whispered, scared.

Steel joined him. "Jesus Christ." He followed Jo Jo's light. Munitions: hundreds of rounds of artillery mortar and small arms sitting in rotted and collapsed crates. On the floor, scores of grenades lay about like small metal fruits. "Move slowly out. You never know what might set this shit off."

"I could not agree with you more," Jo Jo whispered.

The munitions, despite sitting in a dank cave for forty years, were still capable of blowing off. Steel had read about U.S. Civil War cannon balls that had detonated after being buried in the dirt for over 120 years because the black powder inside stayed sealed and dry.

Tony said that his father and uncle had perfected the art of de-activating munitions, probably through trial and error. It was a form of natural selection: Those who were successful lived to pass on their expertise. A whole Negrito industry had popped up. They sold the black powder to the NPA and the fishermen who illegally blasted fish.

"Damn, Jo Jo, where the hell did the day go? I'm tired, dirty, and thirstier than shit," Steel emptied the last drop of water from his canteen. "I'm also sick of digging up bullets and trash."

"So you had enough, boss?" Jo Jo asked hopefully.

"Yeah, enough for today. Let's go set up camp. I'm really hungry. Where are the boys?"

"They went back to the hospital."

"Just so long as they are not in that damn ammo storage room." Steel was too tired to fight Tony about the teeth.

"No, not this trip. But Tony will return so he can take all those bombs out of here; he'll make some good money. It is a shame he'll get all the profit. Maybe we—"

"Jo Jo, are you insane? You've been down in the dark too long. Let's go topside, get cleaned up and have a meal and a beer."

Jo Jo slapped himself on the side of the head. "When Tony's idea's start looking good, it's time to go. A beer? You mean *tuba* don't you?"

"No, I mean a cold beer."

"What you going to do? Have a monkey go get us one?"

"Oh my skeptical friend, there are six cans cooling in the stream as we speak. I put them in the pack we had Tony carry. I'm sure he didn't mind."

They rose early to break camp. By midday they were into the fifth hour of the return trip. Steel stopped for a moment and took a deep breath. He squatted down on his haunches. Jo Jo joined him. It had been a hell of a climb up the side of a steep ravine, hacking their way through a dense grove of banana trees. It was hot and something had stung Steel on his back. He hoped it was just a wasp or a fire ant and not a centipede or spider.

The jungle wasps were enormous but still, better them than a spider. He had once had one bite him on the leg below his knee. By the end of the day his leg had swollen to twice its size and Tony, god save him, had had to perform field surgery to drain the fluid out. Steel had thought he would lose the leg. It took a three-day hospital stay and powerful antibiotics to clear up that mess.

The doctors at the hospital were used to treating Steel, intrigued by the variety of tropical maladies he acquired. They never figured out one internal parasite he came in with, but they shipped a stool sample off to Walter Reed in D.C. and enjoyed the debate over its origin with their stateside colleagues.

"How far is Tony ahead of us?" Steel asked.

Jo Jo looked up and down the ravine. "I have no idea."

Steel yelled out. A few minutes later Tony emerged from the rough brush.

"Captain Steel, I want to show you a beautiful place," he said beaming.

Steel shrugged, "Why not?" They were making good time and besides he was intrigued by what Tony thought was a beautiful place.

"Just at the bottom of this hill." Tony motioned and disappeared back into the brush. Steel pushed for a couple of hundred yards through the tangled mess of vine and trees, before he saw Tony and the other Negritos waving ahead.

"Okay," he called out and waved back.

Steel broke through a tangled mess of vegetation into a small ravine surrounded on both sides by lush bamboo groves. A larger waterfall dropped its stream from thirty feet into a series of small rock cliffs and then a pool of water, twenty-by-twenty and deep by the look of it. "That is beautiful Tony. Where does the stream come from?"

"Out of the ground, there."

"A natural spring. That's rare around here," Jo Jo said.

Steel dropped his pack and walked over to the edge of the pool. He touched the water with his hand. It was cool.

"This is a sacred place for our tribe. We don't take any strangers here. You are the first." Tony smiled.

Steel raised his eyebrows.

"Thank you. It is a very beautiful place." He said it loudly so all the party could hear it.

"Are there any caves around here?" Jo Jo asked.

"No big caves. Just a small one." Tony pointed to a grove of bamboo.

"How about Japanese during the war?" Steel continued.

"No sir, my uncle said only a few. No big camps here."

Steel nodded and sat for a moment to rest. He checked his watch. They were okay on time; he'd just get home later than he'd planned. Everyone followed his lead, the Negritos stretching on the ground around the pool.

Steel's gaze moved along the ferns intertwined among the rocks. Toward the bottom of the falls, just before the water hit, Steel thought he saw a dark shadow. He had seen enough Tarzan movies as a boy to know that there was always a hidden cave behind the waterfall. He strained his eyes, peering into the rock. The only way to get to the base of the falls seemed to be wading through the pool.

He walked over to where Tony was sitting, filling a big plastic water jug. "Is it possible there is a cave behind the waterfall?" He pointed.

Tony looked up and shielded the sun from his eyes with his hand. "No, I don't think so."

"But did you ever swim over to find out?"

"No sir, we don't swim in this water. It is sacred water, only for drinking."

"Damn," Steel muttered. Oh well. He removed the towel from around his neck and dipped his hand into the water, so cool to the touch. His hands had been there no more than twenty seconds when he saw them. Five of them, three to four inches of wriggling leech, headed right towards his hands, honing in with their well-developed heat and vibration sensing organs. He left his hand there, teasingly.

Jo Jo wandered over and watched Steel taunting the leeches. "I read that in remote jungles of Mindanao there is a particular kind of leech that lives in the trees. When it rains, they fall down, land in your hair, and try to attach to your eyes," Jo Jo grimaced.

Steel pulled his hands out of the water just as a big leech moved in. He was unfazed by their aggressiveness. They did, however, dampen his enthusiasm for swimming across the pool; getting a leech on the leg was one thing, wouldn't be his first, but on the balls—that would be another matter. Thankfully, it was sacred water.

"Tony, I hate to go, but we've got a long haul back home." As they set off, he took one last look at the falls. Damn, it looked like a cave.

9

Clark Air Base

Snowden enjoyed going to the office on Saturday mornings. He came in early and worked for a few hours, then hit the gym for weightlifting and a pickup game of basketball. The office was empty. He could catch up on reading and reward himself by watching tapes in private—over and over.

He took a long deliberate sip of coffee from his mug tattooed with the OSI logo. He grabbed the remote for the VCR and eased back into his thick, padded desk chair. He fast-forwarded, starting and stopping until he got to the beginning of the interview.

The suspect was nicely dressed, white, a dependent wife in her late forties. She looked more like someone's mother than a criminal suspect.

Snowden stared hard as she answered the agent. She fielded question after question without fluster, hardly even a twitch, just the occasional fidget with her pearls.

As she gave another tug on the necklace, the agent wheeled a TV forward and played footage from the PX's security cameras. The quality was bad but there was no mistaking the wife, complete with pearls, slipping a perfume bottle into her purse. Snowden paused the tape just as the suspect's face cracked—a prelude to a guilty torrent of tears. He stared at her contorted face. This was it, the moment he relished, when the truth of her crime—her undoing—first played on her face.

Snowden scanned the clock on the wall of his spartan office. He still had an hour of time before he would go to the gym. He perused the stack of tapes in his top desk drawer. Maybe the interrogation of the young attractive airman who recanted the accusation of rape she had made against a co-worker. She had been so convincing.

Or maybe...He noticed a brown envelope sitting on the coffee table against the wall of his office. How did he miss that before? That's not where incoming mail went; it should have been in his in basket. Annoyed, he shut the drawer of video tapes and walked over to the table.

He looked at the address; damn, he had requested it two weeks ago. Snowden's mood soured as he pulled out a letter opener and unsealed the heavily taped package. It was the original report from the agent who performed the Special Background Investigation on Capt. William Armand Steel.

The SBI was done five years ago when Steel had applied for Air Force intelligence training, a routine background check for someone with Steel's level of security clearance. The twenty-five-page report contained numerous interviews with neighbors, co-workers, and friends. Snowden checked the date on the report. Steel was due for a five-year update, just the cover Snowden needed. He pushed back in his chair, tapes forgotten, and began to read intently.

Since that day at the market, he had expected to be confronted, turned in, or blackmailed. Why hadn't Steel come forward? Maybe he hadn't seen him. Or maybe he was playing some sort of sick game. "You mean sicker than the one you were playing that weekend?" The voice in his head mocked him. Snowden ignored the baiting but the voice continued.

"You know Steel needs to disappear, leaving no body." Nope, Snowden shook his head. The voice was wrong. Steel didn't know. Anyway, Snowden was finished with killing.

———•··•———

Steel sighed. This was the epitome of decadence. He lay naked, belly down, on a simple handmade wooden bed with clean, fresh-smelling sheets, receiving the best massage in the city from not one, but two, beautiful girls.

Tessie, despite her small size, had strong hands. She was twenty-years-old and pixie cute with a small tight body and short bobbed hair. She was sitting on a towel across his butt, straddling him like a horse, rubbing his shoulders and back. He sighed again—more of a moan. Her hands were literally pushing the pain from his tired muscles, exhausted after the weekend hike to the bunker. Malou, Tessie's nineteen-year-old sister, stood in front of him, pushing the top of his head against her naked belly and rubbing his neck and scalp. Both girls were stripped down to their underwear. The place wasn't air-conditioned. They always worked up a sweat and did not want to soil their white work smocks.

He hadn't told a soul about this place. It wasn't a massage parlor or a sex shop; it was a beauty salon at the end of his street. He got his hair cut there.

Over a year ago, he had been getting his usual Air Force issue cut when the two sisters, who gave manicures, pedicures, and the like, offered up a massage. Now he came for that service at least once a week. He always smiled and said hi to the American women as they glanced suspiciously out from under their dryers when he followed the sisters to the back room.

The massage was all business, not at all sexual, at least as far as the sisters were concerned. Steel, on the other hand, had to keep his imagination in check. It was embarrassing to flip over and have a tent pole under the towel. It had happened more than once, to the great amusement of the girls, who joked in *Warai*, a dialect which he didn't know.

After about thirty minutes on his belly, Malou asked him to flip over, which he could barely do. He was a mass of Jell-O. He silently obeyed her. Speaking was not required. The girls didn't mind; they enjoyed quietly chatting to each other. They had told him that the woman who ran the shop was sour-faced and serious and wouldn't let them talk to each during the business day.

He enjoyed this part of the massage the best. Dressed in their matching white cotton panties and bras, the sisters sat on top of him, each rubbing a leg. Both were wet and glistening; beads of sweat ran down Malou's small brown breasts and dripped onto his thighs. As they wriggled around on top of his naked body, all oily and smooth, he thought, life can be good, life can really be good.

He had toweled himself off, dressed, and handed each of the girls fifty pesos, about $2.50, as a tip—a lot more than they made doing a dependent wife's toenails. They were both happy; he was satisfied. He paid the shop owner eighty pesos: an hour of bliss for less than eight bucks.

Sometimes, he'd go to an actual massage place. His favorite was the Tajmahal Health Studio. There, for twenty dollars, he got an all-inclusive massage with the extra services that Tessie and Malou didn't provide.

The Taj had a large, ornate book they kept at the front desk. There were photos of over fifty different attendants, each with a number. You simply flipped through the book and picked; Steel had his favorite numbers.

The attendant took you to a small air-conditioned room

with a bed, bathroom, and shower. Some rooms were decorated in gaudy ornate colors, complete with replicas of Roman art and mirrored ceilings. Once in the room, you removed your clothes and the girl would strip down to her underwear to give you a massage.

After about thirty minutes, she would offer additional services—a "sensation" or a breast massage for five or ten dollars. Intercourse and oral sex cost slightly more. He always stuck with the breast massage out of fear of the clap and other diseases.

He left the beauty shop and walked fifty yards, down New York Street to his house. Rosa was waiting for him at the door. "William, did you call Father Rudy back yet? He called again." She was annoyed.

"No, no—I'm sorry I forgot. Maybe I could go over there," he checked his watch.

"Oh yes, William, that would make me very happy. You have plenty of time and you should be feeling so full of goodness after your massage," she said, herself looking more full of sourness tinged with a healthy dose of self-righteousness. "It is so sad that they think they have to do such work in order to survive in this life." Rosa was devoutly Catholic and sure the only reason Steel has not been incinerated by a lightning bolt from the blue was his relationship with Father Rudy.

"Rosa, I told you a million times. The massages are massages only. No *giling-giling*."

She brushed him aside with a wave of her hand. "Oh William, that is not for me to judge. That is for God to judge. Father Rudy asks if you could spare the time to see him. It is important, I think."

He checked his watch, six p.m. "I'll go now. Let me get my—"

She handed him his keys and a glass of ice-tea. "Come straight back after seeing Father Rudy. I'll prepare your dinner for you."

He smiled, walked outside, and opened up the tall metal gates in front of his carport. He jumped into the truck and backed out slowly, trying to avoid a trike cruising by looking for a customer to ferry. He waved to Rosa, who dutifully closed the gate.

Steel sped off. He was hungry and a little miffed Rosa hadn't let him eat first, but she was probably right. He would have tucked into her meal and then had to fight off the urge to relax and read.

He wondered what Father Rudy wanted. Steel wished the father had had a phone in his residence. It was unusual for him to call. He would normally drop by in person to discuss church business, religion, and politics, often accompanied by several glasses of wine. He would try to convince Steel to come to services—his or any. Just find God. Steel wasn't Catholic, or even a Christian. If there was a God, he always felt that he had a lot of explaining to do, like why Steel's childhood was so fucked up. If he had to choose, he would probably be a Buddhist. He really liked the idea of coming back to earth again.

And although he considered Father Rudy a friend, Steel could not stomach Catholic dogma. He thought the church's stance on abortion and birth control was at the heart of the Philippines' dire economic situation. There were too many poor Catholic mouths to feed.

Father Rudy was Catholic but had broken from the traditional Catholic Church ten years ago. He and two sisters ran a small independent church on the outskirts of town called Mabuhay House. Mabuhay House was Steel's connection with Father Rudy.

Steel saw two small figures up ahead, walking along the side of the road. They were poorly dressed kids. As Steel passed, he recognized Renaldo and the other boy from the Flying Machine's parking lot. Renaldo waved happily and Steel returned the wave. They must be heading to the Flying Machine, he thought. He recalled the incident with the guard and slammed on his brakes; the truck skidded across the gravel road. He backed up and rolled down the passenger-side window.

"Hey boys. Where are you going?"

Renaldo smiled and pointed up the street, "*Doon*, there." He said.

"You want a ride?"

Renaldo stood and stared as if he couldn't comprehend Steel's offer.

"Get in," Steel pushed open the door and they slowly climbed up. They looked unsure of his motivations; neither had been in a private vehicle before and certainly not one belonging to an Americano.

"So are you going to the Flying Machine?" Steel asked.

"Yes sir. My brother and I are going to watch some cars," he spoke proudly.

Renaldo seemed unimpressed that Steel conversed in Tagalog. The boy must have assumed that all Americanos spoke it. "What's your brother's name?" Steel asked.

"I call him Bong, but his real name is Manuel."

"Nice to meet you, Bong."

Bong peeked shyly at Steel. Steel noticed neither boy had shoes.

He pulled in front of the Flying Machine, gave his passengers some pesos, and let them out. He told Renaldo to buy some rubber sandals. He could see the one-eyed guard standing in front of the entrance talking to the trike drivers parked there waiting for fares. Steel beeped his horn and waved enthusiastically. He wanted it known that he was the boys' friend.

As he pulled away, a rush of sadness replaced his anger at seeing the guard. Where did they live? Did they have a home, or was it true what the scumbag guard had said, that they were homeless. Some of the street kids were, but many had houses and families who encouraged them to beg and watch cars in order to bring in money. He knew he was the boys' guardian angel. He would have Jo Jo check it all out.

Ten minutes later, Steel pulled up to the small compound, which Father Rudy, over one-hundred boys, and a few adult workers called home. Behind the big metal gates were Father Rudy's church and his beloved Mabuhay House—the only orphanage in the city or, for that matter, the province.

Steel had inherited Mabuhay House from Maj. Gary O'Dell. O'Dell was a heavy-set, red-headed Irishman, a helicopter pilot assigned to the 35th Rescue Squadron. Steel had regularly briefed the Rescue Squadron, and O'Dell was the point man for his visits. They soon became close friends. It was O'Dell who first introduced Steel to Tony, as O'Dell was an avid customer of Tony's World War II souvenirs.

O'Dell was an excellent pilot; he had done two tours at Clark and fought like hell to try to get a third. His commander wouldn't approve it though. He suspected O'Dell of black marketeering or dealing drugs. The commander's attitude was common among the senior officers. After all, why else would someone volunteer to remain in this Third World hell hole?

O'Dell had left a year ago, forced to take an assignment in the states at Andrews Air Force Base where he was part of the presidential helicopter support group. He had three years left to retirement. When he finished the Andrews tour, he planned on returning to Angeles and living like King Rat on his major's pension.

Steel could vouch for O'Dell's vices—he definitely loved women and beer—lots of both. And O'Dell, being a good Irish Catholic, used Mabuhay House to balance out his Falstaff-like drunken debauchery.

O'Dell had been a tireless organizer and fundraiser for the orphanage. Before he left, he begged Steel to take over as the home's guardian angel and financial point man. Every month, like clockwork, a check for $500 arrived by mail from Andrews. Steel would cash it for Father Rudy. O'Dell always joked that the money was child support—odds were one of the orphans was his offspring.

Steel beeped the horn of the truck several times. An older boy recognized the battered blue Datsun, opened the gate, and Steel drove inside.

Father Rudy was waiting, dressed as always in his white padre robe with a big beaded wooden rosary. Steel jumped out and embraced the priest warmly.

"Will. So good of you to come this evening. I hope I am not disturbing you?" Rudy said.

"No, father. Rosa told me you called."

"Yes. We've had a bit of a problem. The roof in one of the dorms is about to collapse. I'm afraid we had some bad termite damage. I should have checked to see if there was a problem before this happened," he said, shaking his head.

"So, let's have a look to see what we need. We'll make a list. I'll talk to Gary and see if we can come up with something creative."

"Thank you Will. As always, you make everything seem possible. Thank God for your help."

"Put in a good word for me will you? Or at least tell Rosa I was here."

A small crowd of boys excitedly circled them. En masse they walked over to look at the roof.

Steel surveyed the damage, chatted with the father. The whole process took about an hour. Steel tried to be as upbeat as possible. He wasn't an expert construction guy. It probably wasn't a cheap proposal. He'd have to call O'Dell later and give him the bad news. This could take some creative financing. He was always mentally exhausted after the visits. It all seemed so hopeless and overwhelming—so many kids. He didn't know how the priest managed it day to day. Right now though, Steel was hungry, and tired ready to hide behind the walls of his home.

10

Manila

A BLAST OF A HORN JOLTED Steel out of a dead sleep. He looked out the truck window into a mass of humanity, a sea of pedestrians and vehicles—cars, trucks, buses, and taxis all belching out thick, black smog.

Thank God he had taught Jo Jo to drive. It was late Friday afternoon after a long week at work. They were headed to Professor Abucayan's house for dinner and a first look at the Yamashita papers. Steel felt a current of anticipation run up his spine, waking him fully. The professor had said he hadn't seen much of interest in the diary, but Yamashita had to have said something.

Steel stretched his arms, pushing against the roof the truck. "Hey, we made pretty good time."

"It was fun driving fast, but we shall lose the time now. It's rush hour." Jo Jo said.

"We're going against traffic, right?"

"You would think so, but it is still a mess."

"Good old Manila," Steel thought.

It was an hour and fifteen minutes by car from the base to the

Philippine capital—a nice bit of highway and probably the only stretch of paved road in the Philippines devoid of trikes and *carabao*-drawn carts. And the best part? No speed limit; or if there was one, it wasn't enforced. You could cruise at eighty or ninety miles per hour.

"So you know where we're going?" Steel asked.

"Yes. I think I can get us there. I've been in that area in the back of a jeepney."

"When did you say you first met Abucayan?"

"He was giving a lecture which I attended on July 23, 1972."

"How the hell did you remember that date?"

"On July 24, 1972, I was arrested and sent to a jail for subversive activities during the 'Third Quarter Storm' at the University."

"Jail? You never told me you did time."

"It is not something I'm proud of."

"I don't know. Isn't it a kind of leftist badge of honor?"

Jo Jo shrugged.

"How long were you there?"

"Three months."

"Were you mistreated?"

"If your definition of mistreatment is being held without charges and tortured, then yes."

"Jesus. How did you get released?"

Jo Jo paused for a moment and seemed hesitant to answer. "My father got me out. General Ver, the commander of the armed forces, owed him a favor."

" Ver owed your dad a favor?" Steel repeated. Steel had met Jo Jo's dad. He was a dirt poor, semi-retired farmer, with a small pension, who wove baskets to make ends meet.

"During the war, he and Ver served together. They were both in the army and captured by the Japanese. He was Lieutenant Ver then and my father was a sergeant. He and my father were on the Bataan death march. My father carried Ver and gave him water. He saved his life. You know *Utang Na Loo*, blood debt."

"So your dad cashed in on blood debt forty years later."

"Yes."

"There's nothing wrong with that. It got you out of prison."

"But I left a lot of my friends behind. I think they always suspected I cut a deal—became an informer."

"Ah shit, that's too bad. Anyway, you know the truth."

Jo Jo silently nodded. Steel had more questions but didn't want to push it. Some of Jo Jo's friends might not have survived Marcos's brutal jails.

Jo Jo found Abucayan's house in a quiet neighborhood filled with neat, middle-class homes. Steel looked at the large green gate and double-checked the street address. It matched the one he had written down.

The house, while large, was simple. Steel reached behind his seat and pulled out a bouquet of flowers and a bottle of wine. After one knock, a young girl opened the gate and led the way to the front door where Abucayan stood.

"Captain Steel and Jo Jo, it is so good to see you both again. I trust your trip here was not too bad with our traffic problems."

"Please call me Will. No, the traffic wasn't too bad. Jo Jo did an excellent job driving."

"Please come in."

"I brought these."

"Oh, thank you." He took the bottle of wine and briefly examined the label. "You can give the flowers to Lettie in person."

He led them into the living room where Mrs. Abucayan stood smiling. Steel guessed she was in her mid-fifties, but she looked younger. She was elegant and taller than her husband. She had tied her gray hair back simply and dressed in a white blouse and a long skirt with a tribal pattern. She wore a large necklace of shells and beads, which looked to Steel to be the work of the Igorat tribe. He wondered how the short, bespectacled academic had won this beauty. Steel handed her the flowers.

"Thank you Captain Steel. They are beautiful. I must find a vase." She clasped his hand warmly.

"Oh, please call me Will. This is my good friend Maximo Bato."

"Pleased to meet you, Mrs. Abucayan. Please call me Jo Jo"

"Then you must all call me Lettie."

"Captain Steel also gave us a nice bottle of wine." The professor held it up for her to see.

The professor ushered them into the living room. The place was beautiful—tribal antiques and tasteful furniture artfully arranged on wood floors. Somebody in this house was from money. You don't afford a spread like this on a professor's salary, not in the Philippines anyway.

But for all its elegance, the living room lacked airflow. It was hot. A couple of slow-moving ceiling fans just pushed the humid air to and fro. Sweat started to run down Steel's chest and back.

Lettie returned with the flowers neatly arranged in a vase, and they chatted for a few minutes.

"Ah, Antonio," Abucayan rose to greet a tall, light-skinned, handsome man, who was being ushered in by the young house girl, interrupting Steel in the middle of a story about Tony and the bunker.

Antonio shook the professor's hand, as he said, "Antonio, this is Capt. William Steel, U.S. Air Force, and his friend Maximo Bato. William, this is Lt. Col. Antonio Devincia, Philippine Army." The professor enunciated the formal title.

Handshakes and head nods were exchanged. Steel noted

that Antonio's hair was long by Phil army standards and his thick moustache was definitely out of regulation. Steel would have never guessed the man was in the military.

"So, Professor Abucayan tells me you are stationed at Clark Air Base; you're an intelligence guy."

"Yes, that's right sir, and you?"

"Ah, I am a grunt assigned to headquarters. I am not happy. I'd much rather be out in the field leading troops."

The professor piped in quickly, "Antonio has seen much combat in Mindanao. He was wounded several times and is a decorated hero. I have a great respect for him. He is not the typical ignorant brute who our armed forces have historically recruited. Of course, maybe I am saying this because he is courting my daughter," Abucayan laughed.

"Yes, I'm afraid you are always overstating my career. I am just a simple soldier."

Lettie moved forward. "Please have a seat and get comfortable. We can have another cocktail. I'm not sure where my daughter is. She should be here by now," Lettie checked her watch.

"Yes, I spoke with her earlier today. She said she was coming. There must have been a late story," Antonio noted.

"Vida, my daughter, is a reporter for the Malaya paper." The professor beamed proudly.

"Have you heard of the Malaya newspaper?" Lettie asked.

"Of course; it always has great articles," Steel said. The Malaya was a left-leaning newspaper, anti-Marcos and always on the verge of being closed down. Steel read it religiously to find out what the left and, more importantly, what Marcos was up to.

"Did I hear my name?" Everyone turned. "Sorry I didn't want you to wait for me. I had a story that I just couldn't put to bed." Vida walked over and kissed her mother on the cheek.

Steel mumbled, staring at the gorgeous woman entering the living room. She was tall like her mother and dressed with a similar elegance in a long dress with geometric designs.

"Everyone, this is Vida, my beautiful daughter."

"Oh, mother."

Antonio quickly interjected, "No it is true. I will drink to that." Antonio raised his glass in a toast.

Steel stood quickly, trying to shake the image of "bed" and this girl. "Hi, I'm Will and this is my friend Jo Jo," he extended his hand.

"Ah, Captain Steel and Jo Jo. My father has told me all about you."

"You can catch up in the dining room. We are all half-starved waiting for you." Lettie led the way, arm in arm with her daughter, followed by Antonio and the professor.

Jo Jo leaned over and whispered to Steel, "Close your mouth my friend, you are drooling."

"That is a shining example of a very fine Filipina," Steel tried to mimic Rosa's voice.

"Yes, she certainly is. But look only. She is taken." Jo Jo glanced at Antonio following the girls into the dining room then patted Steel on the arm. "Don't be intimated by his obvious superior breeding and rugged handsomeness."

The meal was excellent: a grilled skip-jack in mango sauce. Steel poked at his meal, too entranced with Vida across the table to eat. Antonio sat next to her. They were a stunning couple. Antonio was one lucky bastard.

They opened Steel's wine and followed it with bottles from their own cellar. The conversation at the table switched quickly from religion to politics to history, but nothing on the Yamashita papers. Steel should have been disappointed—impatient—but Vida distracted him.

"So Will, what do you think of Marcos's human rights record?" Vida asked.

Steel paused, sensing a trap. "I was wondering at what point I would see the Malaya reporter in action. I'll answer only if I don't end up in one of your articles," he smiled.

"Don't worry, it's only for background."

"Be careful. She is always trying to bait me into divulging army secrets," Antonio laughed, putting his arm around her.

"I can see the headlines now: American captain confirms Marcos's abysmal human rights record." Jo Jo outlined the banner with his hands in the air.

Steel ignored Jo Jo. "I personally think he and his wife are corrupt and have raped the Philippine economy. He alone is responsible for the fact that he is facing a major insurgency movement. The NPA has thrived on their anti-Marcos rhetoric. If he would just spend the billions he is stealing and socking away in Swiss bank accounts on the Philippine people, he might find himself in less trouble."

"Interesting and surprising," Vida nodded.

"Ah, spoken like a true leftist." Antonio applauded slowly, his words slightly slurred.

Steel sat silent. Obviously, Antonio had had a few drinks before his arrival.

Vida probed Steel again. "Don't you think you are being two-faced? You are here, after all, as an instrument of U.S. imperialism. Without your country's support, Marcos would have been long gone."

"Oh Vida, do we have to have such lively discussion tonight?" Lettie injected.

"It's all right. I loved being called an imperialist. I have visions of being on horseback with my Teddy Roosevelt Rough Rider's hat on, walking softly and carrying a big stick. But to answer your question, I don't think we're here to support the politics of your government. Clark Air Base and Subic Naval Base are key military installations in our defense posture for the Pacific. The Philippines is an important strategic location where we can check Soviet and Chinese aggression."

"Well said," Antonio raised his glass. "To our U.S. allies."

Vida continued to stare at Steel. "But the money you pay Marcos and the military supplies you give him keep him and his military goons in power."

"Excuse me. I'm afraid I must draw the line at that last comment. The majority of my comrades are not goons," Antonio interrupted with a hint of mock indignation and put on his best goonish face.

Vida continued. "Yes, yes, all right. You and your boys are not goons, but the majority of the military's leadership are corrupt generals who are basically evil men."

Steel switched to Tagalog. "Vida, I beg to differ. The U.S. is generally not in the business of keeping dictators in power. Ultimately, the Philippine people have kept Marcos in power. They elected him, didn't they, albeit decades ago?"

"Will, I am most certainly impressed with your Tagalog. I don't think I've ever heard such fluency out of an American before." Vida said in English, laughing. "And a nice diversionary tactic."

"Yes, I've never heard such pure Tagalog from a foreigner," Lettie pitched in, clearly hoping for a new topic of conversation.

Ignoring their English, Steel continued in Tagalog. "Thank you. I have to thank Professor Jo Jo here." He pointed to Jo Jo.

"He is my best—well only—student."

Steel continued, "So, I really don't think you can continue to lay the blame on so-called U.S. imperialism crap. The real problem I have found is that Filipinos simply accept their present condition with a 'so be it' fatalistic outlook on life…"

They continued in this vein for another hour, through coffee and dessert served in the living room. As the others wandered off to their own conversations in the reaches of the large room, Steel and Vida kept sparring over empty coffee cups.

"I still can't believe that you think that the presence of the U.S. bases on Philippine soil is not an affront to our sovereignty and dignity," Vida said, her face flush with indignation and wine.

"It is a mutually beneficial relationship. You let us base here, and we offer you our friendship and show the Philippine people what freedom and goodness mean—what America really stands—"

"You've been listening to your base propaganda officer too much. What I see is the exploitation of the Philippine people by a corrupt and oppressive government supported by the U.S.," Vida moved closer to him. He leaned into her, momentarily forgetting his patriotic defense, hoping to catch a whiff of her scent.

"But you really want to know what disgusts me about the American presence? It is the pollution and the exploitation of women that occurs around the bases."

"Pollution and exploitation of women? Oh come on. Yes, we exploit women, but we are not polluters. We are very environmentally conscious. You should see what we go through to keep the place clean."

Vida, tried not to smile. "I've heard that Clark stores nuclear and chemical weapons that are leaking into the ground and poisoning the ground water."

"Vida you can't believe all that. Do you think we'd want to expose ourselves? We have to live on that base," he stared into her deep brown eyes.

She looked away. "Well, we can argue about pollution, but you can't argue with the fact of prostitution and exploitation of children around the bases. There are supposedly thousands of prostitutes in Clark's environs."

Steel took a good look at her as she stared off into space. She was so beautiful. He heard Jo Jo and the professor laugh on the other side of the room. Were they finally talking about the papers? Who cares? Steel was in love.

"I can't argue with you there. You are right. It's not the best situation to have so many Filipina's acting as hostesses in clubs."

"Oh come on—hostesses? These girls are prostitutes and you Americans use them because they need money."

"Be fair. It's not just Americans, there are other foreigners too."

"Don't be ridiculous, William."

Steel chuckled. She switched to "William" in order to emphasize his juvenile position on the issue. "Now you're being unfair. Most of the girls working in the clubs are not prostitutes in the negative sense of word. I see them… er… more as paid girlfriends that…"

"What? Paid girlfriends? You've got—"

"Wait now. Hear me out. Many are educated and have degrees. They're there because they can't find work or they make ten times more dancing in a bar then working in an office."

"Oh, so that makes it all right that they sell themselves for a higher salary? If the bases weren't there, they wouldn't be corrupted or tempted to do that."

"That's ridiculous. You can't say that the bases are responsible for prostitution in the Philippines. I mean, Christ! I read an article in Asia Week that discussed the prostitution business here in Manila. You have just as many hookers here as we do in Angeles—and there aren't any GIs."

She smiled, reached down, and lifted her empty coffee cup, pretending to sip. He could almost hear her thoughts.

"So it seems like you've given this topic great thought. Maybe you have firsthand knowledge of the business in

Angeles," she whispered. "Maybe I am hitting too close to home. You wouldn't want your recreation taken away from you."

"I don't have a vested interested in the prostitution business in Angeles," Steel lied.

"Ah, I see." She said.

Damn, he thought. She saw through that. "Tell me, have you been to Angeles?"

"I've driven through it on the way up north."

"Have you been to Clark?"

She wrinkled her nose and shook her head in the negative.

"Now Miss Abucayan, that's not very fair of you to have such preconceived notions without checking the facts for yourself. Why don't you come visit? I would be more than happy to give you a tour of the place." He decided to be bold. "How about this Sunday? You could come down, and we could have lunch. You could see for yourself."

"See what for yourself?" Antonio asked, pulling a chair to their tete-a-tete.

"Oh, it seems Will is inviting me for a tour of his base. He thinks I have a distorted view of his little America."

"I must agree with him. You are prejudiced against our military and our American friends."

"I am not prejudiced. I believe in the freedoms that the average American has in the U.S. I just don't think we enjoy them here ourselves."

Antonio scratched his chin with a finger, speaking slowly, "We are working on changing that. Myself, and my comrades in arms, are a new generation. We will make revolutionary changes from within. We are simply waiting for our time. When that comes, we will be ready to act and act decisively."

Steel perked up. Antonio's comments sounded like rhetoric from the Reform the Armed Forces movement. It was supposed to be a new secret organization, a kind of a brotherhood within the military, composed of young disillusioned soldiers set on fomenting unrest. They were said to have hundreds of members.

Antonio checked his watch. "So Captain Steel, before it gets too late, would you like to discuss the information Professor Abucayan called you about? If so, we could adjourn briefly to his study. I'm sure Vida would not miss our company."

"What business would that be that you have to leave the room to discuss?" Vida asked.

"Nothing that would interest you, my dear."

"Why not?"

" It is... it is just that you wouldn't be interested. It's a man's affair. I'm sure your mother would enjoy your company for a short while."

Steel cringed. Vida didn't seem like the type to take that sort of sexist bullshit.

"Fine. Be an asshole." she whispered in Tagalog under her breath. "Please excuse me, Will, I'll go to the kitchen with the women. She pushed past Antonio and walked out of the room."

Antonio shrugged his shoulders. "She is very intelligent and free spirited. Most of the time, quite a challenge, but that's what makes her so attractive. Wouldn't you agree?" Antonio said, trying to hide his embarrassment.

"She's an incredible lady," Steel was secretly pleased to see them fighting. All wasn't perfect in beautiful couple land.

Professor Abucayan led Steel, Jo Jo, and Antonio into his cluttered study. It was just as Steel would have imagined. A big desk in the center, heaped with stacks of papers and folders, the walls lined with wood shelves holding hundreds of books. He would love to spend hours searching through the titles. The Professor led them to a small table which was clear except for a brown folder. He opened it and pulled out a bundle of papers.

"Captain Steel, here are the documents I promised to show you—with the translations. My brother finally finished up the last batch."

Steel said nothing, just bent over and examined the pages. They were badly reproduced copies of the originals, with English translations handwritten in the margins. Jo Jo slid in beside him and read over his shoulder.

They pored through lists of equipment, inventories, logistics orders, and army regulations until the words "storage facilities" caught Steel's eye. He pointed and glanced at Jo Jo. Now they were getting somewhere. There were twenty different locations described with terms like "maximum secrecy," "security," and "work to be performed by the 35th Special Engineering Battalion." He quickly flipped the page and saw a hand drawn map, with the words "Facility One" written near a large dot. His heart raced.

The map was detailed but lacked geographical coordinates or labeled locations. It was just a topographical showing a mountain, a valley, and two small streams. He scanned the page, looking for some hint of the location of "Facility One."

Nothing. He turned the page, then flipped through several more only to find more supply orders and routine army correspondence. He flipped back through, there were numbers missing. Pages were gone. They only had one section.

"I see you have discovered the words 'storage facilities'," Abucayan noted.

"Oh yeah. But it seems that there are some missing pages."

"Yes. And unfortunately they're probably the most important ones. The map there seems to be useless without some sort of point of reference." Antonio flipped back to the page with the mysterious drawing.

"You have no idea what happened to the rest of the pages?" Jo Jo asked.

"No. My friend said that this is all he found in the file."

"This is strange. Could someone else have gotten to it first?"

"Not necessarily. Maybe this was all that was recovered," Abucayan noted.

Steel picked up the page with the map. "Damn, there just don't seem to be any landmark indicators. This could be anywhere."

"Yes, it could. I had one of our map sergeants look at it. He said there is not enough information to locate the position," Antonio said.

Son of a bitch. Steel thought, Steel looked straight at Antonio. "Well, I know now why you haven't gone after it yourself."

Antonio forced a laugh. "Maybe. Although I'm not sure that I buy into the treasure legend. But who I am to turn down such an adventure? Besides, I could put all that gold to good use. A man could finance his dreams with such a fortune."

"Fast cars and luxury boats?" Steel poked.

Antonio gave him a disdainful look. "No, enough money to equip an army of righteous men. But that's only a dream. This map will not lead us to a vault or any riches."

Steel wanted to know more. "But will money buy righteous men? Mercenaries?"

"Be realistic, Captain Steel. It is hard to face a wall of weapons with only right on your side. The barrel of a gun in the hands of a freedom fighter will be the determining factor. I've been there and I have seen the good a well trained and disciplined man can do, winning the hearts and minds of the people he is sworn to protect. If you multiply that man by one hundred, or one thousand, then you can make history."

Steel listened with grudging admiration. Vida's lover was a born leader. He had an aura of determination. He was the type of man that men would follow into battle. If he was RAM, Marcos had better hope Antonio didn't find the treasure.

"This is really frustrating. It says that there are twenty facilities. There are how many pages missing?" Jo Jo asked.

"Eight," answered Abucayan. "I can't make sense of this map. How about you?"

"No. It's Greek to me," Steel said, but thought there was something familiar about the shape of the mountain—probably only wishful thinking.

"We had so hoped that with all your experience you might be able to come up with something." The professor seemed on the verge of wringing his hands.

Steel studied the map intently, examining every contour, tracing the curves of the lines with his finger. He figured they wouldn't let him have a copy. He looked at Jo Jo and winked. Jo Jo took the cue and reexamined the map as well. Steel tried to commit it to memory. At the first available moment he would sketch it. Then, back home, he would get out some 1:50,000 scale maps and start comparing. It was a long shot, but what the hell. A lead was a lead.

They discussed the papers for a while longer then Antonio announced that he had to leave. Abucayan collected the papers and tucked them away in the folder. Steel smiled, for all his skepticism of treasure, the professor had no intention of giving Steel a copy. I wouldn't give it up either, he thought.

Antonio firmly shook their hands all around and asked Vida to leave with him. Still clearly unhappy, she told him she had plans to spend the night there with her parents. Antonio played it cool, kissed her and her mother on the cheek, and left.

Steel and Jo Jo were next. They stood awkwardly in the doorway. Steel shook the professor's hand and again reassured him that he would do his best to find a way to locate the storage facilities. He shook Lettie's hand and thanked her warmly and sincerely for the dinner and hospitality. He reached out and shook Vida's hand. Actually, he reached out and held her hand, lingering for much longer than required before reluctantly pulling away.

"Let me walk you both out to your car," Vida said.

As they approached his truck, Steel spoke, "If you decide

about the tour and lunch offer, please give me a call. Here's my card."

"I'll think about it."

"You do that." They stood in silence by the truck for another uncomfortable minute until Steel broke in, "I really enjoyed your parents. They are wonderful people. And I relished sparring with you." He turned to face her.

"I get the sense you really love to debate," Vida said.

"Definitely."

"Bye, Jo Jo."

Rolling his eyes Jo Jo gave a wave to Vida then climbed in the truck. Steel reluctantly pulled open his door. He looked into her eyes one more time. She smiled and turned away, shutting the gate behind them.

Jo Jo threw him the keys. "I know what you are thinking; you are like the moon-faced boys who chase my daughters. I think you are setting yourself up for a fall."

"Naah, I'm a realist."

"Since when?"

"Damn, what's Antonio got that I don't?"

"Well, he's a handsome war hero from a well-connected political family."

"Thanks."

"Not to mention he is leading the Marcos opposition in the military."

"Aside from all of that," Steel started the truck and drove off.

"I suggest you challenge him to a duel." Jo Jo poked Steel in the ribs with his finger.

"You're right. No more impure thoughts about Ms. Vida."

"That will save us both a headache."

"Maybe. But first find a pencil and some paper in my bag. We have to sketch out a copy of that damn map while it's still fresh in our minds. You're a better artist than me." He threw the truck into gear and sped off.

Parked across the street, a small, blue Toyota passenger car with heavily tinted windows pulled out and tailed Steel's truck. Inside, two Philippine army sergeants in civilian clothes, both assigned to a special counterintelligence unit, had orders to follow the American officer. A second car assigned to counterintelligence had left earlier, following Lt. Col. Devincia. There was much interest in high circles about the connection between the RAM, the professor, and the American officer.

11

Angeles City

It was Saturday. Steel lounged in his living room in a round, comfortable rattan chair, sipping from a large glass of iced tea. A ceiling fan circled above him sending down a gentle breeze.

Books and papers lay piled at his feet—the latest course work for his master's degree program in Philippine counterinsurgency at the University of Manila. He had never thought he would stay forever in the Air Force; maybe he would pursue a career in academia.

Today, though, the books did not tempt him. Instead, he replayed last evening's dinner in his head. He couldn't get Vida out of his mind. He had dreamed about her, a jumbled and sexual montage of sharp exchanges and sinuous limbs; there might have been a few glances of breast as well. He struggled to remember.

Steel shook his head—Jo Jo was right. He couldn't become obsessed with her. She was smart, beautiful, sexy, and way out of his league. Besides, she was spoken for. But it was fun flirting.

He tried replacing his image of Vida with a visual of the map he and Jo Jo had tried to recreate on the way back from Manila. They talked over the sketch of the mountain, Steel straining to recall where he had seen that peculiar terrain before. Tomorrow, he would take a trip to the 3rd TAC Fighter Wing's map library and do some research.

He sighed and reached down to pick up a book on Thailand's Communist movement. He was barely into the first chapter when the phone rang. He heard Rosa answer it in the kitchen.

Rosa appeared. "William. Are you in?"

"I guess it depends who it is."

"I am not familiar with her but I believe her name is a Miss Vida Abucayan. She—"

Steel snapped his book closed, jumped up, and raced for the phone, startling Rosa. Rosa held her position in the doorway examining a nonexistent smudge on the wall, leaning her good ear toward her boss's hushed conversation. After ten minutes, Steel wandered back by her, a dopey grin on his face.

"So, you seem very happy after speaking with Miss Abucayan. She did seem very well-spoken on the phone."

"Rosa, she is very nice. She's a journalist for the Malaya newspaper. Tomorrow, I'm taking her for a tour of the base and having lunch with her."

"I like reading the Malaya. That is good, William, a nice Filipina woman. You should go to Manila more often; there you'll find more refined examples of our women."

"I found you here with the harlots, didn't I?" He put his arm around her shoulder and kissed her on the cheek.

She frowned and pushed him away. He walked back to his chair and flopped down, still smiling. He had really never expected Vida to call, especially not so quickly.

The next morning, Steel arrived at the café early. He parked his truck and walked over to a stand of newspapers. He scanned the piles for the Malaya paper. He found the Sunday edition, paid the boy at the stand, and went inside the cafe.

The place was busy, filled with folks waiting for the buses which dropped and picked up passengers at a big stop across the highway. The café tried to imitate those in the west, something like a Dunkin Donuts chain. The donuts weren't bad.

He ordered two chocolate glazed and a cup of coffee and took them to a small booth by the front window, flipping open the newspaper, looking for Vida's name. He ate the first donut quickly and nibbled on the second, washing it down with too many coffees. He didn't see any articles by Vida.

They had agreed to meet at ten. He checked his watch: 10:15 a.m. He wasn't concerned. She would arrive probably on Filipino time, which meant he could go and get another donut and some more coffee.

He looked out the window. To his surprise, he saw Vida getting out of her car. He headed out to greet her. A small group of children and a newspaper vendor quickly surrounded her, begging for money, a paper sale, or both. Steel waved and rushed over.

"Excuse me, kids," Steel said in Tagalog. "Hi there. Wow, you're on time." He pushed through and grabbed her hand. "Not much traffic, I hope."

She smiled and clutched her purse to her side with her free hand. "No, it was easy."

She looked incredible, dressed in blue jeans and a white blouse, her long hair tied back in a ponytail. She was wearing dark sunglasses, a classy Filipina movie starlet come to life.

"Do you want a coffee?" he pointed to the cafe.

"No, I'm fine. How about you?"

"No, I've had way too many already. Let's head to the base. You can follow me and park your car in the lot near the main gate. It'll be safe there."

"Okay. Don't drive too fast," she called out as she got back in.

He led her to the base main gate. Security was tight since the Americans had been killed. The small sentry shack was now surrounded with sand bags and outfitted with concrete vehicle barriers and portable tire shredders. The guards were all dressed in helmets and body armor and were heavily armed. Steel stopped and showed his ID to the policeman, who examined it. "I'm vouching for the driver behind me and taking her to the visitor's lot," said Steel. The guard nodded and waved them on.

Steel and Vida parked their vehicles side by side in the nearly empty lot. Steel jumped out of the truck and almost sprinted to Vida's car. "Steady boy," he thought to himself. He hesitated before pulling her door open, watching as best he could through the heavily tinted windows as she reapplied lipstick

"This is better. No big herd of kids pulling at you." Steel said, as he helped Vida out.

"Yes. That was quite a welcoming committee you assembled."

"Nothing is too good for the award-winning Malaya journalist."

"Who said I won awards?"

"Your mom."

"Oh, that's embarrassing."

"Hell no. It's endearing on your mom's part and impressive on yours. We'll take my truck to tour the base. Then we can have lunch."

"It is so nice of you to host me. I hope you didn't have any other plans."

"Not a thing. You saved me a day of boring school work."

He opened the truck door for her. He was glad Jo Jo had cleaned the inside for him. For once it didn't look like he and an untidy band of Negritos lived in there.

While Vida studied the base through the windshield, Steel studied her, occasionally glancing down to admire her tightfitting blouse. He could see the outline of her breasts, which triggered a partially steamy scene from his dream the night before.

Flushed, Steel cranked the air-conditioning. "Is the air too much?" He smiled, hoping she couldn't read minds.

"No, it feels nice. You know, probably what is most striking about the base is that it's so incredibly neat and clean. You rarely see that here in the P.I."

"We Americans are a tidy people."

She reached down and pulled a small notebook from her purse. "Would you mind if I wrote down some notes?"

"Not at all, but I might have to censor some of your work. I have a big black magic marker in the glove compartment."

"Don't worry. I'll keep your name out of any story. So where are all the soldiers living? All I see are civilian men and women and kids on bikes."

"Those are family quarters. That's where the married personnel live."

"So well kept. And where do the single soldiers live?"

"Young single folks live in dormitories."

"Is there where you live? In a dormitory?"

"Are you kidding? Thank God I'm an officer. We have the option of living off base. I live in town."

"You don't want to live on base? You prefer living with the natives?" One eyebrow rose fetchingly.

"I wouldn't call Rosa a native—at least not to her face."

"Excuse me?"

"Rosa is my house girl. Well actually house woman. I guess housekeeper is more accurate." Steel knew he was rambling. But he didn't want Vida to think Rosa was a girlfriend. Or, worse, one of those house girls who spent most of their time in the boss's bedroom. "Anyway, she is a fifty-two-year-old surrogate mother to me. Or at least she thinks she is. You'll get to meet her. We're having lunch at my house."

"I guess it's only fair since you met my mother."

"Actually, I love living off base—much more freedom. The base is too sterile—sort of a plasticville."

"I was trying not to be too insulting about the base. I would imagine it is very much like being in America."

"That's true, but I don't want to be in America. I signed up to live overseas."

"Ah yes, with your little brown brothers."

He laughed. "You certainly have a chip on your shoulder."

"Chip on my shoulder? What does that mean?" Vida swiveled her head to look at her arm.

"It's just an expression. Another way of saying you have a bug up your ass."

"A bug up my ass? I think I prefer a chip on my shoulder," she laughed too. "Maybe you prefer living in town so you can be near the working girls."

He watched her jot down some notes. She really got her rocks off on the banter—then, so did he. "Good point. I am certainly within walking distance of the bar district. Don't worry, we'll do a tour of Angeles city. I won't hide anything from you."

"So where are we going now."

"The flight line, so you can see some of the aircraft that we use to bomb Communist women and children."

She rolled her eyes.

Steel pointed out the home of the 3rd Tactical Fighter Wing. It was quiet now, unlike on weekdays when the roar of aircraft coming and going was deafening. One squadron featured F-4s, fighter aircraft with two seats, menacing tiger shark mouths painted on the nose cones. They drove past the Wild Weasel squadron who trained to attack enemy surface-to-air missile sites with their specialized F-4Gs.

The next stop was the F-5 fighter squadron. Steel pointed to an aircraft. "These play the bad guys in air exercises around the Crow Valley bombing range. The F-5s pretend to be Soviet-designed MiG21s. It's incredibly realistic training for the U.S. aircrews."

"Do you use this aircraft to bomb Communist guerrilla bases?"

"Of course not. We don't bomb NPA guerrillas. You have your own air force and aircraft to do that."

"Do our pilots come to train at that Crow Valley place?"

Steel thought for a moment. Tricky question. It was common knowledge that the Philippine Air Force trained with the U.S., though he wasn't sure it was the official line. Oh hell. "Yes," he said.

"So you train them to bomb the NPA."

"We train them to operate in combat. What they do with that knowledge is your country's business." This was making him a little uncomfortable. "Why don't we head over to the other end of the flight line. I'll take you to the C130 cargo aircraft area." He watched her scribble even more notes. He wondered if she was still listening. "Would you like to see our nuclear bomb storage complex now?"

She looked over at him. "Ha ha—very funny, William. I am sure that that is stop number one on the public tour."

"It would be if it existed," Steel countered. "I've seen real nuclear bomb storage sites in the States. Even in the U.S., those facilities are very secure. Three rings of fences with barbed wire. Three rings." He used his finger to draw the rings in the air. "And motion detectors. They look like they are hiding something important in them. I'll drive anywhere you want on base. If you find a facility that matches that description, then you let me know. In fact, when you get back to your office, compare what you see here with AP photos of nuclear storage sites in the U.S."

She smiled at him and nodded quietly as she wrote more notes. She seemed to appreciate his honesty.

Steel checked his watch. Nearly a quarter to one, and he was starving. He suggested that they meet at his house for some lunch. Vida agreed. She seemed tired. Maybe the base hadn't lived up to her vision of what a facility of the evil empire should look like. No nuclear bomb sites, no dirty pools of contaminated water. They drove to the visitor's lot where she transferred back to her car and followed him home.

Rosa was in rare form: It only took her fifteen minutes to get lunch on the table, which was set with the best linen and plates, a display obviously meant to impress Ms. Abucayan. Rosa spoke glowingly of "her William" and his love for the Philippines.

Steel leaned over to Vida and whispered. "If it isn't obvious enough, I think Rosa is trying to seduce you."

"I think she's wonderful. You are lucky to have her."

"Most of the time I'd agree."

They finished the main course and tucked into some apple pie and ice cream. Vida relished her dessert with obvious glee. As American as apple pie, she kept repeating. He liked watching her laugh.

"How long have you and Antonio been seeing each other?" He had been waiting for the right moment to pry into her personal life.

"Since we were teenagers; our families are good friends. My parents and his parents have been trying to push us together for years; seems like we have been dating forever."

"Are you going to get married?" he asked trying to appear uninterested in the answer but succeeding only in shooting a piece of pie into his lap with a too-tense jab of the fork.

"I'm not sure. At some level I love him, but I don't know if we are really compatible."

"Yes!" thought Steel, this time keeping his hands away from his plate. Shit, were they trembling?

She picked up her cup and sipped some coffee. "How about you? You're not married? You have a girlfriend in the states?"

"Weren't you listening to Rosa? She was outlining my personal life for you." He imitated Rosa's voice. "William needs to find a nice respectable Filipina."

Vida put her hand over her mouth, trying to stifle a giggle and nervously looked over to the kitchen, where Rosa's shadow clearly marked here presence right outside the doorway.

"She can hear. Don't worry, she has a good sense of humor. Has to, to live with me."

"I don't know you seem okay for a gringo."

Oh yeah, thought Steel. Antonio may be a handsome war hero, but I am a charming gringo. He gave Vida a high wattage grin but chose to bait her rather than push for more.

"You see that's your problem. You and your compatriots base your impression of what Americans are like from the movies. You see, Rambo and John Wayne westerns make us look like we all have guns and kill people. But that's not who we are. We are caring, generous, and forgiving. Sometimes we just support the wrong people—but not because we are evil. We do it because we are generally ignorant about world affairs."

"You mean like supporting Marcos."

"Sure. We are supporting Marcos by being here. We didn't

elect him and we certainly wouldn't stand in the way should the Philippine people un-elect him."

"Let's just say, hypothetically, what would happen if the Philippine people rose up in revolution against the Marcoses? Do you think your government would come to their rescue?"

Steel sighed loudly. "Tough question. I would say probably not. I think we would defend the bases, but we would avoid getting involved in a civil war." Her question made him think of Antonio and the Reform the Armed Forces movement. They were the ones that worried him. The NPA would never be able to topple the government, but the RAM was another issue all together. They were working from within the military, and Steel was pretty sure a coup was the only threat to the Marcos dynasty.

"That was an interesting question. Now I have one for you. Do you think that there is any truth to the rumors that there is a group of young dissatisfied military men plotting a coup against the government?"

"It is possible. It would not be a great surprise. There is no doubt that the hatred of Marcos and his military cronies have seeped deep into the ranks. I have heard vague references to such a movement," she said coolly.

"You mean to RAM?"

"Maybe," she took a sip of coffee.

"I would think it would be the greatest challenge to the Marcos government—not the NPA. Wouldn't you agree?"

Her eyes gave her away. "If they exist, then I would have to agree."

She seemed uncomfortable with the topic. He changed it. "So you like the pie?" Only a few crumbs remained on her plate.

"Very tasty. Did you buy it on base?"

"I bought the apples, and Rosa made it. I bought her an American cookbook. She is quite creative in the kitchen."

As if on cue, Rosa appeared. "Would anyone like more pie or coffee?"

Vida, trying to suppress a grin, replied. "Rosa, that was an excellent lunch. I am very impressed with your skill as a baker. Thank you so much."

"Oh, thank you," Rosa beamed. "Are you planning on writing an article about your trip to Clark and Angeles City?" she asked, clearing away the dessert plates.

"I think I will do something. William promised me a tour of the city as well."

"Oh, I am sure he has told you there isn't much to see here. But I hope you will see that Angeles City doesn't deserve its bad reputation." Rosa cast a meaningful glance at Steel. "Oh, William, Father Rudy called this morning. He asked you to stop by. He said that is there is an urgent problem that only you could help out with. Maybe you could take Vida there with you to meet Father Rudy," she said as she left with the dishes.

Steel shook his head.

"Did you say Father Rudy? Does that mean you are Catholic?"

"Nope. Father Rudy isn't technically a Catholic. It's complicated. He broke away from—"

"Wait. I think I've heard of him. Doesn't he have a boys' school here in Angeles?" Vida asked.

"That's right."

"He is doing some good work. He is progressive, has a marvelous social conscience. Although, you are right; his views cost him his parish."

"So you are Catholic?"

"Yes, of course. We are a Catholic country. But unfortunately I, like Father Rudy, have fallen out of favor with the church. I like to think I am part of the reformed church—not that we are formally established. But there are a lot of us, and we are very vocal."

He was tempted to get into a religious discussion like he had so many times with Rudy, but he was enjoying the feeling of intimacy with her too much to risk turning the conversation back to platonic banter. "I certainly love Rudy and think his brand of religion is pretty compelling, no matter what its label, so if you are in line with him, you are all right in my book."

"'All right in my book.' That sounds so American. Just like the movies. Maybe Humphrey Bogart."

"Humphrey Bogart, good Lord. Where did you see him?"

"I love the old black-and-white movies. My father has quite a collection."

"On video?" Steel asked.

"No. His father was very wealthy. He had reel-to-reel films from 1940's. My father still has them. We even have an old projector that used to be in a movie house. When we were kids we would show them on the weekends. 'Here's looking at you kid,'" she said in a gruff voice that Steel imagined was meant to sound like Humphrey Bogart.

He laughed. "That's great. Casablanca is one of my favorites."

They chatted for another half-hour and then left for a drive through town. The first stop was the red-light district and blow row. He was determined to show her the full impact of the American presence on Angeles City—the good, the bad, and the decidedly ugly. Blow row fit that latter category, though it looked more seedy than sordid in the late Sunday afternoon light. The streets were nearly empty; the girls were doing their Sunday errands or sleeping off a late Saturday night.

Vida looked up and saw a brightly painted sign above a nearby bar. "'Super Head.' Is that the name of the bar? Jesus, that's terrible." She put her hand to her mouth and laughed. "Why am I laughing? That is terrible."

They passed more bars, LBFM's and Pussy Galors and then turned onto one of the narrow, dirt-packed back streets filled with pedestrians and trikes. Driving slowly, they came on a bar called Vampire's, where a group of ten or so working girls assembled out front. Vampire's was known for heavy metal, girls dressed in Halloween outfits, and wild live sex shows.

Two performers engaged in an animated conversation in the middle of the road. One, dressed in a black tube top and matching black mini-dress, looked up at the truck. A flash of annoyance showed on her ravaged face, then she turned back to the other girl.

Steel waited patiently, wishing the two would move. He tapped lightly on the horn. The black-garbed one flashed him the finger without turning from her companion. The crowd of co-workers in front of the bar laughed their approval.

Steel looked into his rearview mirror, hoping for a chance to back up, but a jeepney was directly behind him. He shook his head, reached forward, and flipped a small toggle switch under the dash engaging two Italian-made truck horns under the hood. He had mounted them for travel on the treacherous roads outside Angeles.

Steel waited for a few seconds, then looked at Vida and winked. He pushed the horn. The girl in black jumped into her friend's arms and they both fell over backward onto the ground, all to the great amusement of the crowd outside the bar.

"That's enough to wake the dead," Vida said, her hands over her ears.

"Comes in handy," he said, again maneuvering through the narrow street. He wanted to get out of there.

"This is what I expected—so horrible. These poor women, so corrupt and hardened." She was shaken.

Steel just nodded. As they passed the last bar on the street, two girls out front saw Steel's truck and exposed their breasts, calling out offers of explicit sexual acts. Catching sight of Vida, though, they abruptly pulled their tops back up.

Vida looked away. "Is this it for the tour? That seems like an appropriate way to end it."

"No, it's not very appropriate. I told you I'd show you the whole spectrum of the good and the bad. Let me show you some good now."

"Good luck. It would have to be a lot of good to make up for this." She scribbled more notes.

Steel pulled back onto the main drag.

"You're right. The bars can be really bad places, soul-destroying experiences for the girls working there. There are a few bright spots though. I know lots of G.I.s who have married local girls."

"William, surely you can count the number of girls on one hand that work in those places and marry an Americano."

"Maybe."

"I'm not condemning you all. The bars are not uniquely an Angeles problem. You said, and you're right, that prostitution is all over Manila too."

They rode in tense silence to Father Rudy's compound. Steel cursed himself for finding exactly the outing that destroyed the flirtatious, even intimate, feel of their lunch. He reminded himself this wasn't a date; it was a courtesy to a member of the press—PR work for Americans. Yeah, right.

He pulled in front of Father Rudy's compound and beeped the horn. In a few minutes, several boys appeared, waved enthusiastically, and opened the gate. Once inside, a larger group approached Steel's truck.

"Is this the boys' school we spoke of?"

"That it is."

She waved nervously at the throng of young faces pressed up to the windows of the truck. Several others had already climbed into the back of the vehicle. "Oh goodness, there are a lot of boys here."

"More than a hundred. Sunday afternoon is their day off. During the week, you don't get this big a reception. They don't have school or work in the trade shops today. Father Rudy has several small cottage industries here which keep them busy during the week. All right, brace yourself. Let's go out."

Steel walked through the boys. Some were only as high as his waist, others as tall as his shoulders. There was a chorus of "Captain. Steel, Captain Steel." Or more like "Captain Steeeel" with a long "e." Steel hoisted one of the smallest boys in the air then rounded the truck to take Vida's hand. Steel turned to a red-faced Father Rudy, who was ineffectually waving his hands in an attempt to control his large flock. "Boys, boys! Let Captain Steel and his guest through."

"Captain Steel, is that your girlfriend? She is beautiful. She looks like Tetche Albanyi." One runny-nosed small boy dressed in a dirty white T-shirt yelled up to them.

"You're right. You want her autograph?" he turned to Vida. "You know, you do look like her." Tetchi Abanyi was the sultry movie star currently featured in the movie: *Emerald Forest*.

Father Rudy ushered Steel and Vida into his office, where snacks and drinks were laid out for them. When Vida informed Father Rudy that she wrote for the Malaya under the name Selma Comacho, he sang her praises, declaring that the paper, and her articles in particular, were the voice of truth and reason. Vida was equally effusive in her homage to Father Rudy.

Steel leaned back and tried to quell his rising jealousy. Steel was fairly certain the priest had kept his vow of chastity even after leaving the church, but did Vida really need to fawn over him so? It was unseemly.

Father Rudy interrupted Steel's funk. "So Vida, I am so pleased that you and William have met. God himself sent William to us. Without him and Gary, that is Major O'Dell, another American angel, we would have perished long ago." Rudy made the sign of the cross.

God sent me—now Steel felt like an idiot for being jealous of Rudy.

"I didn't think you would be here so soon, Will. What a blessing you are here. As usual we are facing problems. We had some pipes break and are desperately in need of help with the plumbing. We are resorting to water jugs for drinking and bathing. We are also terribly short of cash to buy food this month because we need to spend money for the furniture shop." He lowered his head dejectedly, which was unusual for the normally upbeat priest. "We can make up the difference in the next several months. We will need an additional two hundred kilos of rice and dried fish. We can get by on donations of fresh vegetables and fruit. I know you just helped us through our roof troubles. This was unexpected." He kept his head lowered and covered his face with his hands.

Steel leaned over, and put an arm around his friend's shoulders. He was concerned. "Don't be so hard on yourself, Rudy. You're just one man," Steel said. "You've done an incredible job here, a superhuman job. I don't see how you do it every day. It won't be easy to raise more money, but hey, I think I can do something. I'll get some emergency food money to you right away. The base will donate some pipes or whatever we need. I have Gary's contact in base supply. We'll take a look at the pipes in a minute and see where we stand." Steel rubbed Rudy's shoulder.

Vida leaned forward, distressed at Father Rudy's obvious anguish. "Yes, Rudy, I'm sure there is something we can do to help."

"Yes, maybe Selma Comacho, spokeswoman for the poor, has some ideas," Steel said smiling to let her know the jab was in good fun, which it mostly was, though he had not quite forgiven her for her earlier gushing over Father Rudy.

She shrugged her shoulders and stared quietly at Steel. Rudy stood up and walked to his desk. "I'm sorry. Yes, you are quite right. We have been through worse. This has been a particularly bad week. I'm just very tired: many sick children and late, sleepless nights."

Steel leaned back and closed his eyes. This was his worst fear. They were bottoming out financially. It would be quite a while until they could build the savings account back up. Perhaps it was time to pull the trigger on an idea he had had about a month ago.

He had thought of it when Kuncker, his boss, had roped him into participating in an Officers' Wives' Club mixed doubles benefit. Kuncker knew Steel had played tennis in school and still got a set in on occasion. When Kuncker pulled a muscle, he also pulled a fast one on Steel.

Kuncker's partner was supposed to have been Irene Dresden, the wife of the base commander and president of the OWC. She thought she wore her husband's colonel's rank too.

She had flaming red hair from a bottle, huge boobs, and an hourglass figure. She was outspoken, pushy, and horny as a mink. During practice sessions for the tournament, she and Steel had played well together. Off the court, she made it clear she would like to continue the game.

She had bragged to him of her big plans for the OWC, flush with money from the tennis tournament and other programs. When she said they were looking for a worthy cause, Steel saw green. With a little charm, some flattery, and a dose of ass grabbing on the court, Steel was fairly certain he could provide her with a worthy cause.

"So William what do you think? Is this finally the end?" Father Rudy said bringing Steel back from his calculations of how much fondling he would need to do before he struck gold.

"No, Rudy. I think a solution is at hand. I have to arrange a tennis match."

"A what?" Rudy asked sounding confused.

"Just put in a good word for me."

"Of course. You are always in our prayers."

"Good, call Rosa. Let's have a look at those pipes. Come along Vida, or should I say Ms. Comacho. Let's see how good your plumbing skills are." He offered her his hand, and she let him help her up from the couch.

Steel pulled in front of his house and switched off the engine. They sat in the cab, staring ahead.

"I still can't get over the sight of you and Father Rudy together." Vida looked into Steel's eyes. "This is all so against my vision of the typical G.I. You are a good person, William. You should be proud of what you are doing for those boys."

"Thanks. I do feel good about it. My friend Gary is the real hero, though. I'm just minding the store for him while he's away. It gives me a chance to heap coals off my head, as another American friend of mine says."

"Excuse me?"

"Heaping off coals; it's just an expression—means making atonement for sins."

"Ah, I see," she said, though the look on her face said she did not. She continued: "I thought the only locals Americanos were interested in were the girls they screw in those bars."

"I'll admit. I like to visit the bars on occasion too, but these days I prefer to be an observer rather than a participant." Steel tried to look noble and not think about the luscious Lychee, who he would have surely bedded a couple of weeks ago had it not been for the trip to the bunker. "Anyway, it is hot in the truck. Would you like to come inside for a drink?"

Vida paused before answering.

"C'mon," thought Steel, a vision of Vida's lovely breasts supplanting the mental picture of Lychee.

"No..." Vida frowned. "I would like to, really, but I'm expected back. I had a wonderful time, though. Much more wonderful than I thought I would."

"Why did you come, Vida?" Steel held her arm gently but looked hard into her eyes. His throat ached.

"To...to get the real story. About the base, the Americanos... what we talked about at the party."

"Look," he sighed, deciding to go for broke. "You're smart and sexy. I'd like to get to know you a lot better. Can I call you when I'm in Manila next? We could go out. Hey, you could show me your red light district," he grinned.

She paused for a moment. "I'm not sure. Maybe," another pause, "I think that would be all right."

"Do you have a card?"

"Yes," she pulled out a small white square from her purse. "I'll write my home number on the back."

He watched her concentrate on the numbers. Her hands shook. As she turned to pass him the card, he leaned forward, took the card with one hand, cupped the back of her head with the other, and kissed her hard. Vida pulled out of the kiss and stared at him with wide eyes. "Oh," she said.

"Oh, yeah," Steel thought and smiled, hand still behind her head.

"Yes, um, tell Rosa thank you again." She squirmed out from his hold and opened the door, stumbling out. "The pie was a revelation."

"It certainly was." Steel said to her back as she scurried across the driveway, leaving the truck door open behind her.

Vida paused at her car, then turned, flushed. "See you soon," she said.

Steel just grinned.

Steel was on cloud nine as he opened the gate and pulled into his carport. He walked inside to find Jo Jo and Rosa sitting in the living room having a glass of ice tea.

"Hey guys, what's up?" Steel said.

"How was your afternoon William?" Rosa sung out.

"It was great." Steel didn't want to talk about in front of Jo Jo, fearing his reaction. But Jo Jo started on an entirely different subject.

"I've got some interesting news from Tony. He came by earlier and said that a group of old Japanese men are in the mountains. They came yesterday with some former Phil army guys and hired June and some Negritos to take them into the mountains. Tony was really pissed. He was in town and missed out. Apparently they were paying well. Enough cash that I might have considered joining them."

Steel stopped in his tracks. Wild. He had heard stories of old Japanese men taking pilgrimages into the mountains. One trip supposedly was undertaken by Japanese men so frail that they had to be carried in on stretchers. Rumor was they were Imperial soldiers returning to the battlefields to pray for the souls of their dead comrades. But there were also stories that the soldiers were going back to the mountains to retrieve the gold they had left behind.

One story that he thought of often was of a group of young Japanese men who had come to the mountains in four-wheel-drive vehicles with scuba equipment. They dove in a large pool of water in a stream at the base of the mountains. They had been following directions written on a cloth map. Steel had visited the stream. One of the old Negritos in the village nearby had said that Japanese soldiers during the war had used it for bathing. He also told Steel that the young Japanese men had come up empty-handed.

Steel focused on the situation at hand. "So, Jo Jo, when did the *matanda haponese lalaki,* old Japanese men, leave and how many were there? Tony didn't say how many?" Steel asked, excited.

"William, did Miss Abucayan say anything more about her visit?" Rosa asked, bored with Steel and Jo Jo's conversation.

Steel ignored Rosa. "Shit, I wonder if Kuncker will give me some leave? We've got to go up there and see what they're up to." He mapped out what he would say to Kuncker in his head. "Hey, Jo Jo why—"

Jo Jo moved closer to Steel, blocking his path, clearly not happy. "Miss Abucayan? She was here? What's this all about?" He turned and looked at Rosa.

Steel fumbled, "Ah, she just took me up on my offer to tour the base. No big deal."

"And she came over for lunch. She really seemed to enjoy my food. Such an attractive and wonderfully smart woman. Did you know she is a journalist for the Malaya newspaper?" Rosa stood and headed for the kitchen.

Jo Jo, fuming, blurted out. "Did you also know that the sexy Ms. Abucayan is engaged to a famous Philippine army officer, a war hero?"

Rosa stopped dead in her tracks. She stared at them both, shook her head, and scowled at William. "Is this true, William, that she is engaged?"

"I...I don't think she's engaged. I never really heard her say she was engaged."

"I think Lt. Col. Antonio Devincia might think otherwise," Jo Jo said.

"Well, she made no mention to me that she was engaged to an army officer," Rosa said, glaring at Steel.

"She's not engaged. She's in transition or something." Steel pushed around Jo Jo and headed for his bedroom. "It's complicated," Steel called out.

Jo Jo followed him, not letting this go. "Devincia is not a man to be messed with. He is a dangerous and violent man. An army friend of mine said he knew of his reputation in Mindanao. Besides, what of the professor? He is not going to be pleased with your moving in on his daughter. We need his help to find the treasure." Jo Jo threw his hands in the air.

Without saying a word, Steel entered his bedroom and shut the door leaving Jo Jo standing outside. "I told you this woman would be trouble." Jo Jo said to the door, then turned and walked away, muttering in Tagalog. He brushed by Rosa who threw up her hands as well and walked into the kitchen muttering, "She could have said something about her fiancé."

12

Zambales Mountains

STEEL STOOD FOR A MOMENT. It was just after dusk and light was almost gone. All his senses were tuned to the sounds and smells of the jungle around him. Above the high-pitched calls of the insects and birds, he could hear Jo Jo breathing heavily. Tony stood still, almost invisible in the dark undergrowth.

Reacting to a crashing sound ahead of them, Steel gripped the shaft of his five-foot-long spear tightly. Its tip was large and metal, honed razor sharp on black river stone. The wood shaft was smooth, well-worn by hunters' hands over the years. He smelled its aroma of smoky wood and animal grease. At this moment, he felt primitive and alive.

A few feet in front of them, five Negritos stood, waiting and watching the jungle brush. Three held black palm wood bows and reed arrows at the ready. In the hands of a skilled Negrito, these weapons could kill a deer or wild pig at thirty meters. One of the other Negritos was armed with a heavy-tipped spear similar to Steel's. It was used in close quarters for two-legged enemies or to provide the coup-de-grace to mortally wounded game.

The dogs barked and yelped in the distance; there were maybe ten in all. These little pig dogs, no bigger than rat terriers, were hot on the trail of a wild pig. The product of thousands of years of adept breeding, these hounds were capable of digging out quarry from thick underbrush and chasing them in a circle within killing range of the hunting party. The scrawny canines worked as a pack of biting, snarling dynamos.

The Negrito pig hunters with whom Steel was sharing this 30,000-year-old ritual were from a nameless assembly of grass huts a twelve-hour walk from June's village. Steel, Jo Jo, Tony, and his team planned to camp near the huts for the evening and set out early in the morning to find the *Haponese*. Tony had queried people in his village to get a general idea where the Japanese were headed. He also had Steel hire a man, an expert tracker from this Negrito group, to help locate them.

They had arrived around six p.m. to find preparations underway for a pig hunt. Children had seen signs of a pig that morning, and the clan of twenty was excited by the prospect of fresh meat.

This was a new location for the clan. They had recently moved from another site, a five-day walk to the south of Mount Pinatubo—even by Negrito standards, this group was backwoods. Aside from a few odd pieces of cloth clothing, there were virtually no signs of the twentieth century, or for that matter, the last six centuries. A couple of machetes, metal-tipped spears, and knives were their only link to his world. The villagers were fascinated by Steel. There was only one person in the group who had ever seen a white man before.

The clan insisted he and Jo Jo come along on the hunt. They hoped his white magic would bring luck, though disappointed that his magic did not include a firearm. Steel was eager to accompany them. He had never seen it done before with this set of primitive weapons—he had only witnessed pig traps and, once, a dead pig hanging in a village. He was especially pleased to have been presented with a spear to use for the hunt.

Steel looked up into the sky, partially obscured by thick jungle canopy. Scant remnants of dusk filtered down; soon it would be completely dark. Without a flashlight, or even a torch, he couldn't imagine how they could see to shoot and kill a pig.

He reached down and scratched his stomach, momentarily surprised by the feel of warm slime. He had forgotten that, caught up in the spirit of the event, he had stripped down to his bare chest and let the women of the village smear a mixture of pig grease, ash, and red plant dye on him. They said it would mask his scent and bring the spirit of the pig to them.

Steel wasn't sure of its spiritual properties, but it did seem an excellent mosquito repellant. He hadn't felt a bite or even heard the faint buzz of a bug. "You ready to kill a pig?" Steel whispered to Jo Jo.

"Jo Jo the butcher of Magalang is ready," he answered, making a hacking motion with the big machete in his hand.

"The dogs are pretty close, I think."

"Yes, they sound like they are crashing in the jungle just in front of us." Jo Jo was flushed with exhilaration.

The sound of the yelping grew nearer. The Negritos began to call out and whistle, vectoring the dogs to their position.

The first pig rushed out of the brush and into the clearing in front of them. It was a black boar with a thick mane of bristling hair, foaming at the mouth and exposing its menacing, gleaming white, four-inch-long tusks. It was covered with leaves and vines after its mad dash through the undergrowth in front of the dogs. In the dim light, Steel thought it looked demonic.

Its sudden appearance and large size incited panic and excitement in the Negrito bowmen. They jumped into shooting positions, letting loose a volley of arrows. Two found their mark, wounding, but not killing, the pig. Behind the boar two smaller pigs blasted out, followed closely by the pack.

The boar, wild with terror, gave a deep, guttural roar and charged the Negrito bowmen, who scrambled in different directions. Steel stood frozen, watching the scene unfold before him. And suddenly, he was in it, drawing back his spear and rushing forward. The boar turned and charged straight at Steel. He grabbed his spear with two hands, like a lance, and lowered it to waist height, aiming for the pig's chest.

He screamed at the top of his lungs and ran at full speed. Just before impact, the boar spun to his left. Steel lunged and thrust the spear into the animal. He could feel the tip penetrate deep into its body, just below the shoulder blade. Steel gritted his teeth as the pig let loose a terrible squeal of fright and pain and fell to its side, kicking its short hoofed legs.

He struggled, holding onto the shaft with all his might, attempting to keep the thrashing pig pinned to the ground. He had to keep clear of the deadly tusks, which snapped viciously within inches of Steel's ankles. Jo Jo rushed forward and hacked at the boar with his sharp machete, splattering blood into the air. Steel pushed down on the spear with his full weight until all movement ceased. Adrenaline surged through his body; he was filled with the primal rage of the hunter.

Slowly Steel came back to himself and let go of the spear, standing back. The Negritos were screaming out orders, trying to tie the lead dogs with lengths of braided vines. It would be a while before they were able to regain control of the frenzied dogs.

He turned his attention again to the boar. It was definitely a large pig. The pig dogs were biting at it, licking blood from its hair. One warrior animatedly reenacted the kill.

Two Negrito bowmen prodded the pig with the tips of their still-loaded bows, examining the two broken arrow shafts protruding from its torso, trying to ascertain whose they were. Each Negrito bowman had his own signature arrows; the color of the feathers told who the owner was. The shafts protruding from the pig were both missing the feathers. Steel smiled, it would undoubtedly be the source of campfire controversy for years whose arrows had actually hit their mark on the big boar.

Jo Jo was squatted on his haunches, examining the kill. "Jesus Maria Joseph, that was a close one. That pig could have killed us both. You saved us with that spear," He said, banging, on the tusks with his machete.

"I don't know what got into me—acting like a lunatic with a spear. Thank god, you were right there with the machete chop."

"It's definitely a big pig. What do you think it weighs?"

"Oh, over two hundred pounds I'd guess."

Steel looked around. The other Negrito bowmen were examining a smaller pig, a sow, twenty feet from the boar. It lay on its side with two dogs pulling at its legs. A great surge of satisfaction washed over him.

The Negritos lit a couple of hand-held torches made out of reeds soaked in tree tar and used them to light their way back along the narrow trail to the huts. They entered the village like a bright parade of Roman conquerors. The trussed-up pigs dangled beneath bamboo poles. Steel had taken his turn lugging the boar through the jungle and silently added another fifty pounds to his estimate of its weight. They had had to lash three poles together in order to make one strong enough to hold the beast.

They dropped the pigs next to a large campfire built earlier by the women, who were now yelling and dancing around the pigs. The Negrito hunters tried to best each other with their boasts: The pig was the biggest in their clan's history; was possessed by the forest devil; had red glowing demon eyes; it charged them and, despite being hit with five arrows, it still lived; the white man killed it with a magic spear.

Steel smiled. This evening's hunt would obviously be fodder for many a campfire tale. For him, the hunt was gratifying. They had found game and killed it with their bare hands. What an incredible feeling to know you could survive on your own, without civilization's support system. The Negritos were dependent upon no one for what they ate—or did—and Steel relished this moment as he shared that sense of freedom.

Steel stood and watched the scene around the fire. The women were already cutting the pigs down from the poles and dragging them close to the flames. He wanted to stay and watch them butcher, but he was exhausted. The adrenaline that had fueled him throughout the hunt was fading. He suddenly felt tired and dirty.

The Negritos descended upon the pigs with their sharp knives and began to cut. Steel looked at Jo Jo standing quietly. Steel suddenly realized that they hadn't said more than twenty words to each other the whole evening. He liked that about Jo Jo. They didn't have to talk. Steel also breathed a sigh of relief that their argument over Vida seemed to have blown over.

"What do you say we head over to the spring and get cleaned up?"

Jo Jo looked down at his chest and rubbed it with a greasy hand crusted with dried pig blood. "I don't know, this is kind of an attractive look, don't you think?" He laughed.

"Yes, I think that old Negrita woman there has the hots for you."

"They said she is a widower." Jo Jo gave him a thumb's up.

They walked by the woman in question. She sat in the dirt carefully dissecting one of the sows with a small knife. She was dark and shriveled like a raisin, with a shock of kinky white hair. "I wonder how many times she's done this?" Steel smiled. There were no old folk's homes—she had an honored place in the tribe until she died.

"She looks like a pro." Jo Jo nodded. "We'll let them finish the pigs. I don't want to watch them. I won't be able to eat if I do."

Good point, thought Steel as they headed for their tent to get their clean clothes and toilet kits.

Steel checked his watch. Almost noon. They had left the pighunters around seven a.m. to pursue the Japanese. Even Steel could see signs of their presence on the trail.

"Sir, we have found them," Tony said approaching Steel.

"Good. How far?"

"*Doon*, there."

Stupid question, Steel thought. "Okay, let's go. Tony, I want to watch them. Can we do that without them seeing us?"

"Maybe, sir. But they have Negritos with them."

"I'd like to try anyway."

Tony nodded and walked off.

"What do you really think they are doing here?" Jo Jo asked.

"Probably religious ceremonies. I would like to think differently. I mean, I hope they are digging for the treasure. It would be great to see. Although, what the hell would we do? Kill them and take it?" he laughed. "I don't think I could stand watching them carry it out. Maybe they wouldn't be able to haul it all and leave some for us." Steel squinted. Sweat was running down his brow and burning his eyes. He unfurled the towel from around his neck and wiped his face. "I would have to say, though, they are certainly going a long way to pray. I mean, I would have to wonder if I'd go this far just to burn your ratty-ass bones."

"Then I would have to say, I'd feel the same for you. I'd say a few words for you in church or maybe at the Flying Machine and leave it at that," Jo Jo nodded with mock gravity.

They walked for twenty minutes before Tony stopped the group. He consulted briefly with one of the pig hunters from the night before; he suggested that they unload their equipment so they could move the last distance more quietly. Steel was happy to comply—anything to dump the heavy pack.

He felt positively free walking through the jungle without it. He watched Tony and Norgot, the hunter, moving silently ahead. They had left Tony's two cousins behind to watch the gear.

Tony motioned for everyone to get down, then crouched on his hands and knees, crawled ten yards, and lay flat. Steel and the others did the same.

They were high up on the side of a hill. Despite the heavy vegetation, their targets were visible fifty yards away. Steel stretched out on his stomach, pulled out a pair of binoculars, and focused on two individuals.

Both were digging. They were lowlanders, not Negritos. Steel watched for a few seconds before one pulled out a human leg bone and carefully placed it onto a small pile.

The others, mostly Negritos, dug at other shallow graves. He could see one Japanese man, too young to be a veteran, motioning to a lowlander Phil. These two appeared to be supervisors. Steel noted the weapon slung over the Phil's shoulder, an M1 carbine—must be the army guys Tony told him the Japanese hired as security.

The weapon was a bad idea. The NPA was apt to shoot first and sort out allegiances later when they thought someone was armed. At the very best, carrying a weapon was an invitation for the NPA, or whomever, to attack and take it. Negritos were a much safer defense.

Off to the side, Steel could see an old, white-haired Japanese man leaning on a tall walking stick. He wore a brightly colored red bandanna around his head and stood surveying the scene with a distinct military bearing. He must be the veteran.

Hiroko Mitsumi stood solemnly, watching his comrades' bones come out of the graves. It had been nearly forty years since he had buried them. These weren't just any bones—they were his men. Then Major Mitsumi, he had commanded an anti-aircraft battalion stationed at Clark Field.

He was sent to Clark to defend the base itself, but his unit was soon told to withdraw to the mountains south of the base in order to build a series of defensive positions and wait for the American invasion. It had been hard to see the unit's beloved guns no longer aimed at the sky but positioned ready to fire at men on the ground.

For two long years, he and his men lived like moles in their subterranean world. Most of the time, they were half starved and plagued with a variety of jungle diseases. Many died, often drenched in sweat and covered in in their own excrement. Their screams of fevered madness still haunted his nights.

When the Americans finally came, the battle for his command bunker was quick and bloody. Of the three hundred men who had started with him at Clark, only 125 survived to fight that day. In less than twenty-four hours, they too were gone—killed in fruitless defense of this mountain, this pile of dirt and rock, so many, many miles from home.

He hadn't been there to die with them. To his great shame, he and another officer, Lieutenant. Nagamo, had been surveying an area near the command post when an American patrol, led by two tiny black natives, burst from the jungle and knocked him and Nagamo to the ground. They had no chance to fight. He remembered lying in the dirt, blindfolded and trussed, screaming madly into his gag, trying without success to drown out the machine-gun fire and explosions coming from the mountain.

For years after the war, he had wallowed in his humiliation,

149

drinking heavily and hiding from his family. He became a street vagrant, living in a bombed-out area of Tokyo, doing odd jobs and begging food from local shop keepers. He contemplated suicide so many times. It was Nagamo, his former second-in-command, who finally saved him.

After the war, Nagamo had found his own salvation in Buddha and become a priest. In the spring of 1946, through some determination and sheer luck, Nagamo had found the alley his former commander inhabited. He had carried him all the way to his monastery at the base of Mount Fuji.

Six months into his stay there, on an autumn morning, Mitsumi had a revelation. It wasn't his fault that his men died. The war had not been just. He must have been spared for a reason.

Mitsumi returned home, married a childhood sweetheart, and joined his family's engine business. The company became a primary contractor for the then-nascent car company Toyota. Mitsumi worked hard, raised three boys, and retired a successful and wealthy man. But he never forgot his men. He knew all their names still; over the years, he tracked down many of their families, offering loans and scholarships.

Now here he was back at the command post. He was keeping a promise he had made at the monastery over thirty-five years ago. He was going to pay homage to his men and bring their ashes home. He wanted to honor their valor and purity of thought but not the regime responsible for sending these brave souls to die.

Ayoko Mitsumi approached his father, holding a small metal box in his hand. He quickly bowed and said, "Father, we found this silver box buried in a grave. It has a name engraved on top of it."

Mitsumi acknowledged his son's bow and carefully grasped the box with two hands to examine the lid. He read the name

"Yoshi Hidesu" still visible after all these years. Mitsumi opened the box; a small black-and-white photo of a woman graced the underside of the lid, a music box with Yoshi's wife's face.

Mistumi closed his eyes. He paused for a moment to steady himself, then spoke. "Ayoko, where is the grave? Please lead me there."

"Yes, father."

Mitsumi bent down and gently picked up a human skull sitting on the ground. It was covered with dirt and small plant roots were entwined in the eye sockets. So strange to think he held Yoshi's head in hands.

It didn't feel at all morbid. He closed his eyes and pictured Yoshi's face. Private Hidesu was so happy. A clown by nature, his antics had been a welcome relief to their dreary existence in the cave. On occasion, Yoshi would dress up like a geisha performing a bawdy tea-party skit to the roaring laughter of the men.

"Father, did you know this man?"

"These are his bones? This is his shining smile," he pointed to the teeth. "Yes son, it was Hidesu-San—a delightful man whose spirit and laughter gave us some humor in an utterly humorless time."

The son bowed, and gazed at Yoshi's skull with reverence. "Then we must honor him greatly."

"*Hai*," his father bowed back and gently laid Yoshi back on the ground.

Steel looked past the two men at several tents set up near the base of a large tree. Another lowlander with a weapon draped over his lap sat on the ground, smoking and relaxing in the shade. To his left, a man in an orange robe emerged from a cave.

It was an old Japanese priest, probably along for the

religious ceremony. The priest walked over to dozens of skulls and bones in a pile three feet tall and four feet in diameter. Sticks and dry branches were stacked next to the bones. Maybe a funeral pyre, Steel thought. The bones would be burned and their ashes saved to take back to Japan.

"Here, have a look." Steel passed the binoculars to Jo Jo.

Jo Jo put them up to his eyes. "*Haponese* down there?"

"Yeah, looks like they are collecting bones for a pyre."

"What is a pyre?"

"A fire to cremate bones," Steel said. "Japanese culture is so different from American, or Filipino for that matter. I mean, we go to so much effort to account for each individual soldier lost in war. We have big labs that try to identify bodies and get them home for burial, while these guys here are probably doing this on their own without government support. They are just burning the remains without trying to sort them out."

Jo Jo could hear the sadness in Steel's voice and watched quietly for a while. He knew Steel thought about his missing father in times like this, but Jo Jo had his own strong feelings too. "I feel bad for the soldiers. But, my father told me such stories about how brutal they were. For what they did to my country and my people, maybe rotting in the jungle is too good a burial."

Steel had never heard Jo Jo express such emotion before. Yet it shouldn't have been a surprise, since the war had deeply wounded Jo Jo's family. Before he could ask a question, Jo Jo changed the subject.

"I can see some caves in the hillside behind them."

"Big ones?"

"Medium."

"You been there before Tony?"

Tony, who had been on his back dozing, crawled over closer to Steel. "No sir," he said sleepily.

"How about Norgot?"

"Yes. He said that he had been in this area but not at the caves. What are the *Haponese* doing? Are they digging for gold?"

"No. Bones."

Tony shrugged indifferently.

Jo Jo handed the binoculars back to Steel. "I wonder how many days they'll be here. I'd like to explore those caves."

"There won't be much left after those Negritos have been in them." Steel pointed to the diggers with his chin.

Steel and Jo remained for another thirty minutes, watching the work. Bored, Tony and Norgot moved back another twenty feet to nap in the shade.

Eventually, Steel shook the two awake and motioned for them to follow him. He wanted to be out of earshot of those below. When they were far enough away, he spoke in Aeta. "Norgot, are there any streams or drinking water close by?"

Norgot pointed into the jungle. "There is a small stream that flows into the area where they are digging."

"Have you followed it before?"

"I think so, as a boy."

"Have you seen any caves along it?"

Norgot paused for a moment then nodded. "I think there is one *doon*." He pointed into the jungle.

Tony did a double take. He launched into a dialect Steel didn't know. It sounded like he wasn't pleased with Norgot, either for holding out on him about the cave or for giving up its location without first consulting with him. Norgot answered in the same dialect.

After they had finished, Steel spoke. "What language is that?"

"It is Piaeta—not much is spoken any more."

Steel made a mental note to ask Tony more about Piaeta. "Tony, why are you so angry? Are you mad because Norgot forgot he wasn't supposed to tell me about the cave?" Steel laughed.

Tony smiled. "No sir. I wanted to know why he didn't tell us earlier about the cave. I asked him to tell me about any caves in this place. He said that he just remembered it."

"Let's go have a look. Maybe we can quickly explore it before we have to leave tomorrow morning," Steel said.

Norgot led them to the cave, another man-made command post, a bunker. Compared to the last they had explored, this seemed smaller, at least from the outside. But it was intact, dynamited shut by U.S. forces. A large natural formation hung over the doorway making it not immediately obvious that the cave was man-made. Once inside, though, the hand-dug tunnel was evident.

"You ready to go in?" Steel asked, loading up his day backpack with supplies.

"Yes, I will say a quick prayer to the Virgin Mary for some good fortune." Jo Jo made the sign of he cross, his ritual before all cave operations.

It took only a couple of hours to explore. They found lots of bottles and trash, but nothing of value. Tony and his cousins, however, were loaded down with saleable souvenirs when they exited. Once outside, Norgot, who had been assigned to remain with the gear, informed them that he had found another cave farther down stream. Steel checked his watch. It was around seven p.m.

"What do you think, Jo Jo? One more?"

Jo Jo thought for a minute. "Let's go there and set up camp, then see if we can do some exploring. I don't think we'll have time in the morning."

Norgot had been right again. Steel peered at the cave with his binoculars. It was nicely hidden but he could see the entrance, sitting fifty feet up the sheer rock face of a hill, wide enough for two men to stand side by side in its doorway. They would have to scale up the side of the rock cliff to reach it. He'd send Tony up first with a rope, and he and Jo Jo would use it to pull themselves up after. They quickly set up camp. He had Norgot collect firewood and prepare the fire while Tony scaled the cliff face.

The ceiling was high enough that Steel didn't have to stoop over to enter. As they walked farther from the entrance and the light from the outside faded, Steel and Jo Jo switched on their flashlights.

Steel scanned his light along the ground. Forty feet into the tunnel, a large green sake bottle was laid out on the ground with remnants of a wooden crate. Next they stumbled across the rusted barrel of a Japanese army Asoka 7mm rifle and bayonet. Shell casings littered their path as they moved farther in—all calibers and types: American Garands and .45 calibers and Japanese rifles. Evidence of a major firefight, thought Steel. He couldn't imagine the hell of fighting in here: shooting and trying to avoid being shot—all in pitch darkness.

Steel moved ahead of the group and stood by himself. He watched the rest who circled around Jo Jo's light like moths, except for Tony who groveled around in the dirt looking for any exceptional souvenirs. A high-pitched buzzing noise in the distance distracted Steel. He tried to focus on the sound, holding his breath to hear better. But before he could even guess what it was, a frenzied cloud of tiny black objects blasted by, through, and into him.

He quickly dropped to his hands and knees shielding his face with his arms. He could hear Jo Jo yelling out obscenities and see the light from Jo Jo's flashlight bouncing across the cave. It was minutes before Steel could raise his head without getting buzzed by the winged intruders. A swarm of bats that numbered in the thousands headed out of the cave for an evening of insect hunting.

Steel stood up and brushed the dirt and bat shit from his pants. "Hey Jo Jo, you alive, man?"

"Welcome to a horror movie," Jo Jo moaned.

"That was fucking amazing. I've never seen so many bats. They must have an enormous roost in this tunnel."

He waited for Jo Jo and the Negritos to reach his spot. He shined his light on Tony. "What are you grinning about?"

Jo Jo tried to look dignified. "Perhaps I panicked a little when the swarm came through. He, on the other hand, was too busy killing them, swatting them out of the air and stuffing them into his backpack," Jo Jo said pointing to Tony's pack.

"How many did you get?" Steel asked.

Tony just shrugged his shoulders. "*Maraming*, many, enough for us all to roast them on the fire tonight."

Steel had seen bats floating inside Tony's stew pot on other occasions. He hadn't yet been able to bring himself to try one. A roasted bat sounded even less appealing. He couldn't image there could be any meat on the tiny creatures.

They walked deeper into the tunnel and found the bats' lair, smelling it first, a strong pungent odor of ammonia. The ground in the cavern was thick with layers of nitrogen-rich bat guano. Steel shinned his light on the ceiling, alive with the movement of hundreds of female bats and their offspring clinging to the rock roof. He looked over at Tony, who was pointing to the bats and chatting to his cousins. Bats were more a menu item than a wonder of nature to the Negrito.

"Tony, you can't take these bats; these are mothers and babies."

"I know, I know, sir," Tony said annoyed, having heard the lecture before. "We will leave these alone so the mothers can raise the young. We will take only the males," he said robotically.

"That's good."

They pushed into another narrow tunnel right off the cavern. On the ground was lots of World War II trash: pieces of clothing, several canteens, a helmet, bottles, and rusting metal. Steel stopped, pulled out his own canteen, and took a big drink then checked his watch. "Jo Jo, why don't you take Tony and Edgar and explore this branch here, and I'll shoot down the other. Return here in fifteen minutes. Let's not get lost. If the tunnels start winding or turning, just head back here."

"Okay."

Two minutes into Steel's tunnel, it had narrowed to an uncomfortable size. He decided to turn back. He didn't have the energy to squeeze through tonight. While retracing his steps, he noticed a narrow side path he had missed on the way in. It was dark and hidden from view. He casually shined his light inside and, to his amazement, a body—a skeleton dressed in rags—was laid out on the floor. The cranny was only about six feet in depth and seven feet tall. If the body hadn't been in a near-fetal position, it wouldn't have been able to fit into the space. Steel pushed into the small tomb.

It was a Japanese soldier. Steel could tell by the boots, helmet, and remains of a uniform. Next to the body was a Japanese military-issue canvas backpack and rifle. A chill went down Steel's spine; he felt as if ghosts of the past were circling in the tomb. This wasn't the first time the tunnels had made his skin crawl; nonetheless, he squatted down, leaning in closer, angling his light to get a better look.

The skeleton was well preserved. Steel was surprised creatures, rats and such, had not invaded the cave and destroyed the body. It looked almost like a skeleton in a Halloween display.

As he scanned the skull, a necklace winding around the neck bones was visible. He carefully removed the chain and held it up to the beam of his flashlight. At the end of the chain was a quarter-sized, gold-colored Buddha with a large red ruby in its stomach.

Steel's heart raced. This was the first time he'd discovered jewelry. He had surmised that American or Phil soldiers, right after the battle, had liberated anything of value. They just hadn't found this guy.

He slipped the chain into his shirt pocket, reached over, and looked into the soldier's pack. He found a mess kit, a blanket, and a small canvas pouch. He opened the pouch. "Shit!" he muttered to himself. Inside was a leather-bound book. Steel pulled it out and carefully flipped through the pages filled with neatly handwritten Japanese characters—must be a journal or a diary. He flipped to the end.

The last pages were smeared with dried blood. Turning from the book to the skeleton and back again, he thought the blood was likely this man's. Another cold chill—more ghosts from the past.

Late in the afternoon of the 17 October, 1944, Sergeant Toshito Mitofumi lay gut-shot on the dirt floor of the tunnel, beyond physical pain. He'd been wounded before, but never this badly. A veteran of ten years with the imperial Japanese army, he had seen combat under the leadership of the great General Yamashita, the Tiger of Malay. He had followed the Tiger from victory to victory, from Manchuria through Malaysia, Burma, and Singapore, before ending here in the Philippines.

Mitofumi had arrived at Clark Field in July of 1943 and was immediately assigned to lead a platoon of twenty men. The position should have gone to a junior officer, but they were short of officers. Mitofumi's platoon was headed to Hill 112, northwest of Clark, where they were to set up an observation and communications relay site, acting as a trip wire, warning units farther up the valley of enemy advances.

His platoon occupied the hill for nearly a year before the Allied invasion. Mitofumi had found a natural cave, which required little new excavation. In it, he and his men had set up their radio equipment and living quarters. Life in the jungle had been difficult. Disease and sickness had cost him the lives of three of his men. Hunger and boredom made days seem like months.

From his mountaintop with powerful binoculars, he had watched them arrive. The Americans swarmed like ants. His men were so few and so weakened. The Americans all had new equipment, were well fed, and looked healthy. He knew Japan's days in the Philippines were numbered. They were too far from home and too far from their supply lines.

His little platoon had successfully performed their mission and had warned higher headquarters of the American presence. But now, there was nothing left. They had fought down to the last man—him. Mitofumi felt the warm blood on his stomach. He was cold, numb. He knew he was dying.

At least the sharp, excruciating pain he had initially felt when the bullet struck had subsided. He had had just enough energy to crawl into his special hiding place and escape from the madness. He lay in the darkness of his tunnel, soon to be his crypt, and waited to die. Most of the gunfire had stopped—along with the terrible screaming.

The Yankee soldiers left as quickly as they arrived, overlooking his hiding place as they rushed through the tunnel, shooting blindly into the darkness. The tunnel was now eerily quiet. He thought of his beloved wife, Miko.

He remembered her as she looked when he had left her five

years ago, lovely in her white kimono. He had not been able to get word to her for more than a year. He doubted she knew he was still alive. He was struck by a sudden desire to write her one last earthly note.

He tried to prop himself up against the wall. He groped around in the blackness for his backpack. He carefully opened it and felt for the candle he kept in the bottom. When he found it, he lit it with a silver lighter he had taken from a dead British soldier in Malaysia.

The candlelight lifted his spirits slightly. He fingered the lighter, softly feeling the engraved inscription on its side. Even though it was in English, he had memorized its words. One of his troops who spoke some English said that the inscription read: "Keep safe—come home to me my darling Edward. Love Beth." Sometimes the words saddened him. Sometimes they made him feel like he had stolen someone else's rightful love. But the lighter had been a constant in his life these past four years. Beth's love touched him too.

He suddenly didn't want to die alone in the cave. He wanted Miko there with him, by his side. He carefully removed a small leather journal from his pack, along with a silver Parker fountain pen—war booty found on the body of a British officer in Singapore.

The book was nearly empty when he got it. Now it was filled with poetry and love notes for Miko. He hoped someday she would read it.

He had written every entry in the diary as though it would be his last. He had never really expected to see her again, although he vehemently wished he could just one more time. He was destined to die for the emperor.

She was so young and beautiful when they met. She was from a family of poor farmers who lived near his first army posting outside of Tokyo. Her father readily consented to their marriage; Mitofumi could give her a much better life.

As he lay dying, he thought that he should be honest with himself and with Miko. It had been Miko who kept him going, who kept him alive. She kept him from committing suicide or wasting his life in a *banzai* charge. The truth was he really had no desire to die for the emperor—or to die for anyone. He wanted to live for Miko.

It was in Burma, in a temple they were looting, that he found the key to his and Miko's happy future. He carried it with him in his pack, guarding it and hiding it from prying eyes. His senior NCO status afforded him this luxury.

He would give Miko a life of a princess. He would build a big house and a temple and pray daily for the souls of his dead comrades and for the people he killed. Faces of the dead visited him at night. His once-beloved army had done many bad things, many bad things, of which he was not proud.

The erratic flickering of the candle pulled him from his thoughts. It was nearly burned out. A small piece of wax remained. He penned one last request, one last wish for Miko, closed his book and put it back in its canvas pouch. He raised his head and looked up at the wall, his gift for Miko still safely hidden there. The candle flickered out and darkness came again to the tunnel.

Steel flipped slowly though the book. "What does it say?" he muttered. What a lonely place to die, he thought. He put the diary back into the canvas bag then into his own backpack, wondering if it held any hints at where other gold could be found. He just had to learn to read Japanese.

13

Manila

Lt. Col. Augustino "Junior" Pangalan sat anxiously awaiting his 10:00 a.m. meeting with Col. Oscar Ocampos. Ocampos, a senior intelligence officer, worked directly under the commander of the Philippine armed forces, General Ver. Ver, Marcos's dog-faced right-hand man, had a reputation for not suffering fools lightly. You didn't want to cross Ver.

Pangalan had counterintelligence reports on the activities of suspected senior RAM officers locked in his brief case. On some level, he felt bad reporting on his brother officers, some of whom had been his classmates at the academy. But they were idealistic and stupid. Rebellion against the president, who was fighting the Communists, was no way to solve the country's problems.

He looked over and smiled at Maggie, Ocampos's young secretary. She was seated behind a large wooden desk, typing a letter at a steady speed on a well-worn typewriter. Tall, sitting erect, and dressed very neatly in a plain skirt and blouse, her long hair was tied back in a bun, and her face hidden behind large dark-rimmed glasses.

He guessed she was in her late twenties, maybe early thirties. He imagined that beneath the severe secretarial demeanor, there was a sexy beauty. She glanced up from her letter and caught him staring at her blouse. He quickly looked down at the briefcase, pretending to be more interested in its contents then what he imagined filled Maggie's bra.

He hoped the colonel would find the reports useful. Some were routine; others were anything but. One in particular involved an American intelligence operative.

Maggie ushered Pangalan into Ocampos's office. Pangalan, still embarrassed that he had been caught staring at her breasts, avoided her eyes. Ocampos was sitting behind his desk reading. He put down his file folder. "Junior, please sit. Some snacks and drinks for us, *diba*?" Ocampos directed the command towards the secretary, who acknowledged his request by raising her eyebrows, a uniquely Filipino gesture.

Pangalan nodded politely in affirmation and, trying not to let his nerves show in his voice, said, "Good morning, sir." He had been up at his desk since six a.m. rechecking his sources. Ocampos was unforgiving. He didn't tolerate mistakes.

"So Junior, what is this urgent report you had mentioned on the phone?"

"Sir, perhaps 'urgent' is a poor title."

Ocampos deliberately read through the papers Pangalan had handed him. "Ah, you are worried about Lt. Col. Antonio Devincia and Abucayan. Abucayan's an old goat, past his prime. Devincia is a hothead and no threat. But this American, Steel, he is a different story. He concerns me. I do not want the Americans involved in our internal affairs. The RAM boys are at best an annoyance to us, but nonetheless, we don't want our dirty laundry aired to outsiders."

Pangalan swallowed hard. He had hoped this report would present an opportunity for him to express his fear about the RAM group. He didn't share his boss's indifferent attitude towards the RAM; he and the rest of the senior military leadership treated the disenfranchised young officers as spirited children, brushing them off with little more than an indulgent "boys will be boys."

Pangalan did not think the RAM movement was just high-spirited young bucks acting out. He feared RAM was more of a threat to the stability of the AFP than even the NPA. Unfortunately, he did not have any hard evidence implicating RAM in treason, just gut feelings.

Devincia was highly popular with the militant young officer unions and secret brotherhoods. He had an impressive combat record and the respect of his troops. Devincia believed in leading by example, not from behind a desk. He was known to be brutally honest and his family money made it unnecessary for him to take an extra paycheck from kickbacks and bribes.

It was, however, his position as instructor at the Philippine military academy in Baguio that had won him a cult-following of young officers who graduated from the academy. Most were sent into the field to fight the NPA and Muslim separatists. It wasn't his formal academic classroom instruction that separated Devincia from the other instructors; rather it was Devincia's out-of-class exercises in which he took young cadets into the field to show them the reality of life in their army. He gave them practical advice on how to deal with the corruption and cronyism they would face at every turn during their careers. Devincia's advice would save the lives of many a naïve recruit once they got to the battlefield.

These were the newly-commissioned officers who bemoaned the lack of helmets, ammunition, or fuel only to discover corrupt commanders were selling the supplies on the black market. The young lieutenants watched as the NPA used army-issued bullets bought on the black market to kill the troops under the officers' command. The lieutenants chafed as these corrupt but connected supervisors received medals for combat and promotions without spending a day in the field. Because Devincia had foretold it all to the officers, he was revered as a seer and followed as a beacon showing the way to service—exactly the reason Pangalan thought Ocampos ought to take Devencia's machinations more seriously.

Pangalan had witnessed the love the men had for Devincia; he could see it in their eyes. And now, many of Devincia's former students were in command positions in key units around the country. Devincia attended meetings of their secret blood brotherhoods, the most powerful of which was RAM. Pangalan had no doubt they were out to change AFP corruption—the cronyism, the payoffs—by whatever means it took.

Neither Ocampos, nor those above him in the chain of command could honestly deny RAM's grievances. But they enjoyed the lavish lifestyles the current system offered them—so they chose to ignore its venality and brush away those, like Devincia, who took aim at it.

Pangalan knew the military was rotten with corruption and cronyism from the top down. He, like many young officers, had been naïve when he first graduated from the academy. He thought he could have a successful career based on honesty and merit alone. He was so proud standing in uniform at graduation; he had even shaken the hand of President Ferdinand Marcos who had been the commencement speaker.

But after twelve years in uniform, he knew the military was simply a pawn of the president and his wife Imelda, a former beauty queen from the Visayan Islands, "the Rose of Tacloban," as she was known from her pageant days. Now she was referred to as "the iron butterfly," ruthless and corrupt with a collection of expensive shoes rumored to be in the thousands. With an iron fist, Marcos had reigned over the Philippines since 1965. Discontent with his government had fueled a bloody Communist insurgency and layers of civilian political unrest.

It was even said that the Marcoses socked away billions of dollars in Swiss banks, thanks to his ownership stake in huge companies in the Philippines and World Bank loans. Marcos was smart and seemed secure in his nest of cronies. The only chink in his armor were bouts of ill health, reported to be kidney and heart problems.

Pangalan took a deep breath. Maybe he should just hold his tongue—again. It would do his career no good to give his superiors news that they decidedly did not want to hear. In the past, he too had brushed off the threat posed by RAM and quietly kept his share of his intelligence budget for personal use. He couldn't survive on his pathetic salary, not living in Manila, not with two college-aged children. He too was invested in the status quo. Against his better judgment, he plunged ahead.

"Sir, may I be frank with you? I want to discuss the RAM."

"Of course, Junior, I want the straight story," Ocampos said in a paternal tone.

The secretary quietly pushed open the door carrying a tray of cups, saucers, a small pot of coffee, and some *pandesal* bread and butter.

"Ah good, *Salamat*, thanks Maggie."

Maggie smiled and placed the tray down on the colonel's desk. Ocampos preferred pouring the coffee himself. He's not so bad to work for, Maggie thought. He only occasionally asked for the routine sexual favors that she saw as part of the job, and his demand on her secretarial skills was light. For her quick typing, proficient waitressing, and attractive, available breasts, she made a good salary, which she augmented with pocket money earned passing bits of information that she picked up around the office to a handsome captain in charge of the base supply office. The tidbits she gleaned during her workday seemed trivial, so no harm done as far as she was concerned.

She had listened to the conversation as best she could through the thin walls of Ocampos's office. She took some notes highlighting the RAM and something about an Americano. She hoped she had just enough details to please Captain Agnasio, maybe enough so he would invite her out to lunch again. He was so handsome in his uniform. She would do anything he asked. Maybe she would even enjoy performing sexually for him, unlike her experiences with the colonel. She lingered in the outer office long enough to make sure Ocampos didn't need anything else, then quietly exited.

But Pangalan was not yet done with the briefing. He took a deep breath. "Sir, I am gravely worried about Devincia and the RAM boys. They are like a worm eating at our internal organs. He is feeding upon our young officers and—"

"Oh Junior, don't be concerned. You know we have Devincia under control." Ocampos poured them more coffee. "He is just, how shall we say, an idealist. He is a good soldier, and men will follow him and die in battle for him. We need officers who aren't more interested in the golf courses in Manila than the jungles of Mindanao. That is a good thing, *diba*?"

Pangalan nodded in agreement.

"His politics are only an annoyance. He lets our young officers vent. We have a secure grip on the senior leadership structure of all the services. Cream and sugar?"

"Please."

Ocampos smiled at Pangalan's naiveté. Ver and President Marcos had insured that all the senior positions in the AFP and the other services were filled with loyal soldiers, invested in the status quo. Generals and admirals were handpicked, many extended well past their terms of command. This was a military in which officers received promotions—and the extra graft rank bestowed-for loyalty to the chain of command first and foremost; competency came a distant second.

"Junior, I appreciate your allegiance to me and your disquietude over the RAM. Don't think I have not been able to read between the lines in your reports. Rest assured, we are watching RAM. I myself manage the project. I will tell you something," Ocampos lowered his voice. "Devincia is going to be promoted to another desk job here in Manila, right up the hall from us."

"But sir, I—"

Ocampos raised his hand. "Junior, I'll give you the old saying: Keep your friends close and your enemies closer. This will show the young officers that we value Devincia. We will reward him for his service to our country, and we will extinguish his revolutionary fire with the piles of paperwork his new position will demand."

Pangalan thought for a minute. Ocampos sounded sure, but Pangalan couldn't shake the feeling that a snake was about to move into the house. "Sir, I find that, er… incredible to believe. I would think the best plan for him would be to send him into combat, where maybe a stray bullet could end his career."

"Ah Junior, if I thought he could be killed, I might consider that. But he is very smart, a survivor. He did not die in his first ten years of fighting. No, he must be here where we can keep an eye on him. His promotion will be made with much pomp and circumstance. Who knows, with extra money and freedom from the battlefield, our friend might come to enjoy the soft life Manila provides its soldiers. He might even take up golf." Ocampos laughed.

Pangalan smiled nervously. But he was afraid there was no chance of corrupting Devincia. In fact, the promotion and prestige would just bring him closer to his goals. Antonio Devincia had the followers—all he needed were the means—and it looked as if Ocampos was planning on handing those over, complete with a military parade and comfy corner office.

"Ah Junior, I can see it in your eyes, you are not happy. Go ahead and allocate some more resources to keep on eye on Antonio. But more importantly, see what you can find out about the Americano. Is he CIA?"

"No sir, I do not believe he is. We have identified him as a U.S. Air Force officer, Capt. William Steel. He is assigned to the 13th Air Force headquarters. He speaks fluent Tagalog and appears to be a staff intelligence officer, not a field operative. Although, there are reports that he makes frequent trips to the Zambales Mountains in search of gold."

"Gold?"

"Yes sir, some lost Japanese World War II treasure."

Ocampos's eyes widened. "That is interesting." He had heard rumors that some of the Marcos's family wealth had come from a discovery of lost Japanese gold. He had thought it nothing but legends. But maybe he would follow up. "Junior, this is very odd indeed. An Americano officer caught up in the romance of treasure hunting and with RAM contacts."

Pangalan nodded. "Yes, but the treasure hunting could be a cover for the Americanos' operations in the Zambales. Perhaps this Steel is more than he seems."

"I agree. For many reasons we should keep an eye on Steel."

"Of course, sir." Pangalan was relieved to have his ongoing surveillance of Steel sanctioned, not to mention now financed.

"Maybe RAM is trying to recruit this young American officer outside of his system. I want to know if he is on his own or an operative of the U.S. government."

"With extra resources, it should be easier to keep an eye on Devincia."

"Good! Good! So Junior, drink some coffee and tell me about your latest golf game."

14

Clark Air Base

STEEL WAS SITTING AT HIS desk in the 13th Air Force intel vault. It was early, and he was enjoying sitting alone sipping strong coffee and flipping through the pile of intelligence reports in his inbox. The AC felt good, especially after the sweltering heat of the U.S. Crow Valley Range Facility. He had spent the last two days there observing instructors who taught U.S. aircrews how to survive in the jungle.

At first, Steel had enjoyed the trips to the valley, but these days he felt that if he had to live in primitive conditions, he would rather it be in the mountains looking for treasure. Although, he never tired of watching fighter pilots out of their element. Most of them he had encountered were type-A personalities, swaggering into Survival 101, sure they could ace the course. Their bravado usually persisted until the final exam.

The exercise began at 0600 hours and was meant to simulate a parachute landing into enemy territory. The pilots were dropped in a remote area ahead of Negrito trackers who were paid to act as enemy forces searching for them. The crews then used maps and compasses to find a safe area where they were to be picked up by rescue forces, all the while trying to evade Negrito trackers. Each crew member had a piece of paper, known as a chit, with his name on it. If caught, he had to present the chit to the tracker.

Like clockwork, the hyped pilots ran off into the bush at the start of the exercise, confident they could evade their pursuers. Steel would sit in the shade and smoke with the Negritos as they gave the pilots their head start.

To make it interesting, the Negritos would wager bets on whom they would catch first, or last, or not at all—although the latter was a rare occurrence. Few airmen made it to the safe area with their chit. When Steel would critique their performance, most expressed shock at how quickly they were found. "I never saw or heard the little bastard until he was standing right in front of me" was a common complaint.

If you pressed the Negritos, they would say they could smell the pilots. Aftershave was their undoing. The scent of Brut drifted in the jungle air for hours.

"Captain S." A voice shook Steel from his thoughts. "Sheeet. Goddamnit Cap S! You and your goddamn coffee."

He and Staff Sgt. Curtis Washington raced into work each day hoping to make the morning pot of coffee. Steel liked his strong, Curtis did not.

"Damn coffee gives me the shits," he yelled again.

"Oh, quit complaining. You should thank me for keeping you regular." Steel turned to see Curtis's smiling face. He had his cup of coffee in hand.

"I watered mine down."

"Disgusting," Steel noted.

Curtis walked over to Steel's desk, sipping from his mug. "I organized the reports while you were gone. I put them on top of your inbox, and yesterday I plotted them on the map," Curtis said, gesturing at points on the map.

"Excellent. Let's have a look. Anything out of the ordinary?" Steel examined the five-by-five-foot map of the Philippines mounted on a corkboard. It was covered with different colored pins, each one a recent NPA- or CPP-related incident. For the last year, Steel had been analyzing patterns to determine NPA strengths.

"Nah, nothing that jumped out at me, just more of the same. Although, there was an ambush of an AFP truck convoy in Tarlac; ten soldiers killed and ten wounded. They used a land mine in the road."

"Damn, that's not too far from here. Americans use that road. That's not good." Steel scanned the map for a few more minutes before returning to his desk.

Curtis followed to his desk next to Steel's. "Hey Cap, one more item." He dug for a moment through his inbox. "I know it's here somewhere. Another report of foreigners with local NPA units: could be a problem for us if the NPA get good trainers."

Steel turned. "You know it's strange there aren't more reports identifying the presence of Soviet or Chinese agents in the area."

"Shit, maybe the security dicks down at the OSI are more worried about busting black marketers than foreign agents. Or maybe there just aren't many agents around here."

"Yeah, maybe." Steel found it hard to believe that there weren't any agents. Clark was a key base in the U.S. defense of the Pacific. The Soviets surely would want to keep an eye on operations here.

"Here it is. It's from the AFP and notes that a probable North Korean agent was operating with local NPA forces."

Steel jumped up from his chair and moved to read over Curtis's shoulder. "You're kidding. H'mm, damn you're right—'suspect North Korean agent.' Great find. Damn, this is a first."

Curtis leaned back in his chair. "I guess it only makes sense. Christ, I mean if I were North Korea I'd have agents here. Damn, our wing deploys to Korea if war breaks out."

"That's right," Steel agreed. "What if they are training, or, God forbid supplying, the NPA with arms? Damn, that would be something. In fact, I'm going to propose to Kuncker that you brief it to the general."

"What? Me. I don't—"

"Oh yeah, you can use the face time. Good for your promotion potential, and I can put you in for NCO of the quarter. Hell, it's a two-day pass and your own parking spot in front of the NCO club."

"Sign me up," Curtis said, smiling.

Steel checked his watch. He was dreading his lunch engagement. He looked over at Curtis, who was busy hunting and pecking at keys on the typewriter. "Hey Curtis, I'm heading over to the club for lunch."

"Got your back Cap S," Curtis said without turning around.

"*Salamat Sigi*, thanks goodbye," Steel said unconsciously in Tagalog.

"Where'd you learn to speak Tag-a Log so well?"

"Listening, going to the movies, and of course chatting with the ladies."

"No books?"

"Yes. I have some books and dictionaries and a guy I use as a private instructor. Why? Are you interested in learning?"

"Maybe."

"You should consider it. Would be good for you to learn a language. Besides, you should see how the ladies react when you can say a few words to them."

"I'll give it some thought." He turned and resumed his typing.

"One more thing, I'm going to the 3rd TAC squadron after lunch."

"No problem. I'm working on the briefing. Thanks again for chance. I hope I don't freeze up and make a damn fool out of myself."

"No way. Besides, remember that the general is just a man. I've found that the higher the rank, the nicer they are. It's the lower-ranking guys who'll stab you in the back."

"You mean lower ranking, like captains?"

"Captains are the worst."

Steel grinned, grabbed his hat, and headed out of the door. He had offered to put on a slide show of Father Rudy's operation at the orphanage for the Officers' Wives' Club at today's luncheon. He had made a good impression on the OWC's president, Irene Dresden, last week after he had volunteered to partner with her in a base tennis competition.

He and the lusty Irene had managed to come in second place in the mixed doubles. She was happy with their performance on the court, and he let her feel him up between sets. She whispered in his ear that they should do lunch soon and agreed to let him present at today's meeting. He hoped his sales pitch would net Rudy at least $500 dollars worth of immediate support. He would also invite the club to the orphanage for a field trip.

He knew the face-to-face contact with the boys would get the orphanage on the club's permanent donation list. The only hard part would be keeping Irene interested in the orphanage but out of his bed. The last thing he needed was Colonel. Dresden gunning for him.

The O Club was packed. There weren't many other options for lunch on the base. He finished his presentation to the OWC and was headed out. As he rounded a corner, he plowed into a tall officer dressed in cammo fatigues, nearly knocking an ice tea glass from his hand. He was familiar and a quick look at the name embroidered on his jacket pocket confirmed his identity—the OSI's vice chief, Snowden. Steel spoke first. "Afternoon sir, sorry to knock into you."

Snowden froze. He gritted his teeth and stared blankly at Steel.

"Sorry sir, I was distracted thinking about a speech I just gave to the OWC. I'm trying to help a place called Mabuhay House—it's full of abused and neglected kids—young boys in need." Hey thought Steel, Snowden could be a good contact; he was in charge of a large organization. "Could I interest you in helping out?"

Snowden was stunned; he averted his eyes. "I'm not sure what you want." Snowden stammered.

"I do believe you've been here at Clark for as long as I have, and you know the situation here with orphaned children."

Snowden felt like a trapped animal. What was Steel's game? Did he get a perverse pleasure out of this?

"All we need right now to help these kids is $500. Yep, $500 dollars seems like a lot of money, but it would sure help us out."

So that's it. It's all about blackmail—$500 dollars. Finally, something I can understand, Snowden thought. "Don't pay the asshole a dime—just kill him," His inner voice snarled. Snowden bit the inside of his lip, trying to keep the voice from leaking out.

Steel continued, oblivious. "Could I come by sometime and talk to you in person about this? You'll really feel good helping us. My friend says it's like heaping coals off your head, helping the boys."

Snowden reached into his cammo jacket pocket and fumbled for his checkbook and a pen. He turned quickly, found a small wooden end table to lean on, and began scribbling out a check.

Steel looked on at first stunned, then flustered. "Hey, um, sir, I didn't mean to put any undue pressure on you this moment. I'm just over-caffeinated and pumped up about the boys after my brief."

Snowden ripped out a check and handed it to Steel. "I hope this is the end of it." He pushed briskly past Steel without another word.

"End of what?" Steel thought. Probably thinks I'm a real jerk. He slapped himself on the forehead, shocked at his pushy salesmanship. He looked down at the check. What the hell? Snowden had just written him a personal check for $500. What a great guy.

Steel jetted out of the parking lot with Snowden's check tucked safely in his wallet and headed toward the flight line. He was in route to the Third Tactical Fighter Squadron for a meeting with their intel folks. While there, he needed to track down Maj. Henry "Weasel" Wallace.

Weasel was the head of their planning office and the squadron's chief plans and training officer. He was also the best F-4 back-seater in the wing and possibly the entire Air Force. More importantly, Henry was a brilliant map man and, after four years of flying low level around the Philippines, knew the lay of the land.

Steel wanted Henry's help finding the location of the Japanese command post Professor Abucayan had shown him. He sketched as much as he and Jo Jo could remember of Abucayan's Japanese map, a crude illustration, but the mountain had some unique features that Henry might recognize. It was a long shot, but what the hell?

Steel was bummed when he popped his head in the squadron office only to discover that Weasel was flying today. He wrote a quick note and had an admin clerk put his drawing in a large envelope and place it in Weasel's inbox. He'd follow up with a phone call tomorrow. He walked back to his truck and headed to his next errand.

The airport terminal came into sight. Steel's Thai friend, Flight Lt. Chamlong Srimuang, or as his American friends called him "Cham," was arriving late this afternoon. Cham, a Royal Thailand Air Force intelligence officer, was visiting Clark in order to attend a conference and would be Steel's houseguest for a few days.

Close in age, Steel enjoyed Cham's sharp wit. He, like Steel, was an unlikely military officer. Before his stint in the military, Cham had been content helping his father run their successful mining business in northern Thailand. Cham's only sibling, an older brother in the army, had been less inclined to join the family enterprise initially, though three years ago he quit the army for the mining business. Shortly thereafter, according to Cham, his father announced it was Cham's turn to get some military experience and "toughen up." Steel always suspected that it was more likely the older brother's jealousy that had landed Cham in the military. Cham opted for the air force, joining the squadron headed up by his uncle, a pilot.

On Cham's first trip to Clark, Steel had showed him some basic tricks of the intel trade and helped him put together flashy briefs. They'd even cooperated on a joint presentation, which brought rave reviews from their commands.

Cham had a mining engineering degree from the University of Montana, and Steel relied on Cham's expertise for his treasure hunts. He would have liked to take Cham on a trip to the mountains and show him firsthand the command posts, but he doubted the meek lieutenant would enjoy the trip.

Cham was also an expert in precious gems. Steel loved listening to his descriptions of the legitimate and the black market gem businesses he operated on the side. Steel figured that Cham moonlighted in gems as a backup occupation in case his father died and his brother booted him from the business. Steel also knew, should be find treasure in the mountains, he'd need some way to fence the stuff; he figured Cham's connections would be the best approach.

They exchanged regular letters and phone calls. Cham had his uncle request Steel for two exchange visits to Thailand. Cham had hosted him in Bangkok, treating him to the best restaurants and fantastic massage parlors.

It was on his last trip to Thailand that Steel confirmed what he had suspected about his friend. Cham had taken him to a *Katoy* club, a place where Thai men dressed like women had mannerisms and physical appearances that made it nearly impossible to tell that they were actually men. Inside the club, Cham told Steel that he preferred *Katoy* girls to real women.

Steel could recall how Cham, nearly in tears, had been concerned that once Steel learned this, he would shun Cham. Whom he bedded was his own business, Steel assured, less competition for the bar girls.

Steel walked into the terminal where Cham was already waiting. It was great to see him. Steel was excited to show him the gold Buddha he had found. Then after one of Rosa's great meals, they would go out on the vil, drink beer, and play pool.

"Hey Jo Jo, you want a beer?" Steel yelled over the loud music spilling out of a colorful juke box.

"No, just a coke tonight," Jo Jo yelled back as he walked

across the floor toward the bathroom. Steel shot him a thumbs up sign and headed over to the back of the smoky bar with Cham in tow.

The place wasn't air-conditioned, but large screened windows and wood bladed ceiling fans turning slowly overhead kept the air well-circulated. The bar's big draw was its pool table, professional quality and custom-made of mahogany. The bar's owner, an eccentric Australian named Blake, had it recovered once a year.

Steel smiled to see the table open. It was a weeknight so the bar was relatively empty.

"It looks like we shall have the place to ourselves." Cham said happily.

Cham's perfect white teeth and big smile were plainly visible in the sporadic lighting. His jet-black hair was short and groomed perfectly. He was dressed, as usual, in black pants and a black silk shirt. Steel thought it looked great even though it hung loose and made Cham look even slighter of build than he was. Steel knew that if he complimented the top, he was almost assured a package would arrive in the next couple of weeks with his own black shirt. That was fine by him, it wasn't his intention, but what the hell, it was a great-looking shirt.

A waitress had followed them to the table and was standing patiently. Steel ordered their drinks in English then switched to Tagalog to say he would pick up the tab. He promised her a good tip if she refused the Thai man's money.

"So Cham, have you played any pool back home?"

"Only once or twice; work has been consuming all of my time. And you my friend?"

"About the same as usual, maybe once a week if I'm lucky."

"I think you are a bad liar, Steel. You take pride in your pool game."

"Hey boss, you order my coke?" Jo Jo said as he pulled up a stool and had a seat at the bar which was in yelling range.

"Jo Jo, are you sure you don't want to play in my place? I would enjoy watching you beat this arrogant bastard," Cham called out.

"No, he's all yours. I am tired of taking his dollars."

"Beating me? Ha. Master Jo Jo here dreams of beating me."

"All the Orientals bow to you," Cham said.

"I might have taken pity on you, but now I'm going to kick your little Asian ass from here back to Chang Mai."

Cham laughed out loud. "Kick my ass from here to Chang Mai."

The waitress approached with a tray of drinks. Cham tried to pay, but she refused to accept his cash, pointing to Steel.

"Hey, it's Thai night tonight. Short obnoxious Thais drink free."

Cham scowled at Steel. "So Steel, you want to make this interesting?"

"Sure. What do you consider interesting?"

"Let's say twenty a game?"

"Pesos or Baht?"

"Dollars." Cham said, chalking his cue nonchalantly.

"That's not a friendly bet." Steel now knew that Cham had indeed been practicing.

"Of course it is. It is a gift. Have I ever defeated you?"

"No, but I'm afraid the house decides, and this poor white boy here say, one U.S. dollar a game."

"Okay. You can break," Cham relented.

The first game went by quickly. Steel was surprised by how well Cham played, sinking every shot while setting up the next. He had obviously been practicing, probably even taken some lessons.

Cham destroyed Steel in the first game, but the second was a little closer. Cham still won, though, sinking the eight ball with a well-played bank shot.

"I think Steel's days as champion are now over," Jo Jo said, applauding Cham.

"Alright, tell me with a straight face you haven't been practicing."

"No really, Steel. I have just this moment had a spiritual awaking about pool. I prayed to the Lord God Buddha, and he answered my prayers."

"Oh come on. You mean you prayed to the Lord God Minnesota Fats."

"Minneysotaay who?"

"Never mind, you bastard. Rack them up, Nellie." A short, heavy-set girl racked up the balls for them. "Two more beers for us and another coke for my father sitting over there." Steel pointed over to Jo Jo who was chatting with one of the waitresses at the bar. He waved back without turning from his conversation.

By their fourth beer, Cham had loosened up considerably, unbuttoning two more buttons on his shirt, shrieking and fluttering his hand with every shot, and—thankfully—missing a few. The beer buzz and a couple of cigarettes helped Steel get his game together, and he was confident this fourth round would be his.

"Alright. It is all coming back now," Steel said pointing his cue at Cham, "Time for the Princess of Siam to get his comebacks." Steel concentrated on pushing the eight ball into the side pocket with a delicate touch. He missed.

"Damn you," Steel yelled.

Cham threw his cue onto the table, walked over and shook Steel's hand. "I cannot believe I won four games in a row. I need to go to the toilet room. You want a rematch?"

Steel checked his watch. "Sure, we have time for one more. Then we have to go."

Cham nodded in affirmation and headed off.

Steel looked over towards the bar. Jo Jo was chatting to Gemma. Long, tall, and sexy, she was a new hire with the same life story as many of the girls working in the bars.

She had been a second-year student at the university, a chemical engineering major, when her married professor got her pregnant and her family disowned her. She moved to Angeles with a cousin, had the baby five months ago, and started working in the club. Steel had enjoyed her company the last couple of visits to the bar and was glad to see her tonight.

Steel had given up on Vida. He had left messages for her at her newspaper but she ignored his calls. It had been weeks since she had visited. She knew where to find him and what he wanted, what he could give her, what he had thought she wanted. Ah, to hell with her. She could marry Antonio and play the role of Filipina housewife for all he cared. Steel didn't need the grief from Jo Jo or Rosa anyway. "Give me a willing house girl any day," thought Steel. Or maybe a bar girl with legs that won't stop, breasts you lose yourself in for days, and pussy so hot it'll drive the last thought of a smart-mouthed Manila bitch from my head. He walked over to the bar. "Hi Gemma. This old goat giving you a hard time?"

"He is not old," she said, laughing. "A goat maybe, but not old." She touched Jo Jo's cheek warmly.

"We are having a lively political discussion about the Marcos regime. Gemma and I had the same political science instructor."

Steel put his hand on Jo Jo's shoulder. "I find it hard to believe that an instructor you had is still alive."

"You are very funny." Jo Jo rolled his eyes.

"So how about it, *LoLo*, grandpa, you want to play some partners?"

Jo Jo cocked his head towards Gemma. "You want to play with me? We can make a magnificent team. Your beauty and my talents."

Gemma smiled. "Sure, why not? Would be fun."

Gemma watched Nellie rack the balls and sipped an overpriced, nonalcoholic mango juice concoction Steel had bought for her—the price of enjoying her company in the bar. Gemma had made it clear to him when they first met that she didn't go home with customers; others were available but not her. She was paid a small salary, but made good money on drinks and conversation. Period.

"Are you ready, Cham?" Steel announced, feeling light headed. The beers had begun to take their toll.

"So we have a ten pesos bet, *diba*?" Jo Jo asked.

"Ten dollars it is." Cham was delighted to team up with Steel.

"Ten pesos. Not ten dollars," Jo Jo quickly corrected.

"*Balut* sir, *balut* anyone," A voice called out loudly to the group. They turned to see a skinny old Filipino, awkwardly holding a small wooden box.

"Now, Cham, would you like to try one? It is a Filipino delicacy." Jo Jo approached the man.

"A *balut*?" Cham's asked.

"Don't listen to Jo Jo. It is not something you want to eat," Steel grimaced. "He is trying to affect your game."

"What is it?"

"They take a duck egg that is nearly ready to hatch and bury it in the ground for a month. Imagine what it smells and tastes like. Fortunately, I've never been drunk enough to try one." Steel chalked his cue.

Cham swallowed hard.

Jo Jo paid the man and offered to buy an egg for any takers. No one accepted. Jo Jo shrugged, and sat down, and began methodically peeling the egg. The stench was overpowering as Jo Jo crunched the fermented duck embryo loudly.

Steel and Cham easily won the first game, and agreed to play a second game, though Steel was enjoying chatting with Gemma. He swore this was the last go. It was getting late and a group of three rowdy Americans were impatiently waiting for the pool table. They were marines from Subic Naval base, Steel guessed. They sported crew cuts and were enormous, with that big shoulder- small waisted physique that the Corp seemed to hand out with their regulation boots. He wondered why they were here, instead of at one of the raunchier places.

He didn't like the way they were eyeing Cham and muttering amongst themselves. Steel sensed trouble.

"Alright Steel, put this one in. It is so easy. Then you have the perfect set up for the eight ball," Cham's voice rose in excitement and Steel winced.

Gemma, sensing the end was near, leaned over the pool table directly behind the pocket for which Steel was aiming. She braced herself with her arms and let her low-cut blouse fall open.

He liked the way her shoulder length black hair hung loosely and framed her chest. The bar light bathed her perfectly shaped breasts in a rosy glow. If he strained his neck, he could see her pert brown nipples.

"Your shot." She smiled at him again.

"Goddamn," he thought. She was attractive and he was so ready.

Cham looked at Steel's face and grabbed at his cue. "Steel, they are indeed beautiful breasts, but I am immune their charms. Give me that. I'll shoot this shot."

"Yes, maybe you should. I am having a hard time concentrating. They are particularly distracting," Steel handed Cham his cue without taking his eyes off Gemma.

"Will you fucking hurry up! I'm getting really tired of waiting for you and that fucking queer," a voice boomed out of the darkness.

Steel turned and could hear the laughter. It was the biggest of the Marines who had spoken, much to the delight of his two buddies. Steel looked over at Cham, who was trying to concentrate on his shot, pretending that he did not, or could not, understand what had just been said. Gemma stood quickly and pulled her blouse closed. Jo Jo took a deep breath and gripped his cue tightly.

"Let's go huh?" Jo Jo whispered.

"Cham, take your time and finish the game. Hell, I might even play a couple more games," Steel said loudly.

"Fuck you," the big Marine staggered, spilling some of his beer. "This is your last game. You and your butt buddies are done right now." More laughter.

Steel pointed a finger at the Marine. "Look you ignorant Marine-fuck, you and your Neanderthal buddies can find something to amuse yourselves while we finish our game." Generations of stubborn Irish ancestors urged Steel on as he turned his back on the Marines, flipping them a finger before exaggeratedly considering his next shot.

The big Marine, moved toward Steel. The two other Marines followed a few paces behind.

Steel automatically fell into a loose Kuntaw stance, one that Jo Jo had literally beat into him. It appeared non-threatening and gave no indication that he was prepared to react.

The Marine marched straight at Steel and attempted to grab his shirt collar, the move of a wrestler not a street fighter. Before the Marine's hands could make contact, Steel dropped one leg backwards, lowering his body into a blocking stance while simultaneously shooting his two arms upward, a perfectly timed move that knocked the Marine's beefy forearms into the air.

The block briefly left the Marine's face vulnerable to Steel's uppercut. The heel of Steel's palm caught the Marine directly under his large cleft chin. The Marine's teeth crunched audibly, and blood erupted from his mouth. He staggered backward, both hands gripping his face.

Without thinking, Steel took a quick step forward and executed a front snap kick, catching the Marine directly in the balls. The pain instantly registered in the Marine's face, his teeth and tongue injuries overshadowed. He staggered backwards into his buddies, who each grabbed an arm to keep the giant from crashing to the floor. Steel thought with satisfaction, "I don't care how much time you spend at the base gym, buddy, there ain't no way to prepare for the shock of a well-placed kick to the flimsy sack of nerves housing the testicles." Jo Jo stood watching Steel in shock.

Steel was no less surprised. Though he had spent hundreds of hours practicing *katas* and self-defense moves and countless more hours punching body bags and sparring with the tough and agile Filipino partners that Jo Jo provided, Steel had never used Kuntaw in anger. The only time he had intentionally punched another human was in the sixth grade when he smacked Ken Swollar in the face after Swollar called him a fag. At the time he wasn't sure what fag meant, but the other boys had whooped with laughter, which had infuriated him. And now, here years later, a homosexual reference uttered by this thug had brought forth the same primordial rage.

The big Marine was unceremoniously lowered to the ground by his two friends, and they rushed at Steel.

Jo Jo dispatched the first Marine with a well-placed jab from the butt end of his pool cue. Jo Jo had stepped forward to administer the blow professionally. The cupped rubber end of the cue neatly bounced off the Marine's forehead with a satisfying pop.

The Marine stood dazed for a second, allowing Jo Jo to execute a lightning-fast punch to the solar plexus. Gasping for air, the Marine emitted a shower of spit from slightly curled lips as his knees buckled, and he hit the floor.

The third Marine, a short muscular grunt who looked like he had played some serious football, rushed at Steel and tackled him. They both fell backwards on top of the pool table. Cham let out a war whoop and leapt onto the back of the short Marine.

Ineffectually swatting at Cham with one hand, football Marine quickly landed several punches on Steel's head before he pushed himself off, twisting and grunting in pain. Cham had locked his skinny arms around the Marine's nearly nonexistent neck and his teeth firmly onto one of the Marine's big, white, exposed ears. No matter how hard he spun and thrashed, he could not throw Cham off. Finally, screaming in pain, the Marine crashed to the floor, dislodging the small Thai.

With bodies, blood, and broken pool cues littering the floor, the sixty-year-old bar manager entered the fray. Barely five feet tall, she was a thirty-year veteran of bar fights and had hardly ever—if ever—been on the losing side. With the speed and agility of a woman half her age, she leapt forward, aiming a stream of Mace into the face of the Marine curled on the ground in a fetal position cupping his bloody ear. Cham, lying in close proximity to the Marine, was hit by collateral spray. He rolled away shouting Thai expletives.

Jo Jo grabbed Steel by the arm and rushed over to pick up Cham from the floor. They half-carried, half-dragged Cham to the bar, pushed his face into a metal sink, and sprayed his head with water, trying to flush away the Mace.

Steel paid his bar tab, and left a generous tip. He assured Gemma that all was well, and they both turned to watch the Marines try to collect themselves. Steel grinned at the biggest of them, who was clearly the most incapacitated. His two friends struggled to hold him erect. *Mamasan* and the bar's blue-suited security guard blocked the men's exit. Looked like they hadn't settled their tabs judging from the way she was threatening to spray them again.

Jo Jo unceremoniously shoved a teary-eyed Cham and an adrenalin-filled Steel out the door. He wanted everyone out of the place before the military police arrived.

Once safely in the truck Cham, with eyes still clamped shut, spoke. "Quite a memorable evening, Steel. You certainly know how to host a night out." Cham smiled as tears streamed down his cheeks.

"Yes, this will be difficult to explain to my boss." Steel winced looking at Cham's puffy red eyes and nose.

"No problem, William. I assume proper people have been paid off."

"Yeah."

"Then no problems."

"What about your face?" Steel said, trying to think of a plausible explanation. His boss was going to kill him for getting a foreign officer and a guest of the U.S. Air Force injured in a barroom brawl.

"Am I still not a handsome man?" Cham grinned.

"You look like a war victim," Jo Jo piped in as he started the truck.

"Oh, how about I got stung by some insects and reacted badly?"

"That could work," Steel said as his body jerked forward with the momentum of Jo Jo's rapid exit from the parking lot. A few minutes later they were passed by a military jeep with flashing lights. Steel wondered if the Marines had gotten out past the *Mamasan*.

15

Angeles City

STEEL WAS STRETCHED OUT ON his bed, naked, arms propped behind his head. He was watching Gemma, also naked, straddling him as if riding a horse. The hot, steamy late-night air settled on them like a blanket.

Gemma's eyes were tightly shut. She seemed oblivious to the heat and, for that matter, everything around her. She slowly ground her pelvis into Steel's. Her body glistened with beads of sweat. He watched as several wound down her chest and across her stomach. Others fell from her breasts onto him. She opened her eyes, looked at him, and smiled, leaning backwards, using her arms for support, finding the best angle. She thrust harder against him, using him. Her breathing quickened and she began to moan, tossing her hair from side to side, in rhythm with the ceiling-fan blades rotating overhead.

"Sir. Is this what you wanted?" Joseph called out. He patiently waited for an answer. Steel pulled his glassy gaze from the bedroom window and shook off the fantasy.

He looked at the hole Joseph was digging. "Yeah, looks like you got most of the big ones." Steel pushed his heel hard into his own shovel, going deep into the gray, powdery, volcanic soil. Last night with Gemma was fresh in his mind. He'd like to replay the highlights again, right here and now, sweaty and covered in dirt.

"Sir, do you want to put the gravel in now or wait until all the roots are dug?"

Steel smiled. "Go ahead and get all the roots first." Joseph was not going to let Gemma back in so easily.

Once they had finished digging out the roots, they would put down some decorative stones, black pebbles, round and smooth, worn by the currents of the small river near the city. He had purchased them for pennies from a cement company that had sifted out the best ones for him from their normal batches of gravel.

Steel had wanted to put some time in his garden before it got too hot. He looked up and briefly checked out the position of the sun creeping higher into the sky. Next door, the large white cockatoo squawked loudly from behind the cinderblock wall separating the properties.

Steel stopped digging for a moment and mopped the sweat from his brow. He sighed deeply and again looked up at the sun. It was going to be a hot day. "How are we doing, Joseph?"

Joseph, who was using a pickaxe to cut through the hard tree roots, paused for a moment. "We are nearly through, Captain Steel." He resumed whacking at the dirt.

"Great." Steel had given up trying to get Joseph to call him Will.

Steel reached down into dirt and pulled out a root from a large bush growing nearby. The manual labor gave him time to clear his mind and think. He reflected on the mixed feelings he had had putting Cham on the plane Saturday morning. Steel hated to say goodbye to his friend and comrade, but it had opened a berth for Gemma on Saturday night. What a great guy Cham was—far from being upset by receiving a face full of Mace, he had relished his part in the melee.

Every time he retold the story of the fight at the O Club or to Rosa at dinner, Cham gleefully embellished his role.

Steel hoped Cham would be able to tell his uncle about it. The uncle, in turn, could relay Cham's part in the decidedly manly fisticuffs to his family as proof of Cham's "toughening up." Poor Cham, thought Steel. He didn't deserve the grief his family gave him.

As he dug, Steel went over his plans for the day. He would shower and eat around 11 a.m. Rosa was off today, so he'd have to get his own meal. He also needed to spend a few hours writing a paper due next week on Louis Taruk, the famed Philippine Communist Huk guerrilla leader active in the 1950s. He had actually met the guy—got him to sign a copy of his autobiography.

Steel enjoyed his schoolwork, but part of him would be glad when he finished his degree, maybe by this time next year if he kept up the same pace. Later in the afternoon he would go to the post office and mail a package to an Air Force buddy of his stationed in Japan. It contained a copy of the Japanese diary he had found in the cave a month ago.

Steel had enjoyed showing Cham the minature gold Buddha found on the body of the diary-totting Japanese soldier. Cham noted that it appeared to be nearly pure gold, and his eyes widened when Steel asked him to fence it. The rough-cut ruby imbedded in the Buddha's belly was a nice size. Cham guessed the necklace was worth around three to four grand, mostly based on the weight of the gold and uncut gem.

It could possibly be worth more if the ruby polished nicely. Cham told Steel this was a good piece—he should find more. Steel told Cham to sell it for the best price and take his thirty percent brokers' fee. Cham smiled and said he would do his best for their new partnership.

Steel hoped the gold Buddha was just a taste of the treasures the diary foretold. Boxes of gold bars and jewels. Unlimited wealth. He'd spend the money well, retiring here in the Philippines, building himself a beautiful home with an incredible garden. He wished he had someone local to give the diary to for translation, but he had already wasted a month looking with no success.

The phone rang loudly from inside the house. "Shit," Steel muttered. Could only be work calling.

To Steel's surprise, Vida was on the other end of the line. She wanted to know if they could have lunch, said she was sorry she hadn't answered his calls—that she would understand if he didn't want to see her. She promised to explain everything.

Lusty thoughts of last night with Gemma evaporated, along with Steel's plans for a day of study, as Steel eagerly agreed and offered to drive to Manila. Vida countered, proposing to meet him halfway. He suggested the Orchid Farm Resort. She had heard of the place and agreed. It had a huge pool in the shape of an orchid flower. Steel joked that she should bring her bikini. She said she would bring a baggy, ugly suit and that he shouldn't expect a beauty queen. Besides, she said with a sigh, she couldn't swim.

Steel wandered back inside toward the shower, shellshocked. He could finish the paper Monday, but what about Gemma? Shit, it figures. In his sex-drunk state last night, had he made another date? He didn't think so. Looks like he was going to be yet another asshole Americano. There was no way in hell that he could have predicted Vida would return. But for some unknown reason she had beckoned, and he was rushing to respond. He was glad Jo Jo and Rosa weren't here to witness this.

Steel walked out of his house, whistling, with a gym bag slung over his shoulder. The wooden screen door banged loudly behind him. Its spring was broken. "Must get Joseph to look at that," he thought. He had washed the morning dirt off and had plenty of time to make his lunch engagement with Vida.

He strolled over to his truck sitting under the carport, threw his gym bag through the window, and walked to the two six-foot-tall solid metal gates that blocked out the world. He unlocked them and scanned the area outside quickly—still not many folks up and about. He watched two housegirls walking down the street, dressed in their Sunday best. Most housegirls had Sundays off. The only other sign of life was a tiny brown figure sitting slumped on the curb. Renaldo lifted his head and shook himself awake from an uncomfortable nap.

"Captain Steeeeel," he said, rubbing the grogginess from his eyes.

"Renaldo?" Steel asked.

"Yes, sir, it is I, Renaldo."

"What are you doing here?" Steel asked, looking around for someone to explain.

"Sir, I'm here to ask some favor for you."

"What's up, little guy?" Steel was surprised that Renaldo had found the house.

Renaldo averted his eyes and skuffed the ground nervously with a badly worn flip-flop. He hesitated.

Steel squatted down. "Go ahead."

"Sir, it is Bong. He is sick. His feet is sick. He put a cut on one and now it is very big and he can't walk on it without too much pain."

"Oh. Bong." That was it. Bong was missing from the picture.

Steel checked his watch. He didn't need this drama today. Tomorrow, hell, even this evening, would be better. Shit. Just not today.

Renaldo stood silently watching Steel, then spoke. "Sir, could you give me money for medicine. I have no money for to buy medicine."

Steel looked him in the eye. It was a common line with some of the street kids to ask for money for their sick mothers.

What they really wanted it for was to support their glue-sniffing habits or for gambling. But Steel could see desperation Renaldo's despair. Besides, Bong wasn't here—not a good sign. "Renaldo, your brother sounds very sick. I should have a look at his foot."

"Sir, you don't have to go. I can take the medicine for to him. I just need the money."

Steel switched to Tagalog. "No, I can't do that. I want to make sure he has the right medicine. I don't think you are a very good doctor."

Renaldo froze. Steel could see in his face this posed a problem. Steel wondered what Renaldo's deal was. Jo Jo had been unable to discover where he lived.

"But sir, I don't want to trouble you. I can—."

"Sorry, buddy, I will be the one to see Bong and get him some help. You can take my help or leave it."

Again Renaldo froze.

Steel, not wanting to play this game, turned and walked back inside his gate and pulled his truck out onto the road. He jumped out and closed the gates behind him. Renaldo was still standing with his eyes lowered to the ground.

"So, buddy, what's the deal?"

Still no answer.

"Okay, *bahal ka,* so be it." Steel jumped into his truck and looked down at the boy, who was clearly upset. "Last chance. I have an appointment I have to go to. If you change your mind, you can come and see me this evening."

"Okay, *lang,*" Renaldo blurted out.

Steel motioned with his head for Renaldo to get in, and he scrambled into the passenger seat. Steel sighed deeply and took off. "What gives, Renaldo? Why can't I see Bong? Where do you live?"

More silence.

"I thought maybe you were lying about Bong to get some money."

Renaldo turned quickly. "No sir, I'm not a liar," he spoke in Tagalog.

"So where are we going? Which way to your house?" Steel gestured around.

"*Doon*," Renaldo pointed west.

"Yes…yes… I know, *doon*. Alright, you tell me where to turn."

They drove in silence, except for when Steel had to ask Renaldo to clarify his hand signals.

"You never answered my question. Why can't I know where you live?"

Renaldo lowered his eyes. "Because I am ashamed that I have no house to live in."

"Oh, shit," Steel muttered and put his hand on the boy's skinny, dirty shoulder. Renaldo's words pierced.

Renaldo's house, a lean-to made of plastic sheeting, lumber, and cardboard scraps, stood just two blocks from Steel's. It and five other shacks sat behind the Blue Hawaii, precariously perched around a stagnant ditch filled with vile-smelling water.

Steel followed Renaldo into the ring of squalid shantics, feeling like an alien. The smell of the foul water, garbage, and cramped humanity was almost too much. He looked over in the direction of his own house, an opulent mansion in comparison, and marveled how they were only yards apart yet separated by universes.

Renaldo led the way inside his hut; Steel had to bend over and half crawl into their hole. It was dark and dank, except for a flickering oil lamp. Bong's eyes grew large when he saw Steel, who must have looked like a big white ghost. Renaldo in a motherly voice assured Bong that it was Okay. Steel unwrapped the scraps of dirty cloth bandaging the foot. He examined it as best he could in the dim light. It was badly infected and swollen, well beyond his medical capabilities. "Christ, I hope gangrene hasn't set it. Why the hell did you wait so long?"

Renaldo did not answer. Steel tried to think quickly. He had to get Bong to a doctor immediately. But Vida was waiting, even if only in a baggy one-piece suit. "Shit, shit shit shit!" He couldn't leave the boys in this filth. He looked around the shack, searching for an easy answer. This was more than just a medical emergency; he couldn't leave them in this filth. Not Renaldo, the boy who was too proud to show him his shitty life and Bong, who needed a doctor—now. Father Rudy was the only answer. "Boys, pack your things. Anything you want to take with you, pack up."

No response. Steel switched to Tagalog and explained it more forcefully.

"Sir, where are we going?"

"Someplace where you will be cared for. Someplace where Bong's foot can heal."

Thank God for Father Rudy. Otherwise Steel would have two new roommates.

He picked up Bong and carried him to the truck. It was like carrying a toddler, not an eight-year-old. Poor nutrition had stunted his growth. Renaldo followed him. He wasn't carrying anything. There didn't seem like there was much worth saving from the shack.

Father Rudy was celebrating Mass. Sister Lorna took the boys in. Steel gave her twenty dollars and asked her to take Bong to the doctor. Saying he would pay his medical bills, Steel briefly explained the boys' circumstances. He told her he'd swing by later this evening and chat with the father.

Steel popped his favorite cassette tape into the radio and barreled down the Angeles-to-Manila expressway. He felt good about helping Bong. Hell, that's what Father Rudy's place was for, the Reynaldos and Bongs of Angeles.

He turned off at the San Fernando exit and dug around in the ashtray for some coins to pay the toll at a small booth. Because he was in a great mood, he told the dour attendant to keep the change, roughly twenty-five cents. The attendant pushed her head out the window and watched Steel's truck drive off, confused as to why the American had said to keep the change. No one told her to keep change. Everyone hated her for collecting the tolls. Crazy Americano, she thought.

The narrow road leading to San Fernando was busy. Vehicles of all makes and descriptions loaded with people dressed up in their Sunday best were headed to Mass and visits with relatives. Steel slowed as a large truck ahead loaded with old tires crawled along. It belched out acrid, black smoke. Steel edged his vehicle out carefully to look for an opportunity to pass.

An overloaded trike inched along in front of the truck. Steel took a deep breath and tried to relax. He was in too good a mood to lose his cool.

The parade went on for ten more minutes before Steel, tired of breathing in the foul-smelling diesel fumes, saw an opening in oncoming traffic. He pulled out and gunned the Datsun. He blasted by the truck, waved to the driver, then easily passed the loaded trike. Steel looked up and noticed an oncoming passenger bus with flashing headlights and blasting horn.

As Steel prepared to reenter his lane, a flash of color ahead grabbed his attention. "Christ," he grunted. Another trike was pulling onto the road. Steel hit the brakes and veered the truck sharply into the narrow graveled berm, kicking up dust, rocks, and vegetation. He struggled to maintain control and slow the truck down.

He missed the trike by inches, and, fortunately, there were no pedestrians walking on the berm. Not so lucky were the three or four fighting cocks pecking in the gravel alongside the road. Steel hit the roosters at around thirty-five mile per hour, sending up a cloud of bamboo stakes, string, and dirt—and of course feathers. He grimmaced with each dull thud on the chassis.

As he manaeuvered back onto the road, Steel checked his rearview mirror. The owner of the roosters stood slack-jawed, watching Steel drive away. Steel made a mental note. He had to find another way home. He didn't want to be stopped by local police and made to pay exorbitantly for the roosters. The owner, of course, would insist they were village champions, arguing to his brother, the town mayor, that they were worth thousands of pesos. "Well," Steel muttered, "they are in Colonel Sanders' hands now."

Steel whipped into the Orchid Farm's parking lot. There were a dozen or so cars there already. He reached to the passenger side for his gym bag; he had a book to read, his towel, bathing suit, and a small present for Vida: chocolate. Exiting the truck, he examined the front end: chicken feathers, vegetation, and caked mud in the wheel wells; fortunately, no damage to the underside.

He walked up the sidewalk through the carefully manicured gardens and past the owner's walled-off residence, admiring the hundreds of orchid plants, some blooming spectacularly.

At the pool Steel scanned the rows of wooden deck chairs, looking for someplace to sit while he waited for Vida. To his surprise, Vida was occupying one. "Damn." He took off his sunglasses and quickly roughed up his hair.

She waved. "Hi, William. I got here a little early. To be honest, I didn't quite know where I was going. Besides, I do not like your wisecracks about 'Philippine time.' I am usually very punctual."

Steel admired her for a second. She looked great, with her big movie star sunglasses and hair tied back in a ponytail. She wore a tight-fitting sundress that was longer than he would have liked, but the color was nice on her. Filipina women, overall, were very conservative in dress. They wouldn't think of wearing shorts or a tank top.

He did like that she was early; it suggested she was as nervous as he and anxious to see him. He awkwardly leaned down and kissed her on the cheek. "Well, Miss Abucayan this is an unexpected surprise. You are indeed a woman of mystery."

"I'm not mysterious, just a woman," she laughed easily.

"This is for you."

She opened his gift. "I love chocolate, thank you." She offered one to him. "Oh these are very nice indeed," she ate quickly, licking her lips.

"So an easy drive for you?" she asked.

Steel lied, not wanting to start their chat with a retelling of the chicken carnage he had wrought. They talked instead about nothing for thirty minutes. He could tell Vida wanted to say something but seemed reluctant. He tried to give her some help. "It's wonderful to see you. I thought I'd never get another opportunity. I hadn't heard from you for a while."

She jumped at the opening. "Yes, so am I," she said sounding relieved. "I'm so glad that we have met again. I thought maybe you would be angry at me for ignoring your phone calls," she said, trying to smile.

"I was a little miffed. To be honest, I told myself to write you off. I know that you are involved with someone."

"I'm glad you didn't write me off. I've had a tough week. I broke off my relationship with Antonio last weekend."

"Oh, I'm sorry," Steel said, feeling anything but.

"I knew in my heart it had ended a long time ago, but I just didn't have the courage to make it official. It was partly because I didn't want to hurt him and also because of our families."

"Ah, yes, the families." Steel tried to look sad.

"That is so true. We want so much to please them, at times sacrificing our own happiness. I know I'm not the good daughter for doing so, but I want to be selfish and happy."

"You should be happy. I think your parents want that too. They will get over Antonio in time."

"You really think so?"

"I'm sure," Steel said, thinking what he'd really like to say is: "Take your sundress off."

"How about your parents? Are they worried about your happiness?"

Steel paused, unsure of how to answer. "Well, they both died years ago. Don't have much family to contend with." He tried not to sound too self-pitying.

She lay her hand on his. It was warm and soft.

They talked for a while longer, holding hands like old lovers. She wanted to know about Steel's childhood. He explained how his father wasn't officially dead but instead MIA in Vietnam; how his mother declared her husband dead and sought to erase his memory with the bounty of drugs available during the hippie movement. She overdosed on heroin in 1969 when Steel was just ten. He was shuffled from a grandmother with failing health to foster homes. Steel hated this story and quickly moved to change the subject. Vida's look of pity was making him ill.

"Let's take a swim," he said.

Vida looked reluctant but agreed and headed off to get her swim suit. Steel quickly changed into his old trunks and sat at the pool waiting for her. She appeared wearing a one-piece suit covered by a near-sheer pool wrap.

"Here I am. God, I can't remember the last time I was in a swimsuit." She lay her things down on her chair and removed the wrap.

"Wow, you look great."

"Oh I was concerned that you would compare me unfavorably to your beautiful bar girls."

"Believe me, you have nothing to hide."

She wrinkled her nose and headed over to the pool. She sat down on the side, and put her feet in. Steel joined her. The pool was empty. The entrance fee put the place out of reach of most Filipinos. The few cars that were in the parking lot belonged to the well-off in the dining room having brunch after Mass.

"Ah, this water is beautiful," she said, moving her legs.

Steel jumped in. "Damn, you look like a swimsuit model sitting there. Come on in."

"Remember, William, I have this drowning problem."

"Oh no worries. The whole pool is only waist-deep. There is no deep end."

She eased into the water holding tightly to the side until she got a firm footing. They laughed and played like teenagers. The orchid-shaped pool had small coves that fanned out from the main body. Cascades of plants and vines hung over the edges. Steel followed Vida into one of the quiet side-alleys; it was shady and quiet with only the gurgle of a small waterfall dropping over black rocks at the cove's end. Vida propped herself with her arms on the edge of the pool, her back to Steel. He came up beside her, close enough for their skin to touch. Hers felt taut, almost pulsing. She smiled at him.

"Oh William, this is so much fun. I haven't done anything like this in ages." She looked into his eyes. "I will admit to you, I so much enjoyed being with you for our tour of your base. And…and, oh, I'm turning red with embarrassment right now." She quickly shielded and unshielded her face with her hands. "When we kissed that was such a good feeling for me, one that I hadn't felt in a long time."

"Me too. I was afraid I was too bold."

"It really scared me. I thought I must be crazy. Here I am almost married, yet I am kissing a handsome Americano I just met. I was confused."

Steel moved even closer, put his arm around her, and ran his hand down her wet hair. "I thought I had scared you off with all my phone calls." He squeezed her tightly. She turned to face him.

"No, I wanted more. You don't know how hard I fought to keep from calling you."

He kissed her softly on the lips. She pushed hard against him and bit at his ears and neck. He reached down with both hands and pulled her to him as she pushed into his hips. He pushed her wet breasts into his face and licked her nipples until they showed through her suit. They explored each other with their hands and mouths until Steel thought he would explode. But he didn't, and flushed and panting, they slowly waded across the pool, back to their chairs and clothes. They dried each other off muttering promises of more to come. Not today though. Soon. Steel hated to wait, but damn this was a classy woman, not some bar girl. She deserved to be wooed. They headed in to lunch.

Louis Ramos watched Steel and Vida from his vantage point well hidden from view. He noticed the others spying on and photographing the young captain and his Filipina lover but was certain he was the most skilled of the professionals on their tail today.

He looked towards a patio dining area with his high powered telephoto lens. He had invested in the best photographic and video equipment; it made a difference. He focused on two people eating and drinking at one of the restaurant's outside tables. Probably Phil counterintelligence thugs, he thought. Badly trained hacks. They had been tailing Steel since he left his house. Ramos smiled as he recalled their baffoonery when their vehicle almost ended up part of Steel's automobile chicken crash up.

Another individual, on the patio, clearly not connected with the table-bound morons, was showing more aptitude. He, too, used a telephoto lens to observe the couple. What a complicated web—the spider watching other spiders eyeing the fly.

Snowden had not mentioned the fact that Steel was of interest to Philippine intelligence when he tasked Ramos to do the job. Ramos figured Snowden had a personal grudge against the American and didn't question why Snowden chose Ramos over his own OSI unit. Snowden was paying his expenses. Besides, Ramos owed the man and didn't mind doing work for him.

He and Snowden went back a long way, working together in the counterintelligence business in Europe. Ramos had talked Snowden into taking the assignment in the Philippines. They had joked about eventually retiring there; a place where a man on a military pension could live well. Ramos, a Filipino-American, spoke the language and blended in with the locals. More importantly, his army pension plus his private-eye business's earnings were more than enough to satisfy his particular sexual needs. Compliant women went cheap here, he thought, with a mixture of disgust at his native country's lax moral fortitude and arousal at the opportunities it offered a sadist like himself.

Ramos turned again to his telephoto lens. The woman was beautiful, must be a model or a movie star, he thought; it would be fun to have to have her tied up on all fours in front of him. He had thought the case was going to be routine, but this Steel guy could be fun to watch. Now, what with Snowden's obsession and all these others following Steel too—he couldn't wait to see what all the fuss was about.

16

Foothills of Mt. Pinatubo

Steel stopped and compulsively adjusted the straps on his backpack. The left one had twisted and was rubbing an old raw spot on his shoulder. It was the second day of their journey, and they had set a grueling pace to try to reach the mountain by midafternoon. This was the biggest expedition he had ever mounted, thirteen individuals in all: Jo Jo, four Negitos, and Lt. Col. Antonio Devincia accompanied by six rugged army scout rangers.

Steel began preparing for this trip two weeks ago after he had received a call from Weasel, who claimed he had found the moutain from Professor Abucayan's treasure map. When Weasel presented the evidence, Steel almost leapt with joy: a mountain in an area east of Mt Pinatubo on Weasel's 1-to-250,000 scale low-level aircraft map matched the formation on Abucayan's chart almost perfectly.

Steel convinced his boss to let him have a week's leave, then, true to his word, he called Professor Abucayan. The next day, Lt. Col. Antonio Devincia returned that call, announcing that he and some army scout rangers would accompany Steel on his trip to the mountain. Devincia kept the call professional; Vida's name did not come up, which was fine. There's women and there's treasure, he thought. No need to mix the two.

When Devincia and the scout rangers first arrived at the rendezvous point outside the Clark perimeter fence, Steel was taken aback by their military uniforms and heavy weapons. The rangers dressed in olive-green jungle fatigues with black berets and backpacks; each carried an M-16 armalite, several with grenade launchers attached. Devincia, sported a Israeli-made Izu 9mm machine gun and a 9mm Berretta in an underarm shoulder holster.

From the moment the expedition first set foot on the trail, Devincia made it clear he would be running the operation and by a military rule book. Steel reluctantly gave him that courtesy; Devincia was a colonel, and rank matters. Steel had tried in vain to pursuade Devincia to drop the military tone, wear civilian clothes, and leave the weapons behind, relying instead on the Negritos for security. Devincia would hear nothing of it. Steel prayed they would avoid a firefight with NPA guerrillas. Not only did he not relish the thought of getting shot or killed, but he had no authorization from his own command to be out with an armed AFP unit.

Tony, on the other hand, was in awe of Devincia's military bearing. It was the highlight of his guiding career—he was leading scout rangers. From the hike's first moments, Tony and the rangers tried to outpace each other. Steel heard Devincia quietly order the first sergeant to let the Negritos lead—but at a slower pace.

Steel thought the instructions to the sergeant were mostly for the colonel's personal benefit. He had obviously not hoofed in the mountains in several years. He was out of shape and was keeping up through willpower alone. It was also clear he was not about to let Steel win this race.

Steel slid his backpack onto his shoulders again. The ten-minute rest had gone by quickly, but Steel still felt all right;

he was more hungry than tired. They had packed out early this morning with barely enough time to gulp down a candy bar and some lukewarm coffee. He was ready for lunch and it was still hours away. He reached into pocket of his military-issue cammo pants, pulled out a pack of peanuts, and popped some into his mouth. The salt tasted good.

"Hey, Jo Jo, you want some peanuts?"

Jo Jo held up his hand signaling no. Steel finished the pack.

They were strung out in a single-file line with Tony guiding. Devincia was in the rear with one of the rangers. Steel tried to ignore the guns and warrior mentality. Maybe on his previous trips to the mountains, he should have been more concerned about security, but still this junior GI Joe crap seemed excessive.

Steel stepped up in order to catch up with the first sergeant. Short and stocky with a weathered dog face, he carried his weapon and heavy rucksack effortlessly.

"So, sergeant, have you been into this area before?"

"No sir. Most of my operational experience is in Mindanao or the far north," he whispered.

"I see." Steel said in a lower than normal tone of voice. Now all the display of military might made sense to him. They were in unfamiliar territory. They were accustomed to operating in the northern Philippine provinces where a robust insurgency gave good reason to keep arms at the ready.

The line stopped. Up ahead, the lead ranger, compass in hand, stood with Tony, examining a map and exchanging heated words. Steel knew the feeling. Tony was fundamentally opposed to maps and compasses. The sergeant commanded them to take break while he headed up front to sort out the directions.

Steel pulled out his own map, and Jo Jo looked over his shoulder. Jo Jo fingered the mountain where the command post sat. "We are not far, boss. I think we are here in the ravine."

"Yes, maybe one or two hours away." Steel turned to see Devincia keeping a polite distance. Steel tried to push down a wave of guilt. Vida said she hadn't told Devincia about the two of them.

Overall, Devincia seemed pleased with the expedition and had offered to bring whatever supplies and manpower Steel needed to dig out the cave. Steel told him to hold off on the engineering unit until they performed reconaissance. He had chased down too many hoaxes.

Steel had concluded that this was not a sanctioned AFP operation, that Devincia was doing it on the sly, and wondered how he had gotten away with it. Was he on leave too? How did he get six armed rangers detailed to him?

Steel nudged Jo Jo, who sat slumped on the ground resting, to indicate that they were moving again. The lead ranger and Tony seem to have sorted their differences.

The column marched again for a few minutes then stopped. Again there seemed to be some discussion going on at the front of the line. This time the sergeant moved quickly, obviously perturbed by another delay. Steel and Jo Jo continued walking, joining the leaders who were bunched up listening to the sergeant arguing with Tony and another Negrito.

Steel could see the source of the confusion: two stakes with bamboo arrows lashed horizontal to them standing in the trail. The man-made jungle road signs pointed to hidden dangers.

"Pig traps!" Jo Jo muttered nervously, scanning the jungle around him.

Steel recalled the first time he had encountered these sorts of signs. The Negritos said that the arrow pointed to where pig traps were set; some were deep pits dug into the trail and covered with thatched mats. At the bottom were rows of sharpened bamboo stakes, waiting to impale a wandering pig. Far deadlier, however, were the traps with trip wires attached to World War II hand grenades or mines. Still other traps consisted of crossbows rigged to shoot sharpened bolts.

Devincia pushed his way forward and addressed the sergeant.

Steel laughed quietly and stepped forward, first addressing Devincia in Tagalog. "Colonel, the Negritos are arguing about what the signs mean." Steel then explained in detail about the pig traps. He then moved over to the Negritos and addressed them in Aeta, speaking at length and tersely.

After he had finished, he turned to Devincia. "Sir, it appears that Pong-pet believes that the Anong clan has a territorial dispute with the Ganchee clan and could have switched the signs out of anger."

"So you are saying that these pig traps could be that way—instead of over there?" Devincia said in English, pointing into the jungle. Steel got the impression that the colonel didn't like talking to him in Tagalog.

"I'm not saying that, sir. He is." Steel indicated to Pong-pet who sat staring off into space, clearly upset that his version had been questioned.

Jo Jo pushed in close to Steel and whispered, "I think too this guy is jealous of Tony because he is the guide and is getting more money."

"Jesus. It's like a goddamn soap opera," Steel grunted. Steel barely knew Pong-pet. He had only used him once, a long time ago.

"So Captain Steel what do you recommend we do?" Devincia said, obviously frustrated.

Steel addressed Tony in Aeta. "You think Pong-pet is wrong?"

Tony nodded yes.

"Alright then, lead us down the right trail—you first. If you are wrong, then you will be the first to find the trap." He turned to Pong-pet. "Pong-pet you understand this? If there is a trap then Tony will be the one to find it. Boom!" Steel waved his arm, and startling a ranger leaning against a tree.

Tony's eyes widened. Steel could see he was trying to figure out whether he was willing to gamble his life on his instincts. He looked around; all eyes were on him. He had no choice: His pride was at stake.

"I will be the one to lead," he said in Tagalog and struck his chest with a closed fist. Steel had never seen such bravado out of Tony. The rangers were a bad influence.

Tony then addressed Pong-pet in a Negrito dialect unknown to Steel, turned, and walked off to assume his position in the lead. The two other Negritos huddled quietly around Pong-pet, who clearly was not pleased.

Pong-pet dropped his backpack filled with Steel's gear and shouldered his long bow. He shot off a barrage of Aeta explatives; Steel only caught the tail end of the diatribe, something to do with Tony's sister screwing dogs, then disappeared quickly into the jungle.

"Pong-pet," Steel called out after him. "Damn it Tony, get him back."

Tony dismissed him with a wave of his hand. "He is going on his own."

"Shit," Steel exhaled.

The two other Negritos stood frozen and confused. Tony had the money, but Pong-pet was a good leader and a friend.

Steel sensed trouble. He walked over to the two Negritos. "I will pay you double your wages to stay." He said it a second time slowly.

It worked. "Capitalism at its finest," Steel thought.

They quickly divided up the contents of Pong-pet's pack and headed off, following Tony. Everyone was walking carefully, concentrating on the trail where Tony had walked. No one was betting one-hundred percent on Tony.

Barely ten minutes up the trail, an explosion in the distance made Steel's heart leap. Steel thought it sounded like a grenade blasting off. The scout rangers assumed crouched firing positions. Steel could hear them lock and load their M-16s.

"Pong-pet," Steel blurted out. He felt sick as he visualized the Negrito lying blown apart on the floor of the jungle, or worse yet, still alive with his legs missing.

Devincia looked in the direction of the blast and shrugged his shoulders. "Looks like that one was wrong. *Bahal na*, so be it," he said with indifference. He motioned for the group to keep moving.

The explosion was too much for the other two Negritos, who jabbered in dialect at Tony. Tony, clearly upset by the explosion, slapped his head in despair. After a brief consultation with Tony, both Negritos dropped their packs and disappeared into the forest in the direction of the explosion.

"Damn it." Devincia yelled out. "Come back here." He pulled his 9mm pistol from his holster and aimed into the dense jungle, but he was disciplined enough to not shoot. He shoved the pistol forcefully back into the holster. "Little bastards! Now what do we do? I should have just brought more of my own men."

"Should I go and find them?" the sergeant responded.

"No, let them go and get blown up. Let's just get going again. We will divide up the necessary equipment and leave the rest."

Steel agreed. He hoped that by some miracle Pong-pet was alive. There was bad karma now, Steel thought. He turned to Jo Jo and whispered, "Damn, Jo Jo this is no fun. No one dies on these trips."

"Yes, by Mother Mary of God, this is not for us amateurs." They both stared off into the jungle in the direction of the blast.

Devincia called for them to move out and catch up with

the group. Steel looked at the packs tied up in the branches of a tree. He hoped someone could retrieve them and get some use out of the shovels and other gear.

"Let's go, boss," Jo Jo said nudging Steel. "I'm going to keep a special eye out for those damn traps. I am pleased I am not leading the group, *di ba*?"

Steel nodded in agreement. He was thinking more of the loss of Pong-pet than the traps. Steel walked over to Tony who was squatting on the ground staring off into the jungle, clearly upset. Steel guessed Tony was unhappy that his fight with Pong-pet had caused all this. He put his hand on Tony's shoulder. "Come on, buddy. Those boys will give us news on Pong-pet."

Tony nodded and reluctantly stood. They returned to the trail.

17

Clark Air Base

SNOWDEN SLAMMED THE FOLDER DOWN on his desk. He was irritable and tired, not having slept well the last several nights. He was having nightmares, waking in pools of sweat, jumbled dreams filled with people from his past.

He checked his watch. It was only 3:30 p.m. He still had a couple more hours of administrative trivia to contend with before he could leave to meet Ramos at seven p.m. Ramos had more photos and info for him; so far, he had discovered little incriminating information on Steel, but, if there were something to be found, Ramos would do it.

Snowden had pulled the Filipino-American U.S. Army sergeant into his team fifteen years ago in Germany. The slight, bookish sergeant was the least likely looking spy you could imagine. Ramos's adversaries always underestimated him, and Ramos, like Snowden, had a dark side which Snowden understood—because of this they had grown close.

Yesterday Ramos had informed Snowden that Steel hadn't seen the Abucayan woman since the swimming pool. But he did frequently talk to her on the phone. Ramos also noted that the Philippine CI thugs were still tailing Steel. Snowden picked up a file folder from his desk and flipped through it until he found a photo of the woman. He eyed it closely. A leftist journalist, she was supposed to be engaged to a rebellious senior Phil army officer. What the fuck was Steel up to? If he were involved with the Phil left or rebel officers, that would be dirt Snowden could use.

Steel is playing a cat-and-mouse game with me, thought Snowden, but he's in over his head. That fucker dared to confront me in the O Club, pimping blackmail money out of me, what balls. Snowden leaned back in his chair and tried to relax, but he heard Steel's words replayed over and over: "Oh, you can help the children. The children need help. Those poor children." The voice coming from Snowden's mouth was oddly high-pitched.

Steel was mocking him, taunting him. The voice was clear: Steel had to go. Steel had to go, but on Snowden's schedule, not the voice's. Ramos was the best, and he would find something to break Steel with. Steel had secrets; everyone did. If all else failed, Ramos would end this.

18

Foothills of Mt. Pinatubo

Two hours later, they made it to the base of the mountain Weasel had identified. After consulting, Steel and Devincia agreed they would set up a base camp and then take forays into the jungle looking for the command post. In all likelihood, it would not be easy to find an opening obscured by forty years of growth, or worse, dynamited shut.

They set up camp close to a stream. Steel suggested that they split up into groups and search the base of the mountain. Devincia dismissed the idea, preferring to remain together but to fan out so they could still see each other. Devincia's constant state of high alert made Steel nervous. He began to wonder if Devincia knew more than he had let on about new NPA movements in the area.

Devincia assigned one ranger to remain and guard the camp. The high-pitched clang of machetes slashing vegetation, interspersed with multilingual, murderous curses, followed the group as they spread out. The stamina of the rangers was certainly impressive, Steel thought, as he watched them hack their way through jungle thick with banana and bamboo groves.

For nearly four hours, they hiked their way around the mountain before an exhausted Devincia halted the operation. It was dusk, light was fading quickly, and unfortunately no command post had been identified. Steel had not given up hope; there was still half the mountain to search.

As Devincia and the ranger sergeant approached Steel, he smiled at Devincia's appearance. His fatigue shirt was soaked with sweat and his tanned face was ashen. He was done in.

"We should return to camp now before darkness," he grunted at the sergeant who followed him.

"Time for a beer, eh colonel?" Jo Jo said.

Devincia pushed passed them, ignoring the joke.

"I'll give you one-hundred pesos for one," Steel spoke up.

"I bet Tony would find one for one-hundred pesos."

"So what do you think? The cave doesn't exist or we just haven't found the entrance yet?"

"Oh, it's there. Just haven't found it yet. Maybe we'll find it tomorrow or the next day. It's got to be on the west side."

"Good." Steel liked Jo Jo's optimism.

They headed back to camp.

Steel crawled out of his tent, stiff and tired. He hadn't slept well. The iodine-treated water he drank made him sick, and a squadron of mosquitoes had invaded his tent. Despite the mosquito net, they had buzzed incessantly in his ears all night. It would be a long day.

Jo Jo was right. Barely two hours into the morning expedition, a ranger found an opening on the west side of the mountain. The entrance led into a long tunnel. At first look Steel thought the setup seemed similar to the large command post they had explored several months ago.

"So, what is the plan?" Devincia asked Steel. He seemed more chipper now than he had the day before.

"I would suggest that we head into the shaft and locate the main section of the command post. This entrance is small and is likely just a secondary shaft. Most command posts have multiple entrances."

"Okay. You lead the way. I will follow with two of my men. The others will remain outside."

"No, Jo Jo goes with us." Steel stared him down.

Devincia didn't push the issue.

Steel led the way into the narrow tunnel. It took a few minutes for his eyes to adjust. He traced the tunnel with the beam of his flashlight. It was man-made, about six feet tall and four feet wide, chiseled through igneous rock.

As always, he was optimistic. Maybe this was the cave that housed the mother lode. They were likely looking for vertical shafts which served as holding vaults: vaults filled with treasure. Jo Jo dutifully manned the metal detector, though it could only determine metallic objects within a foot or two. Further, scraps of shrapnel or mineralized soil played havoc with its sensors.

Steel led the way down the narrow tunnel with Jo Jo on his heels, trailed by Antonio and the two rangers. The farther they walked, the narrower the tunnel became. It was now barely five feet tall, and Steel navigated with his body bent into an uncomfortable stoop.

He felt the walls with his free hand and was amazed that the engineers had chiseled so deep into the mountain. It had been such a waste of manpower and lives to build this. How many men had died in these dark tunnels?

For fifteen minutes they walked silently, listening to their own labored breathing, before they emerged into a small chamber. It was empty: a bad sign. Jo Jo switched on the detector and swung it back and forth. Steel held his breath waiting for the beep signaling it found metal. The detector stayed silent.

There were two tunnels leading from the chamber. The first they chose dead-ended after a short walk. The single-file group awkwardly backtracked out. The next tunnel led to a bigger chamber filled with decaying wooden crates loaded with ordinance. Munitions were scattered on the dirt floor.

"Jesus!" Devincia exclaimed too loudly. He was unaccustomed to the acoustics. He lowered his voice to a whisper. "Those are grenades and mortar rounds."

"They could go off with the slightest disturbance," Jo Jo said simply.

Devincia looked at him and eyed the crates. "Should we attempt to search all the crates? Or maybe the earth beneath them?"

Steel thought for a moment. "No, this is just an ammo storage area. We should continue forward. We can always come back to this spot if other areas don't pan out. The good news is that these crates of ammo signify that we are the first to explore this place. Negritos would have carried everything off if they been here before us."

Devincia nodded.

They walked deep into the complex, a huge catacomb of rooms and tunnels. One room had been a hospital, and it was still filled with metal cots and medical equipment, just like at the previous command post.

Another room, the largest they had encountered, was littered with chairs and tables. It appeared to be a wardroom of sorts. On one table, china, mess kits, and even sake cups were laid out as if for a last supper.

Steel's eyes lit up as his flashlight beam exposed a big red ball on a white background hanging on the wall. A flag, a Japanese flag. He rushed over to it and closely examined what he guessed were faded Japanese signatures filling most of the white space—apparently the signatures of the men in the unit.

He lightly pressed his fingers over the material. Delicate to his touch. He carefully removed it from the wooden bulletin board. Fragile but it held together. It was quite a souvenir. He'd always wanted one.

"Damn, that's beautiful," Jo Jo said admiring the flag as he watched Steel carefully put it into a plastic bag and then into his backpack.

"Yes, unbelievable that it is still intact. It has been hanging here all these years. The cave air and the fact that it was attached to that wooden bulletin board must have helped preserve it."

"So, Steel, have you finished over there? What is the plan?" Devincia whispered impatiently.

"Sorry, colonel, but the flag was too much to pass up. Did you see it?"

Before he could answer, one of the rangers from across the room called out, "Colonel, come and see this table." The sergeant was standing across the dark room looking at something with a small flickering flashlight.

They joined him beside a large table made out of wood and bamboo, covered with a fine layer of dust. On it, a map lay open. Devincia grasped his flashlight with his teeth and, using two hands, tried to pick the map up. As he did, it disintegrated into pieces.

"No damn way to keep it from falling apart," Devincia puffed.

Steel tried to examine a piece of the map for himself. "Too bad. Maybe it could have provided additional clues."

"Yeah, who knows? Maybe it could have told us something," Jo Jo said, as he picked up an object from the table.

"Hey, a Parker pen. We are lucky today."

Steel nodded his head in approval. A Parker in excellent condition was worth some cash.

They turned their attention to the rest of the large room. Steel guessed it had been a wardroom for the officers in the unit, possibly the unit commander's wardroom. But despite the historical items, they had found nothing to suggest that treasure was at hand.

"We should move on. This room just doesn't seem right. We will have to come back," Steel announced.

He shined his light over to the far side of the cave, checking out one last area and gasped as his beam danced on a human skeleton.

"Jo Jo, check this out." Steel walked over to it.

The body sat in a large bamboo chair, a macabre scene that looked posed. The clothes, ridiculously baggy, hung on the skeleton. Steel was drawn to the white skull. Its mouth was wide open, as if frozen in laughter. He looked closely at the Imperial Army cloth hat on its skull and noticed a small neat hole in the temple. "Well, this guy didn't die of natural causes," he said. "It doesn't take a forensic expert to figure out what happened here."

Jo Jo nodded grimly.

Steel inspected the rest of the body's clothing more closely. He recognized the insignia on the jacket lapels. It was an officer's tunic. Femur bones bridged the gap between tattered trousers and knee-high ceremonial dress leather boots.

"Boss!" Jo Jo pulled a long, thin black object from on the chair and elicited a whistle from Steel. A sword. Short of gold bars, a sword was the souvenir Steel coveted most.

"Tell me I'm not dreaming." Steel said loudly, as Devincia and the rangers rushed over.

Jo Jo pulled the sword out and blew off the dust with several choked breaths of air. His mouth was too dry to get the job done properly. He gingerly handed the sword to Steel. "Don't ever say I haven't done anything for you lately."

"Your slate is cleared, my friend." All eyes were on Steel, as he gently examined the handle and scabbard. Devincia quickly concluded that it was a just a sword, sneered at Steel, and wandered back to the map table with his rangers.

Steel slowly slid the sword out of the military-issue scabbard and examined the fully exposed blade in Jo Jo's flashlight beam. It was in perfect condition. He rubbed a thick layer of grease with his thumb and cleared a small spot, which gleamed brightly in the light. Carelessly he ran his thumb along the blade. It was still sharp as a razor and cut him. Fitting, he thought. Samurai tradition dictates that a blade once unsheathed must draw blood.

"Damn, sharp *na lang*. Maybe I could shave with it tonight." Jo Jo rubbed his smooth, nearly hairless cheek.

Steel slid the sword back into the case. "Yeah, shave your nose off."

Steel was pleased. He prayed the blade was a family sword, with a long history—that could be valuable. All Japanese officers and senior NCOs were issued mass-produced inferior swords for battle, but some soldiers chose to carry their precious family blades to war. Imperial army regulations forbade this, but officials looked the other way if the weapon had military-issue scabbard and handle.

He examined the handle closely again. It was a complicated process to remove it and see the tang beneath. If it were indeed a family sword, etched on the tang would be the family name, and more importantly, the name of the master who had produced the blade. Steel had done a great deal of reading on samurai swords. No place in the world was the sword as venerated as it was in Japan.

He had fantasized about finding a famous sword, one made by one of the Japanese masters. These weapons were the strongest and sharpest ever made, even compared to those forged by old masters in Europe. Japanese sword-making had peaked in the fourteen century with the Koto swords.

A skilled sword master at that time would take months to make a single weapon: heating, hammering, folding steel into a blade of unparalleled sharpness and strength. By the sixteen century though, the secrets of the old masters were lost, and the Koto sword's unique combination of artistry and sheer killing power were never seen again.

Steel remembered reading that some blades had numbers etched on the tang signifying the number of men the sword could hack through with one forceful stroke. The bodies of dead and sometimes live prisoners or criminals were lined up like cordwood for the test. The samurai sword of old was a magnificent killing weapon on the battlefield, but the samurai sword in the hands of a twentieth century Japanese soldier was less glorious, more likely used for the execution of prisoners of war, both civilian and military.

Steel looked at the sword again and gazed at the body in the chair. He wondered who he was. Was he from a wealthy family? Steel knew that swords could be worth tens of thousands of dollars. Some families would pay a small fortune for the return of their sword. Was this an heirloom or just a souvenir?

Lt. Col. Misao Mifumu knew the end was near. American and Philippine forces were close by and his mission was to keep this facility from falling into enemy hands. He was alone in the large cavern he called his command post and was seated in his favorite chair. He had taken his time getting dressed in his last clean uniform. He had saved it for the occasion today, when he anticipated he would he would serve the emperor gloriously. The uniform felt stiff, and he took a minute to admire its taut, pressed fabric. His boots were polished and shone brilliantly, even in the soft light of the oil lamp. It was the first time in six months he felt like a professional soldier.

He reached over and picked up one of the delicate sake cups from the set sitting in front of him, silently toasting the emperor. He had emptied the bottle, savoring every drop and marveling how war could subvert one's tastes. Back home in Japan, he would not have served this grade of sake to his batman, let alone consumed it on such an occasion; but alas, here, thousands of miles away from his homeland in this dank cave, the drink satisfied.

He gently set the sake cup back down on the table and readjusted his tunic. Yafumi, his first sergeant, had informed him moments ago that the explosives were set and ready for the order to blow the entrance to the facility. Mifumu had given the order. Now there was just waiting.

He had had a good life with the army. He would miss his wife and his children. His son had grown up strong and would continue his family's four-hundred-year samurai lineage, proud of a father who had served the emperor so well. He had written his wife a long letter and mailed it more than six months ago. He hoped it had reached them by now and-

The enormous blast from the entrance startled him and knocked a small amount of dirt and dust loose from the ceiling above. He shook off his hat and coat and waited impatiently for the second two explosions indicating that the two auxiliary tunnels had been sealed as well.

The second set erupted in the distance but not as loud as he would have thought. The light from his oil lamp flickered. He hoped both charges went but quickly dismissed thoughts that his men had failed.

They had performed this mission in ten other locations. This was the last vault—the smallest they had constructed. The vaults were buried and their locations recorded on top-secret maps. All the locations had had tunnels randomly rigged with explosives; anyone without access to the plans would be in for a nasty surprise if they attempted to breach the vaults.

He sat rigidly at attention and put down any feelings of fear or regret at his decision to remain here, entombed, rather than die on the battlefield. Three years ago, he had been charged with commanding a specialized engineering regiment to build vaults to house wooden crates full of imperial treasure, the emperor's treasure. At first he was insulted. He should be on the battlefield, not babysitting a bunch of engineers. He had even threatened to commit *seppuku* to end his dishonor and shame. Later he learned he had been handpicked for the assignment because of his zealous loyalty and *bushido* spirit.

The heavy wooden crates were filled with gold and silver bars and jewels acquired throughout the conquest of Asia. The treasure was amassed to fuel the empire's war machine. But the needs of the empire had changed. Mifumu knew the war had been going badly for his nation. Civilian political hacks and capitalist merchants had forced the military to make poor decisions.

Defeat was now inevitable. The crates containing the vast fortune were divided among the vaults and sealed to wait for the future, when Japan's imperial star would rise again.

Despite his initial reluctance, Mifumu thought this mission perfect for him. As a samurai, he knew serving his emperor for eternity was his true calling. Yes, his spirit would stand guard like an ancient warrior accompanying an emperor of old on his last journey. He was indeed a loyal samurai to the end.

Tears welled up in his eyes. He poured the last drop of sake from its bottle and drank it, then reached down and grabbed the handle of his sword. It was cool to the touch. Forged in 1600 by a student of the great master Masamune, the sword was a symbol of his family. Its blade had killed hundreds of times. He himself had bloodied its metal often, beheading barbarians from China to the Philippines. He prided himself for never taking more than one stroke to sever a head—he had carved a notch in the handle for every kill.

He wished he could gaze at the weapon's sheen one more time, but he had masked its beauty with heavy-grade axle grease. He did not want the dank air in the cave to tarnish it. It needed to be perfect for his son, or his grandson, when they found him on guard in this tomb one day in the future.

He released the sword, reached down, and opened the leather case holding his pistol. He balanced it in his hand. It felt part of him; it had served him well in combat. He slid back the carriage and a comforting clicking sound pierced the silence as a round chambered.

A ceremonial *seppuku* with a sharp, nine-inch *wakizashi* dagger would have been preferable, but he was without a second to perform the ritual coup de grace, so he opted for a more assured but equally honorable death. He put the Nampo to his head, feeling the cool thin barrel against his temple. It felt odd to be on the receiving end of the weapon. His final thought was of his family, safe in their ancestral home in Nagasaki. The Nampo worked perfectly.

"Captain Steel, have you finished picking through the trash over there?" Devincia's sarcastic tone reverberated through the cave. "We are letting this scavenger hunt take too much time. We need to concentrate on locating the vaults."

"Yeah, it's time to explore the next area." Steel picked up the sword and tied it to his backpack.

It only took five minutes walking down a winding tunnel to reach the next large and empty cavern. The group stood quietly, watching Steel survey the interior with his light. The ceiling was at least twenty feet tall and the dirt floor was hard-packed and smooth. Steel shone his light on a large tunnel at the opposite side of the room. It was big enough to drive a truck through, he thought.

Jo Jo broke the silence. "Looks like a storage room. But someone has beat us to its contents."

"Not necessarily," Devincia snapped. "It is supposed to be buried. Maybe this is where we find the vaults in the ground."

"The colonel could be right," Jo Jo said. "Look at the size of the tunnel on the opposite wall. I bet you the tunnel leads to the outside and it was sealed shut."

"I guess we'll know with a few minutes of exploration. Sergeant, you and Marcos go down the tunnel and report back on its status. We'll see if it is as the captain bets, *diba*," answered Devincia.

"*Opo*, yes colonel." The sergeant and the ranger dutifully marched off across the room and headed into the blackness of the tunnel.

"Don't leave the main tunnel. It is easy to get lost," Steel called out to them in Tagalog.

Jo Jo switched on the metal detector. "I'm going to start over there and work my way across the room."

As Jo Jo swept the floor back and forth, Steel and the other ranger dug at any beep but found only bottle tops, nails, and bits of metal. No shrapnel, bullets, or shell casings. There had been no fighting here.

After thirty fruitless minutes, Steel decided to take a water break. He handed the shovel to Devincia as he walked past, sat on the floor of the cave near the large tunnel, and greedily took a long drink of grape-flavored lukewarm water.

Steel heard shuffling noises from the tunnel, then the sergeant appeared out of the darkness.

"So, sergeant, what is the situation?" Steel asked.

The sergeant seemed pleased to see Steel and was more animated than usual. "It stops maybe fifteen or twenty minutes' walk down it. Looks like it collapsed; there's lots of rubble."

"Yes, completely sealed," the other ranger piped in.

Devincia joined them. "It was likely done by allied forces, or possibly the Japanese themselves. Maybe, just maybe, they wanted to hide this place from prying eyes."

"Yes, that would be good. The Japanese sealing this place off. But we did find an opening, remember. It is more likely that the Americans blew the entrance." Steel took another sip of the grape iodine-aid.

"No way to confirm that theory," Devincia said dismissively and walked back towards Jo Jo.

Steel watched the ranger who was on his knees digging and was struck by the enormity of the task at hand. What happened if the treasure was buried in deep shafts? The odds of finding it were slim. It would take an army of engineers to excavate properly.

As he contemplated the cavern floor from his sitting position Steel noticed a slight anomaly. He looked more closely—maybe a shallow depression. He wondered if bad lighting was playing tricks on his vision, but he was sure he could see variation in the surface of the dirt. He picked up his flashlight, lay down on his belly, and focused on an area where they had not stepped.

"Hey, everyone freeze where you are. Don't move."

The group obeyed his order and he scanned the ground near them. He wished he had thought to do this before they disturbed the dirt floor.

"Steel, what is the problem? What do you see?" Devincia whispered from across the cave. He was frozen with his arms crossed and a look of consternation. Maybe he was thinking about the exploding pig trap from the day before.

"I want to check out something. Can everyone walk over to where the colonel is standing and hug the wall. Walk softly. I don't want to disturb the dirt more than we already have."

"Landmines?" the sergeant asked, eyeing the ground.

"Jo Jo, get out the other lantern and light it." Steel ignored the nervous query. "I want to put as much light in the place as possible."

Jo Jo did as instructed. "Now what, boss?"

"What is this you are doing?" Devincia asked, impatience replacing fear in his voice.

Steel was still on his belly. "Maybe, colonel, just maybe. Come here and join me. You too, sergeant, the more eyes the better."

They both got down on all fours.

"Do you see anything different in the floor level?"

They all studied the floor for a few minutes.

"I see nothing but dirt," Devincia said, and he stood and banged the dust off his clothing.

"Sir, I see something over there and over there," the sergeant pointed. "There are faint outlines of, how do you say in English?" He turned to Steel.

"Depression?"

"Yes. Depressions in the dirt. *Isa, delawa...tatlo and seguro, apat,* one, two, three, four, five. He continued, numbering them."

Devincia crouched down behind the sergeant and tried to look down his finger. Seconds ticked by. "Yes, I see one now—hmm yes, definitely depressions."

"Oh, this is good then," Jo Jo announced.

Steel stood up. "I'm going to walk slowly over to one. You tell me when I am standing in the center."

They vectored him to the spot, then to two others; he marked each with a rock.

"What now?" Devincia asked.

"We pray to the gods of luck and dig," Jo Jo declared.

"*Tayo na.*" Devincia stood and handed the sergeant a shovel.

"Don't disturb the other areas in the cave; we want to ensure we can find the other depressions. Let's pile up the dirt from the hole against the wall over there."

They took turns digging. Steel's heart raced. Could this be it? Could they actually be close to the gold? Even Devincia whistled cheerfully.

They agreed on a four-foot diameter hole. Steel and Jo Jo rotated with the rangers, digging and hauling the soft dirt. Devincia watched from the side of the hole, occasionally snapping out instructions. After several shifts, Steel checked his watch—nearly four p.m. He hadn't eaten since breakfast and was lightheaded, working totally on adrenaline, but no way he was stopping now, even to eat.

He wondered how deep they would have to go. He had no idea. Hell, it could be one-hundred feet down. He never thought he would get this far, and he hadn't given this step much thought. He looked down into the hole and decided it was time to take another metal detector reading. He passed the machine to Jo Jo and held his breath. All eyes were on Jo Jo as he worked. The ping did not sound.

As the hole got deep, Steel realized that they would have to increase its diameter in order to provide enough room for two men and the five-gallon bucket that they were using to haul the dirt out of the hole.

By six p.m. the hole was deeper than Jo Jo was tall. Steel's shoulders ached as he reached down for another bucket—seemed like the millionth—handed up by one of the rangers. The first sergeant took it from Steel and passed it to Devincia, who dumped it against the wall. The pile of dirt was getting large.

"Hey boss," a voice called from out of the hole. "What do you make of this? It looks like wood?" Jo Jo passed up a handful of something crumbled and black.

Steel smelled it. "I think it is rotted wood. Shit! This might be wood they used to shore up the shaft. Or maybe wooden crates?"

"Here's more." Jo Jo yelled up.

"This makes sense," Steel continued, "the depression in the surface of the cave floor was caused by the rotting wood compressing and the dirt sinking. I guess the Jap engineers never factored that in their calculations."

Steel peered over the side and watched Jo Jo examine the wall of the hole. The hole was a good seven feet deep and six feet in diameter, deep enough to make exiting and entering it difficult.

They were all exhausted. Bored with supervising, Devincia had joined the manual laborers and was now stripped down to a white tank undershirt streaked with dirt and sweat. He refused, however, to remove his pistol holster, which hung below his armpit.

"Boss. I think we hit a thick layer of wood." The voice from the hole again.

Steel and Devincia peered in, angling their lights to see and knocking loose dirt down as they jockeyed for position.

"Jesus Marie Joseph, I'm getting buried!" Jo Jo yelled loudly.

"Sorry, *pare*, brother," Steel called out.

"I think we should take another metal reading." Devincia banged on his dim flashlight. His batteries were nearly dead.

"Okay *lang*. Send it down. But keep the dirt up there." Jo Jo yelled up.

Jo Jo had an awkward time maneuvering the detector around the bucket and shovels. He had problems leveling the meter out. It kept making a loud beeping sound.

"Are the batteries low?" Devincia called out.

"The batteries are new. Do you have the dials zeroed out?"

Jo Jo checked. "Seems okay." He tried again. Still the loud beeping.

"Could be a high mineral content in the soil or ironization. Try zeroing out the dials on the side of the walls."

The other ranger digging with Jo Jo stepped out of the way. There was no beeping sound as Jo Jo put the machine to the wall.

"Jo Jo, do that again," Steel called out.

Jo Jo repeated the test, again with no beeps. He redirected the machine to floor.

"I think the detector isn't broken. I think you're registering solid metal," Steel said, sending a shower of dirt down.

"Start digging again. You want some relief?" Devincia asked.

Both men in the hole refused and another bucket of dirt was filled and hauled out, then another, and then ten more.

"Jesus Marie Joseph," Jo Jo yelled.

Steel rushed to the hole. "What is it?"

"Gold," the ranger called out.

"We've hit treasure. We have found it!" Jo Jo and the ranger danced a jig.

"Treasure?" Devincia asked.

"Yes, stand back, here comes treasure from heaven."

Before they could move, Steel and Devincia were hit by a shower of dirt. Steel wiped his face and shined his light on the ground. He grabbed a small ingot of gold and examined it closely.

"What the hell?" He tried to gather spit in his mouth to wet the ingot, but his mouth was too dry. He rubbed the gold on his T-shirt instead. "Hell. Here, it looks like gold to me."

Devincia grabbed it. "It is heavy. Feels like pure gold."

Two bars thudded on the ground accompanied followed by whooping from the hole.

Jo Jo yelled up, "Jesus, there must be dozens of them. We have dug into a metal cover of some sort."

Steel peered again into the hole, and Jo Jo held up another bar, some gold coins, and a small Buddha statue for Steel to see.

Devincia said, "How much is down there?"

"Hard to tell," the sergeant called up. "It looks like a lot. Maybe this is a fifty-gallon oil drum."

"Now that's some money." Steel looked around at the other locations they had marked in the cave. He wondered if they held gold? Only days of digging would tell.

Steel crawled under the light cotton sheet and lay on top of his sleeping bag. Their elation and celebration in finding the treasure was short-lived, exhaustion had set in. Jo Jo, who had fallen straight into bed, was already snoring loudly from his side of the tent. Steel had taken his time, washing up in the stream and eating more than his share of C-rations.

Steel was physically drained, but he couldn't sleep thinking about the day. They had labored for hours after finding the first treasure stash, widening the hole enough for three men to work. It was too soon to tell if anything else was buried beneath the oil drum. Maybe drums were stacked vertically. For Steel, the enormity of the find hadn't quite sunk in yet. They had all agreed to a fresh start in the morning. Devincia announced that they would need to send for additional help. They would need more men, construction equipment, vehicles to carry the heavy gold, and maybe even a helicopter.

Devincia's good mood had been short-lived. When they returned to camp, he cloistered himself with his sergeant, using him to relay terse commands to the group. That pissed Steel off. What the hell were they going to do with all the gold? How would they divide it up? The fact was that it wouldn't be easy to sell, and there was a good chance the government would seize it. Yup, the operation was far from over.

Devincia had posted one of the rangers to guard the entrance of the cave. Others he rotated to positions on the perimeter. Steel could see the need for perimeter security, but it was hard not take offense at the guard at the entrance. Ah, fuck Devincia. Maybe he was just worried about Tony, who Steel was sure was livid for being excluded from the exploration of the cave; left unguarded, it probably would have proved too much temptation.

Steel tried to relax. It seemed like he had been lying on his sleeping bag forever. The night-glow illumination on his watch was hard to read, but he made out 3:00 clear enough. "Damn. Go to sleep," he muttered, as he banged himself on the side of his head. He paused for a moment, listening to a slight whistling sound, almost birdlike, outside his tent. He sat up and stared into the dark outline of a face pressed against the screen of his tent. His heart jumped, and he slowly slid his hand under his pillow, feeling for his knife.

"Sir, it is I, Tony! Sorry for I to scare you," Tony whispered in slurred English.

He relaxed the grip on the knife handle. "What the fuck you doing, Tony?"

"But sir, it is I, Tony! Do not be frightened."

"What's the problem?" Steel whispered and moved closer to the screen.

"I am just nervous because there are people *doon* watching us." He pointed to the hillside.

Steel could smell the *tuba* on Tony's breath. He craned his neck to look through the screen.

"What are you talking about? Who are these people? NPA?"

"I'm not for sure, but they are men, not Negritos or forest spirits," Tony answered in Aeta.

"Tony, are you sure you are not just seeing things? You have had a lot of *tuba* to drink?"

"Oh no, sir. It is true I have had *tuba*, but I know these men are there," he slurred. "They are a long way away on top of that mountain *doon*. They are watching us. I have felt them follow us for two days."

"Maybe it is the Negritos who quit."

"No sir, I think they are not all Negritos, maybe a Negrito is with them. For that I am not sure."

Steel thought for a moment. If they were NPA, then maybe he should wake the colonel. "So they are not close by?"

"What's the matter?" Jo Jo sat up, flicking on his light.

Steel reached over and pushed down his flashlight. "Shh, it is only Tony, he..." Steel peered out the tent. Tony was gone. "Never mind, I'll tell you in the morning. Tony was up and about seeing things."

"Those Negritos scare me with their forest spirits. I hope there are not ghosts in the cave, guarding the treasure." Jo Jo made the sign of the cross in the shadowy darkness.

"Yeah, me too, that little bastard gives me the willies sometimes."

"Let's just sleep and deal with it in the morning." Jo Jo fell back down on his bag.

"Amen to that."

Philippine Marine reconnaissance Capt. Ferdinand Agnacio was huddled inside his lean-to tent made from his poncho, trying to catch a couple of hours of sleep. He was still dressed in his jungle fatigues and combat boots, keeping as little flesh as possible exposed to the hordes of mosquitoes. Nearby, his two patrols of eight marines each and two Negrito guides were asleep in their tents. He had posted one man on guard. They were all exhausted, having kept up a steady two-day march following the group camped by the next mountain.

Agnacio had been briefed that the group he was assigned to monitor were rogue scout rangers and an American officer. Even though his platoon was the best unit in the marines and trained extensively for such a mission, he had great admiration for the jungle training of the rangers he was after. He would have to be at the top of his game to remain unidentified. Fortunately, he had been assigned several local tribesmen who were invaluable trackers and guides.

He was pleased that he had been chosen to lead the mission, which he was informed was of great interest to those higher up in the military. They had been flown by C-130 from their base in the south on short notice. It was no wonder he had difficulty sleeping— his career could be made on this assignment.

At least his men were pleased. They got extra pay and new equipment, including high-tech communications gear, which they were using to send updates to a marine team eight kilometers away, who in turn relayed the information all the way to mobile headquarters. He had hoped that marine headquarters in Cavite were reading his messages. But mostly right now he wished he had some night vision equipment. An American-made starlight scope that he had read about would alleviate some of his anxieties about what the group was up to right now.

I'm not to worry, he thought as he slapped a mosquito buzzing in his ear. They aren't going anywhere. They too had settled down for the night. He wondered, though, what the deal was with the cave.

Steel dug his entrenching tool forcefully into the dirt. He was still more than a little pissed off at Devincia. Early that morning, Steel had awakened to find that Devincia had ordered Tony to guide the first sergeant back to town. Steel should have been consulted. Tony was his employee, not Devincia's. Had he not been so excited about the gold, he would have protested. But Steel had found treasure, actual treasure. Let the asshole play his power games.

He and Jo Jo were up to their waists digging in a new hole, while the two rangers and Devincia manned the bucket. The other rangers were on guard outside. They were all hopeful that the next treasure trove was buried at a similar shallow depth. They would wait until they got some heavy equipment to dig out the first hole completely.

Steel was still nervous about Devincia's cagey attitude. He wondered how this all would work. Devincia would soon have a large group of his men and equipment. He and Jo Jo would get pushed to the side. He didn't trust Devincia in the slightest. And what about the Philippine government? How long before they found the site?

There was also the issue of what he would do with his share, provided he got it. He dug another shovel full of dirt. He wished he had found the gold on his own. Then they would have more control and time to think. He would have liked to discuss this with Jo Jo right now, but they both felt uncomfortable talking in front of Devincia and his men.

Steel decided to ask. "So colonel, how are we going to dispose of the gold? It might be tough to move it without drawing the government's attention."

Devincia squatted down beside the hole and whispered between clenched teeth: "Do not question this. I will make those arrangements." He stood and walked off.

Jo Jo rolled his eyes and shook his head, wishing too that Devincia were back behind his fancy government desk.

"Fuck you," Steel mumbled in a voice that carried further than he wanted.

Devincia rushed back at them. "No, fuck you," he screamed at Steel, pointing a dirt-covered finger.

Steel stood for a moment, slackjawed. Devincia, glared crazed. He took a deep breath and stared at the ceiling. "I have decided you are through here. You are no longer required for our purposes." He quickly drew out his pistol from its holster and chambered a round, pointing it at Steel's face.

Steel gripped his shovel tightly. The seconds ticked by. The two scout rangers stood next to Devincia, looking at him, bewildered. They had seen the colonel act bizarrely before, but they wondered what the Americano could have done to bring forth such fury.

"Come on, colonel, you don't want to be so angry with us. We are on your side. Just put down the pistol," Jo Jo said, stepping forward.

Devincia pointed the pistol at Jo Jo. "Fuck you, too. I decide now what will happen to you," he growled. "Maybe I'll kill you both and say that bandits or NPA killed you." He aimed the pistol back at Steel. "Or maybe I'll kill you and just leave your bodies to rot in the jungle." Devincia waved the pistol in the air. "But maybe I'll keep you alive for a few more days and then decide." Devincia lowered the pistol.

"Yes, you can keep digging. I'd like you to see the treasure. You know I never really thought in one million years that you would find any treasure. It's quite amazing. In fact, I am stunned. I will let you see the treasure; then, I will take it all away from you. I will take something away that belonged to you, so you will know what that feels like." He pointed the pistol back at Steel.

He knows about Vida. How?

"Corporal Cruz, what do you think I should do, let them live?" Steel watched Devincia close one eye has he looked down the gun barrel, aiming. "He has dishonored me."

The ranger looked coldly into the hole. "I do not know, sir," he said blandly.

"Alright then; I will leave their deaths in God's hands. Yes, you and I have spilled too much blood in our lifetimes." Devincia put his hand on the corporal's shoulder.

Steel exhaled and nearly collapsed against the back of the hole.

"Marcos, get your weapon and post guard on them. Kill them if they try anything. Dig well and live," he laughed then walked off.

"What the hell just happened? What the fuck is his deal?" Steel threw down his shovel. "I think we've been double-crossed."

Jo Jo pushed in close to Steel's face. "Jesus Maria Joseph. Maybe he is angry because you are fucking his girlfriend." He threw down his shovel too. "You had to go and mess with a man who has his own personal army: fucking *loco loco* Americano."

Steel did not answer; Jo Jo had a right to be angry.

In silence, they dug for the rest of the day and into the evening under armed guard, prisoners in the dark cave. They found a second cache of gold bars and gold and gem encrusted religious icons similar to those from the first hole. Steel should have been elated, but he was just angry at Devincia for betraying him and at himself for letting Devincia get involved.

One of the rangers brought Steel and Jo Jo food and water. Shit they really were prisoners. They quietly ate their C-rations. Steel was filthy and chilled. He didn't care. He was alive and at least the cave was free of mosquitoes. He shined his light over to the piles of gold. This was his worst nightmare. So close to the treasure, yet so far. He reached down and picked up a handful of gold coins and silently slid them into his pocket.

He looked over at the ranger sitting in the dim candle light finishing off his food, his weapon cradled in his lap. The ranger had forbidden them to speak. Steel wanted to speak with Jo Jo about an escape plan, but all they could do was listen to each other breathe. Besides, Jo Jo's was still pissed—and rightly so Steel thought.

They could probably surprise and overpower the guard, take his weapon, but then what? The others would be waiting outside. Steel wasn't ready for a firefight. He slumped back on the ground. "Good night, *pare*. Sorry for getting you involved in this shit. See you in the morning," he said loudly enough for the ranger to hear him.

"Tomorrow is another day," Jo Jo grunted.

Steel woke up with a jolt, disorientated in the darkness. He checked his watch, angling it into the light of the guard's candle, 5:45 a.m. It should be just daylight outside. His internal clock was on schedule.

He dozed for another thirty minutes until Devincia came into the cave and let them outside into the harsh daylight. Steel covered his eyes and took a deep breath; the fresh air overwhelmed him.

Two rangers escorted Steel and Jo Jo to the stream, and, to Steel's surprise, they were allowed to wash up. The men handed Jo Jo and Steel breakfast of rice, sardines, and fresh papaya. He scowled as he ate, surveying his personal belongings spread around the campsite. Shit, the dicks were drinking his instant coffee. Not that is was any good, but he felt violated nonetheless.

He looked over and could see his sword. It was unsheathed and speared into a log. Someone had used it to split some coconuts, judging from the husks on the ground. That was his fucking sword. He wanted it back. He assumed his flag was lost too. Steel stood and kicked the dirt, knocking rice from his plate. He drew a glare from one of the rangers eating off of a banana leaf. Another ranger aimed his weapon at Steel. Steel froze in his tracks and glared back. The standoff broke when a voice from the jungle yelled, "What are you doing?"

Movement rippled through the rangers. They dropped their cups and plates and dove for cover and their weapons.

Steel watched Devincia grab his Uzi and sink to one knee, nervously scanning the forest.

The voice boomed again, "*Pare,* what are you doing?"

Devincia, waved at the rangers who began to fan out in crouched and low crawls. Steel motioned for Jo Jo to do the same. They all tried to find cover. Steel and Jo Jo hid behind the log with the protruding sword, sliding in next to one of the rangers, who quietly slid a 40mm grenade into the launcher hanging below the barrel of M16.

Again from the forest: "*Pare,* don't shoot! We have the white flag. We want to talk, okay *lang*?"

"Who wants to talk?" Steel wondered out loud, "NPA?"

Two uniformed soldiers stepped out of the jungle. They were Phil marines. One had a white cloth tied to the barrel of his M16.

The ranger beside Steel kept aiming his weapon. Steel, however, was elated. At this point, he'd be happy to take his chances with the government.

The rangers waited until the marines entered the campsite before they lowered their weapons. Devincia stood, slung his Uzi on his shoulder, and adjusted his dirty fatigue shirt. He walked forward. The marine, surprised to see Devincia's rank, popped him a professional salute. Devincia responded with a sloppy, halfhearted one.

Steel smiled. Devincia was clearly not pleased with this turn of events. The government was going to take the treasure. The marine provided his name, informed Devincia, that he and his men were surrounded, and asked for a peaceful surrender. Devincia scratched his head and stared at the marine captain then into the jungle. Steel chuckled to himself. Devincia was no doubt wondering what happened to the ranger who was posted as lookout.

Devincia identified himself and began to talk to the

marine. Steel could tell Devincia was banking on the man recognizing Devincia's name and knowing his reputation. He could hear Devincia tell the marine he had no jurisdiction in this situation and that he, Devincia was on a special mission from higher headquarters. The young captain held his ground. He said that he was sorry, but that he had been ordered not to accept anything but the group's surrender. Steel watched the jungle come alive with marines. There were at least two dozen, all heavily armed. Steel saw two M60 machine guns pointed at them. Devincia was drawing some heavy firepower.

Only one individual approached. Unlike the others, he was wearing a Philippine army uniform. Steel saw Devincia mutter some expletives then walked forward. Steel was surprised to see Devincia pop a salute. Wow, must be a full-bird colonel; Steel marveled at the twist. Too bad they were out of earshot. He would have loved to hear the conversation.

"Ah Antonio, I see you are out enjoying your leave." Colonel Panglio said in a low voice.

"I was, until now," Devincia snarled.

"I think you know this little operation of yours is over. I don't want any bloodshed. Just have your men put down their weapons, and we will go easy on all of you. No questions will be asked. You will just be returned to quarters. No repercussions at all."

"If I choose not to…"

"Then there will be unpleasant trouble. We have you outgunned five to one. And I have two gunships over the next ridgeline."

Devincia paused, weighing his options. There were few. "Maybe, colonel, we can work out a mutually acceptable deal that is—"

"Ah, this is good. You have found something. Antonio, there are no deals. While I personally would love to work something out, the president himself is involved in this one. It is beyond the both of us. So you really found something, eh? Who would have thought these legends real?"

Devincia was speechless. How did the colonel know?

"Ah, Antonio, don't be too shocked. We tapped the professor's phone. He loves to chat. He spilled the beans bragging to a colleague of his. Come on Antonio, what did you find?"

Devincia glared. He was screwed and he knew it. He contemplated taking the colonel hostage. Even shooting it out. But to what end? The entire Phil army would be down on them. No, it was over. Marcos would get the gold, more blood money for his Swiss bank accounts and those of his corrupt generals.

"Well, colonel, as they say, discretion is the better part of valor. It appears you have bested me in this one." Devincia swallowed his anger and with theatrical graciousness, pointed the way to the cave and escorted the colonel in.

Steel watched Devincia lead the colonel past them. From out of the jungle, the marines advanced to within thirty yards of the camp. They were no longer aiming their weapons, but remained at port arms. The rangers too had stood down. Everyone waited anxiously.

Steel looked over to the edge of the jungle and suddenly knew how the marines were able to penetrate the ranger perimeter so readily. Old June and another Negrito stood watching. Steel smiled. Negritos one, rangers zero. He hoped they hadn't killed the ranger. Steel motioned for June to come over. With his M1 slung over his shoulder, June slowly worked his way past the marines.

Steel addressed him in Aeta. "How are you? How did you get involved in this?"

Steel already knew the answer, but wanted to see what June would say. June averted his eyes. He was clearly embarrassed.

"Captain Steel, I am so surprised to see you. I did not know it was you here."

June seemed abashed, or at least he was putting on a good act. "So, June, you're on the AFP payroll I take it."

"Had I known I was leading them to you, I would never had dared to do so, to you my friend. You should have told me you were here. I had not heard."

Steel didn't believe for a moment that June didn't know. "It's okay, June. I don't hold it against you. I did not know what I was getting into. I am swimming with the python." He used an Aeta expression. He put his hand on June's shoulder, telegraphing his forgiveness. Steel needed June for future operations.

The pair emerged from the cave, the colonel beaming and Devincia hanging his head. Devincia called out to one of the rangers, who huddled with his men. They broke ranks unceremoniously, stacked their weapons and started packing their equipment. Steel and Jo Jo were left to sit chatting quietly with June.

After a few minutes, the colonel approached Steel. Steel stood at loose attention. He carefully watched the man, short and chubby with heavily oiled and obviously dyed jet-black hair. He wore expensive Ray Ban sunglasses with rose-colored lenses. He looked like a Hollywood central casting stereotype of a corrupt third-world military officer. Steel studied his nametag for a moment. Panglio? Panglio... ah Colonel Panglio. Of course. He was a senior officer in army counterintelligence, a junior Marcos henchman. He was right under General Ver in the power structure of the Marcos regime.

The colonel, in his clean, well-pressed olive-green fatigues, put an arm on Steel's shoulder and escorted him out of earshot of the rest of the group. Panglio kept the arm in its fatherly drape as he began to talk. "Captain Steel, I am quite shocked to see a U.S. officer here involved with such skullduggery."

Steel smiled at Panglio's word choice. Filipinos, who generally had a great command of English, still favored old fashioned language.

Steel stood silent. Panglio resumed. "It is unfortunate that a U.S. officer is involved with er...let's say some misguided elements of our armed forces." He dropped his hand. "It would be an awkward situation to have a U.S. intelligence operative caught with some of our forces engaged in unlawful acts. In fact, your boss, General Smith, I'm sure would be most displeased if I informed him that you were collaborating with Communists."

Steel stiffened. "I'm not sure I follow you, sir. If I may, as you know, Lieutenant Colonel Devincia is not a Communist," Steel said in Tagalog.

Panglio paused for moment, thinking. "Your Tagalog is quite good, Captain Steel. But I must be quite frank. This is a serious matter for my government. I will say that I found you in the jungle operating with suspect leftist elements." He looked Steel right in the eye and continued in English. "I will inform your general of this, unless you agree to not discuss any of what you have found or seen here."

Ah, that's it, Steel thought. Of course, it's all about the gold. Hell, they could kill JoJo and me right here.

Steel stiffened to attention. "I have seen nothing here, sir, nothing but jungle," he said in Tagalog. "Thank you for rescuing me from my misadventure of jungle hiking."

Panglio smiled and spoke in Tagalog. "You are a smart officer. I have your word of honor then?"

"You have my word as an officer," Steel said grimacing at his show of honor for such an obvious scumbag. But this was the only way he would get home. Besides, he was sure no one in his command chain considered him enough of a professional officer to be held to his word. Steel looked over at Jo Jo.

Panglio caught the glance. "How about the karate instructor? Will he talk?"

Steel tried not to look worried. "Sir, he will not say anything if I ask him not to. He is loyal to me. He would not want to put my career at risk."

Panglio looked at Jo Jo, who was watching them intently.

"Alright, captain I will take you at your word. Just remember that your friend is very vulnerable to, how shall we say, rogue elements taking actions into their own hands, but that unpleasantness is completely avoidable. I will return you both to your base."

Steel saluted him. He felt dirty and disgusted. But he knew it was a matter of survival.

Steel had thought it was going to be a long disappointing walk home. But, after quickly packing up their gear and heading over the mountain to a cleared, flat area where two Philippine Air Force UH-1h helicopter gunships were parked, Steel realized it was more likely to be a short, dramatic, but still disappointing ride home.

Steel shook his head and whispered to Jo Jo, "Why am I surprised? That fat little turd Panglio sure didn't hoof it all the way up here."

Devincia and the rangers got into one chopper and the colonel, Steel, and Jo Jo in another. Devincia looked like an old man, a defeated old man. Steel wasn't sorry that Devincia lost the treasure. No telling what Devincia might have done to keep it. Steel suspected that too many years of fighting in Mindanao had loosened a screw in his head.

A young army private, the designated door gunner who dutifully manned the M60 machine gun, made sure that Steel and Jo Jo were tightly strapped into canvas troop seats across from the colonel. The senior pilot gave a thumb's up signal to Panglio, who nodded, and the two choppers slowly rose out of the jungle clearing. The sliding doors were open, and cool air rushed in, a relief. Steel was sweaty and dirty beyond belief. He shut his eyes and listened to the whop-whop sound of the propeller blades that, along with the streaming air, made speaking impossible.

Steel had overheard Panglio give the marines strict orders not to let anyone go in or near the cave complex. As they gained altitude, Steel could see it in the distance with the marines swarming like ants around the campsite. He wondered how the hell they were going to excavate the cave. It would be near impossible to get heavy equipment in; they would have to use people, and lots of them. Helicopters would be required to haul out the treasure. One thing was for sure, Steel would never know what riches had been buried there.

Steel nudged Jo Jo and pointed down to the cave. Jo Jo looked over and gave a tired smile and thumbs up. Steel then checked the cargo pockets of his cammo pants—the gold he had taken was still there and his sword was tied safely to his pack, minor consolation prizes.

It took less than fifteen minutes before the Clark Air Base perimeter was in sight. "Oh shit," Steel muttered. The reality of how bad his situation was started to sink in. There would be no discrete reappearance back at Angeles City. They were landing on the base—and not just anywhere but on the 13th Air Force parade field.

Steel checked his watch. It was two p.m. Wednesday and right in the middle of the workday. He could plainly see the concrete building housing the intel shop. Next to it was the general's office. Steel looked over and could see groups of people gathered outside the buildings, all probably wondering what the helicopters were doing.

Once landed, the helicopters both slowed their blades, but did not switch off the engines. The colonel ushered Steel and

Jo Jo out, and led the way towards a group of a half-dozen shocked U.S. military officers. Steel's heart sank. He could see Kuncker standing next to Bart, the general's executive.

"Oh, this is really not good. It is so not good." Steel grunted to Jo Jo. "I'm a dead man." Steel's heart fell even further as he noticed Gen. Smith watching from his porch. "Oh well," he thought. "Article 15 at the least. Maybe some jail time. Court martial for sure. Drummed out of the service."

Steel was still out of earshot when Colonel Panglio greeted Kuncker, who saluted him. Panglio extended his hand and they shook. Kuncker tried to move the colonel over to the general's office, but Panglio seemed to be politely refusing Steel and Jo Jo stopped a few paces back. Bart was looking at Steel questioningly. What was Panglio saying?

After they were done talking, Panglio again shook hands with both of the lieutenant colonels, accepted their salutes, turned, and marched back toward the helicopters. Steel saluted Panglio on his way past, and he returned the salute without stopping or speaking.

Kuncker and Bart joined Steel, and they all silently watched the helicopters take off into the clear blue sky. The mid-afternoon sun was hot. Both lieutenant colonels spoke at once. Steel stood at attention waiting for them to finish.

"Steel, what the hell?"

"Alright son! What the hell is up with all this?"

Steel looked over their heads at the gathering crowd of people standing in the shade of the giant cicada trees across the field.

"Well, sirs, it is a real long story."

Bart thought for a moment. "Let's get out of the heat. My office."

"Could we go to the vault first?" Kuncker piped in. "It would be more appropriate to discuss these matters there."

"Whatever. Holy shit, the general is not going to like this at all." Bart headed toward the intel building.

Steel called out to Jo Jo, in Tagalog and told him to wait for a while, but if it took too long, to take a bus home.

"Don't worry about me. I'll be here praying for your soul," he called back.

Steel filed in behind the two officers. The crowd of onlookers, which had grown to three dozen, gaped at Steel's filthy clothes, dirty bandanna wrapped around his head, and army-issue rucksack with a samurai sword tied to it. Steel saw Curtis standing in the crowd; he mouthed, "What the fuck?" Steel just grimaced and shook his head. Oh well, it was time to be a civilian anyway.

19

Clark Air Base

Steel pulled into his usual parking lot behind 13th Air Force headquarters. It might be his former lot, he thought, after the court-martial board got through with him. Bart and Kuncker had grilled him for two hours in the vault yesterday, after which the general, through Bart, ordered Steel to go home, shower, and report back at 0800.

Steel had provided Bart and Kuncker with few details about the jungle trek; apparently, so had Panglio. He said he had found Steel wandering lost in the mountains and given him a ride to the base. Steel, in his story, added that he had been bird watching.

Bart and Kuncker hadn't bought it and threatened everything from a court-martial to a flogging. "It's a disgrace that an officer would so blatantly violate the general's directives." Bart's words were still ringing in Steel's ears. Through it all, Steel maintained that he had been seeking rare species of birds within the five-mile radius of the base. Steel thought Bart had seemed a little disappointed when he returned from the general's office with nothing more than a "remain in quarters" order for the evening. He was sure that Bart would have preferred to publicly hang him.

Kuncker had been slightly more sympathetic, but clearly

didn't believe the bird-watching story either. Kuncker turned paternalistic once he got Steel alone—gave him the "I'm so disappointed" speech which made Steel feel bad. He didn't want to upset Kuncker. He's a good boss. Steel apologized, saying that he understood that, while he had been within the five-mile radius, what he did could be construed as unlawful. He would accept his fate like a man.

Steel exited the truck and adjusted his hat and shirt, crisp and clean. The air was cool with a slight breeze. He looked over at Mt. Pinatubo and thought of the marines standing guard at the cave, of the treasure, and of President Marcos.

That last thought made Steel angry. Maybe after he had served his jail time, he'd go and find the other vaults himself, as a civilian not subject to the Uniform Code of Military Justice. There were supposed to be at least five more stashes. He'd find them someday—without Devincia. Much less complicated exploring as Mr. Steel.

He marched up the stairs and into the general's waiting area. It was 0755. Kuncker and Colonel Morgan, the OSI commander, were seated in Bart's office, chatting. A big butterfly ripped through Steel's stomach. Morgan's presence brought home just how much trouble Steel was in.

He said good morning to Sergeant Green and Mrs. Conroy, the general's admin staff. They both smiled nervously, looking at him as if he were a condemned man. Steel played the part well, pacing silently.

Kuncker stoically ushered Steel into the general's office. Steel thought Bart seemed particularly smug as he shut the door behind them. They all sat except for Steel, who remained standing at attention. A bead of sweat appeared on his forehead. Many more dripped down his back.

The general sat behind his desk reading something, ignoring them. He squinted through bifocals perched halfway down his nose. Steel saluted the general, who slowly returned it then resumed reading.

Steel's eyes wandered around the room, taking in plaques, mugs, and model airplanes—the office of a frustrated pilot turned senior administrator. He wished he could have visited under better circumstances.

Smith sighed as he dropped the paper from his hands and took off his reading glasses. "Stand at ease, captain." He looked up at Steel and then around the room.

"I've read your report on this situation, Kuncker." He paused, picked up a pen, and leaned back in his chair. With the fingers of his right hand, he began twirling the pen like a drum majorette's baton. Steel stared, mesmerized. He noticed the large Air Force Academy ring on the general's finger and the general's solid forearms; he probably played football in school.

A heavy gold-plated bracelet with large pilot's wings emblazoned with a senior-rated flying-hours wreath encircled general's wrist. He had undoubtedly bought it in Thailand, probably on one of his business trips. It might even have been a gift from a Thai counterpart. On the other wrist was a large, silver Rolex watch. Steel couldn't tell if it were real or a Thai knockoff. Behind the watch was a metal Vietnam MIA/POW band. Steel wondered whose name was on it, could be a buddy, or even Steel's own—

Again, a big tortured sigh from Smith. Steel felt like screaming out, "Just shoot me and get it over with."

"Gentlemen, I've read the report. Why don't you give me a minute here with the captain." Everyone stood, confused. Bart took the initiative and herded the others towards the door and out, shutting the door behind them.

"No Bart, you too. Give me some privacy for a moment." Bart looked as though he wanted to speak but opted against it and reluctantly ushered himself out.

Steel stood at attention, puzzled. Maybe the general was going to beat the crap out of him and didn't want any witnesses. That would be a twist.

"Captain, pull up a chair and have a seat."

Steel complied, relieved to be off his feet, but still sat rigidly at attention.

"It seems that when you fuck up, you do it big." Smith shook his head. "Flown down on my parade field and dropped off by Phil top brass as if they were an airborne taxi service."

He leaned way back in his chair and threw his pen on the desk. It bounced onto the folder holding the report. "I think this bird watching explanation is a load of crap. What the hell were you really doing out there? You're not working for someone else, are you? You're not operating on any black programs?"

Steel thought for a minute. Oh that's right. Smith had been on the joint staff at the Pentagon. He would be familiar with various covert programs. "No sir, I'm just an Air Force intelligence officer, nothing more, nothing less."

The general eyed. "But then again, you probably wouldn't tell us if you were a company spook. So what I am left with? You're sticking with the fuck-up excuse, I take it?"

Steel didn't know how to answer. The general's rough language and hulking physical appearance added an air of intimidation.

"I read your personnel jacket. On the surface, you have a good record, but if you read between the lines, it says you're a problem officer. Are you a problem officer?"

"No sir—I don't think so."

Smith picked up the pen and began twirling it again. "Kuncker told me your dad is MIA in Nam. Shot down in '69 near the Laotian border, an F-100 driver out of Da Nang. I did some checking. There has been no word on his status." He watched Steel.

Steel nodded. He paused for moment, then spoke. "Two hundred and forty-two F-100 Sabres were lost in the war," he looked away from the general. He was used to being pitied, the orphaned son of a war hero—or a baby killer—either way, he never learned to like it.

The general pointed to the MIA/POW bracelet on his wrist. "See this? Robert Johnson, he was a buddy of mine at the zoo. Played first-string tight end with me. Great guy. He was shot down in '68 with his backseat Jimmy Robertson. They were never heard from again. He was a good friend, Robbie was."

Steel stared off into space.

Smith continued. "I was only in Nam briefly. Mostly flew F-105's out of Takhli, Thailand," he paused and considered the large family photo on the corner of his desk. "Must have been rough growing up without a dad."

Steel nodded. You have no idea, he thought.

"I would imagine it's the uncertainty of it all—what really happened to your dad? Is it possible that he is alive?" Smith toyed with his POW/MIA bracelet. "I have the same thoughts about Robbie." Smith abruptly snapped up straight in his chair. Steel figured his nostalgia and sympathy had just maxed out.

Smith slid on his bifocals and picked up Steel's personnel folder, flipped it open, and perfunctorily paged through it. "I could be wrong, but I get the impression from this latest incident that you aren't making a career of the service. I assume by your blatant disregard for my direct orders forbidding violation of base boundaries that you just don't give a rat's ass about your career. Am I right?"

"Yes sir, I mean, no sir! I do give a rat's ass about my job. I was within your set radius of the base."

"Oh, bullshit. You know what I mean, the mountains behind us are all off-limits. Only a wild man would challenge my rules on a technicality."

"Yes sir."

"Well, are you making the Air Force a career? I'm curious."

"To be honest, I have no plans of making a career of the service. I do care about my reputation, though. I am truly sorry I violated your restrictions, and I'm sorry that I embarrassed my boss."

"Well, I appreciate a little honesty. Do you feel that you are above the law, captain?"

"No sir."

"Do you realize the consequences your flagrant actions could have?"

Steel nodded.

"Alright then, captain, we both know where you stand. So let's say we just cut through some of the bullshit." He removed his bifocals and dropped the folder. "I am curious about you. You seem like you are really enjoying yourself here at Clark. Why is that, Captain. Steel? Why do you like it here, when so many of my officers bitch and complain and can't wait to go back stateside? I have a stack of requests for transfer on Bart's desk."

Steel was confused by the turn of questioning. "Er...I just enjoy the adventure."

"Adventure? What are you, Indiana Jones or something?" he smirked.

Steel wondered if Smith knew about the treasure. He had never told anyone at the office about his hobby. Why the Indiana Jones reference?

"No sir."

"Steel, I'm going to make a deal with you right now. You come clean with me and I'll go easy on you. If not, well—then...bird watching, my ass. Panglio wasn't away from Manila flying around the mountains for nothing. Morgan gave me the rundown on him. The man's an opportunist and a crook." He stood up, walked over to the window, and stared out onto the parade field.

Steel's mind raced. Continue the lie? He liked Smith ever since He'd caught Steel gambling in the bushes. Smith could have busted Steel right then. "Alright, sir, I'll give you the straight story. You can go to the OSI if you need to. When I first got to Clark, a U.S. helicopter pilot introduced me to some of the local Negrito tribesmen. They began taking me out for hikes in the mountains. They showed me caves and tunnels full of World War II artifacts. I began going with the Negritos by myself, exploring and collecting souvenirs."

The general returned to his seat and studied Steel.

"We began to find human remains on trips, Japanese soldiers. They were obviously missing in action. At first I ignored them. Then on one trip in a small cave, I found a U.S. helmet and a human skeleton dressed in the decomposed uniform of an American soldier. There was a pair of silver wire-rimmed glasses, a corncob pipe, and the insignia of a medical corpsman on the body. I searched for dog tags or any type of identification, but I didn't find them. I bagged up the remains and gave it over to the OSI. They sent it on to Hawaii to the Army's military identification command. I never heard if they figured out who it was."

"That must have hit close to home, finding the body of the dead GI," Smith said, almost to himself.

Steel nodded. "From that point on, I began bringing in bodies regardless of what nationality, especially those with any type of dog tag or identifying personal items, like a canteen with a name on it. The Japanese embassy in Manila mostly ignores me. They come and pick up the bodies when I bug them enough."

"You're serious? They ignore your calls?" Smith asked.

Steel explained to him about the Japanese government's

indifferent attitude towards their thousands of MIA soldiers. Steel told more stories of finding caves full of bodies and war materials but held off on sharing anything about the treasure. Smith wasn't satisfied and pressed Steel again about why Panglio was involved.

Steel took a deep breath; it was come-to-Jesus time. He reached into his pocket, pulled out a small gold, coin-shaped symbol of Buddha and laid it on the general's desk. Smith hesitated for a moment, then reached over and picked it up. Steel started from the beginning.

The general listened intently. He kept inspecting the Buddha medal in his hand. He even made Steel point out the spot on a Philippine map hanging on his wall where he thought the cave was. Steel told the general who Yamashita was and the treasure legend, about Tony and the Negritos, and how Devincia had double-crossed them all. I'm turning into a goddamn girl, thought Steel, babbling my every secret.

Steel covertly checked his watch: 0910. They had been at it for over an hour. "Yes sir, I would imagine the president does know about the treasure."

"Incredible. That bastard Marcos will keep the gold for sure—and the government will never see a cent," he regarded Steel. "Out of curiosity what the hell were you going to do with the gold?"

"Don't know, sir. Wouldn't have been easy moving hundreds of pounds of gold." Steel leaned forward in his seat, all the formality having evaporated between them over the last hour. "Can you imagine how difficult it would be to fence that much treasure or get it out of the country? Not to mention illegal."

Smith nodded. Steel imagined the general was trying to figure out if he could have devised a plan to move the treasure. The Indiana Jones reference made sense. Smith was a fellow adventurer at heart.

They chatted for another ten minutes before the general

glanced at his Rolex. "Damn. Bart must be having a cow out there. Here's the deal Steel. Since you were open with me, you are getting a letter of reprimand from me personally. You are confined to quarters for thirty days. You go out again before I lift the restrictions and all deals are off. You'll get the maximum." He pointed a finger at Steel. "I'm going to call in Morgan and fill him in on some of the details. You are providing a valuable intelligence collection service, or so we will call it. I don't have to explain myself further. You are not to discuss this with anyone. Am I clear on that?"

"Yes sir." It's great to be the king, Steel thought.

"That's all, captain. You're dismissed." He tried to hand Steel the Buddha medal.

"Sir, please keep it as a souvenir for your shelf." Steel, pointed to the general's display case then stood and held a stiff salute, waiting for the general to respond. Instead, he said, "Tell me one more thing. Do you think there is any more treasure?" He looked at the gold piece.

"Yes sir, I do."

"Keep me posted, captain." He returned the salute. "And do me a favor—keep your ass out of trouble while you're still under my command."

"Yes sir." Steel did a smart about-face and walked out the door, his knees almost buckling. God, he was so relieved. General Smith now had a friend for life. Steel had pure *utang na loob*, a blood debt, to the man.

Bart rushed past Steel, scrutinizing his face for a reaction. He got none. But Steel knew it wasn't completely over. Colonel Morgan would likely want a lengthy debrief. He hoped for his and Jo Jo's safety that the information was kept in classified channels.

Kuncker struggled to keep up with Steel, who was walking rapidly towards his vehicle. "Steel, slow down. What the hell happened in there?"

"I got a letter of reprimand and thirty days quarters restriction," Steel called over his shoulder, not missing a step.

Kuncker reached out and grabbed Steel's arm. "Wait a minute. What? Let me get this straight. You land in a PAF helo on the parade field after blindly violating restrictions and get a slap on the wrist. Oh, come on. You fucking embarrass me with your leave bullshit story and spend one hour with the general alone, and this is the outcome? Christ on the cross, Steel. What line did you feed him? Bart and the DO Colonel Milton are going to hit the roof. Milton is flying back from Thailand especially for this. They all want blood."

"Sorry, sir. You can speak to the general. I could be wrong." Steel now regretted telling Kuncker. He should have let the general do it. "Sir, come to think of it, I shouldn't have said anything. Could you please let the general pass the information to you?"

"Whatever. Fucking incredible. Anyone else would be picking up trash along the road in leg irons."

"Look sir, I know I screwed up royally. I got really lucky with the punishment. I figure whatever career I had went out the window, but that's okay. The Air Force was great to me. I think I was productive in return. Sir, I'm still on leave. I'd like to return to my quarters and rest. I have the thirty days to contemplate my sins." He looked Kuncker in the eye waiting for a response.

"Yes, that you do. See you Monday morning. You're a great analyst, but frankly, a lousy officer. This stunt has finished you here at 13th and in the Air Force. I think you'd be happy as a civilian."

"Thank you, sir." Steel turned and walked away.

"Steel." Kuncker called out to him. "Why don't you level with me? What were you really doing?"

Steel thought for a second about being upfront but opted against it. "Bird watching." He smiled.

"Yeah right, and I'm Imelda Marcos."

20

Target Range: Clark Air Base

A IR FORCE SECURITY POLICEMAN Buck Sgt. William 'Willie' Long loved this part of his job: manning the M60 machine gun in the back of the camouflaged painted HUMVEE patrol vehicle. Willie adjusted his dark goggles over his eyes and pulled the chin strap to his Kevlar helmet tight. They were providing security, escorting two trucks; each held three instructors and ten GIs, officers and enlisted men headed for qualification training. Each trainee clasped an unloaded M16, and instructors sported loaded side-arms.

He gripped the roll bar firmly with his left hand and kept the right hand free to rock and roll with the 60 should the need arise. The 60 could fire two-hundred rounds a minute. Willie had one-hundred rounds in a belt mounted in a box on the side of the weapon.

His security police squadron had been busy since the NPA murdered the GIs. There were gates to man, miles of perimeter fence to patrol, and the flight line to secure. The hours were long, but it was good duty.

He loved the Air Force. He got respect for doing his job well. There was no prejudice here, not like the backwater town in rural Alabama where he grew up—no place for a young black man.

And then of course, there was the social life at Clark. Willie saw lots of women off base, too many for his grandma's liking, he was sure of that. He was planning on seeing one fine lady tomorrow evening—Friday and payday. The joke was that U.S. payday was always a Phil national holiday. Let the party begin. But that was tomorrow. Today was all business. He had to stay sharp.

Willie looked down at the two policemen seated below him. Senior Airman Miles, the driver, was one of the brothers he ran with. They were tight. Seated next to Miles, Airman Willard, a skinny white boy from Texas, lovingly cradled his M16. That boy loved his weapon too much. He always seemed a little too ready to use it.

Miles slowed the vehicle in order to keep the two deuce-and-a-half trucks no farther than twenty-five feet behind them. Willie swiveled his head to check on them. In the lead truck were two crates of 2,000 rounds of .223 caliber NATO M16 rounds.

They cleared the back gate of the base. To get to the range they had to drive about one mile from the base down a bumpy, dusty road that paralleled the Sampang Bato River. Willie worried that its twists and turns would provide ample opportunity for the NPA to snatch the ammo in the trucks.

He used his legs like shock absorbers and kept his lips closed to keep from eating dust. He scanned the terrain ahead of them. They were about one hundred yards from Canyon Run where the road narrowed and ran for about fifty yards through a small gulch of thirty-foot-tall rock walls. During the rainy season the river, which snaked through the canyon, made the road impassable.

Willie thought the scenery looked like the backdrop for a western movie. He loved playing cowboys and Indians as a kid— felt like he was still playing now, protecting the wagon train behind him. Willie turned around and noticed the convoy had lagged behind more than he liked. He tapped Miles on the head with his boot. Miles looked into the rearview mirror and flipped Willie the bird.

"Come on homeboy, slow your ass down," Willie called out.

He tapped Miles on the head again. Miles brought the vehicle to a stop. Willie lifted his goggles and grabbed the binoculars that were hanging against his chest, scanning the canyon ahead of them. He swept the area in a 180-degree arc. Nothing seemed out of the ordinary. Below, Willard strained his neck, checking out the area in front. He may be off, Willie thought, but at least Willard took his job seriously.

Willie turned and saw that the trucks had closed the gap to within twenty feet. "Good enough," he yelled. "Let's keep up a good speed and keep'em moving in a tight formation through the canyon. Let's roll homeboy."

Miles pressed the accelerator, and they jumped forward. Willie hung onto the roll bar. He felt uneasy, like he was being watched. Wasn't that what the hero always said right before the injuns came streaming over the hill?

Willie lifted his binoculars once more, checking the ridgeline to his right, then his left. He focused on something on the road fifty yards into the canyon. It was a trench, like the ones that moles dug in his grandmother's front lawn back home. He hesitated. Probably nothing. But he could hear his hardnosed grandma in his head, "Fool. Of course that don't look right!"

Grandma was never wrong, he thought. He yelled at Miles to hit the brakes, then armed the 60, and yelled out: "Willard, lock and load."

Willard happily obliged.

"Willie, what the fuck, over?" Miles yelled.

"Back up now," Willie barked out, scanning the hills and the terrain to the east and west.

Miles did until he hit the bumper of the first truck. Willie turned and yelled to the driver of the big truck to follow him double time. They were reversing. Suspect ambush ahead.

"You shittin' us Willie?" Miles whispered as he nervously looked around them. He reached down and pulled his baby Armalite to his lap.

"Miles, pull up, let the trucks turn around, and head back. I want to cover their retreat."

Miles obeyed. Willard stood up in his seat aiming his M16 and daring anyone or anything to try something. Not on his watch.

NPA Commander Bong peered at the American vehicles from his hiding place in the tall grass on top of the canyon. Why had they suddenly stopped? They were still out of range. He wished he had some binoculars to see what was happening. He wished he had more of everything to fight against the government. His patrol needed weapons and ammo. Ten men and they only had six guns; all were barely serviceable World War II vintage.

For twelve hours they had waited for the convoy of Americanos. It wasn't an easy target but the large number of weapons and ammo was worth the risk. Bong wasn't afraid of the Yankees. Another unit in his sector had killed Americans before, and all the Yankees did in retaliation was to hide in their base.

His plan to ambush the convoy had been simple. It had to be: this was his first mission. He had no formal training, and the local NPA organization hadn't sanctioned the operation. Bong was out to make a name for himself. Step one: blow a homemade mine set on the side of the canyon road, destroying the lead security jeep. Step two: attack the other vehicles with rifles and grenades. Timing would be crucial.

He had watched the Americans perform the same exact convoy procedures along the same route last week. He couldn't believe his luck when an informant in the village near the range told him that a convoy was planned for today.

He peered into the distance. Something was wrong. Apparently his luck had changed. He angrily watched the American vehicles turn and disappear in a cloud of dust. With no truck of his own, he could hardly chase after them. He aimed his M1 at the fleeing trucks. They were in range, but he did not want to face heavy machine gun fire for nothing.

"Damn," he banged his hand onto the soft dusty ground. His ragtag group of farmers stood little chance of being players in the province without weapons.

His cousin, NPA Commander Hector, had said he was involved in a big operation going down today near Clark. Bong wanted to impress his cousin—make a name himself in the organization. What the hell went wrong?

Ten miles southeast of the canyon, parked alongside the Marcos highway, NPA Commander Hector and five heavily armed men sat in the back of a badly rusted dump truck. From the outside it looked like any of the scores on the roads this hot, dusty afternoon. They had hijacked it the day before from a construction company.

Hector tried not to worry about being seen. They were hidden from view by the tall walls of the truck and the spot he had chosen was away from most pedestrian traffic. At least it was shady. Hector took a deep breath and tried to focus on last-minute details.

A whistling from the front cab startled him. His brother, Ka Romeo, who was the driver, motioned at him through the small window. Hector walked over to the opening.

"Hector, we have just received radio confirmation that the vehicles are only ten minutes away," he whispered.

Hector gave his men the thumbs up and listened as Romeo started up the truck's diesel engine. The whole back rumbled and vibrated. Hector lurched to peer out of a crack in the large tailgate.

Commander Hector was thirty-four-years old. He had spent ten years working his way through the NPA ranks to his current position, commander of a Sparrow hit squad, a post he had held for the last three years.

He hadn't started out life as a guerrilla. He was from a family of peaceful rice farmers who had for generations worked land in a small barrio in Neija Ecija province northeast of Clark Air Base. But almost fifteen years ago his world shattered. Late one Saturday afternoon, his new and newly pregnant wife announced she was going to the river by their home to do some washing. He promised to join her shortly. When he did, she was nowhere to be found. Someone in the village had witnessed four Philippine constabulary troopers fleeing the area in their jeep. The next day her badly beaten body, bullet through her temple, washed up on the shore of the river.

After an investigation, the local police announced that Hector's wife was killed in a shootout with NPA in the area. They said she had drawn a pistol—an old rusty .45 that the policemen presented as evidence in their sham of a trial. Hector knew the real story: Four drunken off-duty constabulary men had raped and murdered his wife and his baby.

Something in him cracked: the injustice of the sham trial. He wanted revenge. He wanted justice. But mostly he wanted those fat, sweaty goons who had done this to die.

He got his wish. After the trial a local NPA contacted Hector, and he jumped at the chance to take up arms. He was taken to a camp in remote Kalinga Apayao province and received six months of rigorous physical training, practice handling weapons, and political indoctrination. The months in the mountains did little to cool his anger. On the day he returned home, he calmly walked into a seedy bar and shot two of the men who had murdered his wife. He enjoyed seeing the shock on their faces as he pulled out the gun and pulled the trigger. Even better was watching the large caliber bullets rip through their bodies.

Hector never did track the two others who took part in the murder. But from that point on, he always imagined his targets were those men. Every person he killed in the last twelve years was responsible for his wife's death.

He used a .45 pistol at close range, coolly and calmly. He had become a killing machine and earned his place high on the government's most-wanted list.

His hit today was not from the usual list of targets: informers, soldiers, corrupt policemen. Today it was American imperialists, a hit planned high up in the command chain. Nor was the operation the usual: a pistol at close range. This involved rifles and vehicles, and that made him a little uncomfortable. He found the anxiety strangely refreshing. It had been a while since he had felt anything when killing.

"Ka Hector." A face peered through the window of the cab. Hector acknowledged Benny who was sitting up front with Romeo. "The vehicles are approaching."

Hector closed his eyes and took a deep breath. He needed to focus. "*Salamat*, thanks Benny. All right brothers, it is time." They silently checked their weapons.

He felt the truck roll forward a few feet, preparing to pull out in front of the van with the Americans heading to Crow Valley: a half-dozen military personnel and civilians going to work at the range. Hector had been ordered to take out the van, killing all aboard if possible.

Hector tried to balance himself as he walked back and forth, squinting out of the crack in the tailgate. He was worried about visibility. The walls of the truck were nearly five feet high—good for hiding but difficult to see over. And they needed to see to fire down onto the van.

The truck bounced onto the road. Hector thought he could see the van several cars behind. The truck deliberately crawled along slowly, forcing vehicles behind to pass them. When the van of Americanos passed, it would pull alongside directly into the fire zone—like shooting fish in a barrel.

Hector had come up with the idea of using the truck and shooting down through the roof of the van. The Americans had mounted bullet proof Plexiglass inside their windows and doors; however, he was banking on the fact that the roof offered no such protection from a rain of bullets.

After a few minutes, the white van came into view just one car behind the dump truck. Hector laughed at how easy the van was to recognize: large American-built, dark tinted windows. "Stupid Americanos," he muttered. He would have used a Japanese-made van. It would have blended in with the local traffic.

Hector could see that the van driver was impatient. He kept pulling out, looking for the right moment to pass. "Comrades, be ready," Hector called out. The shooters moved to the side of the truck and squatted.

The van driver pulled out as Hector watched and waited. Timing was crucial. If they popped up too soon, the driver would spook. Hector raised his hand. "Now. Shoot through the roof."

The cadre aimed their weapons over the top of the truck wall and unleashed a loud volley. Hector had been right; the thin metal roof did little to protect the occupants from the hail of .223 caliber rounds. The Filipino driver was killed instantly, and the van swerved off the road and into a grove of banana trees. Two U.S. civilian contractors who repaired surveillance radars in the valley died from a combination of gunshot wounds and the force of the collision. Five GIs originally on the passenger list had pulled out at the last minute, the only break for the U.S. command in the whole grim incident.

As the big truck lumbered down the road, Ka Hector walked back to his men, who were calmly reloading and readjusting their weapons. One casually picked up empty shell casings. Hector wished he could have stopped to check out the van. He wasn't sure if they hit their targets. But they had to move fast to avoid police or roadblocks.

They sped toward the rendezvous point five kilometers up the road, where a jeepney would be waiting to take them to a base camp in the mountains for several weeks of rest before the next operation. Hector hoped his targets would be PC next time, maybe they would be the ones.

21

Manila

RAMOS STARED OUT OF THE heavily tinted windows of his small Toyota, watching the parking lot of Manila's premier shopping mall fill up. He left the engine running so he could keep his air conditioning on. It was eleven a.m., and the air was already hot and thick with acrid smoke from the thousands of vehicles shuttling along the maddening web of roads.

Snowden wouldn't be able to see him in the car, but Ramos had pulled into a prearranged spot outside the center where Snowden could easily make out the license plate. Snowden was again agitated on the phone when they spoke last night. Ramos had never heard the man as unhinged as he had become about Steel. Snowden was obsessed—wanted him tracked. Ramos still had no clue what Steel had done, and Snowden didn't say. Ramos was hoping, since Steel was in hot water with his command, Snowden would back off; instead he wanted more surveillance.

Ramos, in an effort to get Snowden to relax, had introduced him to a bar owner in the Makati district who provided entertainment for special clients. Snowden was supposed to have spent the last several days in a rented apartment relaxing with a bevy of young girls—and a few boys—who promised to take his mind off his troubles. But from his tone last night it didn't seem to have worked.

Ramos noticed a blue Datsun sedan slowly cruise by, then return and stop. Snowden pulled into the open spot next to Ramos' car and rolled down the window. Ramos exited the Toyota and walked over to the Datsun's passenger door; maybe it was time for Steel to disappear. Life was too short to see his *kuya,* brother, so distressed.

22

Safe House: Northwest Angeles City

NORTH KOREAN EMBASSY CULTURAL AFFAIRS Officer Lee Chang dong nervously paced around the small safe house that had been rented northwest of Angeles City. For the last eight months, he had gotten nowhere on his mission to find an American source to exploit for information on U.S. nuclear weapons in South Korea. Lee feared for the safety of his family back in Pyongyang. He had yet another new boss—the third in eight months. True to form, "Dear Leader" was reportedly punishing failure harshly.

Sitting at a table near him were two other North Korean operatives. Both hardened Special Forces types, one was supposedly an experienced interrogator, the other appeared to Lee to be no more than a brut thug. They were huddled with three NPA cadres, pushing around a map and photos. The embassy's interpreter was helping to translate for the NK operatives, whose English skills were limited.

They had been three weeks planning this operation—it wasn't going to be easy. This morning, he had been given the green light. Six hours from now they would begin. Lee opened a pack of local cigarettes. His hand shook as he tried to light one. He had hoped to be able to quit smoking, but he was back to his two-pack a day habit. This and the alcohol he consumed at night kept him sane.

Lee walked back over to the table and joined the group. He'd never been on an operation like this. He had always kept to the high-end, clandestine side of the house. If they were able to accomplish this, he couldn't imagine anything less than full out war with the Americans. But he didn't care about war. He cared about getting the job done and going home to his family.

23

Angeles City

S TEEL STOOD AT HIS BEDROOM window listening. That car horn sounded like Vida's. It wasn't. He walked over to his closet and dug through the hanging clothes looking for the silk shirt Cham had sent him.

He thought, with not a little smugness, that he had borne the last three weeks of house arrest surprisingly well. He kept to his routine; the only casualty was his morning run. He had to settle for the stationary bike.

His garden was progressing nicely: The pond was complete and he had planted the orchids Tony had sent. Steel's college professors were understanding and sent work home. The extra study time allowed him to finish the quarter off with strong grades.

He was still able to communicate with the office, though most everyone except Curtis treated him like a leper, avoiding interacting with Steel as if just a few exchanged words would implicate them in his self-destructive misadventure. Kuncker had barely said two syllables to him, awkwardly using the NCOs as intermediaries. Steel felt smug again for refraining to mention that he had predicted there would be more killings.

The deaths of the American contractors had stunned the 13th Air Force Command. Between the hit on the van and lucky near-miss for the convoy headed to the rifle range, the OSI and the cops had their hands full with all the investigating. Of course the restrictions were reinstated base-wide, so even if Steel hadn't been under house arrest, he couldn't have left his quarters. No one could.

Steel almost retched when he saw the photos of the bullet-riddled van, the bloodied contractors still strapped in their seats. He had taken that van many times. It could have been him bleeding to death on that dusty road. He hadn't known the murdered contractors. He thought he had seen them around: two older guys, both retired Air Force sergeants. Just in the wrong place at the wrong time. Shit. The NPA were cowards that way, going after the easy targets: working guys just getting through the day.

Of course, house arrest had put a screeching halt to his night life, but Steel found he didn't really care. Vida had been traveling most of the time on business. But today she was back and en route to Angeles to see him. They had a whole day and a half together, before she had to leave again. Staying confined to quarters was exactly how he wanted to spend their time together.

He had relayed to her only a broad picture of how he ended up under house arrest, but she seemed to accept it readily. He had given Rosa three days off and insisted she take it. She had hemmed and hawed, claiming he would never survive without her, but early this morning, he finally got her out the door. The last thing this romantic interlude needed was Rosa's frosty judgment. Had he let her know why he wanted her out of the house so badly, she probably would have had Jo Jo over too, both of them sniping at Steel and freezing out Vida—not the sort of scenario he had planned.

Another car horn beep made his heart race. He peered out the window and through the cracks in the gate and could barely make out the outline of a vehicle parked in front of his house. He rushed outside, putting on his shirt as he ran. It was Vida.

She wore beige pants and a white sleeveless blouse. She removed her large black sunglasses and shook her hair out with her hands. Without a word he pulled her into a deep kiss.

He only made it a few steps up the path to his house before he kissed her again, held her face in his hands and looked into her eyes. "It seems like a long time since I last saw you."

"That's the price you have to pay for being with a professional woman." She smiled.

"Worth it at any price." He led her into the house.

Once inside, he pushed her against the living room wall, nuzzling her neck and whispering in her ear.

"May I offer you a cold drink?" Steel murmured..

She pulled away from him, her face flushed, smiled and slowly unbuttoned his shirt. He undid her blouse and unhooked her bra, amazed that his hungry hands hadn't ripped off a few buttons in the process.

He cupped her breasts gently, lowered his head, and tasted her. She grabbed him and pushed into him. He slid his hand down her back onto her tight ass as she yanked him by the hair back up into a hard kiss. As he scooped her into his arms, she curled into him, skin on skin fueling his desire. He carried her to his bedroom.

"Easy boy. Whoa boy." Security Police Staff Sgt. Ronald "Tex" Reed whispered to his horse. He held the reins firmly with one hand and gently patted Old Smokey with the other. But the stallion wouldn't calm. Tex raised his hand, signaling the other two mounted cops in his patrol to halt.

Tex, twelve years on the security police force, had spent the last three at Clark, and he had recently extended for another two years. He loved Clark; it was home to him, his Filipina wife, and their two small children. He had grown up on a cattle ranch in West Texas but soon longed for adventure and signed up with the military to find it. When an opportunity came to join the only horse unit in the Air Force, he jumped at it.

For Tex, next to the open range of Texas, there was no place he enjoyed riding more than Clark's twenty-four miles of perimeter wall. He volunteered to do it as often as he could, especially now that he had been promoted to what would be mostly a desk job: technical sergeant supervising a flight of fifty cops.

The horses were ideal for patrolling the rough semi-jungle and scrub brush areas along the fence line. You couldn't see a thing if you tried to walk through the shoulder-high elephant grass, but sitting on top of a horse gave you an edge. The area around the base dump was especially difficult to access with vehicles and hence prone to infiltrators, mostly petty thieves. That's who the horse patrols were usually after—until the latest NPA killings. Now they were part of the heightened security throughout the base.

Tex strained his eyes trying to catch what it was in the small grove of bananas ahead of them that was spooking Smokey. The sun had gone down two hours ago; there was a half-moon providing a soft glow of light. Tex didn't mind the night operations; he had great night vision. Many of the other cops weren't comfortable with night duty, so it was easy for him to get the shift, especially on Friday's, when the younger troops wanted to go out and party. He couldn't blame them for that. He had done his share when he first arrived.

Tex redoubled his grip on the reins. Smokey was a big, lumbering horse, calm to ride, except when he was agitated, like now. Tex watched Smokey's ears twitching at something and he inhaled deeply; some smell vexed him. Tex didn't trust Smokey's eyesight, but the horse had a good nose.

It wouldn't be the first time that Smokey had alerted him to intruders hiding in the grass. Smokey had been bred for patrol duty. His grandsire had been brought over from California and mated with a local gray Filipino pony, a descendent of the ponies that arrived with the Spanish occupation two centuries ago.

Tex's young partners stood ten yards behind him. "Hey Sarge. what's the holdup?" Airman Martin softly called out.

Tex raised his hand signaling for silence and motioned them to dismount. He waved Martin to the left and Airman Green to the right.

With the NPA out there, he didn't like that they were sitting ducks on top of the tall horses. He too dismounted and dropped his reins to the ground. Smokey was trained to stay put.

Tex got a comfortable grip on his M16 and crept forward. He walked a few yards, pausing to listen. He could hear Smokey behind him snorting and stomping, still spooked. Tex kept moving cautiously through the waist-high *cogan* grass, his men to his right and left. If someone was hiding in the banana grove ahead of them, he hoped to Christ it was thieves and not NPA.

He stopped walking again and tried to wipe the sweat from his brow with the sleeve of his fatigue shirt. It was burning his eyes and blurring his vision. His bulletproof vest and Kevlar helmet were heavy and hot, but he was glad he had them on. At this point, he would trade some itchy heat rash, for the chance to live another day.

Tex walked another ten yards and halted again. He was twenty-five yards from the large ravine that ran parallel to the cinder block perimeter wall. It had been a favorite spot of fence jumping thieves until word had gotten out that nightly patrols were hitting the area hard.

A noise from behind startled him, and he jerked around quickly, resisting the urge to fire. Smokey's head emerged out of the darkness. Tex clenched his teeth, forcing down a cry. "Jesus, Smokey," he muttered.

Tex heard Green laugh nervously. Wide-eyed, Smokey bobbed his head up, his bridle clinking and jangling. Tex whispered to the horse, and Smokey stood still. In the distance, the noise of an engine broke the silence. Tex could see headlights. A vehicle raced out of the housing area towards the perimeter. What the hell were they doing? Tex reached for his radio and raised the volume switch, no longer interested in silence.

"Alpha One. Alpha One, this is Charlie One patrol, over."

"Charlie One, this is Alpha One. Read you, over."

"Alpha One, we have a vehicle in our area southwest of 13th HQ. Is it ours? Over." He waited.

"Negative Charlie One. HUMVEEs are accounted for in patrol areas."

"Roger Alpha One. We have unidentified intruders in vehicles. Charlie One is on it."

"Roger Charlie One. Will send backup over."

"Roger Alpha One we—"

The sounds of automatic weapons fire pieced the air. Tex hit the dirt hard. A bolt of white heat shot through his arm. He held his breath for a second waiting for the pain to increase, thought sure he had been hit. It took a few seconds for him to realize that he hadn't. He'd fallen on a sharp rock.

He could see muzzle flashes erupting from the banana grove.

"Shit. Smokey was right," he muttered aloud. He scrambled to his knees and tried to look over the grass to his men. "Green, Martin, are you hit?"

"No Sarge," they replied in unison.

"Good, keep your eyes open. Don't return fire until I give the order."

He turned to look for the horse. Smokey was nowhere in sight. Tex hoped he had high-tailed it out of there. He reached for his radio, but it had fallen.

From a squat, he popped his head up. The vehicle was moving towards the perimeter. More fire erupted from the grove, bullets whizzed overhead, and again he hit the ground. Tex crawled forward, found his radio, and called in. More cops were en route.

"Shit Sarge, who the hell is shooting at us?" Green screamed out.

"I'm eating dirt, Sarge," Martin's voice was an octave higher than usual.

More bullets cracked overhead. The staccato sounded more like AK47 than M16, Tex thought.

"Martin," Tex called out. "Looks like the shooters have moved from their original firing positions in the grove. Can you confirm this?"

"No Sarge. Let's return fire," Martin yelled.

"Negative. We're not shooting blindly. Green, I'm moving towards you, hold your fire." Tex rolled on the ground, jabbing himself with the nightstick and flashlight on his utility belt.

"Whoever they are, they are moving in the direction of the vehicles." Martin sounded closer than before.

Three more shots rang out from the banana grove; this time Tex saw the muzzle flash.

"Boys keep your heads down. I'm locked and loaded." Tex popped up on a knee and aimed his weapon at the grove, firing in a steady rhythm, shooting off five rounds. "Men, rally on my voice," he yelled.

But before they could respond, several big explosions in the distance rattled the night air. Tex felt the concussion of the blasts before he saw the fireballs. A hot wind raced overhead, showering them with dirt and debris. Tex jumped up to his feet to see what was happening, but encrusted dirt, blood, and sweat on his face blinded him momentarily. Wiping his eyes, he just caught three sets of vehicle lights dancing in the distance. They were driving through the wall.

Green and Martin edged up beside Tex and stared in disbelief.

"Sheeeet," Tex exhaled.

"They blew a hole in the wall," Martin noted and dropped the barrel of the rifle he was aiming.

Stunned and shell-shocked, Tex watched the lights disappear. He could hear the wail of police sirens in the distance. Those thieves must some gotten some prize to go through all that, he thought.

The truck rumbled through the gap in the wall, bouncing over the piles of rubble. Its front bumper was reinforced so it could have rammed through remnants of the concrete block if necessary, but it wasn't. The truck had been stashed base two days ago, under the pretense of moving furniture; staged mechanical problems enabled it to remain there until it was needed this evening. The enclosed back compartment was large enough to carry the ten man NPA unit and their prize.

The driver breathed heavily under his black bandana. He waved to an armed comrade, a ski mask totally obscuring his face, who stood blocking his path. He held up a hand and the driver stopped the truck. The driver nervously called out, "*Tayo na*, let's go, commander. We have the package."

The man gave a thumb's up. "Is the blocking force in yet?"

"No sir. We have not seen them." He peered into his side-view mirror. "Commander, the Americanos are not far behind. I could hear them firing at us."

"We wait for the blocking force."

The driver nodded and resumed looking into his mirror. The Americanos would soon be on them. They still had to drive up the riverbed several hundred yards to where the hijacked jeepneys waited. He had been told that half the group on the truck would transfer to the jeeps, while the other half would move out on foot with the package.

The jeepneys would head for the Marcos highway to distract the police; the real prize would head into the mountains with cadre on foot. He was not happy going with the jeepneys as that route would take them perilously close to town. He prayed there were no roadblocks.

The commander's face popped up in the passenger window and announced that the force was ready to move. The commander hung onto the side of the truck, standing on the running board. He yelled for them to go.

The driver's heart raced. They had actually succeeded in getting this far. He had always thought that the U.S. base was too fortified, impenetrable. He threw the truck into first gear, and it lurched forward. The Americans were going to be very angry. He didn't want to be anywhere around here.

Steel bolted upright, jarred awake by the harsh ring of his phone. Disoriented, he looked around his bedroom trying to find the time. Vida was wrapped around his chest, and he gently untangled her. It was one a.m. Who the hell could be calling?

"Hello," he croaked. It was Kuncker. Vida was awake now too.

"What? You're kidding. Anyone hurt?...One, a civilian guard killed, but where did he?...alright." Steel looked over at Vida's curves bathed in light from the streetlamp in front of his house. "Alright. I'll clean up and see you soon."

"Darling, are you okay?" Vida asked huskily.

Steel jumped back into bed and held her tight. But his mind was on what Kuncker had just told him. He couldn't believe it.

Someone had kidnapped General Smith—at gunpoint. Shit. He was just thinking about what cowards the NPA were for not taking on bigger military targets. Shit. Shit. Was it the NPA? It had to be. The fuckers. What balls.

"William, is there a problem?"

He couldn't say anything to her. "That was my boss. They need me at work. There is a big, big problem. I can't believe this. I've been sitting here alone for all these weekends, and then the one I finally get to be with you, this happens. I've got to go in."

"Oh no."

"I'm afraid so."

"I won't let them take you." She held him tightly.

"It's after one. I have to be in in an hour."

She slid on top of him and kissed him lightly on the lips, then on his neck. She began slowly rubbing her hips into his.

"You are making it very hard for me to leave."

"Yes, I see I am making this very hard," she laughed softly.

He closed his eyes and lay back. He had a few more minutes.

24

13th Air Force Command Center

Steel sat quietly in a straight chair pushed back against the wall of the imposing 13th Air Force Command Center briefing room. The dark furniture, burnt wood paneling, and soaring walls disappearing into heavy molding usually made Steel sleepy. This morning, however, they just put him more on edge, and he shifted nervously in his chair.

He looked over and nodded to Lieutenant Colonel Snowden, who was seated across the room. Snowden narrowed his eyes at Steel, then turned and began chatting to a nearby OSI agent. Steel would have thought it an odd response had he not become the poster child for military fuckups.

Steel continued to wait for his turn to brief the packed room. He mentally reviewed what he would say. He reached down and touched a box of slides under his chair, reassuring himself that the fifteen images would jog his memory when they flashed up on the huge projection screen on the opposite wall.

It had been over a week and a half since the general had been kidnapped. No group had yet stepped forward to claim responsibility, but the OSI was sure the NPA had done it for political reasons. Steel agreed it was an NPA operation, but he had a nagging feeling it was not entirely for political gain.

The general's disappearance had hit Steel hard. He owed

the man; they understood each other. Steel was going to find him.

Steel had a hunch about who was responsible for the operation but had decided against sharing his theory, at least for now. It would undoubtedly have raised eyebrows, and in any case he was still on the outs with management for the helicopter stunt. Kuncker had told Steel the house arrest was temporarily suspended and would resume after the crisis. But Kuncker remained cold, clearly unhappy that he had to rely on Steel's knowledge of the NPA. The reality was Kuncker had no choice.

In the days after the kidnapping, Steel quietly did his job, concentrating on figuring out what happened to the general and where he was being held. He called in all his chits with his Philippine military buddies, hoping that they could fill in parts of the puzzle. Thus far, however, they had little to add to his analysis.

Steel looked around the large conference table facing the briefing screen. After the kidnapping, an all-star team from out of country and Manila was flown in to take command. Today, all the key players sat around the table in big, leather swivel chairs, and many more new faces dotted the room. It would take a written score card to keep track of the agency representatives that had flown in to manage—or muddle—the crisis.

In charge was the Pacific Command's J-2, a one-star Navy admiral who had traveled from Honolulu. He sat at the head of the table dressed in what Steel thought looked like an ice cream vendor's uniform, mostly white with some braids, buttons, and medals thrown in for color; a naval Good Humor man. Steel tuned out the analyst to his left, currently and inexplicably discussing seasonal weather patterns, and thought how glad he was the Air Force uniforms weren't white: He'd never be able to keep his clean.

Steel watched the U.S. ambassador's representative at the meeting, a distinguished looking army colonel ask a polite question to a passing airman. Technically the ambassador was the senior American official in the country, but he had allowed the military to run the show since an officer was the victim.

Washington's response had been immediate and predictable: a dozen terrorism experts and other officials arrived with suitcases full of papers and communications gear. Sitting along the wall to Steel's left in what he thought of as the peanut gallery were military support officers and strap hangers, two dozen of them. Several appeared dazed, having just flown the twenty-odd hours from D.C. to land in the oppressive heat.

The group had come in at the same time as a kidnapping expert from the FBI. Also at the table was the new CIA station chief; with him sat two American civilians. Kuncker had whispered in Steel's ear, in a most reverent tone, that the civilians were intelligence analysts from CIA headquarters in Langley, the top Philippine experts.

One was a reedy young man with neatly combed hair and thick glasses. Next to him was a desperately thin blonde woman in her early twenties, currently loudly stating her opinions to anyone in range. Though her voice grated, she was good looking enough to attract a swarm of randy military officers milling around her seat waiting for introductions.

Steel smiled—the uncomfortable look on the station chief's face said it all. The loud lady analyst was an embarrassment. Steel had heard from friends who worked in DOD intelligence agencies in Washington that the CIA loved to recruit young, bright, but obnoxious Ivy League graduates. The catch was that the cachet of working for the company swelled their already large egos to the point where they became unbearable to work with—dead on the mark with this blonde.

Steel's eyes drifted to three burly guys with short hair and snug fitting polo shirts leaning against the wall. They had been introduced as Marks, Green, and Johnson—U.S. terrorism experts. Delta Force, thought Steel.

He took a deep breath and tried to relax. He had never before briefed this senior an audience. He watched small groups huddle around the room, nervously chatting. Only Americans for this this meeting, they had wanted to get on the same page before dealing with their Philippine counterparts.

Steel could see Kuncker move toward the J-2, hovering over his shoulder, clearly anxious to give the high sign to start the meeting. The J-2, however, was engrossed in conversation with the 13th Air Force vice Commander Colonel Thompson. Thompson, who had arrived back in the Philippines two nights before after a month in Thailand, looked like a deer caught in the headlights.

The silver-haired colonel was in over his head. It was well known he wanted to retire quietly and play golf on the base course. Steel figured the poor guy's golf handicap was about to take a nosedive.

Kuncker finally caught the admiral's attention. He checked his watch and gave the okay to start.

"Ladies and gentleman, we're starting the briefings," Kuncker called out, putting on his most professional voice.

The J-2, short and thin with red hair and freckles, must have been the kid everyone bullied on the playground, thought Steel. He had heard that the admiral had gotten the J-2 job because he was part of the Navy mafia that ran the Pacific Command. It didn't hurt that he had also roomed with the current PACOM commander when they were at the academy.

The admiral called the meeting to order. "Good morning. Thank you for coming here to deal with this crisis. I know some of you have traveled long and far. I want you to understand that this situation is being followed all the way up the chain of command to the president."

The admiral laid out how the team would operate. He announced that they had to complete the agenda on time because a senior Philippine military delegation would soon arrive for a joint session.

Kuncker, who remained at attention behind the J-2, leaned over and whispered to Thompson, who in turn announced that the OSI was now prepared to present an update on the criminal investigation followed by an intelligence brief. Colonel Morgan took the podium and began to read in a somber, monotone voice, which seemed labored for the native Tennessean. Steel could tell he was trying hard to mask his twang. The first slide on the big screen was a 35 mm photo of the general's quarters.

Steel had seen an advanced copy of this briefing, so he let his attention drift around the room. It was a carnival of experts. There was no way they could reach consensus. Too many egos and reputations were at stake. And even if they could come up with some sort of coherent plan, there was the Philippine government to consider. They had already made it clear that they would be directing any rescue operations. Absolutely no U.S. troops were authorized.

The U.S. ambassador had reiterated the Phil position in a letter the attaché presented to the admiral. Delta Force's hands would be tied. They were here in an advisory capacity only, too bad for the general.

Steel knew that the Philippine military leadership was not opposed to Delta Force support entirely; they still wanted guidance and equipment. But it was clearly a matter of pride; the Phils didn't want it to look like the U.S. had to step in.

The exclusion of Delta really worried Steel. There had been a joke around the command that the last place you wanted to be was a hostage waiting for rescue on the Phil military—considering their long history of bungling missions. They were known for getting more hostages killed than for killing kidnappers; he feared for the general's life, thinking the joke wasn't funny anymore.

It didn't take long for the OSI to complete their presentation; then Steel was called to the podium, where he stayed for an hour before returning to his seat against the wall. He took a deep breath when his butt hit the cushion. Overall, he thought it had gone well. He looked over at Kuncker who gave Steel a thumb's up, which was the most positive sign his boss had offered up in weeks. Steel smiled.

For another hour the group discussed how best to support Phil efforts, since the ambassador's letter had made it clear that direct U.S. action was out. The J-2 noted that the U.S.'s vast intelligence collection system was working overtime imaging and probing the electronic airways looking for any shred of information. Aircraft from Clark were flying clandestine reconnaissance patrols searching day and night for suspicious activity.

Phil army sources had reported that the truck used in the kidnapping headed north out of Angeles City towards Baguio City, where it was abandoned in favor of jeepneys. The Phils insisted that the general was being held somewhere in the heart of NPA country. They said that the odds of finding him were remote; and even if they did know where he was, it would be extremely difficult to get him out alive.

Steel checked his watch; they had been at it for nearly three and half hours. Other than the comments made by the shrill CIA woman, what bothered him most about the discussion was the fact that no one questioned the Phil army's information. During his briefing, Steel tried to suggest that maybe they needed some independent intelligence, but the J-2 stuck stubbornly with the analysis passed on by Gen. Ver.

Steel gritted his teeth and slowly raised his hand. He hadn't spoken since he sat down, letting Kuncker answer all the questions. Maybe the J-2 would just ignore him, that would probably be best, he thought. He tried not to look at Kuncker, who would be horrified by what Steel was going to propose.

The J-2 looked over and saw Steel. He pointed to him. "Captain?" Steel stood, with all eyes on him. "Yes sir. I would like to propose to the group an alternative theory. There have been reports of foreign agents, specifically North Koreans, operating in the area with NPA elements. Could it be possible the general's disappearance is connected? For example, I would think that North Korea would benefit immensely from General Smith's knowledge of U.S. war plans. He was stationed in Korea for years and was on the J-8 planning staff in the Pentagon."

Steel paused. He could see the strained look on the admiral's face. He could also hear the murmurs and laughter emanating from one corner of the room. The CIA analysts made no attempt to hide their disdain. He ignored them and continued. "Further, sir, I believe that General Smith is possibly being held somewhere in the area around the base, rather than up north." Steel sat down again and held his breath.

The J-2 leaned back in his chair and raised his eyebrows. Everyone in the room waited for his reply, except for the CIA woman, whose bony white hand immediately shot up in the air.

The J-2 grimaced. "Well, captain, that analysis is certainly from out in left field. Why would the North Koreans take the risk? I mean, kidnapping a U.S. senior military official would be tantamount to an act of war."

Kuncker quickly jumped in. "Well sir, that isn't really the 13th Air Force intelligence position. Captain Steel here loves to game out all possibilities."

Kuncker's interjection didn't surprise Steel.

The J-2 pushed forward against the table. "CIA, what do you think?"

The station chief beat the shrill woman to the punch.

"Far-fetched. There is really no way the North Koreans would ever do this. It would be an act of war. Our sources definitely point to the Communist Party of the Philippines. It has their fingerprints all over it. Our agency believes that they got him and have him locked away up north."

The J-2 looked around the room. "Anyone else here agree with the captain? If so raise your hand." He waited.

The OSI Commander Colonel Morgan cleared his throat. "Well, admiral," he said in his southern drawl, "I must say it is not mainstream thought, but we can't rule it out. General Smith sure was an interesting choice. They could have easily snatched some other high value targets off base rather than mount such a sophisticated operation on base. The general was clearly chosen for a specific reason."

The admiral nodded his head. "That's true. Seems like the NPA went through a lot of trouble to make a political statement."

Morgan continued, "There could be a foreign hand and General Smith just might be hidden somewhere in the labyrinth of hills around us. It makes some sense. Why risk moving him hundreds of miles when ten or twenty would work fine? When you think about it, damn, if I were a North Korean I would love to get at what's inside the general's head. Then, if you excuse my harshness, I'd kill him and make sure his body was never found."

"That's crazy. We've got to be realistic," the CIA woman blurted.

"Thank you, captain, for your analysis." The admiral looked around the room. "Majority rules in my book. We keep the current course and help the Phils look up north. For the general's sake, we need to stay focused."

Steel stared down at his shoes, angry at the CIA—dismissive fucks. His thoughts turned to Gen. Smith. His life must be hell.

General Smith could hear them buzzing in his ears; their tiny legs tickled his eyelashes. That was the only part of his face that still had feeling. He was sure it was a swollen mash of blood and dirt because that's what a face looked like after it had been slapped and punched for days. Forty-eight hours ago, the sound of the flies nearly drove him mad. He couldn't swat at them, not with his hands tied behind his back. Now, however, as he drifted in and out of consciousness, he welcomed their tickle. It meant that he was still alive.

He fluttered his eyelids slightly, trying to focus. He knew he was slipping in and out. Were the brutes still around? He couldn't tell if he was sitting in a chair or laid out on the ground. He knew he had been in a small bamboo hut chained to the wall but had lost track of the days.

There had been several interrogation teams. The first were Filipinos: NPA cadre who grilled him about operations at Clark. They were polite and friendly enough. That went on for two days. They rotated teams, keeping him hungry and deliriously tired, but they didn't get anything out of him. He was proud of that.

On the third day, however, he was blindfolded and the torture started. He became anxious, even scared. He had a feeling they weren't NPA this time; their accents were different. In his confused brain they sounded Korean and that disturbed him.

The beatings had been so severe, he was pretty sure he had sustained brain damage—but not so much that he hadn't recognized textbook torture. At first they had played good cop-bad cop, speaking in clear but broken English, pleading with him to cooperate so they could spare his life. Damn, they had sounded Korean. He hadn't trusted his judgment.

On what he guessed was day—or night—five of the

interrogation, one question had cut straight into his gut. The interrogator with the higher nasal tone had whispered in his ear: "Tell us about Operation Plan 5027. We want to know what targets the 3rd Tactical Fighter Wing have been assigned to strike. Where are the U.S. nuclear weapons located?" Panic had almost overwhelmed the beaten man. 5027 was the U.S. Operational War Plan for the defense of South Korea. They were fucking North Koreans. He knew too much. He knew everything. They sensed his anxiety. He answered nothing: just his name and serial number.

Hours later he remained convinced these were North Koreans. They had abandoned any subtlety and turned to brute physical violence. They sat him in a chair, tied his arms behind his back, and beat him with thin sticks across the face and head. When this didn't work, they had thrown a rope over a tree limb, looped the rope through his arms tied behind his back, and hauled him up so his arms twisted above his head. He had heard and felt his shoulder sockets pop out of joint.

When they finally removed his blindfold, he tried to look at the faces of his tormentors, but his eyes had been too swollen and bloodied to see them. He had seen, however, the sharpened bamboo slivers that they used to poke him. He had screamed in agony then passed out.

When he regained consciousness, he had given them some information, some low-level intelligence. It was a setback, but he'd resist again, give a little, making them work for every scrap. He knew that was all he could do—he was a dead man anyway. They would never let him see the light of day. How could they? They were goddamn North Korean agents. This could start a war.

He tried to focus again. Where was he? Were they there watching him? Was he sitting on that stump? He had no idea.

They had one major problem—time. They were in a

hurry. He wasn't. He had no place to go. That was okay. He could deal with brutality. No one was going to crack him. His alcoholic father couldn't beat it out of him; several sadistic older classmates at the Academy couldn't either. Hell maybe if he held out long enough, rescue forces could find him.

He thought of his wife and his boys. He was not going to die. He tried to purse his lips so he could spit, but they wouldn't work. He sank back into the darkness.

25

Angeles City

"What kind of movies do you like?" Steel called into his living room where Renaldo and Bong were sitting huddled together on a rattan couch. They pulled closer but didn't answer, just grinned at Steel. They were dressed in clean clothes and had both put on weight since he last saw them. They looked healthy, thanks to Father Rudy. "Well, my guess is you two are comedy fans," Steel walked over to a shelf in the living room and picked out a tape. "A Three Stooges, classic." He grabbed the remote, clicked on the TV, and pushed in the tape.

Rosa walked by them from the dining room carrying a tray of plates and bowls from the lunch they had just finished. She looked over at the boys and smiled, "William, they are having such a good time. They are good boys."

"Yes, ma'am," Steel agreed, sitting down next to them on the couch.

Father Rudy had encouraged Steel to learn more about the boys—start taking them on outings. So, taking advantage of his reprieve from house detention, he drove over to the orphanage and picked them up. He'd take them back home later on his way to a local restaurant to meet an antiques buyer who wanted to view the Japanese sword Steel had found.

Steel had made a rubbing of the Japanese script engraved on the tang of the sword and sent it to an expert in Texas who had advertised in a military magazine that he wanted to purchase World War II samurai weaponry. Steel was surprised to receive a call soon after from the Texas dealer who said his buyer would travel to the Philippines and contact Steel directly. From the expert's urgency and tone, Steel surmised the sword was indeed the work of a famous master. He was reluctant to sell it, but if the offer was good... The orphanage could use the cash as could Steel's own dwindling personal bank account—quick money until he could figure out how to sell the gold he had salvaged from the treasure trove.

He had contacted Cham and cryptically told him of the gold coins and Buddha chain he had. Together, they were trying to figure out how to get the gold to Bangkok. It wouldn't be easy. Steel would have to wait until Cham traveled to Manila—in a couple of months—and could use his classified briefcase to transport the gold back home.

Steel had made the mistake of showing Jo Jo his cut of the gold. Partly out of guilt for putting Jo Jo through the Devincia ordeal, Steel patiently put up with Jo Jo's daily parade of wacky ideas to convert the gold to cash.

The familiar Stooges theme music erupted loudly from the TV and pulled him away from his thoughts. "Alright, guys, now this is a funny movie. Crazy Americanos, Larry, Moe, and Curly," Steel lay back and prepared to enjoy.

It was a moonless night, except for the streetlight outside the wall of Steel's compound. Ramos had easily picked the metal gate lock and, with stealth, moved to what he hoped was the window to Steel's bedroom. He squinted, trying to peer inside.

A fast-spinning ceiling fan in the bedroom emitted a steady

high-pitched hum. Between the fan and the chattering insects, no one inside would hear Ramos. He slowly got up on tiptoe and pressed his nose against the metal window screen, trying for a better angle. He saw a dark form motionless on the bed.

Where were the boys? Ramos was sure he had found Steel's Achilles' heel. He had watched Steel take the boys from the orphanage, but now they were nowhere to be seen.

He shook his head, annoyed at himself for suspending the surveillance for a couple of hours in the afternoon. Had the boys left? Interesting that *Kuya* Snowden and Steel shared a secret proclivity, but Snowden's bent didn't just end with boys. Young girls were on his menu too.

What to do now? No confirmation of the boys. He released his grip on the telephoto lens and let the camera dangle around his neck. With a low-light film loaded, he had hoped to snap a few photos.

Ramos inhaled deeply, pulling his face into a frown. He decided to end this nonsense once and for all. He checked the body on the bed. No movement. He reached into his loose, black shirt, pulled a Remington .22 revolver from a shoulder holster, and methodically screwed a thin metallic cylinder into the barrel to silence the coming gunshot. He had loaded hollow point .22 rounds: good killing power but little chance of finding an incriminating intact bullet. He grasped the worn wood grip on the pistol. He liked a revolver—less chance of misfires—unlike a semi-automatic. Besides, if it took more than two rounds to make a kill, you might as well find a new profession.

Tony stared intently at the man in black standing outside Steel's bedroom. Tony and Pong-pet were camouflaged inside a magnificently flowering bougainvillea bush nearby. For half an hour, they had been quietly debating how to wake Steel, then the lowlander disturbed them.

Tony had felt the man's presence at the gate before he heard him fiddling with the lock. The man should have used a mango tree in Steel's neighbor's lot to scale the fence, like they had. But however he got there, it was clear to them that the noisy man had bad intentions for their friend Steel.

The two Negritos watched fascinated until the man pulled out his pistol. Tony moved forward immediately, and, without sound, pulled out a six-inch knife from a sheath on his belt. Pong-pet followed with his own blade in hand.

Tony leapt at the man and grabbed his shoulder just as Ramos shot, causing him to miss his mark. The bullet whizzed by Steel's head, impacting through the pillow and mattress and shattering on the hard mahogany floor.

Ramos instinctively jerked his weapon in the direction of his attacker and squeezed off another shot, sending the round flying two feet over Tony's head.

Tony reached up and grabbed Ramos's arm with one hand and jabbed the long-bladed knife upwards with the other. The blade struck Ramos just under the chin, severing his vocal cord, the tip of the knife ramming into his brain stem. Ramos pitched forward and was dead as he hit the ground.

Tony and Pong-pet stared silently at the body for a moment, then Tony bent over and wiped the blood from his knife on Ramos' shirt. Pong-pet squatted beside the body and poked it looking for signs of life. Satisfied the intruder was dead, he whispered. "Do you think Steel will be angry with us for killing him?"

Tony looked up at the bedroom window, listening for any movement inside. He waited for a moment then shrugged, "I hope he is not dead from the gun."

"Let's check." Pong-pet moved towards the window and

leaned against the wall. Tony climbed on his back and peered in for a moment, staring intently until he saw Steel's chest rise with breath. He slipped off of Pong-pet's shoulders. "I think he is alive."

Pong-pet nodded, then moved back to the body and picked up Ramos's camera. "What is this weapon?"

Tony smiled at his rural cousin. "It is a camera for taking pictures." Tony looked around on the ground, found Ramos's pistol and pocketed it. Squatting on the ground next to the body, Tony thought for a moment and said, "I think it is best Captain Steel knows nothing of this. He will not be happy, and I want his mind clear without problems so he can focus on helping us. I think he is not too good with too many problems."

Pong-pet nodded. Tony continued, "Go down the street, find our cousin in the trike, and tell him to come by the front of the house. But first, help me grab this body and move this man close to the door. We will move the body in the trike, and Edwardo can dump it *doon*." Tony pointed to the mountains.

Tony looked up at the window and smiled. How could Steel sleep so soundly? He must have a strong dream world that keeps him busy. They picked up the body and moved it to the gate.

After the second try, Tony spoke louder and this time banged the screen with his hand, causing him to wobble awkwardly on Pong-pet's shoulders. Eyes still clenched shut, Steel waved a hand above his head trying to clear away the high-pitched buzzing. Failing, he reluctantly opened one eye, then the other.

"Captain Steeeel? Are you there?" Steel sat up. The noise was outside his window. He reached toward his bedside table and fumbled for his knife.

The clock there read 2:00 a.m. He shook his head; a heavy

sleeper, he always had problems waking. He stood and carefully approached the window, knife in hand, wondering who the hell was out there. Jo Jo, or maybe even Renaldo? Steel couldn't see a thing until Tony's face popped up.

"Shit Tony! What the hell are you doing?"

"Captain Steel, I sorry to have to scare you this early morning. But I need talk with to you about important problems."

"Tony, it's fricking 2:00 a.m. What the hell could be that important?"

"I have news maybe on the general," Tony's barely audible response stunned Steel. He put on his pants and headed for the front door.

As Steel moved to close the door behind Tony, he startled at the sight of Pong-pet standing on the porch smiling. "What the hell? Is that Pong-pet? I thought he was blown up." Steel walked over and touched Pong-pet to confirm he wasn't dreaming.

Pong-pet smiled and said, "No sir, Pong-pet is not to dead. A pig was scared and ran into the trap, not the Pong-pet."

"Wow, this is great news. I thought for sure you were dead."

Steel motioned for Pong-pet to join Tony inside. Steel directed them to the couch. Tony perched on the edge, while Pong-pet remained standing, eagerly taking in the room. Steel slumped in a chair and glared at them then asked, "Tony is that blood?"

Tony glanced down quickly. "Ah, yes sir, Tony had killed chickens today." Impressed with his quick thinking, he smiled at Pong-pet.

Steel again wondered if this were just a dream. "What are you talking about, Tony? What do you mean the general?" Word of the general's kidnapping had crossed the world. It was especially a hot topic in the Philippines and around Angeles City. It would be like Tony to try to capitalize on it.

Tony sat quietly. Steel could see he was gathering his thoughts. Steel asked him again, this time in Aeta.

Tony replied. "I think a Negrito has seen a white man in the mountains. I think maybe it could be the general."

"What? What Negrito? What mountains?"

Tony sat in silence. Steel took a deep breath. He was starting to wake up. Goddamn Tony and his lies. Steel looked at the man and was surprised to see him look straight back, something he rarely did. "Tony, I really don't have time for this crap. It's late and—"

"Sir, they killed my uncle."

"What has that got to do with the general?"

More silence. He studied Tony's face. A single tear slid from Tony's right eye. My God, Steel thought, Tony really was upset. "Who killed your uncle?"

"The men who taken the general to the mountains."

"What?" Steel thought for a moment. "Oh... he was the Negrito guard killed by the NPA when they snatched the general. That was your uncle?"

Tony nodded.

"You're kidding."

Tony shook his head and another tear fell. He wiped it with the back of his wrinkled, brown hand.

"What makes you think it was the general?"

"Tompong says that his cousin saw a white man with a rice bag on his head—to hide his face. He was to being led on a rope into the mountains. There were many men with guns, NPA and maybe some Chinese too." He used his hands to pull his eyes, making them slanted.

"Chinese. Did you say Chinese?"

Tony nodded in affirmation.

"How could he tell the man was white if his face was covered?"

"He said that he moved close to them, and the man smelled white."

"Maybe the white man is Japanese, not American?" Steel paused. "No white men in the hills around here—especially ones tied up and led with a rope."

"No sir, I don't think it is Chinese man—it is the general. I know that."

"So where did he see the American and don't say *doon*." Steel said in English, pointing a menacing finger.

Tony stared at the finger and thought. "He said they were going close by to the sacred water spring. You remember the spring, that I showed to you."

"Yes, I remember that place."

"They were going to another valley close to there I think."

Steel stared at Tony. "Tony, why the hell should I believe you? You're just trying to make some pesos off of me."

Tony jumped off the couch. "No, Captain Steel, I am not doing it for the money."

"Then why?"

Tony whipped out the Ramos killing knife from his waistband and pointed it at Steel's face. "Because I want to kill all of them," he screamed out in English. "They must pay for my uncle's death. He was my favorite in this life. He taught me all about the mountains and the spirit world. He was my father to me. My father died when to I was a baby. He was my father to me. They shot and killed him dead. He did not have to chance to fight. He was very old, and he could not see too well, and his gun did not even to work."

"No, his gun not to work." Pong-pet shook his head matter-of-factly.

"It was broken now for many years," Tony gestured wildly with the knife.

Steel swallowed hard. He had never heard Tony speak so

passionately. "I see. Alright, revenge is a good motive." Steel gently pushed the blade away from his face. Tony re-sheathed the knife as quickly as he had pulled it out.

"I am sorry to have lied to you in the past time. I did it in the past for the money and to joke at the Americans. But now, I am truly sorry. You have been a good friend to Tony. You have the Negrito spirit in your heart. Now I am swearing to you on my uncle's spirit that this is not a lies."

"Tony, I believe you."

"Thank you for that," Tony said. "It is also to the true—the forest spirits have told to me. There is other reasons I for too much also want to help find the general. My uncle's daughter, Metta, she is my cousin. She works in the house for to next door to the general, as the house girl. She helps to the general's house girl when he has the big happy parties. The general's wife is the—the er—good woman. She gave money to my cousin to buy expensive medicine for her sick baby. It saved the baby's life. We family have much *utang* to wife to the general. Now she is so sad the crying, crying, crying all the time my cousin say. My cousin ask me to go and find the general so her wife is not crying. I told I do this for her and for my uncle."

Steel shook his head—with the Negritos there was always drama layered upon drama. "Have you told anyone about this?"

"No."

"Damn Tony! I guess it's—"

A light flicked on in the kitchen. Rosa crashed into the living room with a broom in hand, prepared to do battle with any intruder.

"William? My Jose! You scared me. I heard voices," she dropped the broom to port arms.

"Sorry, Rosa. Just us. So what were you going to do? Sweep the robbers to death?" He pointed to the broom. "Hey, while you're up, how about some instant coffee? You guys want some coffee?"

Tony nodded.

"Good. We have a lot to discuss."

It was an hour before Steel was back in bed. He thrashed mangling the sheets, trying to digest all that Tony had told him. Tony had said he knew where they took the general. Christ, what the hell to do? He'd have to notify the task force, tell the J-2 so he could organize the Phils to form a rescue. Steel turned violently onto his back and covered his face with a pillow. There is no way that the J-2 would believe him, not any more than they believed him during the brief. "Yeah, I can hear myself now," Steel said aloud. "Excuse me sir, a Negrito told me that he knows someone who thinks he saw a hooded white man in the mountains. Oh, no sir, he didn't actually see him, he smelled him—or his friend did—and don't worry, I can back it all up. The mountain spirits all confirmed the sighting. Shit."

Steel knew that even if they did believe him, the Phil army would insist on taking the lead. He didn't want the general killed in any botched rescue. Still, Steel had to do something. Would the J-2 have the balls to run a clandestine operation against the Phil government's wishes? He doubted Washington would jeopardize their relationship with Marcos by letting the command go it alone. The U.S. military needed access to bases here. He had told Tony not to tell anyone. Steel needed time to think this through. He'd bounce this off Jo Jo as well. But now he needed to get some sleep.

26

13th Air Force

Walking out of Kuncker's office, Steel angrily snatched his hat from his desk. He had been in a foul mood the last three days, ever since Tony's midnight visit. No one was doing a fucking thing to rescue the general, poor bastard—not Steel, not the command. Curtis walked up to Steel and put a hand on his shoulder. "Hey, Cap, don't mean nothing. You're just trying to find the general the best way you know how. Fuck'em man."

"Thanks, Curtis," Steel smiled half-heartedly.

"No problem Cap. We all think you're the man."

"Yeah, hang in there, captain," Colston, the admin sergeant, called out over his shoulder as he typed.

Curtis, and everyone else in the office, had overhead Kuncker's tirade when Steel suggested they tell the J-2 Tony's story. Kuncker would hear nothing of it, especially the part about a clandestine rescue. Then he lit into Steel again for bringing it up at the J-2 meeting the other day, called him unprofessional, the poorest excuse for a military officer Kuncker had encountered in his twenty-two years of service.

"Curtis, if anyone is looking for me, tell them I have a medical appointment—I'm getting my head examined or something. I'm taking the rest of the afternoon off." He was pissed at Kuncker for reaming him out and frustrated at the futility of the task force.

"Got your back, Cap." Curtis extended his hand.

"Thanks, Curtis," they shook.

Steel walked out to his truck. He didn't have a medical appointment, but he definitely felt sick. The task force was impotent—all fire power, but no fire. They sat around gaming out scenarios and criticizing the Phils for their incompetence. It had been two weeks since the general's disappearance and the number of participants had dwindled; even Steel was spending less time in the conference room. All the really key players from the OSI and the embassy were either out in the field collecting information from the Phils or waiting for them to hand over something.

He didn't give a second thought to cutting out early. He was off tomorrow and possibly even Sunday. Vida was out of town again. It promised to be another slow weekend.

Or maybe not. He jammed the truck into gear and raced out of the parking lot. He hadn't seen Jo Jo in a couple of days. He needed to talk to him.

"*Kuya*, this is not a good idea." Jo Jo put his hand on Steel's shoulder. "I have to be frank with you. You know I think of you as a brother, a younger, hot-blooded not-so-handsome brother. Let the military handle this; they are the ones trained to fight. You are a lover, not a mercenary," he sat down hard on the couch in Steel's living room, making it slide across the slippery wooden floor.

"Jo Jo, I know it seems like a bad idea, but what choice do I have? The general will die if something isn't done. The U.S. isn't going to act on anything I say, and even if they did believe me, they would only pass the info on to the Phil army.

You know they will fuck it up. I can't risk the general's life like that. I owe him. I have the *utang-na-loob*, blood debt to him."

Jo Jo crossed his arms and shook his head. "I hope to Jose that you will think about this for a few days and—"

"We don't have a few days. It has to be done now. Today. Friday. The longer we wait the greater the odds the general will be dead."

Jo Jo put hands on Steel's shoulders and looked him in the eye. "I still can't understand how for once you can believe that little son-of-mother-whore Tony. You never have believed him before."

"I know. It's ironic—I'm gambling my whole life on him. I'll either be a hero or in jail."

"Or dead. Don't forget dead," Jo Jo made the sign of the cross.

"Okay *lang*, death's a possibility too."

"Even if you live, your patron general will likely not be there to save you this time. They will hang you."

"Yeah, that they will. If it goes badly, I'll say I was kidnapped by the NPA and held for a few days, then escaped."

"Oh, now who will believe that fairy tale?"

"That's my story."

"Why don't you contact that Phil marine unit that captured the good Colonel Antonio and rescued us. They were a crack outfit. They could retrieve the general and—"

"That's just not realistic. I can't tell the Philippine government what to do. I can't guarantee that it would happen. The Phil army isn't going to stand by and let the marines run the show. They'll insist on an army-only debacle."

Jo Jo picked up a glass of Rosa's ice tea and gulped it down. "What equipment will we need? And when will we go? I have lots of questions before I'm willing to die for this general friend of yours."

"I'm not ready to die either," Steel checked his watch. "It's getting on three p.m. I've got to make it to the bank before it closes, and I got a couple of other stops to make. We are going to need weapons."

"Are you mad?"

"No argument. I'm not doing this unarmed. I'll get the cash. Think about who we can get weapons from. Off the top of my head, a couple of baby M16 Armalites, extra clips, say a dozen or so grenades, and at least a dozen M1 Garand rifles and ammo—or as many as I can afford. Maybe, two .45-cal pistols as well. I'm figuring on assembling a force of at least a dozen Negritos and you and me. We'll get June involved. We are going to be armed and dangerous."

"It's the dangerous part that worries me."

"I want to leave Sunday morning. I'll drop by Tony's on the way home and tell him we will go Sunday."

"Okay *lang*."

"Okay *lang*. I'll see you in a couple of hours. I can't do this without you."

"I'll be here preparing the gear we have on hand. We'll need a lot of equipment, I think."

"You decide," Steel said as he headed out the front door.

Joseph, the yard boy, saw Steel and quickly walked over to him. "Hello, Captain Steel, are you leaving?"

"Yes Joseph, I have an errand to run. Get the gate for me."

Joseph walked over and opened the gate, and Steel drove out. Joseph watched the truck disappear down the road. He shook his head, worried that he had made a bad decision—not informing his boss about the pool of blood in the garden and the trail leading out the gate. To Joseph it looked like something, or someone, was killed and dragged. He had reported it to Rosa, but she had convinced him that telling Steel was a bad idea. Rosa said Steel was under too much pressure at work to deal with such a problem. Joseph was to clean up the mess and keep quiet.

Maybe Rosa was right. Joseph scanned the gravel path. There was no mess now, thanks to him. "*Bahal na*, so be it," he muttered to himself and closed the gate.

Steel rolled down his window and called out to a lowland boy standing in Tony's front yard. "Where is Tony?"

The boy's eyes narrowed and he frowned. He obviously hadn't seen Steel before. Steel repeated his question in Tagalog.

Tony appeared in the doorway in the process of pulling on a T-shirt, his wife Gina beside him. He looked like he just awakened from a nap. He slowly walked over to the truck. Steel waved to Gina, who smiled and waved back.

"Can you be ready Sunday morning? I want to go." Steel whispered in Aeta.

Tony nodded. "This is for the good news sir."

"Good. Have you heard any more news on our friend?"

"No."

"We'll need some good Negritos. Men you can trust."

Tony pushed closer to the window and whispered in Aeta, "We can go to June and get some men. I don't trust the Negritos here in my barrio. They are too much to the *barangay* soft life. We need mountain Negritos."

"Okay."

"I will tell to the June to be ready for the Sunday morning with some men." Tony gestured towards the mountains.

"Can we trust June to not tell the Philippine army or PC? He works for the PC." Steel was still bothered by June's coziness with Panglio.

"Yes, he does work for the PC and the army, but he plays them like a jungle cat," Tony laughed. "I will tell him to our plan. He loved my uncle too, like the brother. They fought in the war together against the *Haponese*. This is Negrito blood war."

"Tell June I will have money to pay him and his men—U.S. dollars. I will pay them well. I will have weapons and ammo for them. This isn't going to be an easy job. It could be dangerous. Do you understand?"

"Yes sir. We will know the danger of this. We want no money to do this. June will want no pay for this."

"Alright, Tony, we'll come here and get you Sunday morning."

"No sir, you go to June's. I will be there talking to him for the plans. I do not want the people here to know my plans. *Diba*?"

"Good idea. One more thing. Why do you need me? I mean I will just slow up the Negritos. Couldn't you do it without me?"

"No sir. We need for you to get the guns and for to help us make the plan. You can talk to the general and help him move to a safe place. We will find him and you help us to go get him. The NPA have the guns. We might to need guns to fight them. But maybe not." Tony pulled out his knife with the same motion he had displayed a few nights before. He whispered, "The knife can silently work like death in your dreams. Maybe the NPA don't wake up," he motioned across his own neck with the knife.

Steel watched Tony walk into his house, pleased he wasn't on Tony's death list. Tony turned and waved. What a turn of events—he and Tony were allies. Steel started the truck and headed back home, reaching out to pat the large brown bag full of cash sitting on the passenger seat.

There were a lot of $20 bills in there, $7,000 worth to be exact. He had sold the sword for $15,000, a small fortune. He put aside over half of it as a hedge against the mission going badly, and the Air Force giving him the boot. It was his life savings. The other half of the cash he would use to finance the mission. At least there was the promise of selling the gold he had liberated. That was more future financial padding.

He had no idea how much the weapons would cost. He figured if he pulled this off, he'd get the government to reimburse him. The bank manager had seemed suspicious of Steel's request for the large amount of cash. He said he was buying a house. The guy would probably notify the OSI anyway. As per regulation, he wouldn't provide Steel anything larger than a $20. He wished he could have gotten $50 or $100 dollar bills. U.S. servicemen weren't allowed them lest they put them on the black market off base.

On the floor of the passenger side sat two green military issue equipment bags. After his trip to the bank, Steel had stopped by the helicopter rescue squadron to meet with Staff Sgt. Ricky Scott, a highly respected parachute rescue sergeant, friend, and instructor at the Crow Valley Range. Steel talked Scott into lending him a couple of combat medic kits, a pilot rescue radio, a spare battery, and some orange smoke signal flares.

Steel had concocted a story about needing them for a training exercise. Scott shook his head and laughed. While the management saw Steel's helicopter incident with the Phils as criminal, it made him legendary among the troops. "Just get them back to me in one piece," Scott had said.

Steel checked his watch. Six p.m. His next step was the weapons. He knew they were readily available in the shadowy arms markets around Angeles; all that was required was cash.

The arms dealers got the majority of their goods from unscrupulous Phil troops, who sold either their own weapons or those they captured from the NPA. It was ironic, Steel thought, that the NPA also purchased weapons from these merchants. In some cases, Phil military were killed with their own weaponry.

The weapons sellers were dotted among other black marketers hawking goods and equipment pilfered from the base. An OSI agent told Steel you could buy anything from office supplies to F-4 aircraft parts there. There were always ongoing OSI sting operations trying to stem the flow. Sometimes they even nabbed U.S. personnel. The temptation was great to buy low-end items, like food and booze, and even valuables like stereos and sell them for a tidy profit. He hoped Jo Jo could find a dealer with the equipment Steel was looking for at a reasonable price.

"I found a man who will see us everything we need." Jo Jo was talking before Steel even got in the door of his house. "The M16s for $250 to $500 each and the other stuff even cheaper."

Jo Jo said he would go alone and make the purchase this evening. If they got wind it was for an Americano, the price would be raised accordingly. He would provide a down payment of forty percent and pay the balance on delivery.

It was nine p.m. when Steel flagged down a trike in front of his house. An hour earlier he had given Jo Jo an envelope of cash and wished him good luck. Steel couldn't just sit home and wait. He decided instead to check off another item from his list.

He sank down deep into the seat on the trike; there were still restrictions on, and he wasn't supposed to be riding around town. The last thing he needed now was to be busted for this trivial offense. He had bigger crimes to commit.

He had the driver take him to the subdivision where Curtis Washington lived.

He rang the doorbell on Curtis's gate, but nobody answered. Steel rang again and then a third time. No one home. Steel smiled. Curtis must be out on the town. The restrictions weren't holding him back. He jumped back in the trike and told the driver to head for the bar district. He knew Curtis's favorite place, although he had never been there himself.

The driver said he knew where the Soul Place was. They pulled into a dark dirt driveway that smelled like sewer and burning trash. The Palace wasn't visible from the road. Curtis was right: only those who knew of it could find it. It was one of a half-dozen bars with a black clientele. Curtis had said the Soul Palace was more of a private club than a public bar. It was Curtis's home away from home. He told Steel that a Filipino version of soul food and Marvin Gaye tunes were on the menu every night.

The driver pointed to a ramshackle *sari-sari* store and said the Soul Palace was behind it. Steel looked around, hoping he wasn't about to be jumped and robbed. Steel told the driver to wait, grabbed a large manila folder, and headed into the storefront. Inside, an old woman sitting on a big rattan chair behind a cluttered counter scrutinized Steel. He was about to ask her about the club, when he saw the crudely made sign above a door in the back reading "Soul Palace." Steel smiled: One man's dump is another man's palace.

Lionel Richie's soothing rhythms hit him as he pushed through the wooden beads hanging behind the door. Once inside, it took a moment for his eyes to adjust. A smoky mixture of cigarettes and stale marijuana hung in the air. Three girls behind the bar openly glared at him. "No surprise there," thought Steel, "First of all, I'm white; second of all, I'm white; and third, I'm white and violating the restrictions. They probably figured me for an undercover cop."

On the opposite wall through the haze, he could see a white-haired black man slumped on a dirty worn couch. Sitting on either side of him were two topless girls, both wearing jeans shorts. They looked like twins. The man had his arms around both of the girls and was casually fondling their breasts. The girl on his left had her hand inside the front of his loose sweat pants. The old man's eyes were glazed, doped. He barely acknowledged Steel, certainly didn't move his hands from the twins. Steel assumed he was probably one of the dozens of retired GIs who lived in the area.

Angeles City was home to an eclectic group of American ex-pats. Steel had heard stories about a house somewhere on the outskirts of town where drugged-out American Vietnam vets lived with their Filipino wives and mestizo kids. During the war they had been medevac'd to the hospital at Clark. They lived communally off their pooled VA checks. Steel had never found the house. Probably more legend than fact.

A short, fat waitress approached him and looped her chubby arm through his. "Hi *pogi,* handsome, you want something the *giling giling,* sex," she laughed and gyrated her hips. She switched to Tagalog and spoke to the girls behind the bar. "Maybe he is police or maybe he thinks he is a black. But his skin is too white and his dick is too small for sure," she laughed again, shaking the rolls of fat on her neck.

One of other girls added in Tagalog, "Or maybe he wants the Filipina girl who knows how to have sex with the black man?" They all laughed, several high-fived.

Steel smiled and replied in Tagalog. "No sex for me, thanks. I'll just have a beer. But I'll have you know, it is this big." He held his hands up measuring out an absurd length. The girls roared with laughter.

As he sat down at the bar, he heard a familiar voice behind him. "Sheeet, Cap S, what the fuck?"

Steel turned to see a group of black GIs and several girls emerge from a side room. Curtis was foremost, dressed casually in black T-shirt, pajama pants, and rubber sandals, looking like he had just stepped out of the shower. He took a seat next to Steel. "This is a shock. What the hell you doing here, don't you know there's restriction on?"

Steel grinned. "Don't you?" He offered his hand. "So you got a bell and a lookout. The old lady out front rang a buzzer when I showed up."

Curtis smiled. "Yeah, we'd be hiding in the back. We got a lookout for the man."

"You want a beer?"

"You buying?" Curtis smiled.

"Of course."

"Naah, your money's no good here." Curtis motioned for a beer. "Remy, you sweet thing, put all the Cap's fun on my tab," he leaned in close to Steel. "Now tell me what the hell's up. First time I've seen you here—violating the restrictions and everything. I'm shocked and appalled." He laughed and slapped five to a tall thin man who had joined them. "Cap S, this brother be Martin. Martin, say hi to my man, Cap S."

"Call me Steel."

Martin shook hands with Steel, then turned and left without a word.

"Mr. Quiet there."

"No offense. He don't like whitey, especially white officers."

"Goddamn, Curtis, this place is a dive."

"Excuse me, this here's my living room you're insulting," the old stoned black man called out.

"Sorry." Steel answered sheepishly. Apparently, the man wasn't as zonked as Steel thought.

"Otis, he don't mean nothing. This place is a dive."

"You'd better watch your mouth, young'un." The man tried

to stand but fell back onto the couch wobbly-legged, into the arms of the bare-breasted women.

"Sheeet, Cap. You been spending too much time at the O club. Now, you want some good soul loving, you come here. Mama-san and Otis can cook some mean ribs and greens just to name a few. I eat here at least three times a week, and it hasn't killed me yet. Can't say the same about other places."

Steel nodded.

"So anyway, what brings you here?"

"Can we go someplace private?"

"That don't sound good," he searched Steel's face. "We can use the back room." He got up and Steel followed.

Steel laid out his folder on a small table in the back room. He pulled out a map and unfolded it. "Goddamn, it's dark in here. Is there a light?"

Curtis walked over and pulled on a chain hanging from the ceiling. "That's all we got, Cap. Probably don't want to see too much in here anyway."

"Here it is in a nutshell. I think I know where the general is being held. I'm going to find him. I'm leaving soon. I want to show you where I'll be heading so you can point rescue parties to us."

"Cap S, have you lost your fucking mind?" Curtis blurted.

"Keep it down, Curtis."

"Sorry Cap, I'm going to have to be frank with you. Sir, have you lost your goddamn mind? You know the hot water you're in already."

"I know that, but I know where he is, and I'm not about to let the Phils get him killed. And you know the U.S. doesn't have the balls to run a rescue mission ourselves. The only option is for me to try."

"No offense, but you ain't exactly Chuck Norris."

"I know that. I'm taking a group of Negrito tribesmen."

"You mean those little brothers you are always on about."

"Yes. If we can find him, they'll be able to take him back."

"Those goddamn NPA who snatched him are armed to the teeth. They'll shoot your Negritos up. You ain't even got a gun yourself."

The corner of Steel's mouth twitched.

"Don't tell me you got yourself weapons."

"I've taken care of that."

"Get the fuck out of here. When you going?"

"Soon, maybe Sunday morning if I can get the details worked out."

"You mean your funeral arrangements?"

"Oh come on. You already have me dead."

"Nah, I ain't got you dead. I know if you say you can do it, you're just fool enough to get it done."

"Thanks."

"You want me along?"

"Nah, appreciate the offer though. I need you to be around to tell the cavalry where to find us. Here's the plan. When we snatch the general, we will likely be on the run. He'll probably be in bad shape, so we'll have to make a litter to carry him. We will head northwest from this valley. This is where one of the Negritos thinks he is being held."

"Damn. What makes you think he's down here instead of up north?" Curtis pointed to a location on the map.

"It's simple. A Negrito thinks he saw him being led into the mountains."

Curtis raised his eyebrows.

"And it gets worse," Steel closed his eyes and rubbed his forehead wearily. "I think North Korean agents are involved. They are interrogating him for information on U.S. battle plans for the defense of Korea. That's what I think. It's only a wild ass guess. But it's my gut feeling."

"You mean those reports of North Korean agents I found for you," Curtis's eyes widened.

"That's them. A Negrito said he saw Chinese guys with the general. My guess is those Chinese guys were North Korean agents."

"Damn. They'll kill him for sure."

"Yeah, once they are done with him. So that's another reason why I need to do something now."

"Here, show me on the map so I know what I'm looking at." Curtis leaned on the table and stared intently at the map.

"I've circled the area and the escape route we'll shoot for. The plan is once I've got the general, I'll send my best man to the main gate. His name is Tony. He has a worker ID. I'll give him my military ID card and a note saying we are on course. The cops will call the watch. Once you hear about my ID, you can show Kuncker this map. Hopefully 13th can send choppers out to get us. I'll have a radio with us so we can make contact with the helicopters."

"Man. The shit is going to hit the fan on Monday when you don't show up for work."

"Yeah, I know. Don't say anything until you get word from Tony. I don't want anyone coming too soon. If you don't hear anything from me after seven days then give them the map. Tell them you found the note and the map in the file cabinet along with this letter from me. I don't want you implicated. If I can't find the general, I'm going to have to come up with another story to cover my ass."

"Yeah like what?"

"Don't worry about that. I don't want to involve you in this any more than I have to."

"I don't care about that. You just watch your ass, okay."

"Okay."

Curtis leaned over the map. "Alright, let's go over this one more time."

Steel took a deep breath and began again.

27

Barangay Magalang

Steel, M16 in his lap, sat with Jo Jo in the shade of a large mango tree in a ravine a mile from Barangay Magalang. His rifle was still hot. They had each fired twenty-five practice rounds at a paper target. When his weapon cooled, Steel would clean it. He didn't want to chance any misfires. The M16 had a bad reputation for jamming.

Jo Jo had done fairly well, most of his rounds hitting the target. Steel hadn't done badly either and got the center more than once. He was great at shooting paper people. But he hoped to God he didn't have to shoot at living people, especially if they were shooting back.

Steel fingered the two grenades hanging from his combat vest, which fit snugly around his chest. The vest also held four banana clips full of M16 rounds and his .45-cal pistol. Thanks to Jo Jo they were well outfitted.

Steel looked over at June, who was dressed in new fatigue pants, looking every bit the mercenary. He wore two bandoleers filled with M1 Garand ammo and grenades strapped across his chest. At the moment, he was training his squad of ten Negritos. He animatedly gestured to them, holding up his rifle, pointing to its rear sight. Tony lined up with the others, proudly holding his Garand. June was clearly happy to take part in the operation. Steel recalled how June's eyes widened when he was presented with a crate of ammo holding five-hundred rounds and a dozen M1s.

The boom of the M1 echoed loudly off the small hillside. June's marksmanship impressed Steel. June had put ten rounds into a small tight pattern on a homemade paper target before blasting away half the tree that held the target. June's prowess with the weapon confirmed what Steel had read: The M1 was incredible. GIs during World War II revered its rugged dependability and appreciated its large round, which was powerful enough to punch right through trees and sandbags. The only complaint was that the clip didn't hold enough rounds.

One by one, the ten Negritos took turns shooting. Some had obviously handled rifles before. For the others, Steel guessed, years of archery experience translated into good skills with a rifle.

"Damn, boss, those little bastards actually look like a military squad." Jo Jo nodded his head as he watched Tony bark out commands. They were regrouping and repacking their gear.

"Yeah, check out Tony. He's acting like a drill sergeant. Knock on wood, things have gone really smoothly. Too smoothly, maybe," Steel noted.

"Yes, it is hard to believe we're not just going for a treasure hunt."

Jo Jo was right, Steel thought, it was surreal. Late yesterday afternoon Jo Jo had used Steel's truck to drive alone to a small warehouse on the outskirts of town. He had a cup of tea with Mr. Oh, a Chinese arms dealer, negotiated a deal, and paid him $4,000 for the seven wooden crates of firepower. Jo Jo was proud of his haggling; paying in dollars got them a nice discount. He said that anyone watching him would have thought he was picking up produce instead of weaponry.

Steel had hardly slept last night. He was nervous about the trip and about the crated weapons sitting on the floor in his living room. He'd be doing hard time in a Philippine jail if he were caught.

He was already awake when his alarm rang at 0400. He and Jo Jo drove into June's village just before sunrise. Tony and the men efficiently unpacked the crates, distributed and loaded up weapons and equipment, and headed out on foot from the village. They had only paused at this small shaded ravine for a desperately needed orientation with their weapons.

Steel had just finished cleaning his M16 and was struggling to put the plastic handgrips back on the barrel when June approached. He silently reached out, and Steel handed him the weapon. June reassembled it as he spoke. "Sir, I would like to report that my men are ready to go." He handed back Steel's weapon, stood at attention before him, and saluted.

Steel returned the salute from a sitting position. They were all business now, even Tony. Negrito revenge was evidently serious stuff, Steel thought. "So June, the plan is for us to head to an area near where we think they're holding the general and set up camp, then we will try to go to find him."

"Yes sir, we will move to that location, maybe tomorrow. We will be almost there by late tonight, after the darkness. We will stop and then start early morning. We should arrive by the half of the day," he responded in English.

"Okay, we have lots of flashlights to help us on the trails tonight."

"No, we cannot to use the lights. Maybe they will see us to coming."

"That is a good point, but I am not a bat and cannot see in the dark," Jo Jo piped.

"It will be not too much the problem; we have the big moon tonight."

Steel stood up. He lifted the heavy pack and slung it on his back. He carefully put the strap of the M16 around his neck. He was still concerned about the grenades on his chest. He paused, then laid down his M16 and removed the grenades, putting them in a pocket on the side of his pack. Curtis was right. He was no Chuck Norris. Jo Jo nodded and followed suit. Exposed grenades were a little much this early in the war.

June had been right about the full moon, and Steel might have enjoyed walking on the trails had it not been for the forty pounds of weapons, equipment, and water he had slogged for the last ten hours. He checked his watch using a small flashlight with a red lens to subdue the light. It was ten p.m. He hoped they were close to the campsite.

It didn't help that he hadn't slept the night before. His legs were shaking, and he was starting to hallucinate, thinking shadows were people staring at him. Up ahead, he could see Jo Jo's form. He had stopped. Steel approached.

"Boss, I think I heard June say we are setting up camp here."

"Oh, thank God," Steel whispered.

"Yes, thanks to Jose," Jo Jo echoed.

It didn't take long for Steel and Jo Jo to put up their small tent. The Negritos simply laid blankets on the ground. June warned everyone to prepare their food. He would allow a fire for only a short period. The Negritos dug a small pit in the ground at the base of a large tree and made a fire using very dry wood. Steel broke out some C-rations, and he and Jo Jo ate them cold.

At June's village, Steel had offered to give food to June's squad, but he insisted on providing their mess. Steel watched them prepare the evening meal while he ate from a small green can of U.S. military-issue ham and eggs. The Negritos cooked a large pot of rice. When it was done, they mixed in canned sardines, bananas, and a large papaya they had collected along the way.

Steel quickly finished and stripped off his filthy clothes. He hung them over a tree branch near his tent. Jo Jo approached him, shirtless too.

"Boss, I talked to June about posting a guard. He said his men would take turns. He wanted us to go to bed now. They won't bother us."

Steel grunted his approval, crawled into the tent, and lay flat on top of his light sleeping bag. He was too dirty and sweaty to get inside it. That was undoubtedly the hardest march he had ever done. Sleep came quickly—even before Jo Jo joined him in the tent.

Steel woke early. He popped his head out of the tent. A group of Negritos squatted around the small fire pit. Steel could see a flame licking the bottom of a large suspended cooking pot.

Steel woke Jo Jo up and staggered out of the tent to dress and make coffee. As he prepared his own quick breakfast, he watched the Negritos putting together their meal of rice, fruit, and chicken, as well as food for later. Each portion was individually wrapped in a banana leaf and then in a small piece of cut sheet plastic.

Jo Jo grunted and groaned crawling out of the tent. "Morning. Jesus Marie Joseph my aching legs. That was a tough hike yesterday." Jo Jo reached over and felt the lid of the water pot. "Ay!" He jerked his hand away. "I guess the water is ready."

Steel smiled, "Yes, it's been ready for a while."

"My Jose, what are these ambitious little men up to? It looks like an assembly line."

"June says they are preparing food; later there won't be any fires."

"I'm impressed. I think we should have used revenge before to inspire them."

At a sudden commotion in the brush, the Negritos turned and drew weapons. Three Negritos emerged, two of them armed with M1s. Steel recognized Regalito and Henny. The third, who carried a bow and arrow, Steel had never seen before. June began addressing the trio in rapid Aeta. He called out for Angelo, who was wrapping food, to replace Regalito on guard duty. June switched to another dialect with which Steel was unfamiliar. June's tone was soft and paternal. He ushered the trio to the fire for food then approached Steel.

"Captain Steel, Henny has just arrived here with Dunpit. Dunpit says—"

"Where'd Henny find Dunpit?"

"I sent Henny to find Dunpit's house to talk to him about the strangers around here."

"Oh, okay. Make sure you tell me these things. Damn, Henny must be tired. He was out all night."

Steel smiled at the surprised looked on June's face. "Henny found to the Dunpit who says he saw many NPA coming through here weeks or maybe days ago, and they have the white man with them."

"That's great news. He was sure about the white man?"

"Yes, it was in his mind to remember because the man was tied up like the dog to a stick."

"Jesus Christ, poor bastard," Jo Jo murmured.

"How many is many NPA? A number, June?" Steel asked firmly in Aeta.

June called over to Dunpit, who replied something in his

own dialect. "He said maybe twenty or thirty men with the many guns. They have no Negritos with them."

"Any Chinese?" Steel asked.

"I do not think Dunpit knows to the Chinese. He is the mountain Negrito."

Steel eyed Dunpit, who squatted in the dirt in his simple loincloth and beaded necklace. He was delicately eating a roasted chicken leg.

"So June, we are leaving soon?"

"Yes, in maybe thirty minutes. We will have food and be packed. Have you eaten to your meal yet?"

"Yes, thanks, I'm almost done."

June nodded and returned to supervising the fire.

"Christ, Jo Jo, I think I'm right. The general is in the Zambales. God, I hope we can find him quickly. He's got to be in really bad condition being hogtied and marched all this way."

"Yes, he is not a young man and a soft office worker to boot."

Steel looked off into the mountains and tried to picture where the general was being held.

General Smith sat on the dirt floor of his lean-to and ate the rice and banana gruel without complaint. His hands were free and only his left leg was shackled to the tree. Things were improving. He ate every scrap of food they gave him.

His eyelids were still swollen, and his vision blurred. He forced a smile; at least he couldn't see his filthy living conditions. He ate slowly and deliberately, trying not to move his jaw more than necessary. He figured they must have fractured it. Every bite was painful. There were teeth missing. He could feel the holes with his tongue.

But at least the severe beatings had subsided. He was now only subjected to slaps and verbal abuse. He figured they had made a decision to back off; they probably realized they had almost killed him.

He let them think he was a broken man. He gave them just enough information to keep them interested. He milked his injuries to the fullest, slurring his words and pretending to fade in and out of consciousness.

The sounds of footsteps startled him. He opened his eyes wide enough to see the blurred outline of Comrade One, as Smith called him. The short, foul-smelling individual leaned over and dragged Smith by his chain. "Enough food for you right now, General."

The captor patted Smith's cheek, and he winced in pain. "We not pleased with the progress we make with our talks," the man said in broken English. "We must insist you answer questions with more details. We not want to start making your life so unpleasant again, do we?"

"Can we play a round of golf today? I think it's going to rain tomorrow," Smith rolled his eyes and slumped down.

His captor let the general fall back hard on the ground, spilling his food bowl. He screamed in pain, no acting needed. He rolled into a fetal ball, his captor's face a foot away. Smith had to resist the urge to reach out, grab his tormentor by the throat, and break his neck.

"General Smithy, General Smithy, why don't you tell me about nuclear weapons at Osan Air Base? How many are there? It is important that you tell us. Then we can play the golfy. It is going to be a beautiful day today for golfy."

"Okay, let me tell you something," he whispered, gritting his teeth. Damn it hurts to speak. He had screamed loudly enough during the worst of the torture to damage his vocal cords. "It's a big bomb. I call them fat boys. Yes I do. Fat Boys! Hell, maybe I should call them fat girls!" He laughed erratically.

"That is a good name. The fatty boy." The small fiend leaned in closer.

Smith could feel the man's hot breath, putrid with garlic. The bastard was so close, so close. Smith visualized looping the chain around the Korean's neck and—pop. Smith took a deep breath. Now wasn't the time; that was his last resort, to take at least one of them with him. He just wanted to delay. It wasn't the end game yet.

"We have lots of them, fat boys. They are stacked like cordwood, this high." He slowly tried to lift his arm and show a height. "Yes Sir-ee-bob, like cordwood."

"Cordywood? What is this cord-a-wood?"

The general almost laughed out loud. "Well, let me tell you about my Uncle Wacko's farm in Wisconsin. It's…"

28

In the Zambales

STEEL BRUSHED TWO HUGE FIRE ants off the back of his wrist. It was nearly dark, but there was enough light left for him to see the one that had just dug its large mandibles into his flesh. He gritted his teeth as several more bit his neck. He realized he had just missed crawling over their home, an adobe mound rising out of the ground. That would have been worse.

Instead, he inched over a few yards to his left to skirt their fortress. Ahead he could see June, Tony, and Jun-Jun stretched out on their stomachs waiting for him. Tony had sent Jun-Jun ahead of the group to scout out the NPA camp. He had found it quickly, following the scent of cooking fish. He joked that he was hungry and considered sneaking in to steal some dinner.

Steel had been on his belly for at least one-hundred yards, trying to blend in with shrub brush and plants. He had to fight the urge to roll on his side and check out his knees and elbows; he imagined they were cut up and bleeding. He wished he had thought of knee and elbow pads.

He supported his weapon on outstretched arms, trying not to bang it against trees and rocks. All he could hear was his shaky breathing. He hoped the chorus of tree frogs and insects that had begun its nightly symphony would drown out his gasping.

Tony signaled Steel to crawl towards the group. Steel did, figuring they had a good vantage point on the camp. Tony pointed down into the valley of the high ridge on which they perched. About three hundred yards away, Steel thought he could see the outline of a hut nestled amongst a thick banana grove. He pulled out a pair of binoculars and focused on what looked like a man-made shelter. Then he saw the men.

There were a dozen walking near the hut, all carrying weapons. Steel tried to flatten his body even lower to the ground. A squawk of a jungle bird startled him. He looked up into the canopy to see a brightly colored parrot alight from its branch.

"Can you see the NPA now?" June asked pointing to the binoculars.

"I see maybe six near the hut. I'm sure there are many more."

"Can you see the general?" Tony whispered.

"No, just NPA." Steel scanned the entire area around the hut. He handed the binoculars to June.

Steel unfolded his map on the ground, using his compass to orient it. June and Tony peered over his shoulder. Steel studied the terrain around them, then the map, trying to formulate a plan. Bile filled his gut. He wished he knew for certain where they were holding the general. Was he even there?

"Have a look at the map, June. I want you to see where the camp is."

June and Tony poked at the map and then pointed towards the hut. From the puzzled look on their faces, Steel wasn't sure if they understood the concept of a map.

Steel started to worry that they had lingered in this place too long. It was too dark to see anything. They would have to pull back and regroup to plan the attack. He put away the binoculars and retreated at a high crawl. Tony and June silently followed.

They moved back to a new staging area. Jo Jo rushed up to greet Steel, tripping on a tree root. Steel caught him before he hit the ground. Jo Jo peppered whispered questions at Steel, who did not answer, focusing instead on the Negritos huddled in small groups talking quietly. Their original band of a dozen or so had swelled. The new arrivals, armed with bows and arrows, wore black and green striped war paint.

"What the hell, Jo Jo? Looks like our numbers have increased."

"Yes, ten new Negritos."

"That's good news." Steel looked more closely at them but didn't recognize any of the fresh faces. "It's amazing how they just show up. How the hell can they find us in the hundreds of miles of jungle?"

Jo Jo handed Steel a candy bar. "I have no idea. I could barely keep up following June. June did tell me that Dunpit had brought members of his village. June had promised machetes and salt if they helped. They said they would be happy to make war on the lowlanders who killed the Negrito warrior."

"I'll take any help we can get. I just wish we had more rifles." Steel finished the candy bar and drank greedily from a canteen full of tepid water. He scanned the ground and found a flat place to set up the map. He motioned for June, Tony, and Jo Jo to come over.

"We need to know exactly where the general is being held before we can finish the plan. Keeping the general alive is most important. Killing NPA is second," Steel jabbed the map hard with his finger.

"Yes, it is important to keep the general safe," June said, nodding reassuringly.

Tony stood and addressed the group. "I will give to you where the general is when I return from the NPA camp tonight. I will escort Golgi to the camp, and he will look."

"Can you get in without being seen?" Jo Jo asked.

"Maybe I cannot—but Golgi can do it."

"Who is Golgi?" Steel asked.

Tony turned and, in an unfamiliar dialect, grunted out a command to one of the groups of Negritos. A small figure stood and apprehensively approached. Steel tried not to stare, but Golgi was tiny, even by Negrito standards. Steel guessed he was probably in his twenties and maybe four feet tall. He was dressed in a loin cloth, his body painted with vertical black and green stripes. He smiled shyly at Steel, exposing tiny white teeth filed to sharp points. Golgi looked like an evil elf.

Tony pulled the little man close. "Captain Steel this is Golgi."

Steel, smiled and nodded.

"Golgi and Tony will go to the camp tonight and look for the general," June said, reinforcing his leadership role.

Tony continued, "I will take Golgi to the camp and wait on the edge. Golgi is like the forest spirit; even I cannot see him sometimes."

"Why are his teeth like an animal's?" Jo Jo blurted out.

Tony patted Golgi on the shoulder. "The medicine men in Golgi's tribe do it to their best warriors."

"Good to have you with us," Steel said.

Tony whispered to Golgi, who in turn nodded and returned back to his group. Steel illuminated his watch: It was a little after midnight. "Alright Tony, we'll wait here for you and Golgi. We need to attack before dawn."

"Yes, we will catch the NPA in bed asleep," June agreed.

Steel knew it paramount that they strike soon. He didn't want to risk waiting another twenty-four hours. There were too many things that could go wrong. An NPA patrol could find them or the bad guys could move their camp.

"Alright Tony, it's up to you," Steel put his hand on Tony's shoulder. Tony nodded and with Golgi, silently disappeared into the foliage.

"Well boss, nothing to do now but wait. I'm going to try and close my eyes and rest." Jo Jo turned and followed Tony and Golgi into the shadows. Steel, too nervous to sleep, bent over and shined a red subdued flashlight back onto the map, wondering how long Tony would be gone

After a few minutes of staring at the map, Steel slumped down next to it and closed his eyes for a minute. Ninety minutes later, he woke to Jo Jo's frantic whispers. There was just enough moonlight filtering through the canopy to see Jo Jo's form.

"Shit, what's up?" Steel sat. "Is Tony back?"

"Yes, they have just returned." Jo Jo was dressed for action: camouflaged jungle fatigues, black face paint, and a bandana wrapped around his head.

Steel followed Jo Jo across the camp toward June. Clusters of Negritos milled about, chatting in several dialects. "June, have Tony and Golgi come over here," Steel said.

Tony appeared with Golgi trooping behind. June spoke to Golgi and translated for Steel. "Golgi said he saw the white man inside a small hut. He was tied to the tree. He was asleep, not dead. He is tied to the tree with the metal rope. It is not to be cut with the machete."

"My God, we've found him." Steel sat down hard on a tree stump.

"Boss, I'm shocked. It is as Tony said."

"Shit, Jo Jo," Steel said.

"I guess there's no turning back," Jo Jo sat on the ground near Steel.

"I didn't count on him being tied with a chain. We don't have metal cutters."

"Wait. We do have an axe, boss."

"I guess it will depend on how thick the chain is. It's gonna make a lot of noise smashing through it. Damn." Steel added in Aeta. "Anyway, June, what else did Golgi see?"

June asked dozens of questions, which Golgi readily answered. Tony pitched in. There were at least half a dozen men posted as guards around the perimeter and two NPA sleeping right next to the general.

It wouldn't be easy to get in there, thought Steel, though he was heartened that Golgi had been able to wander around undetected. He had even hinted that he touched the chain binding the general.

Both June and Tony agreed that the perimeter guards would not be a problem. They could be swiftly silenced, as could the two with the general. The problem would be moving Smith.

They had to get him out of harm's way before the main body of twenty NPA woke up and started shooting. They were sleeping twenty-five yards away from the general's hut, scattered in hammocks and on the ground under crudely made shelters. There was also a large hut hidden in the brush that was better built than the general's lean-to. Golgi said there were a few men sleeping in there along with equipment. Steel guessed that was where the Koreans lived.

He checked his watch. They had less than an hour before it would start to get light. He gathered Tony, Jo Jo, and June around his red light. They squatted in the dirt and started to sketch out a plan on the ground with sticks.

29

NPA Camp

STEEL LOOKED THROUGH THE SPARSE jungle canopy at large clouds silhouetted against the moon. June said that it could rain soon. Would it hinder their rescue or hide their retreat?

The din of insects was near deafening. Leading the jungle chorus were tiny colorful male tree frogs, ready to mate, calling desperately for partners. The females would lay their eggs in the puddles of water that formed in the wet season. Tony called the frog sounds "the rain song." The beat of life went on despite the insanity of man around them, Steel reflected. Right now however, as he lay hidden on the jungle floor's litter, the clamor of the frogs was a blessing: it masked his man-made sounds.

He scanned the shadowy terrain in front of them, aiming his M16 at imaginary targets. Less than one hundred yards away was the NPA camp. Steel and six Negritos waited for the others to eliminate the perimeter guards.

It was so much easier to think of it as "elimination"—so clinical, surgical. It wasn't the grizzly business of muffled screams, sliced throats, life ebbing from human bodies. But Steel knew that was what was happening right now.

A slight rustling to his left drew his attention. Something

was moving through the dry leaf litter. Whatever it was, it was coming toward him. Was it a Negrito? NPA? Would he have to shoot? A pygmy deer, the size of a small dog, appeared and stopped twenty feet in front of him, its nose and ears twitching rapidly. It could sense them.

The deer bolted. June appeared in its wake, then Tony, and, like ghosts, they approached. Tony had a big grin on his face, as though he had just returned from a night on the town.

June squatted beside Steel. He motioned with his hands, making a pulling motion of a bow string and held up one finger. He pointed to Tony, who Steel could now see was blood-splattered. Tony dropped something at Steel's feet. Steel swallowed the bile rising in his throat. Four human ears lay in the dirt. Tony, still grinning, whispered "*patay*, dead" dragging his hand across his throat.

Steel nodded. This was real. They had killed. They stood quietly for a moment, June looking at Steel for the next command. Steel motioned with his hands and whispered faintly, "Golgi?"

June pointed with his eyes, and Steel looked to his left and was startled by Golgi squatting at his feet. He appeared even more like a miniature devil, spattered in mud, green war paint, and blood. He was something out of a bad nightmare—the kind you woke up from with the sweats. June whispered something. Golgi smiled, exposing his pointed teeth and held up four fingers.

Steel took a deep breath. "Christ," he murmured. The little bastard was the angel of death. He made a mental count: at least six dead. They decided to take out all the sentries. There was no turning back now. The NPA would want revenge.

Steel addressed June in whispered Aeta. "Okay. Golgi goes ahead now and kills the NPA sleeping next to the general's hut. Tony will go with him. We'll follow behind. Tell him to come and let us know they are dead." He made June repeat the commands back.

June quickly translated, and Golgi looked at Steel. With a smile spreading on his bloody face, he held up two fingers. Steel nodded and held up two fingers. Golgi turned and headed off into the night.

Steel flashed a red light toward Jo Jo's position; he would know the sentries had been taken out and that Steel was advancing with the Negritos. He pulled back the M16's cocking lever and nodded with satisfaction as it locked and loaded a round. He checked the safety to make sure it was on and lightly touched his grenades.

He waited a few minutes, and then waved to June to lead them forward. They needed to get within fifty yards of the hut. Steel held his weapon at the ready and concentrated on following June's footsteps exactly, trying to move noiselessly. Even though the bulk of their gear was with Jo Jo, Steel still felt like a bumbling giant looming over June's compact form. Might as well be a one-man band, Steel thought.

He turned to check the Negrito behind him, who was grinning happily. The M1 he carried port arms looked enormous in his small hands. Four grenades dangled from the bandoleer strung across his chest. It bothered Steel that he couldn't remember the Negrito's name.

Behind him crept Gan and Din Din. In addition to their weapons, they hauled a makeshift litter of lashed bamboo poles and parachute fabric. Steel prayed the general was well enough to walk. They'd have a hard time trying to outrun the NPA carrying him.

June raised his hand and assumed a low crouching position. Steel noted the professional stance. Forty years ago, June was probably leading some U.S. military guys in these same mountains, not after the NPA but fighting the Japanese.

June motioned Steel forward then pointed into the jungle. Steel couldn't see anything but shadows and vegetation. He assumed June was pointing to the hut. They sat silently, listening to the frogs, waiting for Tony to contact them.

They didn't have to wait long. Steel heard the Negritos behind him stir, and Tony approached from the shadows. He gave Steel a thumbs up, and whispered, "*Patay na*, dead now" in Tagalog.

Steel held up two fingers. Tony nodded.

They spread out and moved through the jungle with Tony leading the way to the hut. Steel's heart was pounding, blood coursing; he tried to focus. He was feeling the lack of sleep. He inhaled the smell of campfire smoke and human waste. They must be near the camp latrine.

Twenty more feet of uncomfortable, hunched movement and Steel could make out Tony approaching Golgi ahead. They both pointed to a dark shadow. Steel could see the faint outline of the hut.

He caught June's attention and mimed that he should lead his men to their positions between the camp and the hut. June nodded, slipped his rifle on his shoulder, and pulled a grenade from his bandoleer. The others did the same. Steel watched June, Golgi, and four Negritos creep forward, grenades in hand. Tony, the two Negrito stretcher-bearers, and Steel headed for the hut.

Something pattered in the trees above, and Steel swung his weapon skyward: The first cloudburst of the pre-monsoon rain—the rain the frogs were screaming for.

"Shit," Steel whispered an appeal to the rain spirits. "Not now." He held the handgrip of his rifle tightly. He could see Tony staring intently, wanting direction. Steel looked past the hut into the distance. What would the NPA do now that it was raining? Would they move? They would surely awaken. It was too late now to back out. Steel waved at Tony to press on.

The first raindrops had begun to penetrate the foliage and crash to the rich soil. Steel exhaled—perhaps the rain was a blessing. It would confuse the enemy and afford them cover. The rain slammed everything around him. As the rain poured down now in torrents, he wondered how it could go from dry to instant monsoon?

Steel swept the terrain with the barrel of his weapon looking for any signs of enemy movement. None. Tony and the litter bearers stood poised next to the hut. It was maybe eight feet tall and fifteen feet in diameter, crudely constructed against a large tree. Just as Golgi described.

Tony pointed to the entrance, but Steel brushed by the Negrito. "I'll go," he mouthed, handed over his M16, pulled out his .45, and went into the hut.

Inside, he whipped his flashlight beam around, and it fell on one of Golgi's victims, face down and spread-eagle, its head in a large pool of blood. Another body lay to the left on its back, a huge oozing gash across its neck. Where was Smith?

Steel jerked the light. Tucked into a corner, he saw a half-naked man on a bed of banana leaves. Even in the darkness, he looked filthy.

Steel rushed over, bent down on one knee, and touched the man's shoulder lightly. The general turned his head, a look of horror in his eyes, and lashed out. Steel pushed his weight down onto the general's chest and used a free hand to cover his mouth.

"General, I'm American. Don't make any noise." He kept his hand on the general's mouth. "Did you hear me, sir?" Steel grunted the question softly, staring into Smith's eyes. The general's face was battered and swollen. When Steel felt the general's body begin to relax, he removed his hand.

"Who the hell are you? Delta?" The general coughed.

"No sir, it's me, Captain Steel. We've got to move quickly."

"Steel?"

"That's right, sir. Let's check this chain out," Steel whispered, trying to speak loudly enough to be heard over the din of the rain. He glanced back toward the NPA camp, bracing for gunfire. All was quiet. He quickly crawled along the ground feeling for the chain. Golgi was right. It was heavy and secured firmly to the tree.

Steel followed his flashlight beam back along the chain to the general's leg. A big metal lock rested on the general's swollen ankle.

"Shit, the axe won't do anything against this chain or the lock. I'm going to have to shoot through," Steel said in a panic, worried he was taking too much time sorting this out. "Can you stand, sir?"

"I think so, son, with some help."

Steel grabbed the general's hand and pulled him to his feet. He could hear Smith grunting in pain. "Sir, I'm going to have to shoot the lock. Once I do, we're going to have to run like hell." He looked at the general who was leaning hard against a small tree. They were going to need the stretcher. Smith gritted his teeth and nodded, acknowledging the plan.

Steel put the barrel of the .45 against the lock and tried not to obsess on how close it sat next to the general's ankle. He flipped off the safety, clenched his teeth, and pulled the trigger, squeezing off a round.

The sound of the pistol was deafening. Once Steel saw that the lock was blasted away from the chain and Smith's ankle was still intact, he put his arm around the general's body and carried him forward. Smith grabbed Steel and held on tightly, using him like a crutch. Steel guided their way out of the hut with the flashlight in his free hand.

Outside they were greeted by explosions, gunfire, and pouring rain. Tony handed Steel his rifle, and he slung it over his shoulder. Tony dropped to his knee and aimed his M1 into the jungle, firing off several rounds, covering their limping retreat. The concussion from the grenade blasts rattled Steel's skull and shook his rib cage. Gunfire and screams of pain erupted from the jungle behind the hut, where no doubt the grenade blasts were sowing confusion and death among the guerrillas.

Steel yelled at the general to get on the stretcher. "General, we're going to litter you out. You're in no condition to move fast." Smith started to protest and Steel forced him down. Smith fell to his knees with a grunt and said, "Sorry sir, don't argue, get on."

Steel yelled out in Aeta for Tony and the Negritos to grab an end each, his commands interrupted by the blasts of more explosions and gunfire. Tony reluctantly took his side of the stretcher; he clearly wanted to go and kill NPA instead. They counted aloud and lifted the litter.

Steel was surprised to feel how light it was as they rushed forward in the darkness. He looked down at the general, markedly thinner than he was several weeks ago. That explained some of it; adrenaline must account for the rest.

More explosions. He could hear the high-pitched whine of bullets whizzing by and ricocheting in the trees around and above them. Steel bent his head down and yelled to the Negritos to hurry. He flipped his rifle off his shoulder and grabbed the grip, feeling the trigger guard with the finger of his right hand.

The rain had turned the trail into a treacherous mudslide. The general, wide-eyed, gripped the sides of the stretcher; water streamed down his face.

"Where we going, captain?" Smith yelled out from between clenched teeth.

"Getting the hell out of here," Steel shouted back in between forced breaths.

"How many U.S. forces are here?"

"None—just me and some friends."

"You're kidding, right?"

"Wish I was sir, in fact—"

Steel caught sight of someone sprinting up on his right; he raised his weapon and aimed from the hip. The shirtless NPA cadre tried to stop, seeing the rifle, but lost his traction in the mud not twenty-five feet away. He floundered and tried to aim his rifle. Muzzle blasts of bright orange erupted from the barrel.

While still moving forward with the stretcher, Steel flipped off the safety and squeezed the trigger, shooting off a three-round burst. The NPA cadre yelled out, falling backwards with arms and legs flailing.

Steel lowered his weapon and stared back. A sick feeling gripped him. He had just killed a man. Those five seconds were going to be the subject of many a nightmare and guilt trip. The stretcher team kept a firm hand on the litter, continuing to move forward at a steady pace, dragging Steel with them.

"Die you son of a dog. Die," Tony yelled out in Aeta to the squealed delight of Gan and Din Din.

"Jesus, son, did you get him?" Smith propped himself up on his elbows. "I've dreamed about blasting those bastards for weeks now."

Steel smiled half-heartedly and nodded. He released his death grip on the M16 and hung it back on its shoulder strap. He reached for his .45 pistol, turned it over to check that the clip was inside, and passed it to the general, butt first. The general looked at Steel and smiled. "Thanks, son." He turned the pistol over and handled it with an air of familiarity.

"No problem, sir." He should have given it to the general

earlier, Steel thought—the poor bastard needed not to feel so helpless.

The rain stopped almost as quickly as it had begun, though streams still cascaded from the leaves. They would do so for a while.

Suddenly remembering Jo Jo and the blocking force set up ahead, Steel unclipped his flashlight and flipped it on, wildly waving it. "It's Steel, Jo Jo, hold your fire!"

They raced ahead and nearly crashed into Jo Jo's team in place in the middle of the trail. Jo Jo stood armed and soaking wet. "Boss, you did it," he grabbed the handle of the stretcher from Tony. "Jesus Maria Joseph, sounded like World War II out there."

"Yeah, we'll wait here for June and the boys; they will be coming through soon. Jo Jo, you lead the stretcher up the trail a couple hundred yards and sit tight. Gan, Din Din, and you others stay with me. We'll cover you, okay, *Lang*."

Steel walked over to the general. "Sir, this is Jo Jo my pal. He's going to move you to a safer location. I'm waiting here for the rest of the men. As you can hear, they are engaging the enemy and moving this way."

"Alright, Steel. Keep your head down. I haven't told you yet, but thanks for doing this. You got one helluva set of balls."

Steel smiled and nodded.

"Alright, brothers, keep your eyes open and lead us up the trail," Jo Jo said to the men at the stretcher grips.

Steel could still hear fire and occasional bullets whizzing overhead; some sounded closer than others. He knew the battle was moving their way.

Steel turned his attention to Tony, who was aiming his weapon into the jungle in the direction of the gunfire. "Old friend," Steel put his hand on Tony's shoulder and watched raindrops running down his face. It had washed most of the mud and blood from him. He turned and smiled at Steel who said, "You were right and so were the forest spirits."

"Yes, the spirits do not to lie, just sometimes the Tony," he said in English and laughed. He resumed scanning the jungle.

"Tony, this is important now. Take this plastic bag. Inside is money, my ID card, and a letter. You know what to do, right?" He made Tony repeat every detail, which he did on the first try.

"Don't be to worry too much, Captain Steel. I will be to the base fast. I will not to have your—how do say in English?—slow ass to drag over the mountains."

Steel laughed, "Thanks."

"I will have the men in the helicopters come for you. You just be careful and follow June. He will get you out of here. I will talk to the spirits on the way out of the jungle to protect you all. Here, you should to wear this." Tony untied one of his bracelets and retied it on Steel's wrist. "It was my uncle's. He will now protect you from death."

"Okay, my friend."

Tony nodded and put his hand out, offering to shake. Steel gave Tony a hug instead. Embarrassed, he nodded and silently disappeared into the jungle, his M1 leading the way. Steel checked his watch. They had less than an hour before dawn. He wondered how long it would take for Tony to get to Curtis.

The first Negrito to appear elicited a birdlike scream from Gan. The Negrito returned the call as he moved rapidly through the jungle. Amid sporadic gunfire, other calls erupted, and Negritos emerged from the shadows. They were moving tree to tree, walking backwards, and aiming their weapons behind them. Eventually June came into view. He and another carried a wounded Negrito. Din Din rushed to help.

As June approached, Steel could see an ugly wound on

Tek's leg. June, clearly exhausted, grunted in Aeta at Steel, "Captain Steel, we have been followed by NPA. We are slow because I am old, and we have to carry Tck."

Several booms erupted out in the jungle. June laughed. "Ha, I think the pig trap got a two-legged son of pig."

"You set some traps?"

"Yes sir, with the grenades in the trail."

M1 gunshots rang out as the Negritos standing near Steel fired into the jungle. Steel crouched behind a fallen tree and tried to see what they were shooting at. Muzzles flashed and bullets flew. A Negrito tossed a grenade, and Steel gritted his teeth, waiting for the explosion.

The boom shook the ground. Tek sat holding his wounded leg; a chunk of his calf had been blown away. His face was twisted with pain. Steel could see that the wound, bleeding heavily, needed immediate attention.

He pulled out a medical kit and unrolled some bandages, then applied a tourniquet mid-thigh to stem the blood and field-dressed the leg. "June, let's move. The rain has stopped, and we've lost its cover. We have to get the hell out of here," Steel said, crouching beside the wounded man. "We've got to make sure we release the pressure every five minutes from the tourniquet or he will lose his leg." June nodded and ordered Din Din and another to move Tek.

Tek had distracted Steel from the gun battle. There were still pissed-off shooters in the jungle. He peeked around his thick tree-trunk shield and aimed his weapon, though at what, he had no idea. He couldn't see a thing. He pulled the trigger anyway, haphazardly firing six three-round bursts into an area where he had seen muzzle flashes moments ago. "Alright June, let's go. They are waiting for us with the general up the trail."

Some more gunfire from the NPA ripped through the brush. Steel heard one round thud into his tree. He wasn't the only one using muzzle flashes to his fire.

He grabbed a grenade from his vest. He was only too happy to get rid of it. He peered around the tree to ensure he had a clear path. Looked clear enough, he thought. He didn't want the grenade bouncing back in his direction. He pulled it up to his face and quickly tore out the pin. He winged it into the darkness and waited. Finally it boomed in the distance; how effective it was, he had no idea.

He picked up his rifle, and, with June, left the cover of the tree. He had only taken two steps before gun fire erupted directly behind him. A wave of heat hit the back of his legs. He stopped in his tracks.

"Christ, June, I think I've been hit." He watched June crouch and fire several rounds into the night. Steel heard a man scream. "He is dead now," June said matter-of-factly. "He had a pistol."

Steel leaned against a tree. He was confused. Was he shot by the pistol or not? He started walking forward, aided by June. He reached down and felt his ass. It was hard to tell if it were wet from blood or wet from the rain. He moved forward, the backs of his haunches burning.

After about one hundred yards, Steel was overcome with dizziness. He shook his head and tried to focus on the trail ahead. He could hear June talking, but his voice sounded distorted. The world was moving in slow motion. Steel lifted his pants leg and rubbed his hand against bare skin. He pushed his hand close to his face. Blood—his blood. His legs buckled and he crashed into the dirt.

Raindrops splashed on Steel. He heard Jo Jo's voice and saw his dimly lit face close by. It must be sunrise, Steel thought. He couldn't properly hear Jo Jo but felt his hand. Steel realized Jo Jo's voice was muffled by a downpour falling harder and faster than before. He and June pulled Steel out of a large puddle and onto his feet. He struggled to keep his footing on the wet ground.

"We have to keep moving," Jo Jo said, bracing Steel with his body.

"Where's the general?" Steel asked.

"Right here, son."

Steel looked over on the ground next to him and saw the general sitting upright in his stretcher.

"You took a round in your ass. The bleeding isn't too bad. We'll keep our fingers crossed the bullet hasn't hit anything important. We won't know until we can get you to a doctor," the general called over the rain.

Steel nodded.

"What's the plan?" Smith demanded.

"We'll head northeast. I left a map with someone at Clark. Tony left for the base. We have to head north and wait for rescue forces."

"Alright. Then let's get at it," Smith grunted, fighting back obvious waves of pain. It hadn't been an easy stretcher ride for him.

Steel leaned heavily on Jo Jo's shoulder, teeth chattering as his wet clothes and blood loss took its toll. A Negrito supported Steel's other side and they moved forward like a bad six-legged race. He could see the general's stretcher ahead and Tek supported by three Negritos.

"June did you loosen Tek's tourniquet?" Steel asked.

June nodded yes.

Their retreat was shielded by the pouring rain and several Negrito rear guards. Steel hoped Tony was on track.

30

Clark Air Base

CAPTAIN SPAN, THE 13TH AIR Force watch officer, tapped Curtis on the shoulder. "Sargent Washington. Curtis, wake up."

He jolted upright. He had spent the last two nights slumped on a big leather couch in the watch break room. He told the night shift that he was waiting for a call with news of a dying aunt back in the States. The truth was he was worried sick about Steel.

"Washington, you won't believe this. The cop duty officer just called. He said that a local approached the Friendship Gate guard at 1800 hours with Steel's ID card. They said they have a note from Steel addressed to you. What the hell is this about?"

"Shit, you're kiddin!" Curtis checked his watch. Seven p.m.

"I'm not." Span grinned widely. "I'm going to call Kuncker and the DO." He picked up the phone. "Damn this is hot. I thought it was going to be just another quiet night. You want to hear Kuncker explode?" He held up the phone.

Curtis shook his head no, stood, and put on his shirt, tucking it in neatly, then headed to the bathroom to splash water on his face. It was going to be a long night.

"I wonder if this means Steel's dead?" Span's grin suddenly faded.

"Don't say that, captain. He ain't dead," Curtis smiled and thought about the map. Yes, the shit would hit the fan very soon—and he was going to be right in the middle of it. They thought Steel's disappearance was big news. Ha, that was nothing.

"Colonel Kuncker, this is Captain Span at the watch. We have a situation here that warrants your immediate attention. Yes sir, it's..."

"Sargent Washington, what the hell are you telling me?" Curtis stood at attention. Sweat ran down his back and from under his arms. All eyes in the 13th Air Force conference room were on him. He'd never heard of anyone being jacked up as many times by as many officers as he had been over the course of the last four hours. Now, here he was in front of a video screen being reamed out by an admiral, the PACOM J-2 himself, thousands of miles away in Hawaii, where he had returned after his week at Clark. Yes sir, thought Curtis, when I fuck up, I do it in style.

He looked up at the big TV screen and watched the veins in the admiral's face pop out. Curtis kept quietly repeating what Steel had taught him prior to briefing General Smith. He's just a man. He's just a man. Curtis guessed the admiral had gotten the call from his watch as well. It was 0700 Hawaii time. At least he didn't have to get out of bed in the middle of the night like the 13th Air Force crew here, Curtis rationalized. It could be worse.

Curtis took a deep breath. "Sir, like I told my boss, Colonel Kuncker, Captain Steel gave me this here map and told me he would send one of his Negrito warriors with a message when he had found the general. We got the letter, and I gave up the map."

The admiral removed his glasses and rubbed his eyes. "That's what I thought I had heard. I just had to hear it from you personally. Christ on a cross, this is bad news."

"Sir, it's good news." Curtis said, wishing immediately he had kept his mouth shut. "The coordinates are on it, and I hope sir, we can go and get him. If there is anyone who could have pulled this off, it is Captain Steel."

"That's not your call Sargent Washington. Did Steel give any idea why he did this? Did he say he was working with the Philippine government? We heard that rumor."

Kuncker piped up. "Oh no sir, it is pretty clear Steel has done this on his own, or with just the assistance of some natives."

"Let Sargent Washington respond to my questions," the admiral blasted over the monitor.

"Yes sir," Kuncker sat down quickly.

"Don't be afraid, son, I'm not here to try and lay blame on you for this. You were just obeying Steel's orders," the admiral adopted a fatherly tone, though Curtis noticed his face was still bright red.

"To be honest sir, Captain Steel said he loved the general, and he didn't want him to be killed by the Phils on account of the fact that they couldn't save no one in a rescue mission. He also said, begging your pardon sir, he didn't think the U.S. had the balls to do it, you know, rescue General Smith."

"Off the record, unfortunately, I think he's right on both counts. But that doesn't give him the right to undertake this on his own. The Phils are going to crap when they get wind of this. Alright, sergeant, thank you for you honest assessment. I guess we'll have to decide how to proceed from here. Please continue to cooperate to your fullest. That's all."

Curtis nodded at the video monitor.

"So gentlemen, what we have is a map with some coordinates and a note from Steel that says he has rescued the general from the NPA and is headed to a safe area."

Colonel Thompson, the 13th vice commander, pushed the map onto the table and called out for the video technician to focus the camera on it. Steel's map appeared on the screen. "Sir, let me call on the OSI to continue."

Colonel Morgan, the OSI chief, called out. "Sir, this is Col. Morgan, OSI. Well sir, I just received the interrogation report on the native tribesman who brought the note from Steel. The individual is quite cooperative. He speaks relatively good English and has given us details about the general. Apparently, our young Captain Steel was right on most accounts about the kidnapping," Morgan paused for effect. "The general is reportedly on the move with Steel, twenty clicks to the north of Clark, as indicated by the circle on the map. They are engaged in a running gun battle with the NPA and North Korean, I repeat, North Kor-ean agents." Morgan made a point of looking in the direction of the two CIA analysts seated against the wall. They squirmed uncomfortably as all eyes turned toward them.

"Oh—it's that Captain Steel—who gave the intel briefing. Continue Colonel," the J-2's voice reverberated from the speakers.

"Well, the native fella also reports there have been numerous NPA killed in a big firefight during the rescue," Morgan said, forgetting to hide his southern drawl.

"You're kidding," the J-2 interrupted. "How many?"

"Probably at least a dozen—we are not too clear on the details at this point."

"Damn. Continue, colonel."

"This tribesman under Captain Steel's direction reported, quote: 'Golgi and Tony killed NPA sentries—then Captain Steel infiltrated a native hut and shot through a chain and freed the general.' Apparently, the general was safe when Steel ordered the tribesman to leave for Clark. They had him on a litter. It seems he is pretty banged up. Looks like the NPA—or the Koreans—were rough on him."

"Unbelievable," the J-2 said. "That's enough of the map, put me back on." The J-2's grim face flashed up on the big screen. He silently shook his head, clearly disturbed by the news. "Thank God the general is alive. Alright, I'll meet with the CINC right now. Fax me a copy of that debrief and anything else you have. My gut feeling is that we need to scramble some choppers immediately, but that decision will have to be made pay grades above mine. I just hope to God they can hold out out there."

Curtis noted the worry in the admiral's eyes. Curtis wasn't worried. He knew Steel would get them out.

Steel could hear a bird chirping close by and feel the sunlight on his face. He slowly opened his eyes and looked up into a bright blue sky. He was disoriented, but peaceful. Maybe he had died. He focused enough to see Jo Jo's smiling face. "Boss you okay *lang*?"

Jo Jo's in heaven? Okay, maybe not. Steel figured he was still alive.

He struggled to sit up. "What the hell happened? What time is it?" His throat was too parched to speak clearly. He checked his watch. "six p.m.? Holy shit, I've been out a while."

"Yes, you were delirious. Here, have a drink, then sit back and relax. We are safe here." Jo Jo pushed a canteen of water to Steel's lips. Steel drank greedily, coughing up some abruptly as he remembered why they were there. "Where's the general?"

"We've got him comfortable. He is resting. In fact, he is doing better than you. Why did you have to put your ass in front of a bullet?" he added in Tagalog.

"Good question," Steel rolled to his side, grimacing.

"I've bandaged it as best as I can. Fortunately the bleeding has slowed. Are you in pain?"

"Yeah, a little. Are you sure I've been shot? Doesn't seem as bad as I would have thought."

"Yes, I've seen more of your ass then I ever wanted. I have seen the two holes where the bullet passed in and out. You're lucky the bullet went through."

"Fuck, you're kidding."

"No, my friend, you now have the three assholes."

"Thanks. God, why an ass wound? I'm never going to hear the end of this."

Jo Jo smiled. "So what now?"

"We need to move." He tried to sit up again but immediately became dizzy. "I think we'll have to wait a few minutes for me to get my shit together." He felt like he'd been hit by a bus. Steel looked down. He wasn't wearing any pants. "Where're my goddamn pants? I need my map."

"I'll get them for you. I hung them up to dry."

"I need the map and my compass. We need to figure out where the hell we're at."

"I can help there. I am a pilot after all."

Steel looked over and saw the general standing next to him. He was in cutoff pants, barefoot, and obviously wearing one of the Negrito's jungle fatigue jackets. It was absurdly small, unbuttonable, barely covering his dirty bare chest. In the light his face looked even more gaunt and beat-up than it had during the rescue. Steel tried not to stare. "Looks like we got away," he said, trying to sound upbeat.

"Yes, we did. They would have killed me for sure. The bastards were—"

"North Koreans?"

"Yeah. The bastards were trying to beat intelligence out of me." He grimaced, recalling. "The brass in Washington must be crapping through hoops trying to figure out how to handle your one-man rescue operation. Do you think your soldier arrived at Clark yet?"

"Tony? Jo Jo how long has it been?"

"Over a day."

"Tony should definitely be there by now."

"Hope he can get through security and convince them he's not completely insane," Smith noted.

"He has my military ID and a letter. Plus, Sergeant Washington has a map."

"I'm impressed. Seems like a well-thought-out mad operation."

Steel looked at Jo Jo. "Did you post June and—"

"You aren't the only Douglas MacArthur here. The Negritos are guarding us. We are in their safe hands."

Steel smiled. "Jo Jo, you're a good man."

"Let's see that map." Smith leaned over. "You're in no shape to be giving orders, captain."

"Yes sir." Steel pulled out the map from its plastic bag and handed it to Smith, who spread it out on the ground. The general got down on all fours and started orientating the compass. "Let's see here, where'd those bastards have their camp?"

Steel turned on his side and watched Jo Jo and the general work. He noticed blood oozing from beneath the bandages taped to his ass cheeks. He hoped rescue forces were on their way—a thought that reminded him of the radio and flares they had packed.

"Jo Jo, my combat vest. You have it right."

"It's behind your head."

Steel reached around and grabbed the vest. He looked at the M16 magazine clip pouches and recalled the NPA cadre flailing in the mud before he gunned him down. He shook his head to clear the image. He didn't need that now.

Jo Jo saw the bloody bandages and moved over to Steel. "Let me change those bandages. I'll spread some more antibiotic powder too." Steel wasn't about to argue.

When Jo Jo finished, Steel pulled out a green rescue radio and attached its battery and antenna. He flipped a switch and it beeped loudly. Jo Jo and the general looked over. "If we hear aircraft, we can use the mirror, pop orange smoke, and make contact with this." He held up the radio.

"You get high marks for planning, Steel. Good judgment is another story." Smith went back to his map.

Steel scanned the sky. He wondered how long before they would arrive.

Steel awakened when Jo Jo pulled back the sleeping bag. Steel barely remembered laying down for the night on the bed of banana leaves prepared by June. He was feeling stiff and weak. He watched Jo Jo methodically change his bloody dressings. "The blood has slowed. That is a good thing. I'm not a doctor, but as long as we can keep it clean and dry, you should live. Good thing your ass is not a vital organ."

"Maybe not to you. You have some water?" Steel croaked.

Jo Jo passed him a green canteen. "No rescue forces last night, huh?"

Jo Jo shook his head soberly. "I could hear aircraft in the distance. But nothing."

"I hope Tony got through." Steel looked grim.

"I have great confidence in him." Jo Jo nodded vigorously.

"June's still watching our perimeter? The NPA is going to regroup and come after us."

"June has organized our defense. We are safe," Jo Jo said, applying the last piece of tape to Steel's bandages.

Smith walked up next to them. "I heard you. My guess is

your man got through, but I'm sure after what he told them about the NPA, Washington is trying to figure out how to proceed," he squatted down.

Steel squinted into the morning sun and eyed Smith. He had cleaned himself up some, most of the dirt and blood was gone from his face and chest. It was hard to hide the bruising and cuts though. He was still wearing the undersized clothing and had tucked the .45 into the waistband of his pants.

"Well, let's hope they believe Tony and Curtis and do the right thing," Steel noted.

"Yeah, like hurry the hell up." Smith poked the ground with a stick.

June approached carrying a green half coconut shell in each hand. He nodded politely to the general, squatted, and handed one shell to Steel.

"Sir, you must eat and drink to get strong again. Drink this liquid from the forest plants. Dom Dom made it for you. His wife is a spirit doctor. It will help your body heal."

Steel shrugged and choked down the liquid. It tasted like a cross between dishwashing liquid and menthol cough syrup. He handed the empty shell to June. June nodded approvingly and passed him the other coconut. Steel peered inside.

"It is eggs and meat from the wild chickens," June announced.

Steel grabbed the shell and smelled the food, sheer ambrosia. He wolfed it down. He had thought he had smelled cooking chicken earlier but had written it off as a hallucination.

Smith shielded his eyes from the harsh morning sun. "It's a new day. Let's hope our boys are on the way."

Steel nodded and looked up into the sky.

"Delta One, this is Killer One, over."

"This is Delta One, over," the chief radio operator in an

Air Force airborne warning and control aircraft, or AWACS, responded. The converted Boeing 747 had been scrambled from the U.S.'s Kadena Air Base in Japan and arrived on station over the Zambales mountains at 0400 hours. The AWACS was charged with organizing the command and control of the rescue mission for the general.

"Killer One is two minutes away from Zambales 212, over."

"Roger Killer One. We got you, over."

Killer One, or Maj. Gridley 'Gridlock' Green, nudged his control stick slightly left and checked his horizon indicator. Everything had to be perfect. His F-4 was blasting along at eight hundred miles per hour at an altitude of two thousand feet. He was lead for three other F-4s, trailing several miles behind. Officially, they were on routine training. In reality, they were on a short-notice classified mission looking for the general. They were uploaded with ordinance, four five hundred pound bombs and cannon ammo for the guns. Green was excited to say the least. He pushed the switch on his mike. "We have seen signs of habitation, over. I repeat, we have seen indigenous personnel and smoke, over."

"Can you identify personnel, over?" Delta One's voice crackled.

"Negative," Killer One answered.

"Have a look, over."

"We'll go down and have a look."

"Wait, Killer One. We have a beacon signal, over. We got a down pilot beacon coming in loud and clear."

"Holding Delta One."

"Killer One, open your radio frequencies."

"Roger Delta One. The beacon is coming in from a location away from where we are now observing personnel on the ground."

"How far, Killer One?"

"We got a voice Delta One. Repeat we have voice contact with subjects on the ground."

"May Day. May Day. Can you hear me, over?" Steel yelled into the radio.

Capt. Larry 'Bird Dog' Davis, the lead F-4s back-seater, squeezed his mike switch. "Yes, I read you. This is Killer One. Identify yourself, over."

"Killer One, this is Captain Steel, USAF. I can hear you, but I can't see your bird, over."

"Where's is your location?"

"I believe you are west of our position. I'm going to use my mirror to flash you and key my radio."

"Roger, keep your radio beacon keyed and flash us, over."

"Delta One, we have mirror flashes," Gridlock called out to the AWACS. He flipped on the intercom. "Larry you got that? Yeah it's coming from that hillside over there. Got it marked on the map."

"Roger front seat. Got the flash. Holy shit, Batman. I'll tell Delta One we found the eagle. Scramble the hounds."

"Alright Bird Dog, make the call."

"Delta One, this is Killer One, scramble the hounds. I repeat scramble the hounds. Over."

"Roger that Killer one. Scrambling the hounds."

"We've been found." Steel exhaled as if he had been holding his breath for a week. Maybe he had. "I can't believe we actually did it." Jo Jo held the small mirror up to his face and peered through the hole in the center. He was trying to align it with the sun and aircraft flying overhead.

"It can't be that long until the choppers arrive. It's just not that far a flight," the general added.

"Yeah, let's keep our fingers crossed. Jo Jo, make sure June isn't distracted by the aircraft and keeps focused on protecting us. Tell him American helicopters are en route." Jo Jo nodded and headed off into the bush.

It had been three long hours between first contact with the aircraft and the sounds of helicopters in the distance. The F-4s overhead had kept up words of encouragement, noting that an armed rescue team was put to ground and was moving toward their location. They wanted to provide a secure land site for the helos. The F-4s were reporting possible armed unfriendlies in the area.

Steel, still exhausted and in pain, was on his back, eyes shut as June approach. He tapped Steel's shoulder. "Sir, Golgi has seen NPA men coming. You can see them with your looking glass," June said in Aeta, pointing out into the valley below them.

Steel struggled to his feet with June's help. "Shit, that hurts," he winced. "God, I hope it's the rescue team." Steel spied into the jungle with his binoculars, supported on both sides by June and Jo Jo. They were on a high ridge and had good sight lines.

Golgi was right; it was NPA. Steel could see a patrol crawling in their direction. He counted fourteen. One carrying a heavy machine gun that looked like a vintage World War II .30-cal. That could be bad news for the rescue helicopters.

"How many are there?" the general asked, peering over Steel's shoulder.

"About fourteen. Here, have a look, sir." He handed him the binoculars.

"Damn. I see some heavy weaponry as well. A small mortar and heavy gun."

"Yeah. June, have the boys move into a defensive position

over there," he pointed to an area near them. "There is a U.S. patrol out there somewhere. I don't want us shooting at each other."

Smith intently watched the NPA. "It's been a while, but I think I can still call in an air strike." Smith got down on all fours and laid the map on the ground. "Here give me that radio."

Steel hesitated then handed it over.

"Sir, we might want to notify the F-4s, who in turn can tell the team that NPA have been sighted."

The general looked up from his map and stared at Steel for a moment. "What's their call sign?"

"We've been talking to Killer One."

"Killer One this is—er—Honcho over." He shrugged his shoulders, embarrassed by his spur-of-the-moment call sign. "This is General Smith. We have visual confirmation of a heavily armed NPA force. Relay this information to the U.S. ground team. They are—" Smith paused, quickly reached for the compass laying on the ground, and aligned it in his hand. "West. I repeat two hundred yards west of our position. We might need some air support. I repeat. We have heavily armed bad guys closing in on our position. We need some help, over," Smith dropped the radio to his side. "I hope kimchi-breath is down there with them. I owe that bastard a bomb or two."

"Bird Dog, did you hear that? Shit, I think that was the general, and he's asking for close air support." Gridlock released his intercom button.

"I read you, Gridlock. I'll relay his request to AWACS."

"Delta One, this is Killer One. Are you out there, over?"

"Killer One, this is Delta One. We have been monitoring the radio. We have relayed info to ground team. Inform Honcho that we are processing his request. Killer One, be prepared to fulfill request, over."

"Roger Delta One, we will begin preparation, over."

"Damn Bird Dog. Lock and load. This will be a first, dumping bombs in anger. Rock on!" Gridlock yelled.

Steel watched the F-4 streak overhead in a simulated attack. He had heard on the radio that the aircraft had been denied permission to drop live ordinance. Damn. But he wasn't surprised that authorization hadn't been given to fire. The U.S. had no balls. Washington didn't want to rock the boat. He wondered where the rescue team was in relation to the NPA

Steel held his hands up to shield his eyes from the harsh noon sun. He was still too weak to stand for long, and his ass throbbed with pain. He looked over at the general, laid out on his belly, binoculars to his face, watching the F-4.

"Boss, it's not going to shoot, eh?" Jo Jo asked, mesmerized by the fast-moving aircraft.

"No, it's just going to try and scare the hell out of them buzzing at one hundred feet."

"I wish they'd drop bombs on them, instead," Jo Jo shook his head.

"Yeah, shame to do that to the crew, tying their hands and expecting them to fight," the general grunted.

They all watched the F-4 race towards the NPA, who had scattered and hidden when they first heard the aircraft.

The intense, bone-rattling sound from the Phantom's afterburner blasted over the NPA crouched in the scrub brush in the valley below. From the tall elephant grass, the patrol responded with erratic machine-gun fire.

"Those ignorant bastards are shooting," the general huffed. He picked up the radio. "Delta One, this is Honcho. Your birds are taking ground fire. I repeat, your birds are taking ground fire."

Steel strained to sit up. "Jo Jo, make sure June and the guys hold their fire."

Jo Jo yelled, "June, Steel says don't shoot."

June waved to acknowledge he got the order. Just as he did, more gunfire erupted from near the NPA's last position. Jo Jo jumped up and scanned the trees below, "Jesus Marie Joseph, the NPA aren't firing at the sky this time. I think they are shooting at our rescue team."

Smith checked out the shooting with the binoculars. "Damn, he's right. I can see a firefight between the reds and our boys."

More shooting erupted and an explosion from what sounded like a mortar or grenade. Jo Jo turned to Steel, "Should we send June to help?"

"No, let's give our side a few minutes first."

Hundreds more rounds were exchanged in what sounded like a running gunfight. Steel could see June yelling, wanting to know if they should fire.

Before Steel could reply, two more F-4 emerged from the cloud cover. They began another attack run, rolling in on the NPA position. This time the lead Phantom opened up with his nose-mounted cannon and let loose a devastating burst of fire. The second Phantom did the same. "Uncle Sam does have balls," Steel muttered into the din as he pressed his body into the ground.

Snowden watched the F-4s roll in from a position not more than one hundred yards away from the target. A forward air controller on their eleven-man team had brilliantly vectored the F-4s in for a strike on the NPA positions. Snowden thought the cannon rounds and tracers looked like high-speed flaming meteors hitting the jungle brush, rocks, and human bodies.

He watched the aircraft rocket out of sight and surveyed the target area looking for movement. He saw nothing alive. Snowden turned and gave the young sergeant sitting next to him a thumb's up.

Snowden couldn't believe his good fortune. The firefight was exhilarating. He couldn't have asked for a better mission. He had bullied his way onto the rescue team, claiming a counterintelligence operative was required because of possible North Korean involvement. He and three delta guys were accompanying the seven Air Force rescue troops and the forward air controller who were assigned to link up with Steel and the general and provide security and a landing site for the rescue helos.

While he was enjoying the mission, his reason for making the trip was the hope that he could facilitate Steel's untimely demise—let him disappear in the fog of war. Snowden suspected that Steel had killed Ramos, who had vanished without a trace. It wasn't like Ramos not to check in. How did Steel do it? The man was a superhuman devil.

Snowden crouched on the top of a rocky ravine. He had an excellent view. Up on his left, on a parallel ridge, was where Steel supposedly was. Snowden scoured the landscape trying to catch sight of the man. He had foolishly forgotten to bring binoculars.

Movement in the brush below his position caught Snowden's attention. He pushed the butt of his M16's stock tightly into his shoulder and sighted his rifle. He thought he saw an individual take cover behind a rock ledge, not more than forty yards below him. Snowden grunted out that he spotted NPA. Marks, the delta man crouched next to him, followed Snowden's lead and aimed at the rock.

In a few seconds, a head edged out from around the side of the rock. Snowden was surprised to see it was a female, armed with an AK47. He could see her long hair flowing from beneath a blue bandana. He aimed his weapon and squeezed off three rounds quickly, watching the explosion of blood and brains.

"Good kill," Marks whispered to Snowden.

He shuddered. Good as sex, he thought.

Snowden scanned the rocks again. No more movement. The delta guys were motioning that they were heading up toward Steel's ridge top. As the team snaked forward, Snowden moved to the right flank. He aimed his M16 into the scrub brush ahead and advanced awkwardly with his body half bent over. Sweat poured into his eyes, gushing out from beneath his hot Kevlar helmet. Mud and the cammo paint on his face impaired his vision.

Snowden examined the troops around him and figured he had enough time to wipe his brow. Pulling a green towel from the pocket of his cammo pants, he released his chin strap and removed his helmet. Just as Snowden was pushing the towel back into his pocket, Marks let out an expletive and yelled, "Grenade! Hit the dirt!"

Snowden reacted instinctively—the instincts of a counterintelligence operative who was trained in spycraft—the wrong instincts for the battlefield. The shrapnel from a grenade explosion filled the air and a cloud of metal enveloped Snowden. Had Snowden fallen to the ground as quickly as his comrades, he could have survived his wounds; had he been wearing his helmet, the jagged, dime-sized piece of metal wouldn't have sliced through his unprotected skull and penetrated deep into his brain. Snowden crashed to the dirt, dead before he hit the ground.

Hearing the grenade explode below their position, Dom Dom and several Negritos peered over the side of the hill aiming their weapons. Dom Dom could see Americans crouched near his grenade pig trap. A sick feeling filled his stomach.

Pong Pet shook his head in disgust. "Did they not see our signs? The traps were clearly marked."

"No, maybe some are dead now," Dom Dom answered sadly.

Pong Pet thought for a moment, remembering the man at Steel's house. "I don't think we should bother Steel with the pig trap killing Americans. He will only blame himself and be sad. They will think the NPA did it."

"Yes, it would be best," Dom Dom said somberly.

Smith let out a war whoop. "Well, young Steel, seems you underestimated Uncle Sam's balls," he slapped the ground with his hand. "Die you bastards! Goddamn it. I hope they got that damn Korean."

"Apparently we do have balls," Steel called out to Smith, not quite ready to celebrate. He was watching the Negrito forward line. He could see Jo Jo and June. Steel had ordered them to monitor the rescue team movements, still concerned about friendly fire.

The F-4s and ensuing firefight had created quit a stir among the Negritos, who were excitedly peering over the ridge. Some of the hill Negritos sat in groups animatedly talking to each other. Never in their wildest dreams could they have envisioned the destructive power of those small, noisy, silver birds.

"Honcho, this is Delta One, do you read me, over?" the radio crackled.

"This is Honcho. Read you loud and clear. Both aircraft were right on the mark. Nice work gentlemen."

"Honcho, the rescue team is coming in now. They have taken casualties in a firefight with the NPA."

"Roger that," the general shook his head in disgust.

"Americanos," one of the Negritos yelled out.

"Americans hold your fire, we're friends. The general is here," Jo Jo yelled out over the ridge.

Steel had June gather all the Negritos and order them to shoulder their weapons. Several camouflaged, heavily armed Americans cautiously emerged from the brush. Two more followed, supporting a wounded comrade limping painfully along. Four more shuffled up the hill, each struggling to carry a body, clearly dead. Steel's heart sank. They had come so far without a death on their side.

One of the rescue sergeants approached Steel, now laid out on the general's stretcher, while two others checked in with the general standing nearby. The sergeant popped Steel a salute, "Captain Steel."

Steel, still on the ground, saluted, then reached up and offered his hand, "Good to see you Ricky. Shit, who got hit?"

Ricky knelt, "Good to see you sir—alive. Lieutenant Colonel Snowden, an OSI guy, is dead, and Green, a delta guy, took some shrapnel from a grenade."

Steel was stunned. "Snowden?"

"Yeah, NPA bastards got into a firefight with us and one lobbed a grenade. You hit, sir?" Ricky reached down to check out Steel's bandages.

"Yeah, I took a round in the ass, a couple days ago." He looked at Snowden's crumbled body, laid out on the ground, and craned to see his face. Smith, accompanied by an officious looking young pararescue major, whom Steel didn't recognize, walked up to Ricky. The major barked out, "Sergeant Reed, collect weapons from these locals. I don't want them armed in my helos." Steel watched Smith's jaw tighten.

"Excuse me major, these here locals, as you rudely referred to them, are Negrito warriors. Under no circumstances will you disarm them."

"But sir, I have my orders."

"Major, that order is not up for discussion. They return as warriors. Get that man some medical attention immediately," he pointed to Steel, who was now standing, supported by Jo Jo. "There's another over there with even more urgent need," Smith pointed to Tek.

"Yes sir. We'll make stretchers. We have a landing zone picked out over the next ridgeline. I suggest we move out immediately, sir." The major saluted and headed off.

"Roger that, major," Smith returned his salute.

"William, order the boys to move out. Let's get the hell back home. And son, get back on the stretcher," Smith turned and limped over to supervise the major.

"Yes sir," Steel barked out his own commands in Aeta, which sent the Negritos scurrying.

Jo Jo helped Steel lie down on the stretcher. "So William, can we go home now? I really need a shower."

Steel smiled. Jo Jo rarely called him by his given name. "Yeah, you certainly need a shower," Jo Jo, Reed, and two Negritos picked up Steel's stretcher. June supervised the other Negritos as they carried Snowden's body. What the fuck was Snowden doing out here, Steel thought. He was way too senior for this shit, poor bastard.

Reed, handling one rattan pole of the stretcher, looked down at Steel as they marched along. "You know, sir, you're a hero, but you're going to get a rash of shit for getting shot in the ass."

"Yep." Steel said and closed his eyes. It was going to be a sweet helicopter ride, unlike the last time he left the mountains by air. He couldn't wait to see Kuncker's face this time.

EPILOGUE

Angeles City

"WILLIAM, WHAT ARE YOU READING?" Vida asked. She was propped up in his bed, scanning a book on local politics. Steel looked over and smiled. Vida was spending almost every weekend with him. He hadn't been to visit her in Manila; her parents were still upset by their relationship. "A translation of a diary of a Japanese soldier. I found it in a cave. I'm almost done."

"Very interesting," she murmured. "Might make a good story for the paper," she returned to her book.

Steel watched her read. Dressed in one of his rumpled white T-shirts and white panties, she was incredibly sexy. The small black reading glasses perched on the end of her nose were cute rather than scholarly. He couldn't recall a time in his life when he had felt so happy.

It had been nearly three months since the rescue of the general and the helicopter ride from the mountains. He had spent nearly two weeks in the hospital getting pumped with antibiotics. The bullet had missed vital organs, instead nicking his tailbone, severing muscle tissue and damaging some nerves. Fortunately, it had been a small-caliber pistol round and not a high-velocity rifle bullet. Overall, he had been lucky.

Life was easy for him now at work; lots of time off and

a relaxed schedule. He was a hero in everyone's eyes, at least everyone who knew the truth behind the general's rescue.

For political reasons, the whole thing had been hushed up and Steel's actions were immediately classified. Uncle Sam wasn't about to let it be known that one of its own had killed scores of Communist guerrillas in an unauthorized firefight and rescue operation. For its part, the Philippine government, while angry with the U.S. for interfering, reluctantly went along with the story to save face.

The involvement of North Korean agents was buried even deeper. The U.S. government was not prepared to go to war with North Korea. Its response stopped at putting troops on high alert along the demilitarized zone and holding unscheduled and provocative military exercises, plus the U.S. provided Seoul with some highly publicized new military hardware.

Steel felt he had received more than adequate recognition. General Smith saw to it that Steel was reimbursed for all his expenses and the Negritos' salaries. Tony and June were, by local standards, suddenly very rich men. Jo Jo, too, received a monetary award. For Steel's official recognition, he was flown to Hawaii, where the Commander for Pacific Forces presented him the Air Force's top peacetime medal for heroism and bravery.

General Smith was at the small ceremony. He spoke glowingly of Steel's actions, as far as he was allowed. The citation to accompany the medal had been classified: TOP SECRET NOT RELEASEABLE TO FOREIGN NATIONALS. Few would ever know the real story.

Steel was allowed to take Vida to Hawaii, that was the highlight for him. They had many long walks on moonlit Waikiki beaches. Vida tolerated Jo Jo and Rosa's company— Steel had brought them along too, listed as his immediate family on the attendance list for the award ceremony. Jo Jo and

Rosa tried hard to hide their disdain for Ms. Abucayan as they sipped tropical drinks next to the hotel pool.

Yes, Steel thought, life was good. He was energized enough to start back on trips into the mountains: the thing he had left unsettled. He wanted another shot at the treasure. There were more barrels of treasure buried out there in the hills.

He resumed reading the diary his friend had finally sent from Japan. It was riveting. Steel could see vividly the lives of those Japanese soldiers interred in the mountains. What hardships they had endured for their emperor.

It was Sgt. Toshito Mitofumi's last entry, with the soldier's blood staining the page, that Steel read over and over. "I will give you, Miko, a life of a princess. I will build a big house and a temple and pray daily for the souls of my dead comrades and for the people I have killed, for the faces of the dead that visit me at night. I raise my head now and look up at the wall. My gift for Miko is still safely hidden there." The last sentence struck Steel like a thunderbolt. There was something hidden there. He had missed it. "I'll be damned," he muttered out loud.

"What are you damned about, honey?" Vida peered over the glasses.

"Oh, I'm not sure. We'll have to see which crime I'm held accountable for in this life," Steel mumbled, still mesmerized by the last entry. He read it out aloud. "My gift for Miko is still safely hidden there."

He wondered how long it would take Jo Jo to get them packed and ready?

ABOUT THE AUTHOR

Nick Auclair has over twenty years' experience as an U.S. intelligence officer, five of those in the Philippines where he spent his free time chasing after the Tiger of Malay's treasure. He currently lives with his wife on a small farm in Virginia and teaches counterinsurgency at the Virginia Military Institute. The second book in the Steel treasure-hunting series is due out in 2014.

ACKNOWLEDGMENTS

There are many people without whom I could not have completed this book. Thanks to Kate Sparks Auclair, my wife, editor, and chief supporter—when she is not trying to strangle me over improper pronoun use; to my mother-in-law, Fredda Sparks, who line-edited the manuscript twice and lowered her normally highbrow literary standards to help with prickly editorial details like the proper number of words in "shitface;" to Jeff Telgarsky for lending his eagle eye for detail to an early draft; to Liz and Austin Auclair for copyediting the final draft and helping me with social media, even when they had much bigger things on their minds; and to Armand and Mavis Steel Auclair for always being my biggest fans. To StreetlightGraphics.com for their great book cover, professional manuscript layout, and prompt service.

I also owe a debt of gratitude to the officers, enlisted men and women, and civilians working in and around Clark Air Force base when I was stationed there between 1983 and 1987: You gave a young captain the opportunity to have the adventure of a lifetime. Special thanks go to Michael A. Nelson, Lieutenant General USAFR, for saving my career and to Rand for reading the manuscript and helping me survive the Philippines—we had fun.

A final thanks to the people of the Philippines for letting me share your beautiful and exciting country for five plus years. I hope for you the prosperity and peace you so richly deserve.

Made in the USA
Charleston, SC
10 May 2013